SECRETS

OF

THE FIRE SEA

STEPHEN HUNT

TOR®
fantasy

A Tom Doherty Associates Book
New York

This is a work of fiction. All of the characters, organizations, and events portrayed in this novel are either products of the author's imagination or are used fictitiously.

SECRETS OF THE FIRE SEA

Originally published in Great Britain in 2011 by HarperVoyager, an imprint of HarperCollins*Publishers*

Copyright © 2011 by Stephen Hunt

A Tor Book
Published by Tom Doherty Associates, LLC
175 Fifth Avenue
New York, NY 10010

www.tor-forge.com

Tor® is a registered trademark of Tom Doherty Associates, LLC.

ISBN 978-0-7653-6611-5

Tor books may be purchased for educational, business, or promotional use. For information on bulk purchases, please contact Macmillan Corporate and Premium Sales Department at 1-800-221-7945 extension 5442 or write specialmarkets@macmillan.com.

First U.S. Edition: March 2012
First U.S. Mass Market Edition: March 2013

Printed in the United States of America

0 9 8 7 6 5 4 3 2 1

Praise for Stephen Hunt

"The whirliest of contemporary cross-pollinated steampunk visions, with enough in it to keep three or four ordinary books going."
—*The Wall Street Journal* on
The Rise of the Iron Moon

"It has everything you could want in a fantasy novel: light magical overtones and a heartfelt story . . . A highly detailed adventure full of surprises for fans and newcomers to the series."
—*San Francisco Book Review* on
The Rise of the Iron Moon

"A swaggering, eye-filling, brain-swizzling extravaganza!"
—*Kirkus Reviews* on *The Rise of the Iron Moon*

"This is Philip Pullman with a dose of Benzedrine. Hold on to your hat and let yourself get carried away."
—Tom Holt,
author of *Life, Liberty, and the Pursuit of Sausages,*
on *The Rise of the Iron Moon*

"Wildly imaginative and compelling, this charming steampunk yarn plays out against a backdrop of civil war and failed rebellion, layered and complex treachery and love in surprising corners."
—*Publishers Weekly* on *The Kingdom Beyond the Waves*

"A Dickensian atmosphere with shades of Indiana Jones featuring a strong-willed adventuress that will appeal to steampunk fans."
—*Library Journal* on
The Kingdom Beyond the Waves

"Steampunk fantasy and SF with a Victorian-era feel . . . A rip-roaring Indiana Jones–style adventure."
—*RT Book Reviews* (4 stars) on
The Kingdom Beyond the Waves

"A curious part-future blend of aerostats, mechanical computers, psychic powers, self-willed steam-power robots, Elder gods, talking superweapons, and more . . . Harry Potter mugs H. P. Lovecraft and L. Ron Hubbard explains it all."
—*Kirkus Reviews* on *The Court of the Air*

TOR BOOKS BY STEPHEN HUNT

You would not cling to his guiding hand
if the way was always bright.
And you would not care to walk by faith
could you always walk by sight.

Anon

SECRETS OF THE
FIRE SEA

CHAPTER ONE

The Isle of Jago. Hermetica City

Watching the underwater craft carrying the ambassador away from Jago's shores was as good a way as any to pass the afternoon, if you could ignore the distant thrum of the iron battlements keeping the hordes of prowling monsters out of Hermetica City.

Hannah turned as her friend Chalph joined her near the edge of the tall cliffs. Not so near the edge that she might be scalded by the boiling water lashing up from the Fire Sea, but near enough to glimpse the departing ambassador's u-boat on the surface. The u-boat was meeting up with the Jagonese tug that had been assigned to escort it beyond the coral line, before it braved the maze of boiling passages of water that veined their way through the bubbling magma of the Fire Sea.

'They've picked a good day for going,' said Chalph, raising his black-furred arm to point to the u-boat on the surface, guide lines being tossed across to the tug. The sailors were wearing rubber scald suits, coloured yellow for visibility. 'No steam storms today – and I can't smell any cold fronts moving in.'

'That's a pity,' said Hannah. She loved the violence of the arctic rain hitting the superheated waters of the Fire Sea and the parched coastlines of Jago. She felt alive when steam storms broke across the island's shores, geysers erupting from the ocean, hot mists sliding across the basalts plains, lightning painting the landscape and the crack of thunder urging the monsters laying siege outside their battlements into a frenzy. Hannah felt more alive in a storm than she ever did down in the empty echoing streets of their capital's vaults.

Chalph rubbed at his face with a paw-like hand. Like the rest of the ursine race, he had wonderfully expressive eyes – pupils that could narrow to a pinhead or expand out until the rim of yellow around the edges was driven out and the features of his face vanished in a mask of black. 'I wonder how long I've got left on Jago now that the ambassador has gone?'

A blade of fear stabbed Hannah. That Chalph urs Chalph might depart back to his country across the sea, leaving her as good as friendless on the island. 'But you've been brought up here, the same as me. Your house can't just make you go back to Pericur.'

'Oh, they *can*, alright,' said Chalph. 'Why do you think our ambassador is leaving? She supported the claim of the archduchess to the throne of Pericur. The ambassador being recalled back home is her reward. Our conservatives don't like merchants operating on Jago. They believe Jago is sacred soil, that our trade here is an affront to the scriptures. You wait and see. The trade concession the House of Ush had been granted will be cancelled by the new archduchess, then we'll all be back on Pericurian soil within the year.'

'But I'll still be here,' said Hannah. '*We'll* be here. The race of man. . .'

Chalph moved back as a spray of boiling water carried on

the wind and hissed towards his boots. 'The archduchess won't need to force your people from the island.' He clambered over a boulder and pointed to the nearest of the guard towers rising up behind the sloped iron battlements. A large ursine mercenary was just visible inside, the light glinting off the brass of the gas tank on his back.

'Careful,' said Hannah. 'The soldiers might see us, report us for being out on the surface.'

'They don't care we're here,' replied Chalph. 'They get paid for keeping the monsters out, not keeping us in. And that's the nub of it. Your senate relies on our free company fighters to keep the capital safe, not your police militia. The free company may be mercenaries, but they will not dare disobey a direct order from the archduchess to leave Jago, and then who will protect your city?'

Hannah shrugged. 'The militia hate your mercenaries. They never wanted free company fighters here, that was the senate's choice. They'd throw a party on the docks and help load your mercenaries into a boat if the free company were ordered off Jago.'

'And your senate would widen the draft to make up the numbers,' said Chalph. 'Do you want to spend the rest of your life in a guard tower, hoping that the power charging the battlements doesn't fail on your watch?'

'It won't come to that,' said Hannah. But she knew how optimistic her words sounded even as she spoke them. There were press gangs operating across the city now, and even the senate's latest raft of anti-emigration legislation wasn't going to fill all the empty vacancies in every trade from the tug service to clerks for the ministries. 'In the cathedral they're saying that the new ambassador from Pericur is going to be one of your modernizers. He'll argue against any attempt to embargo Jago.'

'Of course he's a modernizer,' laughed Chalph – although there was little humour in his growl of a voice. 'Jago's been a dead-end posting for embassy staff for centuries. The new ambassador is being sent here as a punishment! He was ambassador to the Kingdom of Jackals before. A bit of a demotion, don't you think? From the most powerful nation in the world to this cold, dying place.'

'How can you say that, Chalph? You were born here!'

'You weren't,' said Chalph. 'You should go home. Go anywhere there's a future for you.'

'This is my home.'

'No,' Chalph insisted. 'The Kingdom of Jackals is your real home, this is just where you ended up.'

Hannah shook her head. 'Jago is all I've known.'

'It's all I've known too,' said Chalph. 'But there's more out there than this place.' Chalph picked up a piece of rock and angrily tossed it in the direction of the Horn of Jago, the vast peak rising up behind them out of a cluster of the capital's domed greenhouses. He threw the stone as if he might break one of the tall stained-glass windows along the senatorial palace circling the mountain. Hannah winced as the flare-house at the very top of the summit erupted with magnesium phosphorescence. A brief flash of light to help guide in the traders that had long ago stopped calling on the island.

'It's just that I don't want you to go back to Pericur,' said Hannah, trying to placate her quick-tempered friend. 'Alice says there might be war between Pericur and the Kingdom of Jackals now there's a new archduchess sitting on your throne.'

'War? No, that's foolish talk. I'm sure the archduchess would be happier if the Kingdom's colonies disappeared from our southern border, but traditionalist though our new baronial council may be, they understand well enough the power of the Kingdom's Royal Aerostatical Navy. The archduchess might close the border and hope the rest of the world goes away, but she won't be invading Jackelian possessions anytime soon. Your people have airships, mine don't.'

'The Jagonese are my people,' said Hannah.

'Your parents were both Jackelian,' said Chalph. 'The senate can't stop you leaving the island. You have a choice, at least. More of a choice than I have. I'm bonded in service to the House of Ush. I go where the baroness sends me, just like the baroness has to trade where the archduchess sells her the charter to operate. But you, you can travel to the Kingdom, to Concorzia, go to the Catosian city-states if the fancy takes you. But all you do is stay here. You're wasting your life away on this island.'

'It doesn't feel like a waste to me.'

'It should do,' said Chalph. He pulled out a large Pericurian timepiece from a pocket in the heavy dark leather clothes that were the fashion among his nation. 'You're the cleverest person I know, but you're surely one of the laziest too. The entrance exam is beginning now. You're meant to be back at the cathedral, not watching steam shapes above the ocean.'

'Yes,' sighed Hannah, 'I suppose I am.' She pointed at one of the clouds of mist leaping up off the sea. 'That one's a lion.'

Chalph responded to the game and pointed at another wall of steaming mist rolling up behind the first. 'And look, that one's my future. Come on, let's see if we can't find you one too.'

It was a measure of how determined Chalph was to secure a life for Hannah off Jago that he had personally come to fetch her back to the cathedral. Ursine might be more or less the same height as their counterparts in the race of man, but the dense flesh and thick muscles of the bear-like people meant that a citizen of Pericur usually weighed twice as much as a similarly sized human. And Chalph urs Chalph had dragged his weight up every rung lining the air vent before wrestling open the heavy armoured door that opened out over the black cliffs of Jago.

Now both Hannah and Chalph had to descend hundreds of rungs back down to the subterranean city without slipping – always tricky the nearer you got to the surface; where the heat from the Fire Sea made sweaty, slippery hands – or paws – an occupational hazard when gripping the ladder. Ventilation passage ninety-two was a long way from the cathedral too, close to the submarine pens of the docks – like the rest of the capital, deep underground in the city's machine-hewn vaults. But vent ninety-two's isolation had an advantage. It was Hannah Conquest's favourite way up to the surface. Without a single u-boat sitting moored in the underground pens among the hundreds of tugs waiting unmanned for trade that would probably never return to the island, there were rarely any adults around to see Hannah emerging from the vent shaft and report her to the police militia. It wasn't so much that people feared Hannah and her friends might fall and break their necks – though that was often the stated concern that forbade them to leave the city – it was the fear that a careless child might leave open an armoured door up top, allowing in one of the beasts from the island's cold interior.

Down below it was just as she had expected. Hannah and Chalph emerged from the vent watched only by the dark, empty eyes of passages that led to the underground water locks and lifting rooms up to the sea-bed. There were no tug crew about the docks; most of the sailors would be back home, drawing half-pay while their fire-breaker vessels sat equally idle tied up around the pens. Guiding the Pericurian ambassador's u-boat out through the Fire Sea was a rare flurry of activity for the service this morning.

It was a long way back home through the Eliza Vaults – a

lonely walk past empty warehouses and boarded-up taverns and guesthouses for sailors that no longer visited Jago's shores, before Hannah and Chalph began to pass through the more inhabited parts of the capital, each vault larger than the last as they followed the connected chambers towards the heart of Hermetica City. The two friends travelled on foot, ignoring the cries from gondolas drifting along the city's canals. Chalph was a junior apprentice in an increasingly impoverished foreign merchant house and Hannah a ward of the church, and neither had the little platinum pennies that a gondola owner would demand for a quick ride towards the cathedral.

It seemed to Hannah as if they had crossed every one of capital's arched bridges by the time the waters widened out into the Grand Canal, and here at least Hermetica City still felt like a metropolis. Noise. Smells. Activity. People about the arcaded passages of shops, colonnaded walks that were still polished and cleaned by the district's workers. People, it was always people that made a place. Little private skiffs moving down the canal, paddles turning under the power of chemical batteries with the whiff of eggs about them. Large oared barges moored for use as restaurants along the canal walls, bored kitchen staff leaning out of the windows to talk to idle gondola men. Hawkers' cries filling the air, knife-grinding for a penny a blade, pig gelders offering their services to the increasing numbers of people keeping livestock in their canal-side houses and apartments. Not trusting to the scant food supplies coming down from the greenhouses on the surface, not now so many of their labourers had left for the fertile wheat plains of Concorzia. Where once civilization had clustered around the warm coastline of Jago as the glaciers moved south and enveloped the world under white sheets of ice, now the islanders were themselves clinging ever tighter to the noise and din of each other, leaving the fringes of their capital to the water rats, cavern bamboo and the shadows of their ancient glory.

Even the roof of the subterranean vaults seemed to burn brighter in the centre of the city, the diode plates shimmering above in an approximation of the sun the mist-shrouded island's surface hardly ever saw, especially now, in the winter. Though the seasons mattered little to the Jagonese; not with their flash steam systems, powered by the underground water table warmed by volcanic action within, and the Fire Sea without. If only the island had more people. They could continue to live on Jago for another two thousand years – the machinations of the Archduchess of Pericur and the rising power of her nation on the opposite side of the Fire Sea be damned.

It wasn't long before Hannah and Chalph reached the largest – and, some said, most elegantly carved vault in the city, the vast circular cavern of the Seething Round. Here, flanking the grand canal, buildings stood as high as twenty storeys, sash windows sparkling as brightly as jewels. And there at its centre, Jago Cathedral, the Grand Canal surrounding it like a moat, spanned by three bridges leading across to its chambers. The largest bridge – the south – lay opposite the steps leading up into the Horn of Jago itself, the mountain long ago hollowed out like a termite mound for the richest vaults and streets of the capital, topped by the senate and capped at its summit by their flare-house. Yes, the light of Jago had once burned with far more than the Fire Sea's red glow reflected from its basalt cliffs. For those who ruled the city below from high inside the mountain, it probably seemed as if nothing had changed – and even Hannah, at her tender age, could see that that was part of the problem.

There were extra priests and vergers standing at all three bridges across to the cathedral now. Last month, Jago Cathedral had been broken into at night and the altar raided for silver, its collection boxes smashed. The crime no doubt perpetrated by would-be emigrants desperate to scrape together enough coins to bribe the harbour workers to look the other way when the next supply vessel docked.

Hannah chose the smallest bridge to try to sneak across to the cathedral, but Chalph's heavy six-foot figure following behind her was unmissable. A tonsured priest sucked on his teeth in a disapproving way as they passed. 'You may be late, Damson Conquest, but I can't be letting your friend into the cathedral.'

'Because he's ursine?'

'Because he's a believer, miss. In the scriptures of Pericur, unless you've renounced your faith, Chalph urs Chalph?'

'My house may be of a reforming bent,' said Chalph, 'but I don't believe we're ready to renounce the scripture of the Divine Quad quite yet. Atheists are treated less kindly in my nation than in yours.'

'Then you and your faith shall stay on this side of our good Circlist dwelling, my fine-furred wet-snout friend, while young Hannah can go and make her apologies to the archbishop for an appointment ill-kept.'

Chalph glanced knowingly at Hannah, who was looking annoyed that the priest had used the insulting Jagonese name for an ursine: *wet-snout* indeed. 'This place is just like the rest of Jago, it's a relic. You remember what you're going inside there for . . . it's your future.'

She shrugged. 'I'll meet you out in the park later. We'll see what the future looks like then.'

Hannah walked inside. Jago Cathedral wasn't a relic to her, it was *home*. Wheel windows a hundred feet across painted the nave of the cathedral with brightly coloured illumination, much of it speckled by lines of formulae traced across each stained glass light. Formulae had always been important to the Circlist church – the church without a god. Some of them were scientific, outlining the known building blocks of creation. Others were the proofs and balances of synthetic morality – equations that proved society worked best when people worked together, that kindness to the weak was a thing of glory, to do unto others as you would have done unto you. The quantitative proof for the qualitative teachings of Circlism. Hannah's eyes flicked across the stained glass. There, the elegant proof for the parable of the clear mind – openness of mind versus the infective vectors of a faith-based meme. Every koan and parable taught by the church was represented, through both equations and sublime rainbow-coloured images. Of all Jago's arts, stained glass was the most celebrated: as was attested to by the double-lancet windows as tall as the cathedral's spires, which adorned the island's most important building, the senatorial palace.

Hannah found the archbishop lighting candles in the north transept where a simple steel hoop held a thousand red wax candles, one for each of the koans of the Circlist teachings. The candles were always going out, much as they did – so the archbishop said – in the hearts of the race of man that were meant to subscribe to them.

'I'm sorry I'm late,' announced Hannah.

Archbishop Alice Gray turned around with an appraising look at Hannah. What did she see before her? A young blonde girl with skin so pale it might as well be alabaster? The lazy blue-eyed youngster that hoped to follow the woman who had raised her into the Circlist church? A stubborn, slightly distant little dreamer who always seemed to cause mischief for the prelate who had taken her in as her ward after her parents' death?

'I don't suppose you were off studying for the algebra test

that Father Penley tells me he's setting the church class at the end of the week?' asked the archbishop.

'I'll pass it,' said Hannah.

'Yes, I'm sure you will. Then, undoubtedly you've been helping Damson Grosley fumigate the sleeping rooms for wall-louse.'

'I tried,' admitted Hannah. 'But the brimstone was making me choke. I thought I was going to be sick.'

The archbishop rolled her eyes. 'You're not the only one who is being tried. That is the point of it, Hannah. That's how you get rid of wall-louse.'

Sometimes, Hannah thought, the archbishop must have regretted taking her in aged three as a ward of the cathedral. If only Hannah's parents' boat hadn't been incinerated in the Fire Sea. If only she'd had other relatives still alive in the Kingdom of Jackals, then they both might have been spared such perennial disappointments. If Archbishop Alice Gray had such thoughts, the perpetual look of concern that she wore on her face, whatever and whoever she was dealing with, effectively masked them.

Hannah followed the archbishop into a lifting room, past the belfry – then up into the rectory testing rooms, vestries, refectory, charterhouse and lodgings for the church staff that formed the cathedral's highest level, but the lowest level of the Horn of Jago. Windowless at so low an elevation inside the mountain, and with nothing to look out on anyway except the frill of artillery tube placements waiting to drop mortar shells on anyone – or anything – foolish enough to try to storm either the capital's walls or its harbour.

It was the rectory testing rooms that Hannah was interested in this afternoon, though; always more hopefuls waiting in front of testing tables than there were fathers with seminary experience to administer the tests. While every shop, mill and concern in Hermetica City perpetually displayed

11

staff-wanted signs in their bow windows, the Circlist church had to turn away would-be novices queuing to enter its ranks. Or rather, sign up for the slim chance that the church might post them away from Jago and across the sea to one of the other Circlist nations.

The archbishop talked to the seminary head for a minute, before coming back towards Hannah.

'Father Blackwater has had no message from the church council, nothing in the post sack that arrived with the boat from Pericur this morning.'

'I need to sit the entrance exam,' protested Hannah.

'You are still two years away from being of age,' said the archbishop. 'You need special dispensation from the Rational Synod.'

'Do I?' asked Hannah. 'You're the Archbishop of Jago, you can grant me the dispensation.'

'No.' The archbishop shook her head, a stubborn glint in her green eyes that Hannah knew too well. 'It would be wrong for me to intervene where I have a personal interest. You are my ward; I have to excuse myself from the examination process. It is the right and rational thing to do.'

Hannah lost her temper and jabbed a finger at the other hopefuls waiting for the Entick test, the measurement of their aptitude and mastery of synthetic morality. 'So if I wasn't your ward, if I was just one of *them*, you'd give me your dispensation to sit the church entrance exam early?'

'You're two years away from the age of testing,' said the archbishop. 'And any answer I have to give would be far too clouded by my feelings for you.'

'I'm ready for it!'

'I don't doubt your abilities in casting analytical proofs, Hannah,' said the archbishop. 'There's too much of your mother in you for you to be anything other than a mathematical

12

prodigy. But you need a basis of experience to apply what you learn in the church, that's why there's an age set to take the test. If the church merely wanted to indoctrinate fanatics, if we wanted to train *preachers*, we'd have snatched you from your cot and invented deities to terrify your mind into obedience. You need a clear mind and a wise heart to work with your parishioners, with the experience of humility to know when you're falling short of either of those.'

'I don't even want to leave the island,' argued Hannah. 'I'd be happy to stay on Jago, not try to land the first vacant Jackelian vicarage or Concorzian parsonage that comes up.'

'I'm not concerned about you leaving the island.'

'You are,' accused Hannah. 'You want to keep me here, wallowing in the same ignorance you're sworn to try to banish.'

The archbishop sighed. 'We're not exactly a pit of ignorance here at the cathedral. I think you've been spending too much time listening to your ursine friend Chalph urs Chalph, young lady.'

Hannah could see this was an argument she wasn't going to win, and she was distracting the others taking the entrance exam. Some of the seminary fathers were looking up irritably from behind the piled leather tomes full of questions and equations to solve. A few of the candidates were trying to twist their heads around inside their rubber helmets, rattling the heavy lead-lined cables going back to the Entick machines. The goggles inside the hood measured the dilation of the iris in an attempt to ensure the questions were being answered truthfully, and her heated debate with the archbishop was probably skewing results across the testing room.

'Chalph is no fool. He said I'm going to have to leave the island to have a future,' retorted Hannah. 'Perhaps he's right.'

'"The finger that points at the moon isn't the moon,"' quoted the archbishop.

'Oh, please,' said Hannah, 'of all the koans . . . this is Jago. I haven't seen a moon through the mist for months.'

Hannah didn't hear the archbishop's reply. Someone was coming through the testing room door and her heart sank as she saw who it was. Vardan Flail. The long red robe he wore disguised the high guild master's awkward movements. The Circle knew what mutations he was hiding under that intricately embroidered crimson garb! If a foreigner were to enter the cathedral and see the archbishop standing next to Vardan Flail, they would lay eyes on his fancy red velvet mantle with all its woven transaction-engine symbols, note the archbishop's simple chequerboard-pattern cassock, and come to the conclusion that it was Flail who was head of the church here on Jago, not the archbishop.

A shiver went down Hannah's spine as she smelled the mint-like fragrance that had been infused into the valveman's velvet robes – sprayed, it was said, to disguise the smell of putrid flesh.

'I hope,' said the archbishop, 'that you aren't here to complain about the additional processing cycles that the testing sessions are going to require of your transaction engines.'

'Hope,' came the grinding voice under the cowl, 'or pray?'

'I won't tolerate that filthy language here in the cathedral!'

Which was precisely why he had said it.

'If you had need of extra processing power, I would bring the matter up in the appropriate forum – in front of the stained senate,' said Vardan Flail. 'We have power enough. It's not you that I have come to see, it is your young ward here.'

Her? Hannah looked with disgust at Flail's red cowl, just enough of the high guild master's pockmarked features visible in the shadow of the hood to turn her stomach. What in the name of the Circle did the most loathsome high guild master in the capital want with her?

'I have the results of the ballot,' said Vardan Flail.

The ballot? Hannah's stomach felt as if it was dropping down the city's deepest airshaft.

'Damson Hannah Conquest is one of the names that has been randomly selected for service within the guild.'

'*Randomly* selected by the programs running on your transaction engines,' said the archbishop.

'I don't care for your tone,' warned Vardan Flail. He pointed slowly to the testing equipment and then up towards the diode panels in the stone roof of the testing room. 'You seem happy enough to utilize the processing cycles of the engine rooms and draw power for the lights to keep your cathedral illuminated, but like everyone else here, you flinch at the sacrifices necessary to keep our island's mighty turbine halls humming.'

'I won't do it,' spluttered Hannah.

'Not turning up for balloted service is considered desertion,' threatened Vardan Flail, 'and you are far too clever to let yourself be exiled for that crime, young Hannah Conquest. With your mind you will settle in fine with us as an initiate cardsharp. We won't have that beautiful intellect of yours wasted hauling sacks of broken valves to the smelt or crawling inside the turbine halls' generators to oil the magnets. No, within a year you'll be able to turn out punch cards like you were born to it. Punch cards to control the most powerful transaction engines we possess. You will be able to make a difference that can be measured in the efficiency of everything you code.'

'And end up like you?' spat Hannah.

'These are my blessings,' said Vardan Flail, touching his arm. 'The sacred scars of duty.'

'The senate won't need to exile me beyond the city walls. I can ship out for the Kingdom of Jackals any time I want.'

'Legally perhaps,' sneered Vardan Flail. 'Although dual

nationality and the application of the draft is still a point of law that is open to examination; I should know, I checked the legality of the situation quite thoroughly before I came to see you, little lady. How many new anti-emigration bills have been passed this year? You can spend the few days before your service starts looking at the empty docks and wondering when the next Jackelian u-boat is going to come calling – because we both know there won't be any. And there's not a supply-boat captain this side of the Fire Sea willing to risk the senate's wrath by smuggling out a passenger without official exit papers.'

'This is outrageous!' said the archbishop. 'I will protest to the senate.'

'Of course you will. Everyone who is called to our service protests,' said Vardan Flail, sadly, as if the desire not to end up concealing a twisted body underneath crimson robes was a personal calumny against him. 'The bleating of our chosen is as natural as a steam storm after rain. After every annual ballot the floor of the senate is fleetingly filled with the cries of rich merchants' sons who are too good for our guild – or prelate's daughters who are too fine and unblemished to toil inside our vaults.' Vardan Flail reached out to stroke Hannah's face and she flinched back as his warm, wrinkled skin brushed against her face. 'This isn't your true beauty, girl, it's in there.' He prodded a finger against her forehead. 'Yes, it is in there, and we shall use it well. . .'

Hannah watched in horror as the valveman's claw-like fingers vanished back inside the sleeve of his robe. This wasn't happening to her. This wasn't any future fit for her! She was going to follow her guardian into the church, a quiet, easy life of meditation and reflection in the still peace of the cathedral. Thinking great and noble thoughts. Not bonded into labour for a beast like Vardan Flail, her body swelling and cracking and breaking until she too would have to scuttle through the streets of Hermetica City, hiding herself behind heavy robes from the gaze of everyone she knew on the island. Cursing mirrors, cursing her very reflection in the canal waters.

'Off you go, Hannah,' commanded the archbishop. 'I think it's time the high guild master and I continued our conversation alone in my chancellery office.'

Hannah waited in dread as the two of them left the testing room; the queuing would-be novices uncomfortably averting their gazes from the high guild master.

Then they were both gone and all Hannah could smell was the scent of mint in the air; mint and her cruelly crushed dreams.

'What,' asked archbishop Alice Gray as she shut the door to her chancellery office, 'is this really about? I don't come to the engine rooms and try to recruit your valvemen into the church orders. Is it too much to expect some of the same courtesy from a high guild master? Or is this what we have descended to now in Jago? So few people left to employ that we must poach labour from our neighbours' staff?'

'The courtesy is for a high guild master to take the time to come and serve a ballot notice personally,' hissed Vardan Flail.

'How gracious of you,' said the archbishop. 'Now, what's your real motive? Is it Hannah you want, or. . .?'

'There might be a way,' replied Vardan Flail, 'for me to forgo the services of your ward. A singular loophole in the statutes of the ballot of service that could be exploited.'

The archbishop's green eyes narrowed. 'Go on.'

'The ballot is not allowed to fall on a high guild master's own family. A very wise clause, don't you think? You only have to see how the stained senate works – or rather, how it doesn't – to know the harm that nepotism and favouritism within a guild would create.'

'But Hannah Conquest is not a member of your family.'

Vardan Flail dragged his body to the window looking over the cloister chamber below. 'She would be if you married me, Alice. Your ward, my ward. Everything squared. Or should that be joined on the Circle?'

'So that's what this is really about. You've had my answer on that matter before.'

Vardan Flail looked out of the window, gazing down towards the albino-pink blossom falling from the trees lining the cloister, a rain of it drifting in the draughts from the ventilation grilles. 'The unlikeliest things can blossom in the vaults of Jago, Alice. Look down there, the only trees that prosper well under diode light. Is it so unlikely that a union between the two of us might do the same? The tenets of Circlism set no store on the physical appearance of things, only our true selves. And we're very good Circlists in the engine rooms.' He pulled out a heavily pockmarked palm from underneath his sleeve's crimson velvet folds. 'The flesh fades and what remains is true.'

'Cavern bamboo also prospers like a weed down here. I don't doubt your belief in Circlism,' said the archbishop. 'Sometimes it verges on *faith*—' she pronounced the word like a curse '—but a meeting of minds is never enough for marriage, there must also be a meeting of hearts.'

'There are other things I can offer you,' said Vardan Flail. 'Like immortality.'

'A sketch of my face on paper isn't me,' said the archbishop, angrily. 'And a simulacrum of myself sealed up in the valves of your transaction engines isn't me, either. Our essence is cupped out into other lives after this. That's the only permanence you can trust, all else exists only as currents in the stream.'

'There must be someone else, another man,' hissed Vardan Flail, 'for you to keep rejecting me. Tell me who it is? Who has been courting you?'

'A long time ago, maybe, but not now. I have the duties of my position and the needs of the people of Jago to serve and that is enough for me. It will need to be enough for you too, Vardan Flail.'

'Then I will hold to them,' spat the crimson-robed form, limping towards the door. 'And I will hold to my duties with the fine mind of your ward added to the labours of the guild.'

'Over my dead body!'

'Your body really doesn't matter,' said Vardan Flail, menacingly as he departed. 'Not any more.'

CHAPTER TWO

The Kingdom of Jackals. Middlesteel.

Boxiron walked towards the drawing room, his heavy iron feet echoing on the polished, veined marble. There was a strip of carpet before the doorway and the clunking of his feet faded, muffled just enough to enable him to hear the voices from those gathered inside the drawing room through its closed door. It was luxuriously appointed, this Middlesteel townhouse, but then that was to be expected. Only the wealthy could afford the services of Jethro Daunt and his trusty servant, Boxiron.

The constable guarding the door looked at Boxiron advancing with a curious expression on her face. Steammen were a common enough sight in the Kingdom of Jackals, but they weren't usually quite so ramshackle. Boxiron had none of the grace of the creatures of the metal that bowed their knee to King Steam inside his mountain state. The modern shining skull of a steamman knight was inexpertly welded to the primitive body of a man-milled mechanical, steam hissing out of loose plates as he walked on his awkwardly jerking hinged feet.

'You been out looking for clues?' asked the constable, a simple crusher wearing the black uniform of the city's constabulary.

Boxiron gave a slight shake of his head, the movement amplified into a spastic jerking by his unsynchronized neck controls. No. What would be the point of looking for further evidence of misdoings now? Cuthbert Spicer, Lord Commercial of the Kingdom of Jackals, was just as dead as the finer sensory control servos running along Boxiron's neck, and both their masters now stood inside the drawing room for the culmination of the investigation – Inspector Reason of Ham Yard giving official sanction to the presence of Jethro Daunt and his metal servant.

Not that there was much of a pretence by anyone that the ex-man of the cloth would have been called in to uncover the truth of Lord Spicer's murder without the insistence of the victim's estate. Jethro Daunt's keen intellect might have been arguably better employed here than it ever had been when he was the parson of Hundred Locks, but it was not an argument that you would ever hear coming from the lips of any constable or police inspector, eager to keep amateurs out of their profession. It was not as if the capital's police force needed to feel threatened: for every high profile murder like Lord Spicer's, there were a hundred cases of garden variety grave robbing, kidnapping, counterfeiting and pick pocketing where the injured parties lacked the resources to engage a consulting detective.

'So, what are you here for then?' asked the policewoman on the door.

Before Boxiron could answer there was a shout from inside the room and the door was flung open with some vigour, knocking the constable off her feet, her hand – which had been resting on her police cutlass – flying out to steady herself.

Boxiron raised an arm and the exiting figure ran into it, crumpling as if a garden wall had dropped on top of his head. Knocked down to the carpet, the miscreant fumbled for the small pistol he had dropped and Boxiron took a step forward, his anvil-heavy foot smashing the gun and breaking at least three of the man's fingers.

'I am here for that,' explained Boxiron to the constable. The steamman's leg lashed out, kicking the villain in the ribs. 'And that, and that, and that, and that. . .'

'Good grief!' came a bewildered shout from inside the drawing room. 'Constable, stop that metal fellow, he's beating Lord Spicer's murderer to death.'

'Not like that, officer!' sounded a voice in warning. Boxiron's vision plate was already focusing on the palm of the constable reaching down for her black leather holster, and he began to calculate the arc his right arm would need to shatter her pistol hand. 'The lever! The lever on his back.'

Jethro Daunt lunged out of the doorway and dragged the lever on the back of the steamman's smoke stack down through its gear positions, slotting it back into its lower-leftmost groove. The little engraved brass plate placed there by the manufacturer read 'idle', but Boxiron's previous employers had scratched a line through the script and painted it over with the words 'slightly less-murderous', instead.

'Boxiron can't reach his gears by himself,' said Jethro Daunt, apologetically.

Or rather, no household in their right mind would ever buy a Catosian city-state manufactured automatic that left its regulation in its own iron hands. Boxiron's leg crunched down and the suspect's beating was over; at least, the one he was going to receive from the consulting detective and his assistant. What he was going to receive inside the cells of Ham Yard was another matter. The constable forced the suspected

22

murderer roughly to his feet, translating her embarrassment at being taken by surprise while on duty into a rather rude handling of her prisoner.

Boxiron turned to see Jethro Daunt and the police detective at the door behind him. Inspector Reason standing a shade under Daunt's six foot – the inspector's hard cynical face the polar opposite of the erudite, distinguished features of Boxiron's beak-nosed employer. The others in the drawing room – all potential suspects – were hovering nervously, watching as the suspect was manacled.

'But the Circle damn it, Daunt, how did you know that it was Spicer's own doctor who killed him?' asked the inspector.

'He bobbed us for fools,' explained Jethro Daunt. 'The smell of elderflower in the library we came across wasn't the bottle of scent that had cracked when Lord Spicer fell down inside the room. Its label read Kittle and Abrams, and their firm sell no scent with elderflower as an ingredient. The scent was a decoy to mask the smell of something else . . . a sleeping draught administered by the doctor to make Damson Stow fall asleep, giving the doctor time to wind back the carriage clock and make us think that the murder happened half an hour earlier than it actually did.'

'But how did you know about the clock?' asked the inspector.

'Because when the doctor slipped back to reset it to the correct time, he did so using Damson Stow's own pocket watch, and that runs ten minutes fast – she told me she kept it like that, so that she would never miss her day's deliveries coming into her kitchen. And that's why she also had to die. When the damson realized what the doctor had done, she tried to blackmail him over Lord Spicer's murder.'

'Poor woman,' said the inspector. 'She probably never knew the doctor was the illegitimate child of Lord Spicer and her sister.'

'Raised with enough money to pass through the royal college of medicine,' said Jethro, 'but not enough to paper over the grievances of the family fortune sliding away from him and towards his half-brothers and sister.'

'You almost cheated the hangman out of a handsome crowd,' the inspector said to Boxiron. 'They'll pay more than a penny a seat to see a respected doctor swing outside the walls of Bonegate.'

'Sorry, inspector,' apologized Boxiron. 'My steam was up and my gears slipped.'

'No harm done, eh, old steamer.'

Now securely restrained by the constable's manacles, the murderer winced at the pressure his arms, bent around his back, were putting on the ribs the steamman had cracked. 'My father said I was a god for curing him. But I cured him of everything that was wrong with him in the end. What sort of god does that make me?'

'The only sort there are, I am afraid,' said Jethro, sadly. 'The rather dangerous kind.'

Behind the ex-parson, the other suspects had fallen into a staccato chattering – proclaiming that they had known all along the killer hadn't been any of those left inside the drawing room.

Jethro Daunt shook his head at their naivety and caught up with Boxiron's hulking form just before the heavy steamman departed the town house, his voicebox muttering to himself in machine-like echoes. When his friend's steamman head had been attached to the centaur-like form of a steamman knight, his voicebox has possessed the power to cast a battle cry that could burst a human heart inside its chest. Now it was attached to an inferior piece of Catosian machinery, however, all Boxiron could do was whisper half-mad dialogues to himself

– cursing the Steamo Loas and the cruel hand of fate for how he had ended up.

'You did well enough, good friend,' said Jethro, laying a hand on the steamman's cold iron shoulder. 'You prevented the doctor from escaping.'

'I nearly killed him. My thoughts travel too fast for this body,' said Boxiron, allowing only a small trace of self-pity to escape into his voice. 'Stuck in a loop every time I over-reach myself.'

'The mind is willing but the flesh is weak,' said Jethro, opening the front door onto the neat square in Middlesteel's expensive western district, the railings of the crescent thoroughly polished, a thousand metal spears gleaming in the sunshine.

'It's not my flesh that is weak,' said Boxiron, his legs pistoning down the wide porch steps to the cobbled pavement below. 'That's one burden I don't carry.'

Jethro angled a nose that was too proud for his kind face towards the cab rank at the end of the street, and one of the drivers flicked his whip, sending a midnight-black mare clattering forwards. Just before the hansom cab could reach the two of them, though, it was cut up by a larger coach, this one a horseless carriage with iron wheels as tall as a man at the rear. As his horse spooked, the cab driver swore furiously, shaking his fist at the whining clockwork contraption. But the new vehicle wasn't a rival in the carriage trade, for all that its black iron matched the sheen of the hansom cab's dark walnut exterior.

Riveted iron doors swung open on each side of the horseless carriage, tall men dressed like Circlist monks with simple grey robes stepping out onto the street side and staring down the cabbie, who swapped his obscenities for a final scowl before driving off. On the pavement side of the carriage, a nun aged about sixty stepped out, dressed like her companions – although she had not tonsured her greying hair, but had her locks tied back in two buns above her ears. The monks stood very still, with a calmness that hung in the air like the glint of sunlight on a brandished dagger.

Boxiron stomped noisily on the pavement, his hulking, unwieldy body swivelling to take in the ranks of monks now surrounding them – more exiting from the second iron room at the back of the horseless carriage. Some of the monks carried staffs and Jethro Daunt doubted they were intended to aid infirmities or for the long travels of a pilgrimage. He just hoped Boxiron didn't slip a gear now.

'I have been defrocked,' said Jethro. 'I'm no longer in the church.'

The woman's head rocked to one side. Of course she would know that. It would have been people rather like these pressing the ecclesiastical court to throw him out of his parsonage.

'I understand you have been operating as a consulting detective for the last few years,' said the woman.

'That is true,' said Jethro.

'Of course it is. I wish to *consult* with you.' There was quite a tone of menace in that single word, for all the eerie calmness in her face.

'Well, well,' said Jethro. 'I'll be bobbed. Of all the people in the capital I might have expected to be conversing with about my current mode of employment, your people are the very last ones I would have expected to turn up.'

'As it should be,' noted the woman. 'Of those that know of the existence of the League of the Rational Court, there are even fewer that should be aware when they are about to be touched by our hand.'

Jethro looked at the open door of the carriage and the woman pointing to the empty red leather seat opposite the one she had just vacated. An invitation with exceedingly little choice in it.

And carriage rides with these people were sometimes one-way affairs.

The hand of the Circlist church's League of the Rational Court. The hand of the *Inquisition*.

Hannah Conquest pushed aside the thick brambles to try and find the path. Like all of the great domed greenhouses nestled in the shadows of the Horn of Jago, Tom Putt Park was named after its creator – or at least the merchant notable who had paid for it to be constructed. Nestling against the battlements, far from the city, Tom Putt Park had drawn the short straw when it came to maintenance from the dwindling band of park keepers and farm labourers. They were presently engaged in the serious business of feeding the capital, not pruning the wild-running hedges and copses under Tom Putt's crystal geodesic canopy.

It always felt a curious thing to Hannah, moving through the bush and the greenery of the park. In a very real sense she wasn't walking on the soil of Jago. All the dirt here, and in every other park and farm dome, not to mention the tree beds in Hermetica's vaults below, had been imported by traders' barges in centuries past. Dirt from the Kingdom of Jackals on the far side of the Fire Sea, as well as from Pericur and the other nations on the opposite shores. The native top-soil beyond the capital's battlements was fit only for growing stunted fruitless orchards, those and the island's blackened forests of thorns that cut at travellers with the sharpness of the machetes needed to hack out a passage amongst them. Not that many dared to venture outside without wearing heavily armoured walking machines – RAM suits, as the trappers and city maintenance workers called them. The aging power tunnels that fed the city with the energy its people required always needed upkeep, as did the iron aqueducts

27

carrying in fresh drinking water down from the hills. A job that was almost as unappealing as what Hannah suspected was in store for her with the guild. . .

Hannah found the path again and after a minute came to the flint wall that would lead her to the stone singers. Chalph urs Chalph was waiting by the circle of moss-stained marble statues when she came to the clearing, looking as if he might join in the fertility song the circle of carvings were said to be singing to the stone apple tree in their centre. A reminder of more prosperous times that had once paid for the park and its upkeep. There was little time for wassailing now. The city was lucky if its entire crop could be collected before it spoiled lying on the domes' dirt.

'I've just seen the ballot list posted,' Chalph called to her. 'Although if I hadn't, the look on your face might tell me the tale by itself.'

'Well, I've found my future,' said Hannah. 'Rotting away in the engine rooms as an initiate of the Guild of Valvemen.'

'The draft ballot's been nailed up everywhere in the city. The senate are calling more people than ever before this year for the protected professions.' He licked at a paw-like hand. 'But you have dual citizenship through your parents. You can just leave. . .'

'How, by walking across the Fire Sea?' asked Hannah. 'That twisted jigger Vardan Flail seems to think the supply boat from Pericur isn't going to be selling tickets out of here when it comes to me, not to *anyone* who's been called by the draft, in fact.'

'There must be something you can do. . .'

'I don't want to end up like them,' said Hannah, almost sobbing. 'Have you ever seen what's under a valveman's robes? Working in the engine rooms changes your body, kills you eventually.'

28

'You can claim asylum,' speculated Chalph. 'The Jackelian ambassador, the short fellow with the red nose, he could grant you asylum in his embassy.'

'That old fool? Sir Robert Cugnot is lucky to remember to stuff the cork back in his wine bottle before he turns in of a night. How are he and his staff going to keep me safe? Nobody can dodge the draft now, the militia always finds you. It doesn't matter where you hide, in a friend's house, in one of the empty quarters, they always track you down in the end.'

'Then take the seminary vows like you wanted to,' urged Chalph. 'You're clever enough to pass the examinations and the guild can't draft you if you're already working for the church.'

'Alice won't waive the age limit for me,' said Hannah. 'I begged her. But I'm her ward and proffering me for early advancement is not the right and rational thing to do.'

Chalph shook his heavy dark-furred head in anger. 'And letting your body cook in the energies of the guild's engine rooms *is*?'

'That won't be Alice's choice; it'll be Vardan Flail's. Circle damn the man, I hate him. Always coming around the cathedral, trying to ingratiate himself with Alice, the stink of decay and death on his robes.'

'I'll get you out of here,' promised Chalph. 'The supply boat from Pericur is owned by the House of Ush. I'll find one of our sailors willing to take on board a stowaway, there must be one of them who'll help me.'

'The militia search the boats now before they let them leave. But it won't come to that,' said Hannah, trying to sound more hopeful than she actually felt. 'Alice will argue for me. She's cleverer than the whole stained senate put together. If there's a loophole. . .'

Chalph was about to answer when he turned his head and sniffed the air. 'It – no!'

Hannah couldn't smell anything, but she could hear the distant crackle of brambles as something heavy pushed through the undergrowth. 'What is it?'

'It's an *ursk*,' whispered Chalph.

'How would the monster get inside the park? It should have been fried coming over the city wall,' said Hannah, looking uncertainly in the direction of the noise. 'Ursks are similar enough to your people, Chalph. You must have the scent of one of your house-men coming looking for you skiving.'

'Ursks are nothing like my people,' said Chalph, backing up. He seized Hannah's arm. 'Run! Back to the entrance now.'

Hannah let her friend break through the passage of greenery ahead of her, trampling bushes and breaking creepers with his mass. If it was an ursk . . . Chalph had a keen nose, but the monsters that inhabited the island's interior depended on *theirs* for feeding. She heard the crashing behind them – a savage racket. Just the sort of clatter something twice as heavy as an ursine would make loping after them. How many times had Hannah heard people sitting at the tea-tables in the vaults below whispering that the killing charge running along the city's battlements was failing now, predicting that something like this would happen sooner or later?

Chalph howled in fear and rage as he pushed forward, but there was no one else to hear it in Tom Putt Park. That was the point of coming here, you could be alone without being spotted by priests and housemen and assigned the kinds of tasks that often came to mind when faced with idling young-sters. Chalph's howl was echoed by something similar-sounding, but louder, coming from behind them. That sound came from no ursine! Off to their side another roar answered the first, a quick bestial exchange of information. Two ursks, or more? How had the monsters got over the battlements alive? A section of Hermetica's defences had to be down. Their sloping iron ramparts were over forty feet high, the electric charge they carried enough to hurl back the corpse of any creature unwise enough to touch them.

Hannah urged her cramping legs to hurry. Ursks, what did she know about ursks? Nothing that could help them here. Only stories from the men that ventured outside the walls: trappers, hunters, and city maintenance workers. Tales of bear-like monsters that prowled the basalt plains and volcanic mountains. Twice the size of a Pericurian and thrice the weight of anyone from the race of man. Monstrous, thick-furred killers that hunted in packs and could rip a Jagonese citizen apart in seconds with their claws. Almost – but not quite fully – sentient, with enough guile and cunning to plan ambushes and lure those travelling overland away from the safety of a well-armed caravan. Always hungry, always prowling the capital's battlements.

Hannah tripped on part of the crumbling old path through the undergrowth just as a long, black-furred shape seemed to pass endlessly through the air where she had been standing; the stench of rotten, steam-slicked fur filling her nose. It didn't matter how many of its pack had broken through the wall alongside this monster. Hannah and Chalph were unarmed. This single ursk would be more than enough to kill them a dozen times over.

Still on the ground, Hannah scrambled back in terror, gaping at the foul thing that landed snarling in front of her, a nightmare carved in flesh.

Jethro Daunt climbed into the horseless carriage's forward compartment and Boxiron made to clamber up behind him, but the nun shook her head at the steamman and pointed across to an organ grinder entertaining a group of children in the crescent's garden opposite. 'Not you. We require the one playing, not the one dancing.'

The red light behind Boxiron's vision plate flared in anger, but Jethro shook his head at his friend. 'There's really no call to be impolite, good sister.'

'Of course,' said the woman. 'My apologies, steamman. Your talents are not what I require presently.'

'I use my talents to keep my softbody friend here safe,' spat Boxiron.

The woman merely smiled in reply.

'We're in the open, it's daylight and we've just walked out of a house filled with Ham Yard's finest detectives,' said Jethro to the steamman. 'Save your top gear for the moment, good friend, I believe my life is safe.'

Boxiron looked at the large monks climbing back into the rear room of the carriage. 'You may be without gods, but if I find a hair out of place on Jethro softbody's head when next I see him, you will find cause to wish you had someone to pray to.'

Opposite Jethro, the nun shrugged nonchalantly. 'The funny thing about those Steamo Loas you worship, creature of the metal, is that even on closer examination, they're still mostly steam.'

As their carriage pulled away, Boxiron began to clump angrily back towards their lodgings at number ten Thompson Street.

'He's hardly subtle,' said the nun, watching the gas lamps whisk past now that her horseless carriage was speeding up.

'As you said,' noted Jethro,' it's not what he's for. He's a topping old steamer, really.'

'And what are you for, Jethro Daunt?'

'I'm all for whiling away my remaining years on the Circle's turn with as much serenity as I can find,' said Jethro, rummaging around in his pocket to withdraw a crumpled paper bag filled with black and white-striped sweets. 'Would you care for a Bunter and Benger's aniseed drop? They're quite wondrous.'

The nun looked at the bag with barely disguised disgust. 'You realize those foul things are highly addictive? The sugar is mixed with poppy opiates. Parliament should have outlawed them years ago.'

'Slander on the part of their competitors, I am sure,' said Jethro. 'They help me to think. I don't suppose you are going to tell me your real name, or your rank within the Inquisition?'

'Not if you insist on calling us by that vulgar name,' said the woman. 'You're a little too educated to be reading the penny dreadfuls.'

'The League of the Rational Court, then, if you prefer,' replied Jethro. 'I would say you are a mother superior.'

The woman picked up a heavy folder from her side, its contents protected by a wax seal. It put Jethro in mind of a ministry dispatch box, the kind you might spy from the visitors' gallery at the House of Guardians, being carried by a politician on the floor below.

'Deduced from my age or the size of my carriage?'

Jethro pulled out his pocket watch, the chain dangling from his green waistcoat. 'From the time, good sister.'

The woman raised an eyebrow.

'Half an hour to read the petitions a mother superior accepts before lunch, another half an hour to get here for midday.'

'That would suggest you know where the league is based.'

'You'll be surprised at what can be whispered in dreams,' said Jethro. 'Even postal addresses, sometimes.'

'Which gods do you hear the most, now?'

'You mean the gods that don't exist?' smiled Jethro. 'On balance, I would say Badger-headed Joseph is my most frequent visitor, although I find what Old Mother Corn whispers to me is often the most reliable.'

The woman broke the seal on the folder and opened it, lifting out a parcel of papers tied tightly with red cord. 'It's small bloody wonder we threw you out of the church.'

'I wonder about it,' said Jethro. 'I wonder about it all the time. But haven't I kept my end of the bargain? Not a hint of scandal, no stories about me in the penny sheets.'

'Not as the ex-parson of Hundred Locks,' said the woman. 'But you've been keeping busy as the proprietor of Daunt's Private Resolutions. Quite a reputation you've built up among the quality, solving cases, hunting down criminals.'

'So you say.'

'I find it slightly grubby, myself,' muttered the woman. 'All those years the church spent training you in synthetic morality and here you are now, applying your finely honed mind to uncovering sordid infidelities and unmasking common poisoners.'

'There's exceedingly little that's common about such crimes. To keep the gods from the people's hearts, you must first understand the people,' quoted Jethro. 'And while I acknowledge your disdain for my new calling, I believe expediency has driven you to seek out those same skills as much as it has pushed me towards a career outside the church to keep my coal scuttle full and the bailiffs from my door.'

'The irony isn't lost on me,' said the mother superior, passing the parcel of papers across to Jethro.

'What is it?' he asked.

'A murder,' said the woman.

'It must be important for you to come to me.'

'Clearly.'

'Important enough for you to give me back my parsonage if I asked for reinstatement in the rational orders as my payment?'

The reverend mother laughed heartedly, the first real emotion Jethro had seen her demonstrate. 'We don't let people inside the Circlist church who believe in gods. Not as parishioners, and certainly not as parsons. I do believe your ancient gods have driven you quite mad.'

'As I told your people at my hearing, I don't believe in them,' retorted Jethro.

She shrugged. 'Well, perhaps they believe in you, rather than vice versa. It doesn't matter. The distinction is irrelevant and besides, we're asking you to investigate precisely because you're *not* in the church. Believe it or not, we do have a few minds in the league that are almost as proficient in synthetic morality as the much-vaunted Jethro Daunt. Aren't you going to open the folder? You will quickly see why we believe this case would be of particular interest to you.'

'No,' said Jethro. 'I'm not interested in your money, I'm not interested in working for the Inquisition, and most of all, I'm not interested in continuing this conversation.'

'We can offer you a hundred guineas to take the case, triple that upon a successful conclusion.'

'I've already got a hundred guineas,' Jethro told the woman. 'I get to choose the members of my flock now.'

The woman sniffed disapprovingly, then banged on the roof of her carriage for it to draw to a halt. 'Keep the folder. Read the papers. It sounds as if you already know where to send your note indicating that you agree to be engaged.'

'Not in a hundred years, good mother superior,' said Jethro, opening the door and starting to climb down the steps extending towards the street with a clockwork clack. 'Not even in a thousand.'

The nun leant out of the window. 'Is it just the precepts of synthetic morality that have helped you solve all the cases you've taken, Jethro? Or do the voices you hear at night whisper other things, too? What do all those ranks of pagan gods really murmur to you?'

'That the intellect is only a lie to make us realize the truth.'

'Just send word,' tutted the woman at Jethro's blasphemy. Her carriage pulled away, the hum of the engine disappearing as it rounded a corner.

Jethro looked at the collection of papers in his hand and pulled his cloak tight against the cold of the afternoon. The folder's contents would do for a five-minute crackle of kindling in his fire grate, if nothing else.

Jethro Daunt knew many things: the things that his finely tuned mind could extract from the pattern of life swirling around him, and the things that the ancient gods hissed at him in his dreams. But what he didn't know was what in the name of the Circle had possessed the Inquisition to think that he could possibly be coerced, tricked or cajoled into working for the same organization that had hounded him out of the church.

Jethro ran his fingers thoughtfully through his long sideburns, the black running to silver now, and cleared his throat as he always did before he sucked on an aniseed ball and his brain began to whir.

'How extremely diverting,' he whispered to himself, balancing the papers in his hand.

Then he strode back towards his apartment.

Twisting on the overgrown path where she had fallen, Hannah flinched back from the snarling, intertwined forms – Chalph lost in the larger black mass of the ursk. Chalph, brave suicidal Chalph, who had charged the beast when they were cornered. Not only was the creature attacking them at least twice the weight of Hannah's ursine friend, its fur was matted across a leather-thick skin hardened against the steam mists and geyser plumes of the volcanic landscape outside. You would be hard pressed to have opened its hide with a sabre, let alone the tooth and claw of a mere ursine cub.

But a turret rifle, *that* would do it. As the ursk angrily tossed Chalph off itself, throwing him back into the brambles and rearing up on all fours, its chest exploded open. Toppling backward, the ursk fell to the side of Hannah and landed like a collapsing mountain an inch shy of Chalph's leather boots. Hannah glanced up to see a three-foot long rifle being lowered, the rotating ammunition drum clacking to a halt as the finger depressing the trigger uncurled and the clockwork-driven mechanism slowed. Hannah scrambled back as the cable attached to the shooter's brass tank of compressed gas went limp and dropped past her nose.

Hannah pointed back through the brambles they had flattened while fleeing the ursk. 'There's at least one more over there.'

The free company fighter that had come to their rescue – at least a head taller than Chalph at seven foot – growled in acknowledgement. 'And it knows what the bark of a turret gun sounds like, as it should.' The soldier sniffed the air with her black nose. 'It's heading over to the other side of the park.'

Chalph picked himself up from the dirt. 'Stom urs Stom, what are the free company doing inside the park?'

'Our job,' growled the over-sized soldier. She had a leather patch covering her left eye socket and looked like a brown-furred buccaneer as she scowled down at Hannah and her friend. 'The guard post reported seeing ursks coming over the wall. It looks like a section of the battlements have lost their charge.'

'How can that happen?' demanded Hannah. It was a rhetorical question.

'Lack of repairs would be my guess,' said Stom. 'Not enough people left on the island to maintain anything the way it should be kept. Now, stay close, this one's friend might be circling around to take us from the rear.'

The soldier strode forward as Hannah and Chalph trailed in her wake, Chalph's triangular black nose snuffling the air for a clue to the second monster's whereabouts. 'But its scent is coming from the other side.'

The soldier angrily raised her paw-like hand. 'Hold your tongue, Chalph urs Chalph. It's pissed on the undergrowth over there to draw us off in the wrong direction.' She thrust a finger to the left. 'I hunt that way. Stay behind my rifle to stay alive.'

'Chalph was just trying to help,' said Hannah.

'When I want a price for grain I will ask a junior clerk from the House of Ush's advice,' said the soldier. 'The first time you underestimate an ursk, little furless cub, is the last time you underestimate an ursk.'

They passed an overgrown gazebo built from flint sealed with white mortar. Chalph whispered to Hannah as the mercenary forged ahead through the abandoned park. 'Stom urs Stom is the captain of the free company. Don't ever cross her. Even the baroness is wary of her.'

In front, the soldier raised her paw and Hannah and Chalph stopped. Stom urs Stom peered suspiciously around a thicket of birch trees. They were almost at the edge of the park, the greenhouse's crystal walls rising above their heads. Hannah could hear the wind from outside close by. They must be near where the ursk had cracked the dome to gain entry after scaling the battlements. Stom stalked forwards, her dark leather clothes disappearing through the trees. Hannah heard her curse and quickly followed. A manhole cover had been wrenched out of a stone conduit running around the base of the greenhouse wall, just large enough for an ursk to drop through. Hannah looked over the edge. She could just see a fast-flowing stream of water below, its heat striking her face. A flash-steam conduit, part of the city's heating system – and it would eventually lead to the vaults of the capital below.

'It'll die down there,' said Hannah.

'An ursk can swim through superheated geyser water before diving for an hour in a frozen lake,' said the soldier. 'What's down in those drains won't kill it.' She patted her rifle. 'What's in here will.'

Voices sounded from the break in the dome, ursine voices talking in the modulated growls of the Pericurian language. Stom urs Stom moved towards the smashed panels of the dome and barked orders at her fighters.

The reality of what had just occurred sank into Hannah. Ursks and the other creatures of the interior had occasionally breached the battlements before, when the wall's killing power failed, but they had always been shot down outside. She couldn't ever remember a time when they had got into Hermetica City's vaults – it was the citizens' greatest fear.

Hannah realized the fact that she and Chalph had been in the abandoned park – the same park the ursks had smashed into – would put them under suspicion of complicity in the creatures' intrusion. Chalph, the apprentice merchant, one of the venal wet-snout foreigners profiting from Jago's hard times. Hannah, the lazy church girl whose parents weren't even Jagonese, the reckless outsider who was known to climb air vents to travel beyond the vaults.

They were both in a great deal of trouble now.

The streets were alive with people when Hannah and Chalph followed the hulking mercenary captain down into the central vaults of Hermetica City. The diode lamps in the roofs of the caverns had dimmed for the evening, while the street lamps burned a brilliant yellow. Mobs of citizenry ran around the canal-lined streets carrying chemical braziers, most clustering tightly around the green-uniformed police militia with their long rifles. Heavy free company soldiers swept their turret rifles' barrels across the surface of the canal from gondolas running low in the water. The vaults were the territory of the Jagonese police militia. The fact that so many mercenary fighters had been allowed down from the battlements at all was a sign of how bad the situation was.

Stom urs Stom stopped on a bridge and one of her ursine fighters came running up alongside a Jagonese militiaman, halting to beat her chest with her paw in a salute. Stom looked at her fighter. 'Why are the city lights still on evening time? We need full daylight to hunt properly.'

'We have sent word to the Guild of Valvemen,' the militia-man interjected defensively, 'but it may not be possible to switch the city to daylight quickly enough to serve the search.'

'Why should it be otherwise?' growled Stom urs Stom. 'When it seems the guild can't even keep the battlements fully charged now?'

The militiaman snorted as he heard this. Hannah knew there was an intense rivalry between the local police militia and the foreign mercenaries who had usurped their ancient position as the battlements' sentries, and this man did not take kindly to the city's institutions being belittled by wet-snout savages. He slotted the base of his staff of office in a control socket on the highest point of the bridge, sliding up a panel to expose a line of keys enamelled with shorthand communication symbols, and began tapping out a message – no doubt a call for extra police to be dispatched towards their position.

From lower down the canal there were shouts from one of

the gondolas, the guttural cry of a free company mercenary followed by the howl of depressurizing gas from the brass tank on the fighter's back. As she fired her turret rifle spouts of water erupted where her pitons struck. A forest of bobbing torches and the insistent cries of the crowd up on the streets indicated that the mercenary had found one of the intruders.

'There!' cried Hannah as a black shape glided under another gondola. The gondola slammed into the air, unseating both the gondolier and his mercenary passenger. The man fell into the water screaming and disappeared thrashing inside a bubbling maelstrom, while the mercenary hit the water silently. She must know that she would be next, after the ursk swimming underneath finished off the weakest victim – the gondolier. She didn't even try to swim to the side of the canal.

'Shoot the water!' the militiaman next to Hannah shouted at the mercenaries. 'Shoot the water, she's dead down there anyway.'

But none of the massive Pericurian mercenaries was listening. A couple of seconds after the gondolier had disappeared, the mercenary fighter was pulled under the water, vanishing as quickly as if she had just winked out of existence. Almost instantly a massive plume of water gushed up in her place, showering the bridge where Hannah stood with steaming water.

A guttural humming sounded from the mercenaries, and they raised their fists towards the vault's roof as they sang the death hymn for their comrade. Hannah glanced down at her clothes. The water that had spattered her was tinged crimson with the blood of the ursk and of the dead foreign mercenary.

'It was her kill,' said Stom to the militiaman, patting the belt of spherical grenades looping around her waist. 'That is why we did not fire. It was her kill. Turret rifle bolts are slowed by water. The ursk we hunted knew that.'

'She killed herself,' said the militiaman in disgust. 'You people truly are savages.'

Hannah looked at the tall mercenary commander silently scanning the water. No. The ursine were a force of nature. Fractious, quick to temper, but magnificent. Quite magnificent.

'There might be more monsters in the canals,' said Hannah.

'If there are, the presence of the crowds will keep them in the water,' said Stom, grimly.

But word of the ursks infiltrating the city was to come quicker than any of them had anticipated. Another militiaman came running up to the bridge and after a brief exchange with his superior, the green-uniformed man turned to Stom. 'Your fighters are requested to deploy in the Seething Round, wet-snout. There has been an attack there.'

Hannah looked with horror towards Chalph. An attack on the vault where she lived.

'Where?' demanded Hannah. 'Where inside the Seething Round?'

'The cathedral,' replied the militiaman. 'It's the archbishop. She's been torn apart by the bloody beasts.'

CHAPTER THREE

It was the same dream that Jethro Daunt always had. He was back inside the confessional of his parsonage at Hundred Locks. They didn't even know – many of the refugees who came to him – what a Circlist church meant. Its stone didn't look much different to that of the churches across the Kingdom of Jackals' borders. It wasn't as if the refugees could look at the flint walls and know there were no gods inside them. The churches in Quatérshift were filled with the paraphernalia of the Sun Child, and a light priest's cassock wasn't so different from a Circlist parson's clothes – the golden sunburst of their deity replacing the silver circle. But there were no gods in this church, *no* gods.

Jethro sweated on his side of the confessional, his cubicle a claustrophobic trap. He heard a scratching on the other side of the grille, a claw dragging across the filigree of equations etched across the walls. Not one of the refugees, this time, then. One of the *others*. The ancient things that usually visited his dreams afterwards. Black and silver fur brushed against the grille, and a snorting like that of a bull wading in a water meadow sounded from the other side. Badger-headed Joseph.

43

An ancient god that was meant to have lightning for sight, except Jethro never got to see its eyes.

'Fiddle-faddle fellow,' growled Badger-headed Joseph, in the kind of voice that you would expect to come from something half-man and half-beast. 'Are you shy, Jethro Daunt, little man, little fiddle-faddle fellow? Too shy to open the Inquisition's post?'

Jethro glanced down towards his lap. There was the package, still unopened, the gift of the Inquisition's highly placed emissary. 'It is not my business; it is the Inquisition's. I reject it and I reject you, Badger-headed Joseph.'

More scratching sounded from the other side. 'Do you reject curiosity, too, fiddle-faddle fellow? Part of you must want to know what's in the folder. *Whose* name is in the folder? The same part of you that stuck your hand in the fire when you were a child. When your grandfather warned you to watch out for the embers.'

'I am Jethro Daunt, I am my own man. I serve the rational order.' He tried humming the algebra-heavy mantra of the first hymn that sprang to mind, but the scratching grew louder, breaking the concentration needed to enter a meditation.

'Take care, little fiddle-faddle fellow. You make your intellect your god – it has powerful muscles but a poor personality. Not like me. Here comes the rain. . .' There was a moaning noise of relief on the other side of the confessional booth and a powerful stench assailed Jethro's nose. The ancient god was urinating against his side of the booth.

'This is a rational house,' shouted Jethro, retching. 'It has no place for you, Badger-headed Joseph. No place for the old gods. I cast you out!'

'You're not a parson anymore,' growled the voice behind the grille. 'Make me happy, fiddle-faddle fellow; indulge your curiosity with the packet.'

Jethro Daunt woke with a start. His bedroom was dark save for the illumination of the triple-headed gas lamp in Thompson Street burning beyond his window. Just enough light to see the tightly bound folder from the Inquisition.

He looked at it, the echo of his grandfather's warning as his hand reached for the fire grate whispering across the darkness.

Boxiron thumped along the corridor. He had trouble enough approximating sleep during the small hours, the hearing folds on the side of his head wired into the inferior routing mechanisms of the man-milled neck join randomly amplifying the sounds of the night.

Opening the door with far more vigour than he had expected – or requested – from his arm servos, Boxiron was faced with a sight strange even for their chambers at Thompson Street.

Jethro Daunt was in the middle of the floor, the folder from the Inquisition cut open with a letter knife. Papers and notes sodden with the consulting detective's tears were scattered across a rug in the centre of the room.

Glancing up, Jethro noticed the steamman as he entered. 'She's dead. After all these years, she's dead.'

The light in the centre of Boxiron's vision plate flared with anger. This was the Inquisition's work. It wasn't just Jethro Daunt who was an expert at staring into a softbody's soul. Curiosity. Curiosity could always be counted on to undermine Jethro's resolve. Every time. The Loas damn the devious minds of the Inquisition.

'You're going to do what they want, aren't you? You're going to take their case.'

Jethro rested his spine against the foot of the bed and stared up at the ceiling, a blank look on his face. A mask. 'Of course I am.'

And where Jethro went, Boxiron would inevitably follow.

As he so often did, Jethro began to hum one of his mad little ballads as he leafed through the papers spread around him. He didn't hum church hymns anymore, that pained him too much; but he had picked up many ditties from the drinking houses their informers frequented. *'Well of all the dogs it stands confessed, your Jackelian bulldogs are the best.'*

The steamman noticed the stack of unpaid bills on the table in the room, a little higher every day. Boxiron hoped that the League of the Rational Court could be counted upon to pay more promptly than Lord Spicer's estate.

It was a terrible sight to see inside the cathedral – normally so tranquil and shaded – now lit by the brightly burning diode lamps of the police militia as they moved about the nave, throwing open the doors leading down to the crypt and checking the transept for any sign of ursks. Nobody was protesting the presence of the heavily armed free company soldiers with them. The green-uniformed police militia was interviewing the few monks and vergers left inside the cathedral. Hannah and Chalph pressed past for a view of the confessional booths along the side of the far wall.

'We weren't here,' Hannah heard a verger telling a militia officer. 'Hordes of people came across the cathedral's bridges begging for help. We were out with the people carrying torches alongside the canals. Only she stayed behind.'

She. Hannah looked unbelievingly towards where the police were kneeling outside the confessional booths, blood flooded across the flagstones. Dear Circle, those were the archbishop's robes on that stump. That *decapitated* stump.

'Alice!' yelled Hannah, trying to press forward.

'Who let her in here?' frowned Colonel Knipe. Jago's imposing silver-headed police commander limped forward on his artificial leg.

46

'Is it Alice?'

'It is the archbishop's body,' said the colonel sadly, pushing Hannah and Chalph back.

'Where's her head? Where's her head?'

'Don't look at the body, this isn't something for you to see,' ordered the colonel.

She couldn't take it in. There wasn't even a skull left on the woman who had raised Hannah as her own daughter. And some of their last words. . . . The accusation that Alice had been trying to trap her here. . .

'Where's her head?' Chalph demanded.

'I wish I knew,' said the colonel. 'It's not inside the cathedral. The ursk that did this must have ripped pieces off the archbishop to feed on later.'

Chalph sniffed the air. 'I can't smell any ursk scent in here.'

'You think her head fell off of its own accord, sprouted legs and ran away?' snapped the colonel. He tapped his metal leg, the clockwork-driven mechanism inside whirring back at him. 'I know things about ursks, wet-snout. The only difference between filth like those monsters and your people is about twenty stone in weight and a leather shirt.'

'Pericurian free company soldiers are the only thing keeping Hermetica City safe,' cried Chalph in outrage.

'What a good job your people are doing,' sneered the colonel. 'I told the senate that paying for free company mercenaries to patrol our walls was a mistake of the highest order. When you fight for money, money is all you value. You wet-snouts let this happen, cub. You want to scare us all off your sacred soil, but it's not going to happen. We've been here for two thousand years and we'll be here for another thousand before your damn archduchess holds one inch of Jago's mud for her scriptures.'

'But there's no claw marks on the confessional's walls,' observed Hannah. 'Let me see the body!'

Colonel Knipe snapped his fingers and two of his police militia came forward grabbing Hannah and Chalph.

'I don't have time for this! You can see her body at the funeral like everyone else – get these two out of here.'

Chalph snarled as the Jagonese militia pushed him rudely out of the cathedral, shoving with their lamp rods and rifle butts, no doubt venting the frustration they felt at the usurpation of their role manning the battlements by Chalph's race. They were only slightly kinder in their handling of Hannah.

In the crowd that had begun to form outside on the bridge, Hannah spotted one of the junior priests – Father Baine – the young man who usually clerked for the archbishop.

'Is it true?' he called out, seeing Hannah. 'The militia won't even let us back into our own rooms.'

'I think so,' said Hannah. 'There's a dead body by the confessionals and it's wearing Alice's robes. Sweet Circle, I think she's dead. The ursks. . .'

'May serenity find her,' mumbled the priest, shocked to the core by the confirmation of his prelate's murder. 'Have they shot the ursk that did it?'

Hannah shook her head. 'They're searching the crypt levels now.

Father Baine looked at Hannah and then more nervously at Chalph standing at her side – as if he was expecting the Pericurian trader's apprentice to triple in size and transform into one of the bestial ursks in front of his eyes.

'They may not find anything down there,' whispered the young priest. 'The archbishop told me before our afternoon meditations that Vardan Flail had threatened her life and that the high guild head was no longer to be admitted to the cathedral. Not even on Circle-day for the open service.'

Vardan Flail had threatened Alice? The brief heated conversation in the testing rooms between them leapt back to Hannah. The odious little man leaving for the archbishop's chancellery two steps behind Alice.

'Did she say if the argument was about me?'

'Your call-up on the ballot list, yes.' The priest ran a hand through his prematurely thinning hair. 'But that's not all that they argued over. Vardan Flail mentioned to her that if she married him, it would invalidate your draft, but the archbishop told me she'd spurned such a clumsy offer.'

Chalph growled in surprise by Hannah's side. 'Marry Vardan Flail? Who would want to mate with such a twisted creature?'

'He was not always what you see limping through the vaults,' said the priest. He looked at Hannah, eager to impress her with his knowledge. 'Why do you think he was always making excuses to come to the cathedral? He had set his cap on the archbishop from the first day she arrived on Jago. In the early years, Vardan Flail was the only friend the archbishop had on Jago – everyone else's noses having been put out of joint by the church thinking it could presume to appoint an outsider to the position, over all the Jagonese priests who had been waiting for preferment.'

Hannah was shocked. She had always seen Alice as an archbishop first and her guardian second – but never as a woman, a woman that might marry. Hannah had been going around all these years with her eyes closed. A well of despair opened up inside her. How little she really knew the woman who had raised her – how little she ever would, now.

Father Baine leant in close. 'We turned Vardan Flail away, just as the archbishop had ordered us to. On the south bridge, about five minutes before the city's breach bells started sounding. Flail was furious, cursing us and wishing a plague upon everyone who worked inside the cathedral. He could have slipped back after the alarm sounded, murdered the archbishop while we were out with the people keeping a watch on the canals.'

'I knew there was no ursk scent inside the cathedral,' said Chalph. 'I tried to tell the colonel, but—'

'The colonel loathes everyone from Pericur,' said Hannah. 'It suits him just fine to blame the ursks for Alice's murder – he can stoke up more resentment against the free company soldiers now, point to how many years his militia stood watch on the walls without ever letting any of the creatures from outside break into the capital's vaults.'

There was a crowd gathering on the bridge. Word of the archbishop's murder was spreading through the Seething Round. Using their lamp rods as staffs, the militia were holding them back. Archbishop Alice Gray might not have started off as a Jagonese churchman, but she had been popular enough with the people of the island by the time she died.

'I think the archbishop expected something like this would happen,' said the priest.'

'Had Alice talked to you before about Flail?' asked Hannah.

'It wasn't what she said,' explained Father Baine. 'It was what she didn't say. There were letters she was drafting; the ones she didn't ask me to write for her. Some were composed in church cipher, but I saw who those were addressed to once – the League of the Rational Court.'

The Inquisition! Sweet Circle, that was one arm of the church Hannah had hoped never to encounter.

'It's not just bodies that are twisted in the guild's turbine halls,' said the priest. He tapped his prematurely thinning hair. 'It's their minds. The way they cling to Circlism out in their vaults, it's almost faith!'

Heresy. Superstitions perverting the church without gods.

The implications of the archbishop's murder collided with the weight of emotional wreckage spinning around Hannah's mind. And with the archbishop gone, Hannah would have no one to speak for her in front of the senate. She was going to end up an initiate of the Guild of Valvemen, indentured to a master who had murdered her guardian!

'We have to prove that Vardan Flail killed the archbishop,' said Chalph. 'If we can do that, prove that your draft ballot was a personal matter in a vendetta, the senate will have no choice but to nullify it.'

Prove it when the colonel's police militia wanted the very opposite finding. What hope did they have?

But it was the only way Hannah was going to survive – if the deadly energies of the guild's vaults didn't finish her off, then Vardan Flail would be only too eager to ensure an accident befell her and silenced her wagging tongue.

Jethro and Boxiron waited in the shipping office for the agent behind the wooden counter to flick through his box of yellowed cards. This was the last shipping agent on the harbour, and it looked as if they were about to receive the same answer they had been given by every other office they had visited.

'Sorry, Mister Daunt,' said the clerk. 'I hate to turn away custom, but there ain't no call for passage to Jago no more.'

'There must be at least one vessel on your roster that makes regular stops there?'

'Not since the southwest passage fully opened,' said the clerk. 'They're dangerous waters, the Fire Sea, and there are easier ways to get across to the colonies now. It's their own fault, bloody Jagonese. Their tugs used to charge skippers a small fortune to see us safely through the boils. Now there's another way to sail to Concorzia, who'll pay their fees, eh? Not any of the vessels on my lists, that I can tell you.'

'Myself and my good steamman friend here need to get to Jago,' insisted Jethro.

'Well, you won't be going direct, fellow, that's the truth of it. Last I heard, Pericur still runs a service out to the island once a month. Take a steam ship across the Sepia Sea to Concorzia and travel north overland to the ursine lands, and then you can wait there for your boat to the island. That's how I'd do it.'

'What about a direct passage to Pericur?'

'Not on my list either,' said the clerk. 'Their great and mighty archduchess hoards their trade routes for her kin, and it don't seem like I got the furry hide to qualify for her graces, do I? Like I say, travel to the colonies and then head north overland for the Pericurian border. I can sell you an airship berth rather than a steamer cabin if you're in a hurry. You'll be walking the streets of New Alban in three days and there's plenty of wagon trains from there up towards Pericur.'

'We are on church business,' said Boxiron. 'Is there really nothing you can do?'

The clerk traced an ironic little circle across his waistcoat and shrugged. 'Then may serenity find you.' He walked away leaving the two of them to their own devices.

'Then may it find us on a luckier day.' Jethro shook his head and made to leave the dusty little room, but a younger female clerk – seeing her master had left the front office – stopped scribbling in a ledger and waved her inky nib in Jethro Daunt's direction.

'There is a way for you to travel directly to Pericur. There's a free trader with a trading licence from the archduchess moored down in the submarine pens. No shipping agent here will recommend him to you, though. He's an awkward bugger and he's not registered with any of us.'

Jethro eased a coin out of his pocket and slipped it across

to the girl. 'Thank you. I would have paid you a commission on the recommendation, whether the boat was a free trader or not.'

'It's not just the lack of a fee for us,' warned the girl. 'There's talk about this boat and the kind of cargoes it's been known to handle. You'll be shipping out with a right crew of rascals. A gentleman of your quality, sir, you might want to take a berth on an airship of the merchant marine and go the rest of the way overland from the colonies like was suggested to you.'

Jethro tapped the iron shoulder of his hulking steamman companion. 'Have no fear, good damson. Boxiron and I can both be persuasive, in our own different ways.'

'Then count your fingers after shaking hands with any of the crew, sir, and ask for the *Purity Queen* down on the docks. You won't miss her when you see her lines.'

She was correct in that, there was no chance of missing the craft. The u-boat in question was a double-hulled affair, lying low in the waters of the pens like a giant metal catamaran, a single conning tower rising out of her middle, the bridge low and square and home to a flock of screeching seagulls. The bowsprit of the closer hull ended in a snarling moulding of a boar, her companion hull an iron lion's head, the ferocity of both figures diminished somewhat by the spattering of guano from the cloud of noisy seagulls above her.

'Look at the carvings of the mouths,' noted Boxiron, his voicebox quivering. 'That vessel has real teeth: those are torpedo tubes inside the jaws.'

'Ex-fleet sea arm,' said a familiar-sounding voice behind them. 'Decommissioned and sold off into private hands. There's empty gun mounts on the fantail behind her bridge, and the torpedo tubes have been deactivated. Allegedly.'

Jethro turned and was startled to see a face he knew standing behind them; a middle-aged woman with gorilla-sized arms, and next to her a girl half her age whom Jethro didn't recognize. 'Professor Harsh,' said Jethro. 'Bob me sideways; I haven't seen you since, what, that business with the tomb of Kitty Kimbaw? Are you mounting another expedition, good lady?'

'Not this time,' said the professor. 'I'm head of the department of archaeology at Saint Vine's College now. I'm reluctantly leaving the fieldwork to my more youthful associates these days.' She indicated the young woman standing next to her. 'This is Nandi Tibar-Wellking, my assistant, about to embark on the solemn task of adding some extra letters after her name, and these—' she indicated Jethro and Boxiron '—are the two dears who helped me prove that the curse of Kitty Kimbaw's tomb owed more to a heavily bejewelled statue that had been stolen from a side-passage than it did to supernatural vengeance from the disturbed mummified remains of its occupant. Mister Jethro Daunt, ex of the church, and Boxiron, ex of the Steamman Free State and various other parts.'

'It is good to see you again, Amelia softbody,' Boxiron nodded towards the professor. 'Would your assistant be shipping out on the *Purity Queen*? We've been led to believe that this vessel has something of an unsavoury reputation.'

'Yes,' hummed the professor, 'knowing her skipper, I would be surprised if it were otherwise.'

'Do you know her commander well enough to recommend us for berths?' asked Jethro.

'I don't think you'll have much of a problem in that regard. Tramp freighters are lucky to get whatever cargo they can, and there are no bigger tramps than—' she pointed towards a figure weaving out of the conning tower and crossing the gantry to the quayside, followed by a pair of submariners in striped shirts '—him!'

I can see them both now. One having caught a lift with the other, so to speak. We should be away directly with the tide.'

Out on the docks, threading their way through the fishermen spreading their drying nets, four flatbed wagons drawn by shire horses rattled into sight, their beds piled with wooden crates and a single passenger. The passenger was ursine, a large ginger male wearing Jackelian clothes – looking for all the world as if he might be a country squire out for a day's hunting with his hounds. All he lacked was a birding rifle and beagles to complete the picture.

'Ah now,' waved the commodore as the carts halted in front of the *Purity Queen* and the bear-like figure on the back jumped down, landing on a fine pair of knee-length riding boots. The Pericurian moved through the crowd of stevedores coming over to haul the crates down to the u-boat's hold, and walked towards the commodore. 'I received your baggage yesterday, so I thought you might be arriving in a grand old fashion this morning, Ambassador Ortin, rather than helping keep your cargo safe.'

The ursine creature blinked in surprise and adjusted a monocle resting in front of his left eye. 'Technically speaking, dear boy, I am not presently an ambassador, as I no longer hold the position here in the Kingdom and haven't yet been sworn in on Jago. A point the new incumbent at the Jackelian embassy was only too keen to underline by ensuring my airship berth to Spumehead was cancelled and replaced by a cheap narrowboat ticket.'

'Well, however you've arrived Mister Ortin urs Ortin, you're here now right enough and I'll make good on my contract to deliver you to your new posting. Just as soon as the transaction-engine parts your arse was so kindly keeping warm are loaded on board my boat.'

The commodore barked a flurry of orders at the stevedores shouldering the cargo towards his u-boat, and then with a nod to the professor, Jethro and Boxiron, he led the Pericurian diplomat across to his vessel.

Professor Harsh leant in close to speak quietly to Jethro. 'I won't ask what you'll be doing on Jago, but I would be grateful if you kept an eye out for Nandi on the island.'

'In addition to the eyes of the good commodore?'

'I trust Jared Black,' said the professor. 'That is, I trust him well enough to guard my spine when sabres are drawn and pistols are pulled, but the commodore has an unhealthy knack for getting into mischief and you're not the only ones trying to arrange a discreet passage to Jago.'

'Your young assistant's work, good professor, it isn't the sort of archaeology that involves jewelled artefacts and murderous dispute over precisely who has the rights to secure them?'

'Nandi will simply be trawling Jago's records in their transaction-engine vaults,' said the professor. 'But a little knowledge can be a dangerous thing.'

'So it can,' agreed Jethro.

After the academic had extracted a promise of safe-keeping for her assistant and was walking away, the transaction-engine drum in the centre of Boxiron's chest began to rumble as it turned – usually a sign that the steamman was drawing down extra processing power for his ruminations.

'What are you thinking?' asked Jethro.

'Much the same as you, I expect,' answered the steamman.

'Yes,' Jethro hummed thoughtfully.

That the good professor knew their business on Jago must be an investigation, and if she was asking for the help of Jethro Daunt and Boxiron, it was only because she suspected her assistant's dealings was likely to put her in even more danger than consorting with the pair of them.

Bob his soul, but not all the truth of the academic's business on Jago had been told here.

are wanton enough to think they are able to put one in front more than they can count, they deserve to lose all their...

This for fear, lady, or Why will it be fought in the Rational Synod... as your had been told him.

CHAPTER FOUR

Hannah was about to go into the archbishop's chancellery when a monk stopped her with a message. 'Your friend Chalph is waiting for you outside on the north bridge.'

'Thank you, father. Could you tell him I'll be finished here in a little while?'

He nodded and departed as she entered the office. It was still strange seeing someone else sitting behind Alice's desk, even if Father Blackwater – the head of the testing rooms – was only acting as their senior priest until another archbishop was appointed. A fiercely clever man who hid his true thoughts behind the odd veiled comment or dry remark, Father Blackwater was a Jagonese priest through and through. Which was precisely why the Rational Synod would never confirm him to the archbishop's post he obviously thought he deserved.

Hannah entered and took the seat where she had sat opposite Alice Gray so many times over the years. Meeting an ursk wearing the robes of a priest would not have seemed as alien to her.

'I have mixed blessings to report,' said the father. 'As I feared, the senate will not allow me to oppose your draft ballot.

I am not regarded as having the seniority to even speak on the floor on your behalf.'

Her heart sank. 'Then I am finished.'

'Not yet, my dear,' said the priest. 'On the other side of the equation, we have found this—' he flourished an envelope '—among the personal effects of the late archbishop. It stipulates that in the event of her demise preceding your majority, you receive her grant of authority to sit our entrance exam early.'

Her waiver! Alice had granted her dispensation after all. Hannah was overwhelmed, the grief over losing her guardian momentarily lifted. But . . . Hannah did the calculation in her head, working out the date of the next church board examination. 'I'll already be drafted into the guild's service by then, father!'

'We can't nullify the guild's draft order,' said Father Blackwater, 'but Vardan Flail can't nullify a written waiver from the archbishop that precedes your ballot notification, either. Her letter was written weeks before your name was ever posted on the draft ballot.'

Weeks before? It was as Alice Gray's clerk had said: almost as if she had been preparing for her own death. How many run-ins had there been between Vardan Flail and Alice in the previous months that Hannah hadn't been around to witness, before Hannah's name was 'coincidently' teased out at 'random' for entry into the lists of the Guild of Valvemen?

Father Blackwater pointed to the chess set waiting lonely on the table in the corner of the chancellery, and Hannah remembered the gentle snorts that Alice would make while planning her next move. 'Stalemate, Hannah. You will unfortunately be in service with the guild for a while, but the guild cannot forbid you to take our tests, and if you pass, you will be free of the curse of the draft for the rest of your life. You will be part of the church.'

He said the words with satisfaction, as if there could be no higher honour. A couple of days ago Hannah would have agreed with him; that life had seemed almost inevitable to her. But with the death of Alice Gray, the cathedral's bright stained glass seemed so much dimmer, the formulae and lessons of the Circlist teachings mere parroting of the echo of great thinking done by minds long since dead. In their stead grew the cold hard seed of something else planted in a ground far more fertile than the volcanic basalt outside the capital's battlements. Vengeance, vengeance and the fell craving for it.

To Hannah's surprise, vengeance could be like one of the mathematical puzzles of synthetic morality. You could lose yourself considering it, studying its shape. Vengeance could become as much an obsession as some of the paradoxes that had driven church priests insane when pondered for too long. There was a beauty in vengeance's pursuit and gratification to be gained in solving the riddle of the murder. Gratification that would climax in Vardan Flail being led by a hooded executioner across Snapman's Bridge and made to stand on the trapdoor while the crowds gathered on each side of the black canal.

It took a heinous crime to earn a death sentence that wasn't commuted to banishment or life indenture by the senate judiciary, but Hannah was determined to see that Vardan Flail was one of the few that received it. And if she had to serve that twisted monster in the guild's own vaults, then that would just take her a step or two closer to realizing her new goal.

Jethro Daunt pulled himself up the final few rungs of the u-boat's conning tower and emerged onto the observation deck, almost immediately finding the goggles of his rubber scald suit misting up from the heat of the Fire Sea.

Standing against the rail wearing a battered greatcoat and

holding a telescope was Commodore Black, his black-bearded face tinged orange from the glow of the magma. 'Come up for your turn of fresh air, Mister Daunt?'

'That I have, good captain, and I'm already regretting not bringing my coat.'

It was a curious, unhealthy mix outside, the intense waves of heat from the Fire Sea's magma interspersed with jabbing arrows of a freezing artic wind from the north. Too much exposure to this was likely to bring any passenger – or sailor – down with a fever.

'A savage, strange sea,' said the commodore. 'But old Blacky has got used to it. I've sailed further and deeper inside it than any other skipper, and left many a good friend's bones on the shores of its wild islands while doing so.'

'I'm hoping for a rather more pedestrian voyage.' Jethro looked down at the boiling waters their u-boat was pushing through on the surface – *boils* in nautical parlance – searing, shifting channels of water veined through the bubbling magma. He rummaged in his pocket and pulled out a paper bag filled with striped sweets. 'Would you care for a Bunter and Benger's aniseed drop, good captain?'

Commodore Black put aside the telescope he had been using to sweep the burning waves. 'I won't be troubling you for one of those wicked things. You know what they put in them. . .?'

'Defamation on the part of their commercial rivals, I am certain.'

'I'll stick to eating what goes well with a drop of wine. No need to suck those blessed things for your nerves, Mister Daunt – a nice boring voyage is what you'll get aboard the *Purity Queen*. Jago barely lies inside the rim of the Fire Sea and The Garurian Boils here are settled waters. The magma keeps to its course and so do the boils we sail through.'

Commodore Black pointed to the north. 'One hundred and seventy miles ahead is a buoy station of the Jagonese tug service. That's when the magma gets unpredictable and choppy, but the island's sailors will lead us through the safe channels – for a price.'

Jethro stared where the old u-boat man was pointing, but all he could see from the conning tower was a burning ocean of red seamed by black cooling rock, the passages of super-heated water they were following marked out by curtains of rising steam.

'You've never sailed the Fire Sea before, Mister Daunt? Never been to Jago. I can see it in the way the flames are casting a mortal spell on your gaze.'

'My business has occasionally seen me travel across the nations of the continent,' said Jethro, 'but never over the ocean.'

'Yes, now, your *discreet* business,' said the commodore, teasingly. 'But you've travelled widely enough to know that a master of a boat is rightly addressed as captain, be they an admiral or a commodore.'

A cracking sounded in the distance and a geyser of molten rock and gas fumed into the air, adding to the chemical stench of the place – sulphur, by its reek.

'Someone told me that at the docks,' Jethro dissembled. 'An ocean this wild, it seems hard to believe that the people on Jago can predict where the ebbs and flows of the magma and the passages of water through them will lie within an hour's time, let alone days and weeks ahead. It's a wonder anyone can follow the boils back to Jago.'

'Ah now,' said the commodore. 'It's an easy enough matter predicting a safe passage when you have caverns filled with mortal clever transaction engines. Machines that could give King Steam a run for his money when it comes to the thinking game. And when we get to the buoy station and the master there summons up a tug to see us safe to their black shores, we'll no doubt pay for every penny of their engine room's power and the model of the Fire Sea they have sealed up down there with them.'

'That will be a sight to see on Jago, good captain,' said Jethro. 'Cities where they have actually tamed the wild power.'

'Electricity,' said Commodore Black. 'Yes, nowhere else in the world, only on Jago.' He pointed to the currents of magma sliding past the watery channel of the boils they were navigating. 'Something to do with all that blessed molten iron swirling around out there, or so a fine steamman friend of mine would have it.'

'You sound like you don't approve, good captain.'

'I've used the wild energy to tickle the armour of wicked savages trying to break their way into my hull and had cause to thank it,' said the commodore. 'But for more practical purposes I'll take the thump of good honest steam power, the hum of high-tension clockwork and the burn of a little expansion-engine gas any day of the week. The kind of dark power the Jagonese use is as good for your blessed health as taxes.'

Jethro nodded. The commodore was as superstitious as most u-boat men. It was small wonder when a small metal bubble of air was all that stood between them and death under the darks of the ocean. The Circlist church always did have its work cut out in the harbour towns of the Kingdom. U-boat men were almost as bad as airship sailors with their strange rituals and their profession's cant.

He raised a hand to shield his hair from a few rogue cinders drifting across from a fire plume that looked to be erupting ten miles to starboard. It was no wonder that no airship could cross above the Fire Sea intact – the combination of plumes, wild thermals and fierce artic storms made an aerial crossing a one-way bet: with a grinning skeleton drawn on the reverse of every card in the deck. Jethro remembered reading about a few foolhardy Jack Cloudies who were never seen again after attempting the voyage in the early days of Jackelian aviation.

Commodore Black pressed the telescope back to the brass goggles protecting his face and Jethro looked on as the whistle of a magma fountain off their starboard became the whisper of Badger-headed Joseph. *'The blood, the blood of the earth is your sea.'*

Jethro gritted his teeth. The old gods never normally bothered him during the day, only within his dreams. He wiped the steam off his goggles and unnoticed by the commodore, stepped back and rubbed at the side of his head. This was his choice, sailing to Jago. His. Not the Inquisition's, not *theirs*. Only his.

An invitation to dinner at the captain's table wasn't something that Jethro expected, but perhaps for Commodore Black it mitigated the guilt he felt at the extortionate rates he was charging his passengers to travel through the inhospitable currents of the Fire Sea. Although looking at the square navigation table in the captain's cabin that had been pressed into service for dinner, Jethro suspected the location of their supper had more to do with the wishes of the coarse men and woman that served as the u-boat's crew – desiring to make free with their ribald table manners in the mess, rather than feeling they had to be on good behaviour in front of the 'cargo'.

The Pericurian ambassador-in-transit – Ortin urs Ortin – demonstrated the highest manners at their table, every facet of Jackelian etiquette smoothly performed in almost mocking counterpoint to Boxiron's jerky shovelling of high-grade boiler coke into his furnace trap and the noisy siphoning of the water the steamman needed to feed his boiler heart. The young academic Nandi Tibar-Wellking was a fairly neutral observer of the two polar extremes at the table, but recalling his own time in the company of her professor, Jethro rightly guessed that Nandi had been well taught and exposed to the intricacies of dining at foreign tables. If the cabin boy acting as steward had served them sheep's eyes and fried scorpion tails rather than their usual fare of scrambled duck eggs, Spumehead rock crab and pot-roasted lamb, he doubted she would have even blinked.

Commodore Black's appetite tipped the table's balance back towards the ribald; he ripped apart the meats with gusto and matched Boxiron's siphoning of water with an equal capacity for sweet wines, jinn and beer. If the boat's master had an excuse for his thirst, it was that even with the *Purity Queen*'s cooling systems running on maximum, it was hard not to drip sweat onto their food as they maintained their course through the outer boils of the Fire Sea.

Ortin urs Ortin tactfully overlooked the rattling from Boxiron and instead addressed the young academic, his Jackelian accent so polished he might have been born a squire to its acres. 'You mentioned that you have not been to Jago before, damson, but I am interested to know what your book learning in the college suggests the island's people will be like?'

'Very similar to the Jackelian citizenry,' answered Nandi, balancing a soup spoon between her fingers as if she was penning a dissertation on the subject. 'And with good reason, ambassador, when we look back to what classical history texts have to say on the matter. The two largest tribes settled on the northwest of the continent were the Jackeni and the Jagoli, but when the cold time arrived, the Jagoli fled the advancing glaciers and journeyed to a new island home, whereas the Kingdom's ancestors stayed put. Prior to that, the early Circlist church had converted both tribes, and there were plenty of intermarriages between the two peoples. In many ways, the modern Jagonese are truer to the traditions of our ancestors than we are – as, unlike the Jackelians, their civilization never fell to the Chimecan Empire. When all else was darkness and ice, their island kept the traditions of democracy burning. They kept their freedom when our kingdom was a vassal province of the empire and our people were being farmed for food. Jago kept their science through the age of ice, and they kept their history.'

'The people of Pericur hold the island in some reverence, I believe, good ambassador,' said Jethro.

'The scripture of the Divine Quad,' said Ortin, adjusting his monocle, 'teaches that the island was once a paradise, where the ursine were shaped and breathed into life by the whisper of the world. There we lived on the Island of the Blessed until the two male members of the quad, Reckin urs Reckin and Amaja urs Amaja, fell to bickering between themselves and had to leave the island for the crime of destroying their home. And the whisper of the world became tears of fire at their fall from grace, filling the sea with all its flames.'

'Then you believe Jago is sacred soil and that neither the Jagonese nor your people should be there?'

'That is a conservative view. I am certainly not one of those who believe that, but I do believe there must be some practical truth to the scriptures. That the ursine once lived on Jago before we lived on Pericur.'

Nandi took another mouthful of soup. 'And why would that be?'

'Let me show you,' said Ortin. The ambassador ducked out of the commodore's quarters and returned a minute later having retrieved a leather-bound tome of Pericurian scripture from his cabin. 'In the scriptures, Reckin urs Reckin was unfairly cast out of paradise for the covetousness and lusts of his ravening brother, Amaja urs Amaja.'

The ambassador opened the holy book to a beautifully illuminated page showing the two couples of the Divine Quad. The two deities on the left were clearly ursine, glowing in beatific purity, while the pair to the right – a furless male and female – were almost definitely from the race of man. '"And the fur of Amaja urs Amaja and his wife was singed from their bodies as they waded into the fires of the sea, begging Reckin urs Reckin and his beloved to forgive their brother his foolishness in destroying their home, the selfish Amaja urs Amaja watching his brother and his wife borne away by the Angels of Airdia to new lands." The people of Pericur had followed the scriptures of the Divine Quad for thousands of years before we ever laid eyes on someone from your nation, Damson Tibar-Wellking. It came as quite a surprise when we discovered the same covetous devils painted on the walls of our temples colonizing the territory to our south in Concorzia, not to mention trampling the sacred soil of Jago deep inside the Fire Sea.'

'But the timescales are all wrong, you must see that?' said Nandi, perplexed. 'The Jagonese settled the island long before we first established contact with your people in Pericur. Your race and ours have never lived alongside each other: the Jagonese migrated from the freezing wastes of our continent – they were never native to the island.'

'Aye,' interrupted the commodore, 'and the only time the black blasted rock of Jago looked like a paradise was when sheets of ice covered the rest of the world and the people there had the blessed heat of the Fire Sea to keep their greenhouses warm and their vaults heated from the cold.'

Ortin urs Ortin tapped his book. 'And yet here your people are, and here we are too, just as the scriptures say. I am a reformer, damson and gentlemen. The great liberal houses of the Baronial Council have paid for this u-boat's hold to be filled with the latest transaction engines from the Kingdom's workshops. I would see our archduchess's rule tempered by a properly elected council of her peers; I would see our cities pushing towards the heavens with the sway of pneumatic towers; I would see the best of your Jackelian science and culture being used to improve our nation; but for all that, there are still some things you must take on faith.'

'Don't be so quick to change, lad,' warned the commodore. 'I have visited Pericur, and I say that your cities of oak with their strange blessed wooden minarets wouldn't be much improved by the smogs of our mills and the beating engines of our industry. Your scriptures say that Jago is a dark isle where only those who would be cursed abide. You walk down the streets of Hermetica City after we have docked and tell me that you don't feel cursed just being there, and then ask yourself why their land is locked away behind the Fire Sea.'

Ortin urs Ortin raised his glass in salute towards the commodore. 'May I always be reminded of the scriptures' truth by my Jackelian friends without any gods at all.'

Jethro winced. *Without any gods at all.* If only the Pericurian ambassador knew the truth of that.

'There are other books than your people's scriptures that must be considered,' said Nandi kindly, her voice coming alive with the passion of her quest. 'Jago is not just the oldest democracy in the world; their transaction-engine archives are the oldest in the world, too. When the rest of the continent was burning encyclopaedias to stay warm, Jagonese traders were preserving what knowledge they could find, keeping the Circlist enlightenment alive during the depths of the long age of ice.'

'Their transaction engines may be ancient, lass,' said the

commodore, 'but they're dangerous. They don't run things on steam out there. The Jagonese will poison your lovely head with their knowledge.'

'I am aware of the dangers, but I'll take precautions,' said Nandi. 'New knowledge is never acquired easily. The island has historical records stretching back unbroken for two millennia that have never been properly mined.'

'Aye, and now our boats can bypass the Fire Sea to get to the colonies it's all they have to sell,' spat the commodore. 'That and safe passage to a fat fool like Blacky who's still generous enough to come a-calling to their bleak isle.'

Jethro didn't comment that the commodore seemed only too willing to pass the cost onto his passengers.

'Saint Vine's college must consider your research worth funding, Nandi softbody,' said Boxiron. 'If it wasn't for the college's share of this voyage's cost, I suspect Jethro softbody and I would be heading to Jago via Pericur by way of a colony boat.'

'I won't argue with you on that,' said Nandi. 'But I don't think my research can take all the credit. When my sponsor at the college, Professor Harsh, was my age, she studied under a Doctor George Conquest. He later travelled to Jago with his wife to pursue a similar vein of research to mine, but his boat sank in the Fire Sea as he returned back home to the Kingdom. All his work was lost.'

'And the good professor wants his work finished,' said Jethro.

'I believe it would be fitting,' said Nandi. 'And now the professor is sitting on the High Table and she has the authority to spend the money to ensure it happens.'

'It's a wicked shame,' said the commodore, 'for a beautiful lass like yourself to be locked away in dusty archives studying the shadows of what has passed. What use is that to us,

Nandi? Forget Jago, lass, stay on my boat and I'll show you all the mortal wonders of the oceans. There are wild, beautiful islands deep inside the Fire Sea untouched by the footsteps of the race of man; there are the seabed cities of the gill-necks carved from coral and shaped in living pearl. And if you've still got a taste for archaeology after you've seen all that, I'll show you some of the broken, flooded towers that lie collapsed along the sides of the Boltiana Trench. You can put on a diving suit and run your hand along marble statues that haven't been seen by anything apart from sharks for a hundred thousand years.'

Her dark skin seemed to blush, and Jethro wondered whether it was the attraction of the offer or the glow from the magma outside the porthole that was lighting her burnished features.

'Thank you,' said Nandi, 'but there is important work awaiting me on Jago. The Circlist church was kept alive on Jago when the Chimecan Empire were raising idols to their dark gods across the continent – without Jago there would be no rationalist enlightenment in the Kingdom today. We'd likely be dancing around maypoles on the solstice, wearing the masks of animals and our old gods like—' Nandi paused to recall a name.

'Like Badger-headed Joseph,' said Jethro.

'Exactly. You've studied prehistory, Mister Daunt?'

Jethro rubbed at his temples, which ached as if trapped in a vice. 'I used to be a parson, before I found a more accommodating line of work. But I can still disprove the existence of every god and goddess of every religion on the continent – current or historical. Some things you never forget.'

At the head of the table, the commodore narrowed his eyes; he obviously disapproved of Jethro Daunt's old career. 'There's five types of gentlemen I don't normally carry on the *Purity*

Queen, sir. That's members of the House of Guardians, lawyers, spies, officers of Ham Yard, and last but not least, church crows – of any denomination. But seeing as you've taken up a new business now and come well-recommended by a fine lady like Amelia Harsh, I shall make an exception in your case.'

'Thank you, good captain,' said Jethro. 'I fear neither myself nor Boxiron would be comfortable swimming through the boils or trying to scramble over the flows of magma.'

But it wasn't the steaming waters of the sea that Jethro Daunt felt he was drowning in. It was the swirling currents of his thoughts. His case. The demands of the Inquisition. The visitations from gods he was trying to deny. And now tales of the history of Circlism on the island and the concerns of a long-dead university doctor and a venerable professor worried for the life of her student.

Jago, all the answers lay on Jago, smouldering lonely and dark amidst the angry solitude of the Fire Sea.

Hannah glanced behind her as she ducked down the corridor leading to Tom Putt Park. She could have sworn one of the police militia had been following her through the vaults below. But it looked as though Hannah had lost the militiawoman in the maze of surface corridors that led to the constellation of greenhouses huddled around the foot of the Horn of Jago. She was clearly in class hours and the last thing she needed was to be dragged back to the cathedral just for heeding the urgent-sounding message that Chalph urs Chalph had left her.

Yes, heeding a friend's note – that sounded so much better than truancy. She found Chalph by the statues of the apple singers, the overgrown path to their clearing now trampled clear by the repair crew that had sealed the greenhouse, not to mention all the sightseers who had come to see the ursk corpse before the dead beast had been dragged away for incineration. It was strange, but the presence of the Jagonese in Tom Putt Park seemed more of a violation of her private space than the attack by the monsters that had scaled the city's wall. The wild beauty of the park had been hers and Chalph's alone, and now half of Hermetica City must have pressed through to gawp at the spot where she and Chalph had nearly met their deaths.

Chalph, when she laid eyes on him, had a hemp sack thrown over his shoulder and had been crouching down behind the statues as if he was one of them.

'It's me!' called Hannah. 'Didn't you smell me coming?'

'I have caught a flu,' said Chalph, coming out of hiding. 'I've been outside in the cold, pretending to be part of a free company detail escorting the Guild of Valvemen.'

'You've what?' Hannah was astonished at her friend's audacity. 'In the name of the Circle, why?'

'In the name of your godless faith, this.' Chalph held up his sack and pulled out some battered iron components. 'The guild's people were checking the machinery charging the battlements when they found it.' He showed her an iron box with holes in the side where a line of cables hung out like baby elephant trunks. Each rubber cable had been severed halfway down its length, the insulation sawn through to reveal the thick copper wiring underneath. 'The section of the battlements the ursks came over had been shorted deliberately. Someone wanted the wall's charge to fail.'

Hannah examined the box with her hands, feeling the cold metal, not believing what she was hearing. 'But who would want to do that?'

'I can tell you this much,' said Chalph. 'The Guild of Valvemen were half-expecting to find this. I was pretending I could only speak Pericurian and I heard what they were whispering. There were three sets of damaged transformers like this on the failed section of the wall, and the guild's workers were all for hiding the sabotaged parts and taking them back to their vaults.'

The guild were involved in this? Their job was to maintain the walls, the machines, keep the city powered and keep the transaction-engine rooms humming. But then, it was a guild that was run by Vardan Flail.

Chalph pointed in the direction of the park's domed surface, near to where the ursks had smashed their way down into the capital's flash steam channels. 'That's not all; I checked where the hole in the park dome had been repaired. There was broken glass scattered on the outside of the dome, as if it had been cracked open from the inside of the park.' He opened his fingers three inches wide from claw to claw. 'That's how thick the panels they were repairing this dome with are. I checked with one of the city's glass blowers: dome glass is designed to withstand steam storms and magma plume falls from the Fire Sea. An ursk would not be able to smash into the park without a very large hammer and chisel.'

'We're the only ones who use the park,' said Hannah, numb with the implications of what her friend had discovered.

'And it wasn't me they were after,' said Chalph. 'It was *you*, Hannah. It's just the same as how politics in the Baronial Council work back home when things cut up rough. You don't just poison the head of a house, you poison the aunts, the sons, the daughters, the brothers – you assassinate everyone at once! Leave no one alive able to come back and try to take revenge against your house. Tooth and claw, Hannah, tooth and claw.'

'This is Jago, not Pericur. We have the police, the stained senate, the accumulated law of a thousand generations.'

But there were Alice's mutilated remains lying in state inside her own cathedral. Had the failing of Hermetica's battlements simply been a distraction to ensure the entire city was otherwise engaged when she was murdered? One that should have also ensured her ward was ripped to pieces inside the abandoned park. . .

'It's never fair,' said Chalph. 'They might not even care about you – you just happened to be the ward of the wrong person. A loose pawn to be tidied from the board.'

Hannah passed the sabotaged machinery back to Chalph. 'We have to show this to someone, to Colonel Knipe.'

'In a vendetta, you trust only your own house and family,' said Chalph. 'The militia wants to blame the free company for the ursk attack. The colonel's not going to listen to either of us if we accuse the most powerful man on Jago outside of the First Senator.'

'The church is my house, Alice was my family. . .'

'I could tell the baroness, but I don't think she will help us. No Jagonese is going to trust the word of a foreign trader from the House of Ush. Sentiment is already being whipped up against the ursine here in the capital – people have been shouting at me about food prices and shortages of grain down in the streets: accusing the house of profiteering. Calling us dirty wet-snouts. Saying that the archduchess is trying to starve the Jagonese off the island, saying that the free company fighters let the ursks into the city on purpose to scare the last of the Jagonese away.'

'The Guild of Valvemen,' said Hannah, a feeling of certainty rising within her. 'Their people would know exactly where to strike to shut down a section of the battlements. That jigger Vardan Flail is behind all of this, I know he is.'

Her suspicions were silenced by a woman's shout carrying down the park's path. It was a police militiawoman, the same one Hannah thought she had seen following her earlier – but she had company this time. Four individuals cloaked in the long robes of valvemen.

'Damson Hannah Conquest,' the militiawoman said in an accusatory tone. 'You were not in the cathedral when we called.'

'I finished early,' lied Hannah.

'You have not even started,' hissed one of the valvemen.

'Your ballot notice has been served,' said the militiawoman.

Served? With a start, Hannah realized what day it was. Since Alice's murder time hardly seemed to matter at all – one day, one hour, each much the same as the last – all of them blurring into a single amorphous mess. This was the day her service to the guild should have started!

Two of the valvemen advanced on Hannah, grabbing an arm apiece, the third seizing her behind her shoulders.

The militiawoman lowered her lamp staff to point menacingly at Chalph as he stepped forward to help Hannah. She brushed her cape back with her other hand to indicate the pistol hanging from her waist, and that she wouldn't hesitate in drawing it if the ursine tried to stop them. 'You don't want to assist a draft dodger, Pericurian, you really don't!'

'I wasn't trying to escape!' Hannah protested, struggling. 'I forgot, that is all.'

'Set the example,' one of the valvemen hissed from beneath his cowl, the smell of mint on his clothes making her gag.

The others took up the cry, the quiet stillness of the neglected park broken by their screeching mantra. 'Set the example. *Set the example.*'

Hannah was dragged out of the dome, screaming and scuffling. Dragged towards the vaults of the guild. To serve the devil who had killed Alice Gray. The man who had already tried to murder her once.

*　　*　　*

As the *Purity Queen* approached the soaring coral line that ringed the island of Jago, Commodore Black ordered all of his passengers apart from Nandi to clear the bridge, keeping his word to the professor that he would keep an eye on her.

Now they were bobbing in front of the coral line's iron gate and Nandi had to stop herself from gasping. Of course, she had seen illustrations of the gates in the texts back at Saint Vine's, but the scale was totally different watching them slowly draw back above her to reveal the cauldron-like barrels of cannons on the fortress. The fortifications were wedged between the coral peaks above, a frill of gunnery ominously tracking their vessel – a silent presence and ancient reminder of why the Jagonese had never fallen to the predations of the Chimecan Empire.

Jago, the fortress of learning and the last redoubt of the Circlist enlightenment during the long age of ice. All this and more, once. But the world turned, and the retreat of the glaciers had undermined her pre-eminent position in the world. Studying history at the college, first as a student, then as Professor Harsh's assistant, the single thing that had struck Nandi most was that nations, civilizations, empires, all had a lifespan, much the same as any person. They grew from seeds, they blossomed, they aged, and finally they passed away into the twilight. When you were a citizen of a proud nation like the Kingdom of Jackals, living in its summer years – when you trod the wide streets of Middlesteel feeling the throb of commerce and could turn your eye to the sky and see only the slow-moving sweep of the Royal Aerostatical Navy's airships – it was exceptionally easy to forget that the show of permanence all around you was just an illusion from the perspective of history. The same feeling of immortality a legionnaire of the Chimecan Empire would have felt millennia ago. The same deceptive feeling of durability that a Jagonese burgher would have experienced in centuries past, cosseted by achievements drawn around them like a blanket while the rest of the world huddled and froze in the ice. But the wider world's summer had become Jago's winter. Nandi would be studying a failing civilization on Jago while there was still some flesh clinging to its bones, and that was quite a privilege. It grated on her nerves that she had to travel here in near secrecy, bypassing the jealous fools who would have seen her place on the expedition cancelled. Just because she was a poor scholarship girl.

Passing through the coral line, their u-boat remained on the surface for the short approach through the coastal waters, cutting through a broken haze thrown up by the collision of the boils and the residual lava. This, she remembered reading in the college's text, was what the weather of Jago would always be like. The coastline of the island was a scorched wasteland burned by the Fire Sea, but travel a few miles inland, and Jago's true position in arctic latitudes became apparent, a dangerous night-cold wilderness of ice haunted by creatures as fierce as the freezing landscape they inhabited. What civilization there was left on Jago clung to the fiery coastline, leaving its glacial interior to monstrous beasts. Nandi saw a final flash of magnesium light through the mists, shimmering out from the flare-house on top of the Horn of Jago, and then the mountain disappeared and boiling water covered the bridge's armoured viewing window. As they sank beneath the Fire Sea, Nandi could see the tug that had guided the *Purity Queen* in sinking before them, bubbles fleeting towards the surface from its pressure seals.

The *Purity Queen* followed the tug down, the water outside turning darker with every league of their increasing depth. As they neared the seabed, the commodore ordered his two steersmen to follow the tug's example and head for the mouth of one of the titanic brass carvings of octopi, cuttlefish and nautili wrought into the underwater base of the island's submerged basalt cliff-line. Nandi saw that they were entering a long tunnel illuminated by a strip of green lights running along its side. The tunnel ended in a door which irised open to admit the *Purity Queen* into a large dark space which started to drain of water and descend at the same time, a lifting room and dry-dock combined. As their descent drew to an end, the front of their lifting room opened out onto an underwater anchorage giving Nandi her first look at the great harbour vault of Hermetica City. The warm green stretch of the underwater pool was bounded by the concrete arc of the harbour at the opposite end of the chamber where hundreds of tugs similar to the one that had guided them were moored inside gated locks. From above glowing yellow plates partially hidden by wisps of condensation cast a diffuse light over the port's warm waters. If Nandi hadn't actually been present during their underwater approach, she might have taken the subterranean vault's walls for a cliff-side and believed that they had simply sailed into one of the mountainous harbours back in the Kingdom's uplands rather than entering Jago's underground civilization.

'We're the only vessel in harbour,' said Nandi, staring around her at the quiet lock gates, power houses, travelling dock cranes, sheds and warehouses. At least, they were if she discounted the idle tugs of the Jagonese home fleet. It was a lonely feeling.

After the *Purity Queen* had moored up, the commodore ordered all hatches open and reached for his jacket. 'Best take yours too, lass. It's warm enough during the day in the vaults, but at night they vent in air from the plains above to make it cooler underground.'

'Just like the real world,' said Nandi.

'It's different enough in Jago, lass,' said the commodore. 'I've never had a liking for this place. If it wasn't for your blessed professor twisting my arm, I'd be Pericur-bound and leaving Hermetica City's underground vaults to the Jagonese with a welcome-they-be for them.'

Nandi looked at the customs officials joining the tug crew on the dockside outside the bridge, a gaggle of velvet-cloaked functionaries pushing past the sailors in their rubber scald suits. 'You don't like living underground?'

'You can't be claustrophobic in my trade, lass. Maybe it's the crackle of the wild energy they've tamed to power this place, or the dark creatures from the interior you'll hear singing and whining outside the city walls up on the surface. Maybe it's just that the more they try and make this place seem like home, the stranger it seems to me, but I've no love for this island or the shiver I feel when I walk its sealed-up streets.'

Out on the dockside the collection of velvet-cloaked officials had been joined by green-uniformed militiamen whose main function seemed to be to keep back the townspeople filtering through the otherwise deserted harbour front. Nandi and the commodore were the first out onto the gantry that swung across to the *Purity Queen*'s deck, Nandi fishing in the pockets of her short tweed jacket for the letter of introduction she had been given. Sealed in red wax with the crest of Saint Vine's college.

By the time the police had finished warning the commodore of the penalties if he were to take onboard any Jagonese passengers without senate-stamped exit visas, Jethro Daunt and his curious jerking steamman friend had followed Nandi out, no doubt enjoying their first taste of solid land for weeks. More and more Jagonese were heading for the line formed by the police, presumably the hopeful emigrants that the *Purity*

Queen's master had just been warned of, waving and calling at the crew coming out of the u-boat, brandishing money, papers, or just their empty hands. The tug service's sailors must have spread word among their friends and family. A rare chance to get off Jago.

One of the men standing by the custom officials strolled over to Nandi and Commodore Black. Judging by his dark frock coat and stovepipe hat, he was Jackelian rather than a local. He nodded at Nandi and the commodore before clearing his throat. 'I am Mister Walsingham, an officer attached to the Jackelian consul here. I have cleared your arrival with the Jagonese Board of Aliens.' He passed each of them a wax-sealed wallet. 'You have full papers, captain, your crew and passengers have subsidiary visas attached to your own – Jagonese law can be swift and severe, do try to make sure they don't start any brawls in taverns.' He smiled weakly towards Nandi. 'The crew, that is to say, not your passengers.'

'Any that do will answer to me before they answer to the Jagonese magistrates,' said the commodore, balling a fist.

'A tight ship, eh. Good, good. If you need us, the Jackelian embassy is inside the Horn of Jago. But do try to stay out of trouble here, there's a good fellow. We don't have much leverage with the locals these days, so if any of your sailors end up in the police militia's fortress, they're rather on their own I'm afraid.'

'A grey little suit,' said the commodore as the officer walked away, 'and just the same as a thousand of his friends in the civil service back home, no imagination for anything save creating new taxes to lighten my pocket-book. As much use as a blunt stick in a sabre duel. We're on our own here, lass.'

But not quite as alone as would suit Nandi. 'You don't have to wait for me, whatever the professor told you. I'm hardly likely to get into trouble researching ancient history.

You can leave me here in the capital, deliver your cargo to Pericur, and then pick me up on the return leg of your voyage. The more time I have to root through Jago's archives, the better I shall like it.'

The commodore scratched at his dark, forked beard. 'A promise is a promise, now. Your fine professor has gone out on a limb for me more times than I care to count and I wouldn't want her to use those great big arms of hers on my noggin. Old Blacky's crew and the *Purity Queen* will stay here and feed pennies to a suitably grateful tavern owner while you avail yourself of the archive access Saint Vine's College has so handsomely paid for.' He winked at her. 'Besides, shipping to Pericur and back via the island will mean double navigation fees for these Jagonese pirates and they've had their thieving hands deep enough inside my pockets as it is.'

Nandi felt a brief stiffening of the same hackles that Professor Harsh so frequently raised. Wrapped in cotton wool, handled with kid gloves, overlooked for any foreign archaeological dig where there was even a hint of danger. Where else were you going to find sand-buried cities but in Cassarabia, with its bandits and wild nomads? Creeper-covered temples were two-a-penny in the jungles of Liongeli – but so were sharp-clawed thunder lizards, feral tribesman and river pirates. And here it was again. Jago, the heart of the enlightenment, but Commodore Black was still going to wait around while she poked through the Guild of Valvemen's archives. What were he and his crude, lewd crew of rascals and brawlers going to do for her? Start a fight with the guild if it didn't grant her the complete access the college had paid for?

What no one else seemed to realize was that every dig, every position she was barred from, was just another reminder of the hole left in her life by the death of her father, his bones lost in the sands outside the Diesela-Khan's tomb thanks to a single poisoned rifle ball. Nandi had ostensibly come to Jago to fulfil Doctor Conquest's work, but in reality she was completing another expedition. One that had ended disastrously in the great southern desert. When she was finished here and standing back on the soil of the Kingdom of Jackals, her work circulating through the corridors of the college, then her father's restless spirit would finally have his grief eased. Perhaps if she took her own sweet time in her studies, the commodore might grow bored and make for Pericur anyway, giving her an extra month or two alone here in Jago's capital.

Nandi moved aside as the Pericurian ambassador led a delegation of Jagonese dockers forward towards the u-boat's cargo hold. It looked as if he was unloading some of the crates carrying the transaction-engine parts. His embassy, Nandi suspected, was about to be upgraded with the fruits of the latest Jackelian science.

Commodore Black walked away to present the papers he had been given by Mister Walsingham to the local customs officials, and by the time he had finished with them, he looked to be in a dark mood. 'The raw-faced cheek of it, lass. We've been allocated rooms in city-centre lodgings with not a choice in the matter, and we're to be escorted there by these green-uniformed popinjays as if we were prisoners being given our afternoon constitutional by the warders.'

'Maybe they don't trust us,' said Nandi.

'They trust sailors well enough,' said a voice behind them. 'They trust them to act like sailors in any port and they'd rather not have Jagonese men and women claiming marriage rights with any of your lads or lasses when you sail out of here.'

Nandi looked at the short, broad man that had spoken – dressed in a Jackelian waistcoat with a battered leather trapper's coat over it, rather than the brocaded velvet clothes of the islanders. No local, this, and too scruffy to be one of the Jackelian embassy staff.

'Ah well,' said the commodore. 'Lucky that my friend is here to study and not to find her fine self a husband.'

'I've been married twice,' said the man. 'But never to anyone on Jago. I'm an outsider and they only tolerate me because they find my skills useful.' He pointed to a set of cages on the side of the docks, iron bars holding back snarling, hooting specimens of the local wildlife. Nandi recognized the giant bear-like ursks from the illustrations in her college tomes, huge feral versions of the Pericurian ambassador who had travelled here with them. And by their side a cage filled with something else she had only glimpsed in books before, *ab-locks*. Leathery-skinned bipedal creatures with ape-like faces. They were a head or two under a man's height, furless on the front but with a silver mane striped down their stooped backs.

'My name is Tobias Raffold,' said the trapper, 'and I've been contracted by the Jackelian Zoological Society to deliver these creatures back to the Kingdom.'

Nandi noted the metre-long gap between the ursks' cage and the one holding the ab-locks, the inhabitants of each crate snarling furiously at one another.

Tobias Raffold picked up a crowbar from the floor and drew it along the bars, turning the creatures' growling attention towards him, hands snapping at the bars and trying to reach through to claw at him. 'The only thing they bleeding loathe more than us is each other. Ursks and ab-locks rip each other apart when they cross onto each other's territory.'

Nandi watched the ab-locks' fierce red eyes burning as they pushed up against the bars. 'They can be tamed, can't they?'

'Not at this age,' said Tobias Raffold. 'Trap ab-locks when they're young and geld them and they can be taught basic orders well enough. They're used in the Guild of Valvemen's vaults to porter for them. Ab-locks last longer than us before they're killed by the energies of the turbine halls.'

'Feral or tamed, I'm not carrying the likes of these in the *Purity Queen*, Mister Raffold,' said the commodore. 'I don't transport live cargoes. They can die, they can escape, and even if they don't their stench and racket will make my crew restless. They're not a lucky cargo for old Blacky.'

The trapper waved a wad of money at the two of them. Jackelian paper notes drawn on Lords Bank. 'I can make it lucky enough for you.'

'Not with those you can't,' said the commodore. 'I've been paid well enough to sail here and I already have an outbound cargo for Pericur. Taking these mortal whining things on board is a mite too close to slaving for my tastes.'

'Don't give me that cant,' said the trapper. 'You've got a cat on board your bloody boat to keep down the rats, haven't you? Abs and ursks are nothing more than dumb beasts.'

Commodore Black wrinkled his nose and turned his head away from the whining ab-locks' clamour. 'Not dumb enough for me, Mister Raffold. You can wait for your regular Pericurian boat to put in and ship your pets away for the mortal Jackelian Zoological Society. I'll not be taking them with me.'

'I'll have to wait a month for the next Pericurian boat, man. I just missed the last one!'

Nandi and the commodore left the Jackelian trapper on the dockside, cursing the old u-boat skipper for a superstitious fool.

As the two of them caught up with the other u-boat passengers and their guard, the gathering crowds coming to see the u-boat parted to allow another police escort to pass in the opposite direction. The second group of police militia were pulling an ursine towards the harbour, heavy chains bound across long leather robes inscribed with the symbols of the Pericurian religion. They passed closed enough to Nandi and the others for Ambassador Ortin to take a quizzical interest in one of his fellow nationals being so rudely manhandled.

'That is a preacher of the Divine Quad you are mistreating,' Ortin urs Ortin protested to the officer leading the way. 'Dear boy, can you not—'

Nandi and the ambassador lurched back as the ursine priest threw herself at the new arrivals, the police struggling to hold her. 'You filthy heretic, you'll burn in hell for this! Your presence here is hastening the apocalypse. This is sacred soil – sacred soil that you defile. Your fur will be burnt away with the wrath of Reckin urs Reckin. You will be left as hairless as these twisted, dirty infidels, the foul descendents of Amaja urs Amaja. You will burn along with all those malignant traders with their blind eyes that can see only profit, standing on the cursed soil where our ancient temples once stood. Their eyes will burn in their sockets for their sins, then they will know true blindness!'

'You've had your answer, sir,' said the officer in charge of the group as his men fought to bundle the giant priest away. 'Now move along.'

'What is going to happen to that lady?' demanded the ambassador.

'She stowed away on the boat from Pericur,' said the officer. 'Now she's going back. She attacked some of your own traders down in the main market, turning over their stalls. You know we deport any of your preachers that try to sneak in. We could have arrested her for the damage she did.'

'A zealot,' said Ortin, sadly. 'Treat her as kindly as you can.'

'Nothing for the archduchess to complain about, sir.'

Nandi watched the disappearing figure of the preacher, still yelling about the end-times and the fall of paradise, railing against the laughing Jagonese crowds who were jeering and taunting her. 'Does all of the race of man look like devils to you, ambassador?'

'I think there is a little bit of the devil in all of us, dear girl,' said Ortin. 'Whether you have a fine pelt like we do, or even if you don't.'

Nandi nodded in agreement. So many tensions came from the misreading of history. All so avoidable.

The preacher's voice grew fainter as they walked towards the capital.

'The last judgement is coming, all of you . . . *doomed*!'

Jethro looked out of the window of their lodgings while Boxiron finished unpacking the last of the travel cases he had been too tired to start the day before. It was a grand hotel, the Westerkerk, but the fact that the connected rooms they had been given were almost as large as their lodgings back at Thompson Street did not disguise the fact that this place was as a good as a prison cell for them. As soon as they'd arrived they had noticed the police militia posted at all the hotel's entrances, and while the soldiers were obviously busy turning away Jagonese claiming they had business with the *Purity Queen*'s crew, Jethro knew that their presence was a double-edged blade.

'We have quite a view of the cathedral across the Grand Canal,' noted Boxiron.

'A view,' said Jethro, 'but not an unobserved way to present the Inquisition's credentials to the cathedral staff.'

'The law enforcers here are not like your friends back in Ham Yard,' said Boxiron.

'Indeed they are not,' said Jethro. 'If they changed the colour of their green uniforms for a redcoat's cherry attire, they might almost be taken for a military force.'

'You marked the coral defences ringing the island on the way in,' said Boxiron. 'The commodore told me they have battlements surrounding the capital's surface structures almost as impressive.'

Jethro rubbed his chin. 'An interesting frame of mind, don't you think? All your enemies are external, all your defences facing out to protect you. But what do you do if you find there is a rot within? How would you cope with that?'

Boxiron did not get a chance to reply – there was a knock at their door and when the steamman opened it, Ortin urs Ortin stood there, filling the doorframe with his impressive furred bulk.

'Good ambassador,' said Jethro. 'You're not rooming in the hotel, are you? I thought your embassy would have taken you in.'

'The deputy ambassador claims that she wasn't told I was coming and that she's taken the opportunity of my predecessor's departure to remodel my apartments. I won't be able to move into my embassy rooms for weeks.'

Jethro frowned. 'You suspect a slight?'

'Of course I suspect a slight, dear boy,' said Ortin urs Ortin. 'I am a rare male office-holder in a matriarchal society, and it seems my banishment here is not to be made a comfortable one. But even they can't stop me taking up my duties. I have a summons to present myself to the stained senate this morning, as do you. . .'

'Me? I'm a private party, good ambassador, not a representative of the Kingdom's foreign office.'

'There's still a couple of reformers left on my staff here, despite the best efforts of the archduchess's conservatives, and my house's friends have caught wind of a few worrying circumstances brewing here,' said the ambassador, moving to the window. 'And that's one of them.'

Jethro followed the direction of the large furred finger and saw an officer of the police militia striding towards the hotel.

'Colonel Constantine Knipe, a particularly charmless fellow who seems to hold a low opinion of my appointment here that's not far removed from that of my own enemies in Pericur. He's already intercepted me and warned me to restrict my duties to a bare minimum and now I suspect it's your turn. Well, at least I've beaten the old fruit here to you. I counsel saying little. . .'

True to the ambassador's words, Colonel Knipe arrived outside their rooms a minute later, his appearance preceded by the clump-hiss of his mechanical leg. He glowered at Ortin urs Ortin as though his presence implied that all three of them were involved in some plot. Then Knipe turned his attention towards Jethro, his eyes skipping briefly past Boxiron – the steamman surely an exotic oddity on the island – and waved a sheet of paper at the ex-parson. 'Jethro Daunt, citizen of the Kingdom of Jackals. The same Jethro Daunt, I am presuming, who was the consulting detective that retrieved the *Twelve Works of Charity* when the painting was stolen from the Middlesteel Museum.'

'The same, good colonel. Although it would be truer to say that the painting never actually left the museum, it was merely switched and falsely identified as a forgery by the thief. You are exceedingly well informed.'

'Our representatives in the Kingdom still collect your penny sheets,' said the colonel. 'And our transaction-engine vaults are still one of the wonders of the world.'

'So I have heard,' smiled Jethro. 'And I see from the paper in your hand that their retrieval speeds match all that I have heard about their superiority.'

'Why have you been summoned to the senate floor, Daunt?'

'That, I'm afraid, only your stained senate can answer,' said Jethro.

'Your services have not been engaged by them?'

'No,' sighed Jethro. 'Sadly, my visit here is of a private nature.'

'There is nothing private on Jago when it comes to keeping our people safe,' said the colonel. 'I will have the reason for your appearance on our shores. We haven't had a Jackelian u-boat call for over thirteen months.'

'If you will,' said Jethro, stiffly. 'I have come here to pay my respects to a recent grave. That of Damson Alice Gray.'

'The archbishop?' said the colonel, surprised. 'What is she to you?'

'She and I were engaged to be married, although sadly the loss of my original living prevented our union.'

Colonel Knipe looked shocked, as though he wouldn't have been more disturbed if Jethro had admitted he and Boxiron were grave robbers come to whisk the woman's corpse out of her grave for sale to medical students in need of surgical practice meat.

'If the Jagonese embassy back home have been thorough in sending you copies of the *Middlesteel Illustrated News*, you will find the posting of our banns in your archives, I am sure. A little relic of my personal history buried among so much of yours, good colonel.'

'You have missed the funeral,' noted the colonel.

'Word travels slowly from Jago these days,' said Jethro. 'But I am here now.'

'Better for you to have missed the funeral,' said the colonel, his manner softening slightly now that he thought he understood the rationale for Jethro's presence on Jago. He pointed at Ortin urs Ortin. 'One of your friend's primitive cousins was released into the city thanks to the incompetence of the

Pericurian mercenaries the senate has seen fit to hire to protect us. You have your memories of the archbishop as she was, not as she was left after the ursk attack. It is better that way.'

'A terrible accident,' said Jethro. He did not say that he hadn't been able to properly remember Alice Gray's face for many years. He could recall their courtship, the places they had visited together, but the cruelty of time had erased her features from his memories. He was a different man now. Like so many men, he had defined himself by his relationship with her. What she had left behind would have been wretched, wrecked and worse even without the old gods' touch of madness.

'We killed four ursks in the canals that night,' said the colonel. 'Not much of a recompense for a life lost, but some consolation. I believe we still have one of the furs on the wall in the militia fortress. I could let you have it, if you think the use of it as a rug would bring you peace when you look at it.'

Jethro nodded. 'You are exceedingly obliging, good colonel.'

'I shall take you to the senate,' decided the colonel, graciously. He waved Ortin away, noting that the ambassador was expected to present himself first. Jethro watched the Pericurian leave eagerly enough, happy to be out of the militia officer's company with all his talk of skinning ursks. When the ambassador had left, the colonel shook his head knowingly. 'And on the way I will tell you what you need to know to keep you safe here.'

'Safe?' said Jethro. 'I understood the Jagonese were exemplars of courtesy and the abidance of laws.'

'By nature, our people are,' said the colonel. 'But the wheel has turned and things on Jago are not as they once were.' He stared at Boxiron, 'Is it safe to talk in front of this one?'

'I trust Boxiron with my life,' said Jethro. 'And despite the best efforts of the Jackelian underworld, as my living presence here attests, I have yet to be disappointed.'

'Are you from the Steammen Free State?' the colonel asked

Boxiron. 'Or an automatic milled by the race of man? You are not as I imagined you.'

'I am a little of both,' replied Boxiron, his voicebox juddering.

'My friend's is a sad and difficult story,' said Jethro, 'and it would pain him to relate it. Suffice it to say, Boxiron is a better and more reliable friend than all others have proven over the years. He's a topping old steamer.'

Satisfied, the colonel led Jethro and Boxiron out of the hotel, across the square and towards the imposing steps that led into the passages and vaults hollowed out of the mountainous Horn of Jago itself. Jethro was quite glad the colonel didn't suspect what Boxiron really was, or he wouldn't have been so happy to lead the two of them in front of the senate.

Jethro glanced across at the cathedral before the steps took him inside the mountain, the church building rising stalagmite-like to join the roof of the capital's vast central vault. That was where his business lay, not in front of the rulers of Jago.

What could the senate possibly want of Jethro Daunt that he had to give them?

CHAPTER FIVE

The thing that disconcerted Nandi the most about Hermetica City's atmospheric station was how clean she found it compared to stations such as Guardian Fairfax back in Middlesteel. None of the smoke, the dust, the grime, no cease-less thump from the constant labour of steam engines to keep the transport tunnels under vacuum. This system was powered by electricity. She shivered at the thought.

There weren't many people in the station – but then, this line only served the distant vaults of the Guild of Valvemen, their chambers buried many miles away at the foot of the hills that served as the gateway to the cold, dark interior of the country. Outside the battlements and no doubt out of mind, too. Practically a city by itself. No farm or park domes out there, nothing on the surface. All buried deep and far enough away from the capital for Jago's citizens not to be concerned about being poisoned by the power electric the guild's turbine halls generated.

Nandi stood by a cluster of statues in the centre of the concourse, watching the crimson-robed valvemen moving over the polished stone floor like red ghosts – waiting for the capsule that would take them to their vaults to arrive. She was puzzling over the inscription at the foot of a sculpture of three Jagonese women hugging each other – *Here lays Eli, still and old, who died because he was cold* – when she spotted the commodore coming towards her.

'I thought you might have forgotten I was due to make my first visit to the guild's transaction-engine rooms today,' she said by way of greeting.

'Ah, lass,' said the commodore, 'I would have come sooner, but for the curiosity of that colonel of police, Knipe, and his insistence I satisfy it with every petty little detail of our voyage here. As if the Jagonese shouldn't be grateful that there is still an honest skipper willing to brave the perils of the Fire Sea to pay them a call.'

'I had my turn yesterday evening,' said Nandi. 'After they escorted us to the hotel. What was my research, why was Saint Vine's paying the guild's fees of access so eagerly? How I am to immediately report anyone offering me large amounts of money as a dowry to marry them. What I know of Mister Daunt and the old steamer that follows him around. . .'

'You see now,' declaimed the commodore in triumph, 'why it is old Blacky avoids this blasted port. They are an insular, suspicious bunch on Jago. They have dug themselves a pit here, pulled themselves in and let themselves stew in their own juices for a few centuries too long.' He indicated the guild workers on the concourse around them. 'And these red crows are the worst of all, their bodies crumbling under the wicked weight of the dark energies they tame. But this is where you've come to study, and so I'll wait with you to see you safely away from the cursed place.'

'I'm not your daughter,' said Nandi. 'I don't need protecting.'

'Nobody will ever be my daughter,' said Commodore Black.

'I'm sorry,' Nandi apologized. 'I should not have said that.

I asked one of your crew back on the submarine who your boat was named after.'

'You're not my daughter, Nandi, but you have more than a little of her fire. She died doing what was right. I wish I could say I taught her that, but I'd be a wicked liar if I did.'

'I'll be safe enough here,' said Nandi.

'This city, this whole island, is a mortal tomb,' said the commodore. 'It just hasn't sunk in with the locals here yet. And I know your Professor Harsh well enough to know that she would have lectured you all about the dangers of tombs.'

'There are no stake-covered pits here,' said Nandi.

'Not the kind that you can see, lass,' said the old u-boat man. 'Which makes them even more dangerous in my book.'

'What if *I* need to do what I feel is right?' asked Nandi. 'Will you try to stop me?'

'I'm not that big a fool, lass.' He patted the sabre by his side. 'But I'll be close by, waiting to take up the point with any blackguards that do.'

Nandi shook her head and accepted the inevitable. It seemed that in convincing the professor that she could manage the expedition to Jago on her own, she had merely swapped one would-be protector for another. If her father had been alive, he would have come here with her. Nandi couldn't have stopped him, though perhaps he would have used his influence over the professor to stop *her*. The commodore and the man her father had been were as different as the sun and the moon, but they shared one thing – they would both die for her, that much she knew. Nandi shifted the leather satchel she was carrying, inscribed with the double-headed crane seal of Saint Vine's college and weighed down with her papers, blank notebooks and pens and ink. 'You won't have to wait much longer, look. . .'

Three iron capsules arrived in quick succession, whipping

through the rubber curtain to be caught by the turntable at the far end of the concourse, then rotated in front of the passenger platform as if they were offerings to those waiting. Nandi and the commodore had been sent a capsule all to themselves, to spare them the guild workers' company – or perhaps the converse. Their capsule also came with a guide; a single valveman in the same intricately embroidered crimson robes worn by the guild workers boarding the other capsules.

'No one on the platform to check for tickets,' remarked Nandi.

'Ah, anyone who wants to go where we're going is mortal welcome to it,' said the commodore. 'If there was any justice in the world, the guild would be paying us to visit their dark lair, not the other way around.'

Their guide led them into their windowless capsule and in a female voice told the two of them to make themselves comfortable on the red leather bench seats running along one side. When they were seated, the valve worker touched a button and the door irised shut with a clang, followed by a slight thump as the loading arm pushed them forward – into the atmospheric system. Then a whoosh. An increasing sense of acceleration as the pressure differential built up, sending them hurtling along the airless tunnels towards the great engine rooms of Jago.

Commodore Black turned to their guide. 'Tell me, lass, is there no pilot on this blessed contraption of yours?'

There was a slight shake of her heavy red hood. 'No. The atmospheric capsules are controlled by the machines.'

'Machines, always more machines on Jago,' said the commodore. 'Machines to open the gates on the great ring of coral that circles your island, machines to heat and light your vaults, and yet more of the blessed things to bring down the air from the terrible land above. You've more machines down here in your city than in King Steam's land.'

'And transaction engines,' added Nandi, expectantly. 'Filled with the lost knowledge of the ages.'

'It's never been lost to us,' said their guide.

'Archived away unstudied, then,' said Nandi. She rummaged around in her bag and brought out her letters of admittance and travel. 'Your colonel of police has already seen my papers, but my college is very insistent the right people receive these and I get access to all of the records we paid for.'

The valvewoman took the grant of access, and as she read her previously steady hand began to shake. Did she have the palsy? Had one of the engine-room afflictions weakened her arm?

'Are you well, lass?' asked the commodore. 'Do you need a tot from old Blacky's hipflask to steady your hand?'

'The names on these papers,' said their guide, 'the two original names listed under the prior grant of access.' Hannah Conquest pulled her crimson hood down. 'They're the names of my mother and father!'

As Jethro walked towards the senate, the combination of noises produced by Colonel Knipe's artificial leg and Boxiron's clumping footsteps on the iron gantry seemed to merge into one rhythm. Down below lay an atmospheric station almost identical to those of Middlesteel, save for the presence of Pericurian mercenaries waiting for the capsule-like trains. A large turntable in the centre of the concourse was retrieving new capsules emerging through the rubber curtains that sealed the airless tubes the carriages travelled along.

Struggling in the shadow of the bear-like mercenaries were Jagonese loaded down with bundles, crates and chests of possessions, pushing, pulling and hauling their burdens off the transport capsules and out into the vaults of the capital below.

Colonel Knipe noted the direction of Jethro's gaze. 'You

must feel Alice Gray's loss, Mister Daunt, to have travelled all the way to Jago to see her grave?'

Jethro nodded.

'There,' said the colonel, 'is our loss. The senate has ordered the closure of Tarramack, the second city of Jago. Her people are being relocated here to the capital, whether they care to come or not. When the evacuation is complete, the atmospheric line out to Tarramack will be blown and the tunnels caved in to keep us safe in the capital. Then there will only be us left. Our loss is not as sudden as the one you feel so keenly, it has been happening over centuries. Slowly, like a disease, or like old age, dying a little more each year.'

'Those people couldn't stay in their homes?' asked Jethro.

'A couple of thousand in a city built for hundreds of thousands?' The colonel drew a circle in the air. 'There were twelve great cities looping around our coast, connected by the atmospheric line. In a week's time Hermetica City will be all that is left of them. When your city's population is reduced beyond a workable level, things break down faster than there are people with the time or knowledge to fix them. I was in the city of Flamewall when we discovered that the hard way, manning a tower on its battlements. I left my leg behind there along with the graves of the woman I married and our two young sons.'

'I am sorry,' said Jethro.

Colonel Knipe hardly seemed to have heard him. 'No, better an orderly withdrawal and the planned decommissioning of Tarramack. The refugees hate us now, but they have their choice of homes in the deserted quarters here in Hermetica City.'

'Does everyone come?' asked Jethro.

'Some hide,' said the colonel. 'Holdouts that don't want to be resettled. A few turn outlaw. They won't last long on their own, not when the creatures outside the walls get into a city.'

'These are the problems you said you would warn me about, good colonel?'

'Partly,' said Knipe. 'And those that follow as a consequence of it. There are parents here, proud people, good people, who'll thrust their daughters at you as if their children were two-penny bawdy house girls in the hope you'll take them away from Jago – their sons, too, if they thought you had a taste for it. There are others who would slit your throat if they suspected you carried the foreign coins needed to bribe a u-boat man to look the other way on hatch duty. And as for the Pericurian mercenaries that guard us, you've had a taste of the misery those brutes' incompetence can bring you, with Alice Gray's death. This is what Jago has come to, our ancient redoubt of civilization. The world has forgotten who we are, and now it's just waiting for the last of us to forget too. Then there'll just be the ursks and the ab-locks and the other monsters of the interior hunting each other by the flames of the Fire Sea, amongst our broken ruins.'

'It is never too late to change,' noted Boxiron, stumbling along nosily behind Jethro. 'There are many threads of the great pattern, many paths that may yet be taken by your people.'

'Yes,' agreed Jethro. 'What about the senate you're taking us to see, what course do those that you've voted for favour in this matter?'

'Voted for?' laughed Colonel Knipe, grimly. 'They're the main part of what I wanted to warn you about, Jackelian. Jago's other cities may have been abandoned, but their political wards remain, controlled by one or two voters with ancient property titles. Our senators' seats have been as good as hereditary since long before I was born. When you speak to the First Senator, make no promises. Dissemble if the fool presses you. If you are lucky and his functionaries don't get your words on paper, he will have forgotten what he asked you to do by the next time you see him. His mind will have flitted onto a new fancy.'

Jethro nodded and continued walking, humming a tune under his breath. '*The bulldog as well as to bark may go whistle, just as an upland pup is doomed to be flogged with a thistle.*'

The Jagonese may have chosen to site the bulk of their capital in the warm subterranean caverns along the coast, but the vaults hollowed out within the Horn of Jago followed the usual laws of wealth – the higher they travelled inside the burrowed mountain, the greater the prosperity of its citizens, until the clothing of the merchants and mill-owners became so baroque that Jethro thought it a wonder they could still move under the weight of elaborate brocaded jackets and velvet cloaks. Each zone of wealth within the mountain seemed to have its own lifting room and territory, every guild and organization represented with their routes jealousy guarded, and although the passages' guards would not bar the colonel of the police militia, Knipe led them through the horn using a circuitous route to avoid unnecessary antagonism. By the time they had reached the senatorial levels inside the mountain, the public lifting rooms had become hall-sized, the padded crimson leather of their walls reflected in crystal mirrors and manned by public servants in senate livery. The last such lifting room they rode upwards deposited Jethro, Boxiron and the colonel in a long, echoing corridor lined with busts of First Senators long since departed. Each bust was as tall as a man and created the eerie impression that a company of invading stone giants had been captured and decapitated, their heads left here as a warning. In each of the gaps between the busts a waist-high wooden rack waited.

Jethro indicated the racks. 'For umbrellas, perhaps?'

Colonel Knipe shrugged. 'For holding the senators' rapiers and foils. Duelling was outlawed five hundred years ago on

Jago. It may be hard to believe now, but our cities were incredibly overcrowded once. Settling matters of honour at the point of a sword was commonplace, and the senate considered duelling a useful mechanism for society to release pressure.'

Yes, Jethro could see how centuries before, the comforts of a warm city and dome-grown crops would have seemed a paradise when the alternative was freezing on the surface and possibly ending up as food for the ancient Chimecan empire's plate. The memory of the Chimecans' vicious heel on the continent's throat had faded into the annals of history an age ago, and yet still Jago abided. Narrowly.

A line of Pericurian mercenaries stood sentry over a triangular-shaped door eighty feet high at the end of the corridor. After Jethro and Colonel Knipe had been thoroughly searched and the militia commander sufficiently humiliated – forced to un-belt his pistol and hand it over – one of the mercenaries behind a marble lectern threw a switch and the massive doors were powered slowly open.

'Your staff of office, too, colonel,' said one of the mercenaries, as the three of them were about to enter.

'A colonel of the police militia is permitted their staff on the floor of the senate,' barked Knipe.

The ursine guard shook his large furred head. 'The tradition has changed now, by order of the First Senator.'

Colonel Knipe's eyes narrowed at the insult, but he surrendered his staff anyway. 'Why not, there are hardly any of our traditions left to honour. One more lost won't make any difference.'

Inside, Jethro saw where the stained senate obtained its name: the mid-peak of the mountain was hollowed out into a vast octahedron-shaped chamber, the lower half filled with marble seats, public galleries and stands for the assembly's functionaries. The upper half of the octahedron was a ring of sloped stained glass that bore testament to Jago's lost greatness. Some of the scenes were historical, pictures of the great exodus from the continent to the island – galleons trapped frozen in ice while others burned in the Fire Sea, the surviving settlers standing tall on the shores of Jago and surveying the land. Ramparts being built and defended against rolling hordes of the island's monstrous natives. Acres of rainbow glass paid tribute to the height of Jago's mercantile era – docks spilling over with trade goods, food and spices from a hundred foreign nations. These scenes were interspersed with Circlist imagery, the illustrations of ancient koans and parables mixed with mathematical formulae so dense and elaborate the effect was of an illuminated manuscript set in glass. Light chased across the thousands of panes that had gone into each scene, and for a moment Jethro thought he was seeing lightning, but then he noted its regularity and realized it was the flare-house's sodium glare high above them. Beckoning in a world that had laid Jago aside.

Jethro hadn't known what to expect of this assembly, but it certainly wasn't *this*. None of the rude, urgent jostling and violent ritual of parliament back in the Kingdom. This vast echoing senate was as depopulated as the city it ruled, elegantly robed politicians dotting the chamber here and there, like patrons arrived early at a Lump Street theatre for a play that had received scathing reviews the night before, scaring away the bulk of the audience. Jethro noted some of them were sleeping. There were more senators and officials standing in the centre of the chamber than sitting down, clustered around something, and, as Jethro drew closer, he saw that it was an architect's model of a city built on top of a large round table.

'First Senator Silvermain,' announced the colonel. 'I have the two visitors from the Kingdom you requested to see.'

'Their presence was requested,' announced a politician in

his sixties, straightening up from his observation of the model. He had wild, white curly hair and a hangdog face, his neck hidden by a long scarf despite the comfortable warmth of the chamber. 'Yours was not, Constantine Knipe.'

The police colonel gave a slight bow. 'As the senate wishes.'

'The senate wishes for you to go. You and your sly eyes, always watching.' The First Senator pointed to the elaborately liveried servant standing behind him carrying a tall gold staff of office. 'You think you're fit to have a senatorial rod carrier following you with the First Senator's staff? You're not! You haven't the breeding for it – and without the breeding you're nothing, Knipe.'

The First Senator waited until the colonel had left, then beckoned Jethro and Boxiron to come towards the architect's model. 'We're watching *him*. Watching him talk to senators who think they can fill our chair. But not when we're cleverer than he is, with free company soldiers we trust. Protecting us. Take off your shoes.'

Jethro thought he had misheard the politician. 'I'm sorry, Your Excellency?'

'Off with your shoes, man, and your socks too.' He tapped the round table. 'Sit there and do it. Him too.'

'I am a creature of the metal,' said Boxiron. 'A steamman. These are my feet, not iron boots.'

'Capital,' said the First Senator. 'But your fleshy friend here is not, he is clearly of the race of man, we can all see that.'

Jethro did as he was bid, and as soon as his socks were off, the First Senator was kneeling down, performing a detailed inspection of his feet. 'See, no calluses, neatly clipped nails, the feet of a gentleman – but not pedicured, not pampered, the feet of an honest man. These are wise feet.' The First Senator indicated that Jethro should pull his socks and shoes back on while the courtiers and other senators standing about the table sounded rumbling notes of agreement; as if they had known this would be the case all along.

'You were a Circlist priest,' continued the First Senator. 'You stared deep into the souls of men. As you can see, we possess that talent too.'

Jethro stood up from the edge of the table. 'I was merely a humble country parson. But I fear my soles have given me away.'

The First Senator missed the irony in Jethro's voice and fixed him with an earnest stare, his eyes as glassy as marbles. It was like staring into the shifting magma of the Fire Sea. Hypnotic and dangerous. 'They have betrayed you to a good end. We have need of men like ourselves. We have need of the Jethro Daunt who was clever enough to solve the greatest theft ever to be reported from one of the Kingdom's museums. We can read the future in the lines of your feet, and we see that you have been sent to help solve our robbery.'

'Something has been stolen from you?' inquired Jethro, remembering the militia colonel's advice not to commit to anything in front of the First Senator.

'Oh, they are planning it,' said the First Senator, his hand sweeping grandly across the architect's model on the table. 'A conspiracy to steal this away from us. The future, the future of Jago. What is a mere missing oil painting compared to such a devious theft?'

Jethro was no architect, but even he could see there wasn't enough marble in the Kingdom – let alone on Jago's basalt wastes – to build the imposing boulevards of the city grid laid down on the table. Jethro tapped the table's surface. 'This scale must be wrong; from what I've seen there's not enough space in the vaults of Hermetica City to contain even half of these constructions.'

'There is no scale for the human imagination,' laughed the

First Senator. 'This is not a reworking of Hermetica City you see laid out here, Jackelian. This is New Titus, the first of seventy new cities we are planning to circle the coast of our great island nation. A bright necklace of civilization ushering in a new age of enlightenment.'

Jethro thought of the atmospheric terminus he had passed, the forced relocation of the last refugees living outside the capital. 'You have the people for such work?'

'We sense the wheeze of old thinking, of departing life,' said the First Senator. 'You have only just arrived here, but already you are becoming infected by Jago's curse. There is no place for old thinking in our new age. You Jackelians have shown us that, with your airships and your proud pneumatic towers pushing towards the heavens. But your Kingdom would be nothing without us. We passed the torch of civilisation to you when you needed it most; now your nation is to do the same for us. We are sending the creatures of the island's interior to your Royal Zoological Society. They will find a way to breed them in captivity for us.'

'Breed them?'

'We already have ab-locks tamed and labouring for us in the Guild of Valvemen's vaults. When we can breed them in captivity without having to trap their young outside, then we will have workers enough to achieve any task, any dream. And what if we should be able to tame the ursks, too? What need then to pay for our Pericurian friends to guard our battlements for us?' The First Senator shifted excitedly between each foot and jabbed a finger towards Boxiron. 'You have brought the future with you, Jethro Daunt, with your metal servant. You have shown us the way, as a man of wisdom often does. We have also placed an order for a hundred automatics with Dentley and Sons. Our mills here stand ready to disassemble them and learn the craft of their production.'

Jethro's eyes narrowed and he noticed the juddering of Boxiron's large arms growing more violent at the politician's words. Dentley and Sons, indeed. The Kingdom of Jackals' manufactories were less sophisticated even than those of the Catosian city-states when it came to creating their crude simulacra of the life metal, and if the First Senator had known the first thing about how a steamman knight's skull had come to be welded onto the primitive frame of a human-manufactured butler, he would have all his imported metal servants tossed into the Fire Sea when they arrived.

'Our new cities won't be built by *us*,' continued the First Senator, oblivious to Jethro and Boxiron's reaction. 'Only populated by us. And how our people will live, like kings and queens, even the lowliest Jagonese commanding a legion of servants numerous enough to befit the Archduchess of Pericur herself. Servants of flesh and metal who will toil ceaselessly to please our every whim. Our people shall labour no more, but instead turn their minds to the arts and sciences, to the enjoyments of culture and leisure. It will be an age unlike any other. A perfect age. A paradise of ease and plenty.'

'It is a most ambitious plan, Your Excellency.'

'Only if it comes to fruition,' said the First Senator. 'Empty caverns have been surveyed, great plans – as you see before you – have been laid. But there is a conspiracy here to stop us; those who cling to the old ways that have failed us, those who fear change. We can trust the free company fighters to support us – the Pericurian soldiers know who pays the bills, but they are dull brutes. We must do their thinking for them. But the high guild masters, the senators in the opposition, many of the traders and the city councillors, they are beyond the pale, all of them. They live like princes already and would deny our people their chance to share in the age of glory we have planned for them.'

'Such conspiracies often have a way of coming to light.'

The First Senator continued without acknowledging Jethro's obtuse reply – neither a confirmation nor a denial, merely a statement of fact. 'Move among our people, our Jackelian friend, uncover the conspirators.' He winced as Boxiron shifted his weight and loud clunks echoed around the vast chamber's stained glass walls. 'But you must ask your friend to tread carefully.' He indicated the handful of senators dozing in the benches above. 'Some of our ministers are made of glass, too much noise from your servant's iron boots will surely shatter them.'

Jethro and Boxiron left as quietly as they could, the excited shouts of the First Senator following them out, echoing around the empty senate hall. 'Our new city isn't a stolen painting, it is a stolen future! Find it for us, Jackelian, find what the traitors and schemers have stolen from us!'

'Well,' said Boxiron, after they had exited the vast triangular doors of the stained senate's chamber, 'you can stare into softbody souls. What did you see in there?'

'Bob my poor soul,' said Jethro. 'A blasted echoing void, hollowed out by the fires of Jago.'

'I claim no great understanding of your people,' said Boxiron, 'but even by the standards of this clumsy body I find myself grafted to, the ruler of Jago is clearly deeply defective.'

'You,' said Nandi, looking at the young girl wearing the robes of the Guild of Valvemen. 'Damson Hannah Conquest! I was asked to try and find you, but when I visited the cathedral the priests told me you weren't there.'

'I don't work for the church,' said Hannah. 'At least, not yet. I don't even live there now. You're from the same college my mother and father taught at, then, Saint Vines?'

'A Jackelian girl, here?' said the commodore, surprised.

'You're new to the guild, lass, that much I can see from how your body hasn't been taken sick yet. What's the likes of you doing in the guild? Don't you know what happens to those that work in its cursed ranks?'

'I know all too well,' said Hannah. She hitched up the crimson robes around her legs, showing a line of red weals forming above her ankles. It looked as if someone had been rubbing at her skin with sanding paper. 'But believe me, I'm not planning to stay inside the guild any longer than I have to. Why were you looking for me?'

'My professor asked me to make a call on you,' said Nandi. 'I don't think the college has ever been happy that the church made you its ward out here.'

'My father was an only child, the same as my mother,' said Hannah. 'I have no uncles or aunts in the Kingdom of Jackals, no grandparents left alive.'

'The college knows that,' said Nandi. 'Do you think we would have seen you turned out to a poorhouse back home? You are a living dependent of members of the college who died on duty. You should have become a ward of the Chancellor's Court of Benefactors, like me. College service, the same as your parents, and my studies and board are paid for by the college. Even if you don't want to study at Saint Vines, you have the rights to your parents' accrued pension and death benefits. Double in fact, as your parents were both tenured doctors at the university.'

'Why have I never heard anything about this?' asked Hannah, confused.

'The college has written to you at least once a year, asking you to accept a benefactor's scholarship from us.'

'I've never received a single letter from you,' said Hannah, sounding desperate.

'Ah then,' said the commodore. 'An inheritance that hasn't

come your way. A sad tale, right enough, and a story I have heard before. Normally attached to some poor young cabin boy or girl pressed into service against their will, while their money finds itself falling into someone else's wicked hands.'

'I was a ward of the Circlist church,' spluttered Hannah. 'The church takes enough in tithes and stipends that they don't need to rob children of their pennies.'

'But here you are all the same,' said the commodore, 'a fine Jackelian girl pressed into service on Jago with the terrible Guild of Valvemen. Say that you were pressed, lass. You did not volunteer for this terrible service?'

Hannah gritted her teeth. 'I did not volunteer.'

'Well, whatever the truth of it, there's mischief here, that much I can see.'

Nandi nodded in agreement, as the capsule rattled through the atmospheric tunnel, bringing them closer to the Guild of Valvemen's distant vaults with every second.

Someone had been trying to harm Doctor Conquest's daughter, and suddenly Professor Harsh's insistence that Nandi travel to Jago in the company of a swaggering privateer and his wild crew didn't seem so very strange after all.

Jethro and Boxiron walked towards the confessional against the cathedral's wall. Jethro found it hard to imagine Alice Gray as the archbishop of this vast stone expanse, so different from the small warm seminary rooms where they had come to know each other. It was as far away from the green water meadows, ancient oak forests and shire villages of the Kingdom as it was possible to get. Which, along with filling the archbishop's seat, had been the point of coming here for Alice. As far away from *him* as she could travel. What would their life together have been like, Jethro mused, if the old gods had not appeared to haunt him and ruin his name within the church? Would he and Alice have had children and what would they have been like? It would have been wondrous, the life he had been cheated of. Wondrous.

Jethro had decided not to present the Inquisition's seal to the cathedral staff just yet. If someone inside the church knew who had sent him here, then it was conceivable that Colonel Knipe would find out, and then, Jethro suspected, he and Boxiron would find their comfortable quarters at the hotel traded for armed confinement on the *Purity Queen* until the vessel left port. Or worse. And he had no desire to see the inside of the police militia's damp fortress cells at first hand.

The old priest, Father Blackwater, showed them the confessional booth where the archbishop's body had first been discovered. 'You will find far more peace at her grave, Mister Daunt.'

'I need to see where Alice died,' said Jethro.

Father Blackwater pointed at the polished flagstones. 'She was lying there. That was her usual confessional just against the wall. The ursk must have dragged her out. There was so much blood. I've never seen anything like it before.'

'That will happen when the head is removed from the body.'

'May the Circle bring serenity to the savage creatures that did it,' coughed the father.

'I believe I'm getting the offender's fur as a rug, if you are interested.'

The old priest appeared quite ill at the thought.

'Forgive me, good father,' said Jethro. 'I tend towards black humour these days.'

'We never knew that the archbishop had been engaged to be married,' said the elderly priest.

'The dissolution of our betrothal was an unhappy event for both of us,' said Jethro. 'You know what the great families are like: she was a highly cultivated lady and no one was ever

111

going to be suitable enough for their daughter.' Certainly not a parson who had allowed himself to start believing in ancient Jackelian gods. 'A minute if you will, for me to meditate alone here.'

'If only the archbishop had come with us into the city to help carry the torches,' added Father Blackwater.

Jethro nodded as he slipped into the confessional booth. But how like Alice to have stayed. Stubborn and proud, unwilling to abandon the sacred duty of taking the rational confession. Upholding her first duty towards the people, to balance their minds and purge the troubles of the soul – keeping her patients clean of hostile memes and false beliefs.

As promised, Jethro emerged from the booth a couple of moments later. He stared up at the vast circular rose windows, the shadows of the mathematical patterns depicted there falling across his face. 'A thought, good father. Without a head attached to the corpse, how did you know the body wearing the archbishop's clothes was actually that of the archbishop herself?'

'Our police militia are very thorough,' said the old priest. 'I saw them fill a syringe from the body and it was later matched to her blood code held in the guild archives.'

'What form did their thoroughness take?'

'The police interviewed everyone, they matched the archbishop's blood code, they sealed off and inspected the area where you are standing – the gentlemen officers of your kingdom's Ham Yard could not have done a more exacting job. We are an advanced nation, Mister Daunt, not a backward isle of secluded bumpkins.'

'Please do not take my morbid curiosity as any such slight,' said Jethro. 'The grandness of the cathedral's walls and the beauty of your stained glass speaks deeply to me of the sophistication of your people and the seriousness with which you treat the Circlist enlightenment. I understand the Jagonese way is to cremate the bodies of the deceased, not to bury them as we do back in the Kingdom?'

'In the old days the archbishop's body would have been placed in a boat and pushed out into the Fire Sea to burn,' said the old priest. 'We never dig a grave on the surface – the creatures out there violate them all too readily. Our present tradition is to lower the body on a granite platform close to the magma. The ashes that are left behind are then buried in the Vault of Remembrance. The cathedral fathers and sisters have their own wall there, which is where Alice Gray's remains are interred. I can walk you across there in a minute. . .'

'Another day, good father,' said Jethro. 'I think I need to remember Alice as I knew her in happier times, before I am ready to visit your remembrance vault and say goodbye for the last time.'

'As you wish. May serenity find you, Mister Daunt.'

Boxiron watched the priest walk away to greet a party arriving for the first cathedral service. 'It is not serenity I sense within you, Jethro softbody. What did you discover inside the confessional booth?'

'There was a note slipped under the pillow; curiously it is addressed to us. Also, something had been written inside on the wall. Written in blood, before it had been scrubbed off.'

'The note?'

Jethro cleared his throat. 'An anonymous request for a meeting late at night. A request addressed to the two foreign agents of the Inquisition. I can only presume that means us.'

'A trap?'

'Possibly,' said Jethro.

Boxiron's steam stacks coughed a pungent black cloud out above their heads, the smoke dispersing into the apsidal chapels behind them. 'And could you discern what the writing in blood said?'

'No. Only that someone had tried to remove it and I was lucky to find the traces. Blood had been splashed over the words to look like spray from the slaying, then rubbed off quite thoroughly.'

Someone who is being clawed to death by an ursk is unlikely to have written "the black-furred monster did it" on the walls of the confessional,' observed Boxiron.

'As unlikely as a decapitated corpse being capable of reaching out and scratching a last denouncement at all,' said Jethro. He cleared his throat and tapped the side of his cheek with a finger. 'I think it is time we put your special skills to some practical use on Jago, my steamman friend.'

'Yes,' Boxiron agreed. 'I believe I agree with you. I am meant for other things than padding around senatorial chambers and cathedral vestries.'

Jethro knelt down to the place where Alice's corpse had been discovered, running his fingers across the stone. It felt warm to the touch, as though the passing of her life had burnt an indelible mark inside the cathedral. What had she written inside the confessional booth before she died, what in the world could have been that important to her?

Yes. It was time for affairs to be pushed up a gear.

Without windows, the only way Nandi could tell that the atmospheric capsule had arrived at its final destination was the sense of deceleration followed by a gentle bump as they cleared the rubber curtain of the receiving station's lock. The young academic wasn't sure what she should have been expecting outside the capsule's confines, but it wasn't a man-made waterfall cascading down the Guild of Valvemen's entrance chamber.

Water was gushing out of the ceiling, flowing down sloped iron walls and hitting the floor like thunder before disappearing down sluice gates running along a concrete channel in the floor. The iron had gone green and was streaked with calcium deposits which were being scraped away by guild workers dangling down the iron slope on ropes.

Commodore Black wiped away the sheen of fine water dampening his cheeks and addressed Hannah. 'That's a mighty cascade, lass.'

'Condensed water from the turbine halls below,' said Hannah. 'After the flash steam has been tapped from the bedrock to feed the turbines' rotors and generate the electricity, it's pumped up through a cooling system and comes out as water.'

Commodore Black looked in horror at the water on his hand, regarding it as if it might be poisonous. Hannah shook her head and took them to a bank of lockers next to the atmospheric station's platform. 'The water's not dangerous, the electric field is strongest in the turbine halls and they're buried as deep as anything in the guild's vaults.'

'Dark power to supply the capital,' said the commodore.

'More than just Hermetica City,' noted Hannah, opening the locker with a key tied onto her robe's belt. 'The power plant beneath here used to supply all the cities of Jago and could again if needed. The steam taps below provide free energy.'

'Free if you discount the damage done to your bodies,' said Nandi.

Hannah indicated the suits hanging up in the lockers, all-encompassing leather aprons sewn with hundreds of dark lead squares. 'I'm not planning to be around long enough to find out. It's the accumulated background charge of an electric field that disfigures your body. These—' she indicated the suits '—are for outsiders, but they're really for show, to make you feel better when visiting. You're not going to be around long enough for your body to start changing, and even if you were, these wouldn't help you. You might as well walk around here naked for all the protection such suits will offer.'

'I'll take a blessed suit anyway,' said the commodore, wheezing as he lifted one out.

Nandi did likewise, struggling under the weight after she had belted the heavy lead apron around her.

'I'll escort you to the transaction-engine vaults,' said Hannah, 'I've already reserved a study cell for you with a card puncher and the access to the guild archives you've negotiated.'

Unlike the other guildsmen in the receiving station, Hannah kept her hood down, a small act of rebellion – or vanity, given her face was yet to be scarred by tumours.

'You mentioned you weren't planning to be here that long,' Nandi said to Hannah as they followed her out of the atmospheric station, the protective plates of their lead aprons clunking as they walked.

'I was put forward for the church entrance examinations before I was drafted by the guild,' replied Hannah. 'The guild have to let me sit the tests. And when I pass. . .'

'That's the spirit,' said the commodore. 'It's a wicked shame to see a fine Jackelian girl having to labour under the tyranny of these red-robed crows.'

'I only wish I had more time to study for the examination,' said Hannah, as the passage they were walking along widened into a barrel-vaulted chamber, stone pillars on their right supporting an open portal, voices echoing from within. Inside, row upon row of guild-robed figures were kneeling and humming a mantra.

Nandi frowned. The Circlist chanting contained little of the joy and warmth that was to be felt amongst the congregations back in the Kingdom. Here, there was a dour, plaintive edge to the sound.

Hannah poked her thumb towards the worshipping masses. 'They actually lead a more ordered life here than back in the cathedral. Meditations every hour of the day when the guild's duties aren't being observed.'

Nandi peered around the pillar and into the long chapel hall. 'So full.'

'Circlism has a deep resonance within the guild.' Hannah explained. 'The irrelevance of the physical body, your soul poured back into the one sea of consciousness after death. Your life cupped out again into another, happier, life further along the circle.'

Nandi tugged at the young girl's richly embroidered red robes. 'These aren't to protect you, are they? They're not even to hide you from the sight of others. They're to hide the sight of your body from yourself.'

'You won't find many mirrors here in the guild's vaults,' agreed Hannah.

Nandi listened to the voice of one the guildsmen at the front of the hall calling out to the crowd that they were all the cells of the liver, absorbing the poisons of the flesh, keeping the rest of the body alive. There was more than a grain of truth in that analogy, Nandi decided. She pointed to a figure lying in state on a podium at the front of the hall. 'Is this a funeral?'

'Of sorts,' said Hannah. 'That's the body of a guild highman up there. Before his corpse is lowered into the Fire Sea, part of his essence will be transferred into the transaction engines to become a valve-mind, joining the council of ancestors in advising the guild.'

The commodore shook his head. 'That's little better than the steammen, lass, with the Loas of their ancestors appearing like blessed ghosts when they're not invited, disturbing the rest of us innocent souls with their nagging.'

Nandi had to agree. Life working inside the Kingdom's colleges was difficult enough for young faculty staff, with members of the High Table clinging to their positions on the academic council well into their dotage. And that was without the prospect of having simulacra of them echoing around the college's halls long after they had passed away. She was just thankful they didn't have valve technology back home.

'It's just hope,' explained Hannah. 'The hope of something beyond all of this. Without hope, I don't think the guild could force anyone to work here.'

'Let's go on, lass,' said the commodore, turning his back on the packed hall. 'I've no taste for a sermon so early in the day.'

Nandi smiled. The commodore wasn't so very different from the rest of his rough and ready crew. Voyaging away from the Kingdom for years at a time, exposed to heathen gods and the temples of foreign religions, the enclosed corridors of a u-boat brewing superstition. No wonder places like the guild's vaults, clinging to Circlism, made him nervous.

They continued their journey through the guild's heart. At one point they had to halt when a pair of thick iron doors in the side of a tunnel pulled open to reveal a switchback series of ramps disappearing lower into the guild's depths. The three of them waited as a line of ab-locks filed through, the same simian-like creatures that Nandi had seen caged on the capital's docks. These creatures bore little relation to the wild, unneutered animals captured by the stocky little Jackelian trapper whose demands for passage had been spurned by the commodore. Although each animal was the size of a man, the ab-locks in front of Hannah appeared somehow diminished as they slowly trudged, hunched, into the vault's depths. They had been defanged and the claws on their fingers sliced off. The leathery skin on the front of their bodies hung swollen

118

and misshapen by the dark energies they had absorbed working the turbine halls, and the silver fur on their backs was left sticky and thinning compared to the lustrous sheen of the wild animals caged up on the docks. Whether it was due to the methods of taming employed by the guild, or their energy-sapping exposure to the power plant, these ab-locks seemed broken in every way, a state not helped by the guild handlers walking the line, prodding and threatening with toxin clubs whenever they detected some hesitance on the part of the exploited animals.

Commodore Black shook his head in anger at the sight. 'There's only one thing the wicked House of Guardians ever did right, and that's chase off the slavers from Jackals' coast. But it seems they didn't send their warships out far enough.'

'Does a shire horse in its harness look any different?' said Hannah. 'You might not say such things if you stayed here a season and heard the wild packs of ab-locks howling beyond the walls with the ursks and other creatures out there, probing our battlements for a break.'

The distant thrum of the turbine halls rising up from far below was cut off with a shudder as iron doors clanged down, locking into the floor. Only a few wisps of vapour from the flash steam system were left drifting along the passage.

'I helped set up your access to the archives,' said Hannah, moving the two visitors along the corridor. 'I'm not an expert, but I had to pass very deep down the storage layers on your behalf. You must be researching amongst our earliest records.'

'True enough,' said Nandi. 'Did your church guardian ever explain your parents' work to you?'

'Archaeology,' said Hannah. 'It was never my strongest subject. There's a lot of history on Jago and I lost track of the First Senators' names after the first five centuries' worth.'

'History. Well, that's half the truth,' said Nandi. 'Your father was an archaeologist, but your mother was a mathematician, and their area of study touched both disciplines.'

'I had presumed she was using the transaction engines here to run mathematical proofs,' said Hannah.

Nandi shook her head. 'After Jago was first settled, the island survived as the only nation to remain free of the grip of the Chimecan Empire, although its early years were blighted by the constant threat of invasion.'

'Ah, then, Nandi,' whined the commodore, 'let's not talk of that ancient terror with its dark gods and human sacrifices. We're well shot of the old empire. They've been dead a millennium and long may they stay that way.'

'It was your father, Hannah, who dug up a book back in the Kingdom, a text dating from the centuries when Jackals was a slave state of the Chimecans and the early church was driven completely underground. It suggested that the reason Jago wasn't invaded was that the church on the island had developed a weapon that threatened the empire's gods, a mathematical weapon that would have disrupted their hold on the world if the empire had dared to invade Jago.'

'A likely tale,' said the commodore. 'And where did the man discover this mortal account, in a Middlesteel drinking house?'

'Sealed in a glass jar found buried in a village in Hamblefolk,' Nandi went on, ignoring the old u-boat hand's scepticism. 'We dated the book at the college to the late Chimecan era, and it was dug out of a farmer's field where one of the first Circlist churches was said to have been re-built after the end of the age of ice.'

'The guild's archives cover that period,' said Hannah. 'But I've never heard of such a thing inside the cathedral. A weapon that could slay gods? If our church had ever crafted something like that, I think it would be recorded and still remembered by the priests.'

'Aye,' said the commodore. 'If you want to know why the old empire never took this dark, bleak place, you only have to look at the cannons on the monstrous coral walls surrounding the island and the flames of the Fire Sea lapping against its terrible cliffs. The shifting magma would claim the best part of any fleet fool enough to sail against Jago without the services of the island's pilots to see them safely through the boils.'

'Now you sound like the grey-hairs back at the college,' said Nandi. She looked across at Hannah. 'Don't listen to him. Your father and mother believed enough in what they found in that book to come here with you and search for records of the weapon in the guild's transaction-engine chambers. The foundations of the Circlist enlightenment were laid in mathematics, and around the edges that has a way of blurring into the sorceries of the world-song and our understanding of the universe.'

'From knowledge comes enlightenment,' Hannah quoted from the church's book of common meditations.

'I worry we're on nothing but a fool's errand here, Nandi,' protested the commodore. 'But old Blacky will be true to his word and stay with you all the same, to make sure you don't linger here overlong and singe your fine academic mind in the depths of the guild's dreadful vaults.'

Nandi caught her first glimpse of the vast depths of those vaults when the walls of their passage fell away and they found themselves crossing a bridge across a human-carved canyon, buffeted by waves of heat from the legendary thinking machines of Jago. Unlike the great transaction-engine rooms of the Kingdom's civil service, these vaults were powered by electricity, not steam. No transaction-engine drums turning down there. Instead, millions of glass valves studded the walls of the subterranean canyon, pulsing and burning with light and information. Only when they reached the floor of the first of the canyon-like vaults did the scale of the chamber truly become apparent. Guildsmen marched alongside a hundred ab-lock slaves pulling a cart heavy with valves, replacements for where the erratic course of the dark power had burnt out the thermionic tubes. Each glass bulb that made up the crystal forest of valves was as tall as an oak tree. Here was the true power of Jago. Not the dark energies of electricity generated by their turbine halls – that was just what it took to energize this incredible artificial mind fashioned out of cathodes, anode plates and glass.

The annals of over two thousand years of history were stored here; as well as the machines that kept the capital's vaults illuminated and whispered fresh air down to its streets; that regulated the battlements' killing force and pushed the transport capsules along the island's atmospheric tubes. Not to mention machines which held the model of the shifting sea of magma and the safe channels of superheated water which allowed Jago's tugs to navigate the boils outside. And Nandi was to be allowed to access it all. Humanity's oldest surviving library.

She could hardly wait.

Entry into the Hall of Echoes was forbidden to all save the High Master of the Guild of Valvemen, and Vardan Flail couldn't help but enjoy a little swell of pride each time he stepped forward to the entrance wall and the machinery inside detected his presence, confirmed his identity and admitted him to pass through to the dark chamber. Pride that it was he who had risen to this position over all his fellows through cleverness and guile and true understanding of the guild's intricacies and needs.

It never stayed dark inside the chamber for long. When the high guild master started talking, squares of light would form on the cold black stone wall, images from the memories of the hundreds of guild heads and high officials who had been judged worthy to become valve-minds. Freed from the weak needs of the body and the pain of decaying flesh, they were pure intellect, moving through the transaction engines with the speed of electricity itself.

'I have raised my objections with the senate,' announced Vardan Flail. 'But they will not act in our favour this time, of that I am certain.'

In response to his words, lines of illuminated squares shot across the stone, pictures flowing almost too fast for him to follow. There a remembrance of the senate as it had existed centuries before, here an image of a nose smelling a plant. Beautiful, meaningless, wise and foolish – it was like staring at the firing synapses of a brain. Then the chain of pictures slowed and stopped while disembodied voices started echoing around the chamber. The wisdom of his ancestors within the guild.

<Keep her.>
<Let her go.>
<Kill her.>
<Protect her.>

The clamour grew louder and more discordant, then, as was the way, the suggestions started to slow and finally coalesce into the community view.

<She must not be allowed to leave.>

'She will be allowed to sit the church entrance exam,' said Vardan Flail, scratching with his left hand at the bleeding flesh of his elbow. 'And she is clever, a mathematical prodigy. In the little time she had been with us she has already mastered every level of instruction set we possess for the transaction-engine core. She will pass the church's entrance exam.'

123

<Stop her.>

<Fail her.>

<Work her.>

<Keep her. >

Again the disembodied voices clamoured their way to a crescendo before coalescing into the majority opinion.

<*She must not pass the church's entrance exam. You know what must be done.*>

'I do,' hissed Vardan Flail.

Hannah Conquest must not be allowed to pass the church tests. And there was one way he could make sure of that. . .

CHAPTER SIX

Boxiron's silver skull swept left and right as he and Jethro walked towards the rendezvous, the steamman still uneasy that the note the ex-parson of Hundred Locks had found under the confessional booth's seat might be a trap.

It was darker here than in the streets that ran along the Grand Canal, the sun-like plates on the vault's roof poorly maintained and malfunctioning as a result. This vault, called the Mistrals, was still inhabited, but barely. Its paving was cracking, the albino stems of cavern bamboo starting to push out into the passages. This was the oldest part of the vault, too, a maze of buildings and narrow streets, the waters of the small canals the pair passed slow-moving and pungent with few working filters to clear them.

Boxiron and Jethro had to duck lines of drying clothes left drooping in the warm air by whoever still lived in the crumbling apartments. The directions they were following from one of the hotel's porters appeared accurate, as was the observation that this part of the vault's air recycling system had broken years ago – giving its passages a close humidity that was deeply unpleasant to walk through.

If the gloom and the dereliction of this area of the capital had been intended to disconcert the two of them, then those they were meeting would be disappointed. Boxiron didn't have much of his old steamman knight's body left, but his skull still had the proud vision plate of a knight of the Order of the Commando Militant. Boxiron switched to his ambient light profile and the shadows around them became a bright green patchwork of clear empty passages and deserted bridges, red targeting icons for weapon limbs he no longer possessed settling over any sign of movement – the scuttling of rats or the brief flutter of curtains in a fourth-storey window above.

'I have calculated the chances this may be a trap,' Boxiron warned Jethro.

'So have I,' said Jethro. 'But I have a feeling about the message under the seat. The sort of murderous creature that did what was done to Alice isn't the sort to shilly-shally around with slipped notes and uncertain ambushes.'

A narrow humped bridge led across the empty canal and Boxiron detected the mass of the vault's eastern wall looming up ahead of them. In front of the wall, a long line of stone columns stood sentry. Not holding the distant roof up, but coiled with steaming copper pipes – bleeds that would, they'd been warned, erupt with fire when the pressure inside them grew too intense. This was one part of the vault's systems that had to be kept in good repair – the alternative being the poisoning of the population from the veins of subterranean gas that bubbled beneath their feet. The steam from the pipes grew thicker, until they were wading through a river of fog that came up to Boxiron's chest unit. This was fast turning into the ideal spot for the out-of-the-way murder of a couple of foreigners.

Boxiron's combat instincts automatically overlaid the shifting steam with a grid that could differentiate between gaseous and organic movement: green lines running across the dancing haze, then suddenly deforming as a geyser of flame blew out ahead of them from one of the pipes, the heat-shock rippling over Boxiron and Jethro's heads.

<So desperate.>

Boxiron twitched. The memory, the terrible memory of a mansion burning back in Middlesteel, flames licking out of the bay windows and sparks leaping across to light bushes in the sprawling, overgrown garden.

<So desperate.>

And there she was, Damson Aumerle, a black silhouette clawing at the curtains on her great house's third floor, transformed into a demon capering in the flames of hell, the flames of —

<So desperate.>

Old Damson Aumerle, so desperate to resurrect the ancient human-milled butler that had been in her family for generations, so starved of affection that she had come to think of the stuttering automatic servant as her—

<So desperate.>

—that she pushed aside the grave robbers she had paid to loot the battlefield at Rivermarsh for the skull unit of a steamman knight, an advanced positronic brain to replace the decayed Catosian transaction engine in her beloved friend's —

<So desperate.>

— the hearth lighter in his hand, his metal fingers releasing the blazing hot iron towards the dry grass of the grounds. Had he done this, had he started the fire because he had been—?

<So desperate.>

'— to see you,' cried Damson Aumerle, her ancient eyes ablaze with relief as Boxiron raised his arm to see the primitive machine fingers of his hand for the first time. Not his hand. His hand was that of a steamman knight, not this pathetic, human-created simulacrum—

<So desperate.>

Aumerle House going up in flames. The flames of—

<So desperate.>

Jago.

'Are you alright?' asked Jethro, steadying his steamman friend.

'Looping,' said Boxiron. 'That's all, Jethro softbody. My combat filter is drawing too much power for the pathetic boiler of this body I find myself trapped within.'

Jethro checked that Boxiron hadn't slipped a gear, but the steamman could feel he was still only idling in first. 'Don't worry about me. Movement ahead.'

A figure came out of the steam, wearing the robes of one of the cathedral's priests.

'And there is one still hiding back there. . .' called Boxiron.

Another figure emerged, a dark leather-clad ursine. Barely an adult if Boxiron wasn't mistaken.

'You have good eyes,' said the ursine.

'My vision plate is one of the few parts of me that is good,' replied Boxiron.

'I saw you, good father,' noted Jethro to the priest. 'Back at the cathedral.'

'I am Father Baine,' said the priest. 'I'm the archbishop's clerk at the cathedral. My companion is Chalph urs Chalph, of the Pericurian trade concession here.'

Jethro drew out the message that had been left in the confessional booth. 'I should have known from the elegance of your calligraphy. A scribe. What makes you think that we are with the League of the Rational Court?'

'I knew the Inquisition would come when she died,' said the young father.

'Archbishop Alice Gray?'

'Yes,' said Father Baine. I nursed old Father Bell on his deathbed, the priest who was clerk to the archbishop's office before me. He told me how it was here.'

'That we would be coming?' said Boxiron. 'An exceptionally prescient member of your race, then.'

'No, metal brother, he was the one who told me that all of the appointees to the archbishop's chair on Jago have been ranking members of the Inquisition.'

That was news to Boxiron, and from the surprised look on Jethro's face, news to him also.

'I think if there was anyone the least likely to be an agent of the Inquisition, it would be Alice Gray,' said Jethro. 'Besides, there's been hundreds of appointees since the island was settled. How can they all have been members of the Inquisition?'

'I only know what I was told,' said Father Baine. 'And that the archbishop had a private encryption machine that wasn't like any of the others in the cathedral. She was placing correspondence in the church bag addressed to the League of the Rational Court. You must have heard rumours that the Inquisition was first established here on the island.'

'Rumours breed around the Inquisition,' said Jethro. 'And I suspect it suits their purpose for it to be so.'

'Yet here you are,' said Father Baine, 'you and your friend. They sent you, didn't they?'

'Here we are, good father, at any rate.'

'Tell them,' urged the ursine cub. 'Tell them what we've found out about the church woman's death.'

Jethro listened while Boxiron focused in on the ursine and the priest's eyes, measuring their blink response while they recounted what they had uncovered. About how Alice Gray and her ward Hannah Conquest had fallen prey to a high guild master and his terrible love for the archbishop, the premeditated investigation of the police militia cut to fit the cloth of their political infighting against the ursine mercenaries. The sabotaged wall, the sabotaged dome. A young woman snatched by the guild using the rule of the ballot draft. When the ursine and the young father at last fell silent, Jethro glanced towards Boxiron and the steamman raised an iron finger toward his inferior pressure-leaking boiler heart. His signal that the story was true. Jethro crossed his fingers in response, indicating that his church trickery and the body language of the pair in front of them was pointing to the same deduction.

'There it is,' concluded Father Baine. 'Can you help us?'

'My friend Hannah needs protection,' added Chalph ursk Chalph. 'At the very least you can take her off Jago with you and back to your homeland.'

'I believe your intentions are good,' said Jethro, 'and what you have discovered sheds some light on Alice's death. It's obvious to me that she wasn't killed by ursks – allowing the monsters into the dome was indeed a diversion to throw the city into confusion.'

'You'll help us?' asked Chalph.

'I shall,' confirmed Jethro. 'At the very least, I know a few things about the church entrance exams that will give Alice's ward, this Hannah Conquest, a fighting chance of escaping servitude to the guild.'

Boxiron listened as Jethro explained how the young priest and his ursine friend were to stay in contact using dead-letter drops under the bridge they had crossed to get here, with a cipher based on passages from the *Book of Common Reflections*. Then the young pair were gone; presumably relieved they had successfully engaged the services of Daunt and Boxiron.

'Jethro softbody,' said Boxiron, a suspicion itching at him.

'If you had served in the militant order of your people's church, you would tell me, wouldn't you?'

'I have never been a member of the Inquisition,' said Jethro. He smiled and added, 'Although if I had, I doubt I would be able to tell a heathen steamman who might pass such a secret to his pantheon of ancestors.'

'I fear the Steamo Loas have forsaken me,' said Boxiron.

'Bob my soul, but I could do with a few less deities in my life, too,' said Jethro. 'What did you think of that pair's theories on Alice's murder?'

'I have seen your race commit the darkest deeds in the name of love, but I can sense that you have your own theory on this matter.'

'I have some thoughts,' admitted Jethro. 'I used to know about passion. What happened back in the cathedral, in the confessional, that was cold. I think it would be good to discover what Colonel Knipe and his police really know about Alice's murder, not just what they've cooked up to find fault with the mercenaries from Pericur. Luckily for us, we now have the acquaintance of a young ursine who I believe might be able to help us.'

'Then it's time,' said Boxiron.

'Yes.'

Time for him to go all the way up to five.

Top gear.

Nobody noticed the figure moving through the atmospheric station. Just another crimson-robed guildsman whose footsteps were lost in the roar of the water cascading down the sloped iron walls of the station. When he accessed the terminal that indicated which transport capsules on the turntable were allocated to which team on the duty roster, it was the most normal thing in the world. Just another valveman checking what time he would be departing to the capital's central vaults, and which piece of machinery he would be overhauling, repairing or maintaining when he got to Hermetica. And when his eyes alighted on a particular capsule and it was temporarily shunted into a maintenance bay, nobody would have thought to challenge a guildsman who then purposefully strode towards said capsule, overriding the door controls and entering it.

Once inside the windowless capsule, the guildsman lowered a tool case to the floor, prised open a floor panel, and carefully lowered a bomb down inside, before setting the timer and resealing the floor. The carriage was ready for use again.

Ready to be shunted back onto the turntable, ready for the bomb's circuit to be completed ten minutes into its journey. The journey reserved for the guild's guests and the young woman looking after them – Hannah Conquest.

Nandi sat down where Hannah indicated, at a granite bench running in front of a featureless stone counter, with none of the hardware of the transaction-engine rooms she was used to back in the Kingdom of Jackals. No brass arrays, steam cables, iron panels or spinning drums. The only familiar-looking device inside the guild's study cell was the punch card injection tube and the card writer – and even there, Nandi was glad Hannah had been assigned to her side to translate the symbolic logic. She hardly recognized any of the foreign iconography on the writer's keys. Even the top cardsharps back home would, Nandi suspected, have been flummoxed if they had been sat down alongside such a machine.

Behind them, Commodore Black was staring out of the window of the cell they had been allocated halfway up the wall of the canyon, a grand view over the sound and fury of the valves below. It was as though he was still standing on the turret of his u-boat, expecting the floor of the rock-hewn cavern to surge with tidal waters.

'We've got the card writer to make queries,' Nandi said to Hannah. 'But how about receipt of the output? Is there a central spooler bank with runners to bring the tape to us?'

Hannah shook her head and lifted Nandi's hand up, pressing it against the featureless rock wall above the counter. It felt cold, and there was a grainy texture to its surface that was not visible to the eye. Then it started to itch, as if she was pressing her palm against a hundred small needles. An image formed on the rock wall in front of Nandi as she felt the prickles warm her skin, a large black oblong filled with scrolling yellow words and shuffling icons on the right. Nandi noticed Hannah smile at her surprise.

'There are quite a few advantages to using electricity rather than steam to power your transaction engines. The guild's stone screens will show you whatever you've requested from the archives.'

It took a little getting used to, but Nandi was soon able to settle down to her studies when she realized she could just treat the cold silicate surface like a more sophisticated version of the spinning abacus-like squares on a Rutledge Rotator back home. It was strange to think that once, if the ancient legends were to be believed, the world's temper had been stable enough for the power electric to be tamed by every nation, not just on Jago. A reliable source of power for lamps and the unknowable half-petrified machines that archaeologists dug out when they burrowed far enough down into the rock's strata.

As the day progressed – excavating deeper and deeper into the annals of Jago – Nandi got some inkling of why the man in whose footsteps she was following, Dr Conquest, had been so effective when paired up with a mathematician of his wife's calibre. The traits that made for a good archaeologist were rarely married to the mathematical prowess needed to code transaction-engine queries – one reason why Nandi still preferred the physical library at Saint Vine's to the steaming heat of their college's ancient transaction-engine room. But with Nandi's archaeologist's instinct paired with Hannah's diamond-sharp mathematical clarity, she could drill through the mountains of irrelevant material, stripping away the layers of dross to mine the seams of gold hidden inside the archive. Each record Nandi found contained a hundred links to related information – some direct, some inferred. Hannah's fingers were a blur across the punch card writer, the clack of keys a tattoo of symbolic search patterns and algorithmic re-indexing. There was a brief sucking noise as each finished punch card was drawn away down the tube in the wall like a miniature atmospheric carriage, then information began to crawl across the stone screen as the request was absorbed, processed and the matching records displayed.

The history of Jago could be read by Nandi in the shifting patterns of the world's climate: the short flourishing of trade after the island was first settled written in a thousand bills of exchange for wire, grain, dyes, spices; then the dwindling of commerce as the age of ice turned crueller, glaciers extending further south, and the Chimecan Empire rising like a vampire out of the world's ruins, devouring all the kingdoms struggling to survive. At last there was only the desperate struggle to remain alive, Jago standing alone, huddling in the warmth of its subterranean cities as the organized cannibalism of the Chimecans saw the peoples of Jago's old trading partners farmed for food. This was the period Nandi focused on, opening links to as many layers of the archives as she could, trying to gather up as much of the period as was possible within her grasp. Everything she came across had been erased from the other libraries of the world – books tossed onto fires by desperate freezing citizens living wild and trying to escape the tribute in living flesh demanded by the empire. She almost felt like one of them, an ancient Jackelian serf scrabbling around the forest floor for branches to burn, one eye on the darks between the trees in case she needed to flee. There had always been an edge of snobbery to how the students from families wealthy enough to pay for their studies regarded Nandi and the scholarship undergraduates from the wards of the Chancellor's Court of Benefactors. *Brass spoons*, that was their nickname in the halls and quads of the college – unable to afford a silver one, the obvious unkind inference. Nandi could hardly believe she was here, that the college had paid the guild's access fees and it was *she* who had been allowed to come. There were moments when this all seemed like a dream, about to disappear around her at any moment.

Nandi moved onto the work of sifting through the material, each new record, document and scroll opening up as many avenues as reading them closed. Finally, she struck pay dirt. A document where the annotation layers had actually been filled in by Hannah's father. There was a quick flurry of activity as Hannah designed a punch-card query for them to cross-reference the other records edited by the same access code, then the trail followed by Dr George Conquest opened up before Nandi. Six months of painstaking work by the Conquests laid out for her edification. Hannah gave a yelp of excitement, saving Nandi the job of giving voice to identical feelings.

Nandi plunged into the documents, earnestly at first, but then with an increasing sense of unease at what she was reading. By the time she had finished, her elation had evaporated to such an extent that even the commodore had noticed the change in her mood.

'What have you found in there, lass, to steal the wind from your sails so?'

Nandi tapped the screen on the black wall of stone in front of her. 'It seems that there was indeed an undertaking by the early church to create a weapon capable of undermining the Chimecan Empire's dark gods.' She looked across at Hannah. 'Your father pieced the story together from thousands of records. It seems a single female priest, Bel Bessant, conceived the idea. She must have been a prodigy, even by the standards of those who've mastered synthetic morality.'

'Why so blessed glum them?' asked the commodore. 'You have the beginnings of the history you sought to tease out from this dark place.'

'The beginnings and the end of it, both,' said Nandi. 'The undertaking never amounted to anything. Here's one of the final findings Hannah's father made, the record of a criminal prosecution carried out by the stained senate's judiciary. Bel Bessant was murdered. It gives her murderer's name as that of her lover, a priest known as William of Flamewall.'

'A Circlist priest killing another priest?' said Hannah, clearly shocked by the notion.

'A mortal priest's heart is as prone to the passions of love's malady as any other,' said the commodore. 'The curse of love can make the best of us forget our minds.'

Hannah got up from behind the card puncher. 'What did this William of Flamewall say when they caught him?'

'They never did,' said Nandi. 'Read the bottom of the document. He was tried in absentia.'

'There's nothing else?' said Hannah, clearly not believing what she was reading. 'No transcripts from witnesses as to why he might have killed her?'

'Not in your father's records. We could try to find them ourselves, but your father spent six months here researching

136

the archives. If he and your mother couldn't find them. . .'
Nandi sighed. 'All this way for nothing. Read your father's
notes in the annotation layer. His final conclusion was that
the rumours were just a bluff. Bel Bessant had developed
enough of a sketch of the possibilities of a god-slaying weapon
that the Jagonese only had to leak their plans to the empire's
agents for the Chimecans to forget all about bringing the
island under the heel of imperial rule. All this way out to
Jago, for what? For nothing.'

'Let me see, please,' said Hannah, swapping places with
the young academic on the granite bench and scrolling the
pages of retrieved documents down the stone screen. 'This
document was annotated the day before my father left Jago
to return to Jackals.'

'So it seems,' agreed Nandi.

'But that doesn't make sense,' said Hannah. 'The church
told me I was left in their care on Jago because my parents
were going back to the college to secure extra funding for
continued access to the archives – and they didn't want to
expose me to the dangers of an additional return trip through
the Fire Sea. If this was as far as their research went, if they
were really finished here, then why leave me behind on the
island?'

Nandi leant over Hannah's shoulder to stare at the screen.
The words of wisdom once given to Nandi by her mentor at
Saint Vine's echoed back at her. *'If it's too neat, if it's wrapped
in a box and left for you to find like a gift, then keep your
eye open for a trapdoor and a long drop down to some sharp
sticks.'*

But why in the world would either of the doctors Conquest
have wanted to make people think their work here was
finished, when it wasn't? One reason leapt suddenly to mind.
If the pair from the college had enemies sniffing around their

heels and had been laying a false trail, would they perhaps have hidden some clues for friends from Saint Vine's to follow in their footsteps?

'Hannah,' said Nandi. 'These comments are all from your father. If your mother had left any notes behind, where would they be?'

'In the search strata,' said Hannah. 'You can write comments on how you arrived at a particular record there; that's where you store reminders of the search algorithms you used in case you need to repeat them.'

'See if there's anything accompanying this chain of documents, made on or around the same date as your father's last access.'

Hannah went back to her card puncher and rattled out a query to peel back the underlying layer of her parent's findings. There was a sucking noise as the tube carried the product of her labours away into the injection system, then the stone screen started to flash and the image on the cold silicate surface reformed as a green block covered in mathematical sigils. Nandi couldn't even begin to scratch the surface of understanding this, but Hannah craned her neck out of the heavy guild robes and the wrinkling of the girl's nose and the dance of her eyes across the wall seemed to indicate she could follow the mathematics well enough.

'This,' Hannah tapped a lone stretch of code near the bottom of the image formed on the stone wall, 'this isn't anything to do with how my mother navigated to these files or her bookmark set – it's a Joshua Egg.'

Nandi looked blankly at Hannah.

'Ah now,' said the commodore. 'That's a rare piece of cleverness.'

Hannah shot a glance towards the commodore, which seemed to be a mix of surprise and admiration at his knowledge.

'You wouldn't have much occasion to use a Joshua Egg on a u-boat.'

'No lass, but if a lock's secured by a transaction engine and it's well-designed enough, the locksmith will usually throw one inside to encrypt their key for opening the bolts, and if there's one thing old Blacky's got, it's an aversion to being locked up.'

'This is a lock?' Nandi asked their guide.

'A Joshua Egg is transformative maths,' said Hannah. 'Highly recursive. When you solve it, you get another Joshua Egg and a piece of encoded information spat out. It's like a game of pass the parcel – you rip a layer off the package and you find another smaller parcel and maybe a present waiting inside for you. This is about as long as I've seen one, though, so there must be quite a few iterations inside.'

Nandi's eyes narrowed. The commodore was full of surprises, and so, it seemed, was the work of the doctors Conquest. 'Can you solve it?'

'It would take days by hand,' said Hannah. 'Maybe weeks if it's particularly tricky, but—' she waved towards the window and the wall of valves glowing on the other side of the artificial ravine, '—I don't have to do it by hand. With enough raw power I bet I can crack the first iteration in a couple of minutes.'

'Get to it,' said Nandi, trying to keep the hunger – or was it desperation – out of her voice.

Hannah jumped back on the card writer and transcribed the Joshua Egg and her method for solving it, filling up at least twenty punch cards with a tattoo of holes; the injection tube to the massive transaction engines patiently carrying each card away until the suction tube seemed to be hissing angrily back at them like a maltreated cat. Her volley of instructions released, Hannah leant back from the counter and the three of them waited for the girl's cards to find their mark.

The results came suddenly, and not in the form of a new display on the stone screen, but with an angry yelp of surprise from Commodore Black as a fork of static lightning flashed past the balcony behind him, searing the back of his neck. Hannah ran to the study cell's balcony rail, followed by Nandi. Hooded figures were jutting out from balconies on either side of their study cell, staring in disbelief at the sight. Glass valves on both sides of the ravine were ablaze with light, a nimbus of static electricity cascading down to the forest of valves on the floor. Intense bolts of energy danced between the giant glass bulbs, ricocheting among the relays.

'What mortal dark gale is this?' shouted the commodore over the roar from outside.

'I think it's a switching storm,' Hannah called back. 'One of the oldest guildsmen described them to me once, but he said we'd never see their like again. The transaction engines are overloading, but we're only handling the capital's needs down here now. There's enough spare processing capacity in the guild's chambers to support eleven abandoned cities. This shouldn't be happening!'

The clash and clack of the jumping lines of energy were joined by a rumbling noise from huge iron pipes running along the ravine's walls, cold water from the frozen wastes above ground being pumped down to cool the overheating machinery.

'This is our doing,' whined the commodore. 'Trying to prise open a nest of wicked secrets that were never intended to be known.'

Hannah shook her head vehemently. 'It's not us. It can't be. It doesn't take that much processing power to solve a Joshua Egg, however complex it is.'

Nandi stared out, fascinated and horrified by the leaping forks of energy. It was as though the valve-minds were gods whose rest had been disturbed, and this their rage. The study cell door flew open suddenly, diverting Nandi's attention, and a male guild worker sprinted inside waving an ebony-coloured punch card. 'Black card! Everything from vault nine to twenty-two.'

Hannah ran over and snatched the black card, feeding it into their injection tube.

'Why is your hood down?' demanded the guildsman from inside his own cowl. 'In the presence of outsiders. You shame us.'

'Shut up,' replied Hannah, almost casually.

The punch card disappeared inside the wall, bouncing back seconds later, followed by the dimming of the valve-light immediately outside their window.

Grabbing his black punch card back, the guildsman ran frantically out of the room without another comment on Hannah's state of undress.

Nandi saw that the image on the stone screen was freezing in place. 'We're finished for the day then, I take it?'

'They're freezing all non-critical processes in several transaction-engine vaults including this one,' said Hannah. 'They'll have the guild's senior card sharps and engine men down here all day and night, trying to work out why the chamber outside was overloading.'

Nandi looked at the stone screen, the image of a document half-formed on the rock surface. This was something new! The first layer of the Joshua Egg had been packed with a present after all! She ran her fingers across the archaic words on the document, translating them to the modern form. Could it be? *Yes.*

'This is part of the church's record of the trial of William of Flamewall,' announced Nandi excitedly to Hannah and the commodore. 'Look! It states that he poisoned Bel Bessant with metal oxides from the dyes he had access to. He was an illuminator of manuscripts and a stained-glass artist. That's how the militia discovered he was the murderer – they traced the poison in Bel Bessant's blood back to her lover's own dye mix, but William of Flamewall had already fled the capital by then.'

There was nothing more; the document's image had frozen mid-scroll on the cold stone. What else might they have found if Jago's legendary transaction-engine rooms hadn't failed them in quite so catastrophic and spectacular a fashion?

'An ancient murder,' said the commodore. 'With a good many more in the centuries since to trouble the island's police, no doubt. But it's not the capital *we* need to flee, it's these terrible guild vaults with their sick transfiguring energies and fearful storms of energy. If you've finished here, Nandi, let's head back to the safety of our prison of a hotel.'

'Finished for the day,' said Nandi.

And the day only. There were still a good few questions Nandi had about the work of the two doctors Conquest.

Standing close to the cascade of water down the iron walls, a robed figure watched Hannah Conquest, the aging u-boat man and Nandi Tibar-Wellking board the transport capsule and waited for it to safely clear the rubber curtain, leaving the guild's atmospheric station. The circuit of the bomb he had placed on board would have been completed now the carriage was under power.

He had followed his orders to the letter. The figure allowed himself a sliver of a smile – not that anyone could see it under his hood. He would be boarding a capsule with the other guild workers soon, but he wouldn't be going where those three were heading.

Oblivion's eternal embrace. In about ten minute's time.

*   *   *

Given his two companions' distant evolutionary origins as forest-dwelling primates, it was ironic, Boxiron considered, that it should be his inferior cobbled-together body that experienced the least trouble ascending the air vent to the surface of Hermetica City.

Chalph urs Chalph had the advantage of youth, though, the young ursine climbing the rungs ahead of Jethro without the sweat that was now soaking the ex-parson's face. The three of them were getting near to the cliffs overlooking the Fire Sea, Boxiron steadily pulling his not inconsiderable metal weight up behind Chalph and Jethro. Then the ledge was in sight, giving onto a bare stone passage that led to a heavy steel door with a wheel-shaped handle to open it that wouldn't have looked out of place on the commodore's u-boat.

They exited via a concrete bunker topped with rusted iron ventilation grilles, to find themselves on top of a black cliff with a view down to the boiling waters lapping against the shores of Jago far below. Chalph raised a finger to his lips and pointed to the massive iron battlements to their right, then indicated that they should proceed through the plain of boulders and concrete air vents towards the garden domes nesting under the towering presence of the Horn of Jago. It wasn't too hard for the three of them to stay hidden from the guard posts dotting the battlements – the ravages of a steam storm had recently passed, leaving behind a warm mist that cloaked them from the eyes of the Pericurian mercenaries – which should be focused on the monsters prowling outside the capital's walls anyway.

Chalph took them to a concrete building standing a little taller than the steamman's own height, wedged in between two air vents. There were three iron circles stamped into the wall around the back of the structure, each the size of a drain hole cover.

'This is it?' asked Jethro, his beak-nosed face swivelling about to make sure they hadn't been spotted by any of the sentries.

Boxiron judged they were safe enough. The nearest of the geodesic domes was one of the abandoned overgrown parks that dotted the outskirts of the capital. There wasn't likely to be anyone inside.

'This is what you asked for,' said Chalph. He lifted a steel tool out of his leather pocket and inserted it into a hole in the centre of one of the covers, levering the tool around until there was a muffled clunk – and then he heaved the cover out, pulling it away and resting it down on the stony ground.

Jethro looked meaningfully at Boxiron and the steamman lurched forward to check the machinery inside. It was a nest of cables, clicking mechanics and etched steel circuits lit by a bank of flickering valves hanging from the roof like lanterns. It appeared primitive to Boxiron, but no doubt it served its purpose, allowing the guild's transaction engines to control this stretch of the battlement's defences.

'What do you think, old steamer?' asked Jethro. 'Can it be cracked?'

'All in all, I prefer the locks and systems of a Jackelian transaction engine.' But it would do. There was a connection from the guild's vaults to the wall's control system and what was sauce for the goose could easily become sauce for the gander.

There really hadn't been many options open to a desecration like Boxiron after he had burnt down Aumerle House during his brief fit of madness. Shunned by his people, no longer a steamman knight, only a grave-robbed hybrid wandering the rookeries of Middlesteel begging for high-grade coke and water for his boiler heart. But desecration or no, Boxiron still had the mind of a steamman knight, a mind far superior to the

Jackelians' primitive transaction-engine locks. And after the flash mob had found him and enlisted him into their criminal ranks, they had outfitted Boxiron's human-milled shell with many useful extras. There weren't many locks, doors or transaction-engine safeguards – physical or artificial – that could stand up to his talents.

Boxiron sprung the concealed hatch on his chest and pulled out the highly illegal cables he would need for this piece of work, adjusting the variable heads to match the Jagonese non-standard sockets. Once he had patched in a workaround to bypass the machinery's obviously hostile protective valves, he pushed the other jack into the transaction engine's diagnostics system. *Why, this old steamer, officer? He's just checking the jeweller's here for a malfunction on their doorway. Move along now. Nothing to see here.*

Boxiron dialled back the power to his body, trying to limit the spasms of his twitching iron fingers. It was like holding his breath, painful and potentially dangerous if the retained smog from his boiler heart started contaminating the rest of his systems. *There.* The connection was made, and Boxiron smashed through the protocols limiting the battlement's diagnostics to reporting only – establishing a two-way connection.

'If you can't find anything in ten minutes,' said Jethro, 'you need to return. This mist looks like it could burn off soon.'

'You worry too much, Jethro softbody,' said Boxiron. 'This is what I'm for.'

The one function he could still perform with excellence. No more for him the honour of the battlefield, or whatever mundane tasks his body had performed for Damson Aumerle that had so endeared his frame to her. All that he had left to him was *this*.

Boxiron noted Jethro's hand on his gear stick, a gentle yank and a squealing navigation though the rusty slots on his back, before he felt it reach the final groove with all the impact of running into a brick wall. *Top gear.*

The light flickering across Boxiron's vision plate pulsed off as his consciousness entered the transaction engine like a bullet, hurtling towards the guild's vaults at the speed of electricity.

He encountered a diagnostics handler at the guild's destination gate, sleepy at first, then outraged that the battlements had malfunctioned so badly they had sent it this. And what was *this*? Boxiron sent the diagnostics handler insane while it was still wondering how it could possibly report this oddity, making the handler's corruption look as if it had accidentally fallen into a recursive loop. The guildsman who had programmed the handler so many centuries before had templated portions of the diagnostics' code from the main core, and the lights of shared developer tokens sparkled like open doorways throughout the system as Boxiron traced them across the guild's transaction engines.

Boxiron squeezed himself through one of the more central tokens, just far enough to observe the hundreds of handler functions shuttling back and forth outside, some carrying pieces of data from the archives in response to guildsmen's queries, far more shifting regular data streams between the capital's many systems: air circulation, gas leakage, temperature, the mortars and gunnery telemetry from emplacements around the foot of the Horn of Jago, power fluctuations from the distant, deep turbine halls. Boxiron changed his appearance to mimic one of the handlers, and then carried himself – looking for all the world as if he completely belonged there – towards the goal of his little foray.

He didn't even need to rip into one of the catalogues of port addresses to find the militia's hub – squatting there so similar to Ham Yard back home, bristling with privacy guards and firewalls that spoke more of the self importance of the bureaucrats that maintained its routines than its effectiveness against a steamman mentality. Boxiron circled it. Oh yes, all of this would be fine for stopping a human card sharp bent on creating a little mischief, but how long could it stand against a mind such as his?

Well, longer than it would have if Boxiron didn't need to be unobtrusive. A diagnostics handler bent out of shape would just be written off as one of those annoyances sent to plague the Guild of Valvemen's coders. But the central store for the police militia smashed to pieces? That was quite another thing altogether. Boxiron presented himself to the police store like a good little handler, and while the archive was extending itself across to him, he isolated the handshake protocol and extended a virtual environment around it so realistic that the protocol never realized that what it was experiencing was a subsection of Boxiron's own mentality. After it was safely cut off and isolated, it was a matter of simplicity to break the protocol apart and reverse engineer it, then push his own tame copy back towards the police archives. The next bit was where Boxiron was going to get clever – he had even agreed with Jethro exactly how it needed to be done. He wasn't actually going to steal all the police records pertaining to the arch-bishop's murder. He wasn't even going to copy them and try to make off with them in his memory. This was going to be a clean job. So clean, in fact, that the Jagonese civil service were going to do the work for him.

Boxiron found the police militia's case file for Alice Gray's murder and, seizing control of the archiving function, reset the clock on its timing synchronization forward five hundred years of their present date – long enough for the facts of the archbishop's murder to naturally declassify themselves. Then he sent a copy of the open files to the Jagonese public records office, along with instructions that they were to be immediately output onto paper, stamped and sealed inside an envelope as importation paperwork, then set aside for a certain Chalph urs Chalph of the Pericurian trade delegation to collect. Once Boxiron had reset the clock on the archive back to its original date, the record was automatically reclassified and all references to the copy automatically deleted as if they had never existed. Just to be on the safe side, Boxiron traced the physical bank of valves where the militia information had been stored in the guild's transaction-engine vaults and rotated that wall of valves to the top of the physical cleaning rota. The valves would be decharged, cleaned, re-powered up and not even a residual imprint of his crime would be left.

Boxiron was on his way back to the destination gate when he saw it; a rotating green force, half cyclone and half frenzied spinning top. It was throwing itself down one of the major query channels; upending the clearly terrified data handlers and absorbing them into its gyrating mass before spitting them back out again to shakily resume their transit. By the Steamo Loas, this was something new – something sentient and dangerous scouring the transaction engines for an intruder. It could only be one of the valve-minds he had heard about. It must have discovered the breach and realized the collapsed diagnostics handler was not the result of a bug. Boxiron's chameleon-like exterior couldn't withstand the likes of that whirling monstrosity. If it got hold of him it would instantly realize he was an intruder and the chances of his mentality making its way back to his clunking, human-milled body would be minimal.

Throwing caution to the wind, Boxiron selected an alternative query channel and sped towards the destination gate he had originally broken through, moving far faster than any mere data handler could possibly manage. It almost felt good;

to be in a realm where the pathetic joke of a body that his steamman head had been joined to was not an encumbrance. But it would have felt a lot better if the green cyclone hadn't immediately changed course and come roaring after him.

Boxiron increased speed and the valve-mind matched him. The gate was too far away and the distance between the steamman and the valve-mind too slight – and growing slighter with each millisecond.

He was never going to outrun this enraged behemoth.

CHAPTER SEVEN

It was Commodore Black who gave voice to what Nandi was thinking as their capsule started to decelerate. 'This is too blessed early to be stopping. It took us an hour to get out to the guild's vaults, and we haven't even been travelling for six minutes.'

Hannah stood up and checked the panel at the front of the tube-shaped carriage. 'The destination arrival marker is showing here, but you're right. We're a long way from reaching Hermetica City.'

A rattle sounded from outside, the unmistakable noise of clearing a rubber tunnel valve, then they slowed to a complete halt. Commodore Black reached into his jacket and drew out a snub-nosed pistol. He broke it and slipped a crystal charge into its breech, then pushed back the clockwork hammer mechanism. Nandi looked at the old u-boatman, horrified.

'You've a nose for history, lass. I've a nose for ensuring poor old Blacky's bones aren't added to the dirt you and your college friends like to trowel through.' He pointed to the front of the windowless carriage. 'Get down there, ladies, as fast as you like. Trigger the door when I give you the nod.'

Nandi shook her head and reluctantly pulled a small knife out of her boot. Used only for the purposes of excavation, until now.

'I see the professor's taught you a few of her other skills, then,' said the commodore. 'That's fine. But if it cuts up rough, you leave the killing to me.'

Hannah saw the commodore's signal, triggered the release handle and two iron levers pushed the door up and out with a squeal. It was dark outside; pitch black until Hannah switched on the carriage's external lamps. Commodore Black moved through the door, Nandi following close on his heel. They were in a large echoing cavern, freezing air blowing in from above them. The carriage had been shunted next to a dark platform.

'It's an atmospheric platform,' said Hannah from the doorway, her voice probably louder than she intended across the echoing space.

Nandi stooped down and ran her fingers along the concourse through a layer of dust. 'It hasn't been used in a long time.'

Hannah emerged tentatively from the capsule, glancing around. She walked to the concourse wall and rubbed off a layer of frost and grime from a stone mosaic bearing the name of the station.

'Worleyn,' said Hannah. 'As in Worleyn steel. This was a mining centre for metal ores, the only town apart from the guild's vaults sited away from the coastal ring. It was abandoned before I was born, though.'

Nandi looked up towards the ceiling of the station. Now she was getting used to the darkness she could see there was a dim light coming from above. Not a diode panel, though. A domed skylight partially covered over with snow above, cracks of daylight slanting through. They were close to the surface here.

'Mining is a sight too much like hard work for me,' said

the commodore. 'Let's be out of here on that broken carriage of yours and leave this empty ruin to its ghosts.'

'It's not broken,' said Hannah. 'There's no guidance system in the carriage; it only goes where it's sent. The fault that sent us here must lie in the line machinery. We need to find the controls for this station's platform turntable, then use them to rotate us back for another run towards the capital.'

Nandi was moving towards the end of the station where Hannah was indicating the controls might be, when a fierce flash of light and intense heat hit her, smashing her off her feet. Her ears were ringing when she tried but failed to pull herself up into near darkness. The light from their carriage had gone – the carriage had gone! Replaced by shards of glowing metal littering the platform behind them, burning debris lying raked across the empty hall.

Commodore Black recovered first, and moved over to Nandi and Hannah, feeling their limbs for signs of shrapnel wounds. 'That was no malfunction on the carriage, that was a blessed bomb!'

'It was meant for me,' coughed Hannah. Her heavy robes had been torn by the blast. 'I think the guild have just found out what I've been doing with their transaction engines in my spare time – poking about in the details of the archbishop's death to prove it was their own bloody high guild master who murdered her.'

'They're not subtle about it, then,' said the commodore.

'If we'd been in a tunnel when the bomb went off it would have looked like a cave-in,' replied Hannah. 'We'd have been buried under tonnes of rubble.'

'Let's be off before they find they've failed,' said the commodore. 'Can we call another carriage here, lass?'

'We can try,' said Hannah. 'The station master's bay should be close to the maintenance yard.'

Nandi bent down and picked up a burning piece of seat leather, wrapping it around one of the still-hot pieces of metal carriage rubble to form a make-shift torch for the three of them to navigate by.

They found the equipment where their young guide thought it would be, but it didn't take long for them to discover that the machinery on the station was no longer powered. The rat-eaten schematics on the instrument board indicated that the connection to the energies of the guild's turbines was on the surface, shared with the old opencast mine's ore mill.

Hannah offered to go to the surface first, having – she claimed – ample experience of climbing the air vents back in the capital. But the commodore was having none of it, and the two young women followed him up the rusty ladder to the surface from inside the abandoned station. Nandi felt an inrush of freezing air and a scattering of snow as a hatch clanged open above them, bright white light flooding down their dark passage.

The station's powerhouse had been built behind the dome of the atmospheric station's roof. The three of them were surrounded by deserted snow-covered buildings at the foot of a series of hills that had been chewed into by drift mining. There was a rise of iron battlements on the other side of the hills – not much of a barrier against whatever might be outside now that the protective wall wasn't charged.

When they got to the shadow of the powerhouse it wasn't the drift of ice frozen around its foundations that nearly made Nandi scream before she caught herself – it was the figure captured within the ice.

Nandi peered closely. The corpse was doubled up on the ground; a single hand reaching claw-like towards the switching machinery boxed against the powerhouse's stone walls. The floor of the ice block was crimson, as was the trail that led to the powerhouse – he had been bleeding profusely as he had crawled towards his final resting place.

'He was trying to summon a carriage,' whispered Nandi. 'The same as us.'

'Not quite the same as us,' said the commodore. 'Someone's put a wicked ball in his gut. Old Blacky they just tried to blow to bits like a firework.'

'I know him,' said Hannah touching the ice around the corpse. 'I know him.'

'I don't think you can, he's been here a long time,' said Nandi. 'The body is frozen desiccated under the ice.'

'His face,' said Hannah, trembling and not – Nandi suspected – from the biting wind. 'I recognize his picture from Hermetica's news sheets, from when my parent's boat was lost in the Fire Sea. He was the captain of my parent's boat. His name is Tomas Maggs.'

'He looks good for it,' said the commodore, tapping the ice around the corpse with the butt of his pistol. Nandi had to agree. Captured in the ice of this remote place when he should have been burnt to a cinder by an unpredicted closure of one of the boils' channels by the shifting walls of magma.

And if the captain of the Conquests' boat had been alive when the pair had both disappeared, then their deaths may not have been the result of any terrible accident at sea after all. . .

Boxiron risked a millisecond's worth of processing time to cast his senses behind him again. He was losing ground to the pursuing valve-mind with every loop and twist through the guild's transaction engines – having to keep away from the destination gate in case this twisting green monstrosity realized where he was heading and called in help to trap him inside the valves.

There was something about the valve-mind's behaviour, too, something that Boxiron couldn't quite put a finger on. It was trying to run him down to ground, but not engaging in any action more hostile than that – and hostility was something that the steamman suspected this thing was well capable of. And it was acting on its own, too. If this had been the great engine rooms of Greenhall, back in the Jackelian civil service's vast palace of centralized power, then he would have had a whole pack of sentry routines baying on his trail by now. Whatever the valve-mind's motives, Boxiron had to get back to his body before the thing captured him – it was always dangerous separating out your mentality for a visit to the artificial planes contained within a transaction engine. The dangers of the natives aside, too much time here and the systems of his clunking body might not even recognize Boxiron when he reinserted his id back inside his shell. His own body could reject him.

With the valve-mind nipping furiously at his mentality, Boxiron swerved across one of the main data channels and let loose with a trick that had been gifted to him by the same artful mechomancer who'd turned him into the steamman equivalent of a battering ram for the ignoble art of breaking and entering Jackals' locks and engines. Boxiron slashed down with a piece of self-replicating code that scattered like hell's own rainfall above the crowded channel of data handlers below. Without the reassurance of the comfortable system chatter nudging them along, pushing them towards their different destinations, they flew upwards, blindly groping for orders, for reassurance, for the familiar. More and more of them uplifted, shooting higher into the abstraction layers of their environment – and found the valve-mind.

They swamped it, desperately accreting around its skin like a swarm of bees. And as quickly as it could open up communication with the corrupted traffic and command them away, more and more of the infected handlers pushed in – some re-infecting the cleared handlers that had just been ordered away. Like a battleship whose shell had been weighed down with limpets, the valve-mind sank lower into the data channels and Boxiron had the lead he needed.

The steamman's mental projection had almost reached the destination gate when he felt a fierce bite of pain in his consciousness, an acid burning spreading out from the sting. Behind him, the valve-mind had extended a nest of tentacles whipping about its sinking form like a spastic octopus. Darting to the side, Boxiron slipped under the tendril that had pierced him, the valve-mind blindly grasping out, trying to relocate him. Ignoring the stinging irritation of the wound, Boxiron backed away at full speed, closing the gap to the exit.

As his consciousness picked up a message he could have sworn was projected out by the valve-mind. <The girl. The girl.>

Then he slapped into the black passage of the line back out to the capital's battlements and the crippled iron shell of his body coalesced around him once more, clumsy limbs jerking into life, all of his imperfect feeling restored through the degraded connections soldered into his steamman skull. Back again. And there was the extra pain of the valve-mind's wound on his mind, still smarting; something to dwell on beyond the accustomed sensations of decay his body was feeding him. His vision plate pulsed into life and he found himself resolving on the image of Jethro Daunt, with the furred visage of Chalph urs Chalph gazing anxiously at him from behind the ex-parson.

'Jethro softbody,' Boxiron's voicebox crackled into operation. 'Is this what I'm for?'

Jethro helped him break the connection to the battlement's

control machinery and gently shook his head. 'It's only the smallest part, old steamer.'

The steamman allowed the two of them to help steady him until he found his sense of balance again. 'Then by the beard of Zaka of the Cylinders, why am I so good at it?'

Jethro and Boxiron had nearly reached their hotel in the central vaults of Hermetica City, when a group of large, black-leather-clad ursine soldiers stopped them. Jethro's first thought was that their foray into the police militia's records had been detected and tracked back to them, followed a second later by the realization this couldn't be the case. Given the rivalry between the senate's mercenary army and the police militia, the ursine thugs were the last people the police would turn to.

Jethro and his steamman friend found themselves politely – but firmly – being escorted back to the surface. Not through the air vents, but up into the Horn of Jago, then out along stone corridors that belonged to the fortifications and mortar positions at the foot of the mountain, past the green-tinged farm domes, and finally into a metal-walled guard complex that joined the battlements. There were plenty of free company fighters from Pericur inside the complex, but no sign of Chalph urs Chalph. If Jethro and his steamman friend were about to be punished for their break-in, surely they would have dragged the young ursine here to share their fate? The mercenaries stood back as first Jethro, then Boxiron were forced to enter a vertical passage and climb a ladder inside to the top of the wall.

Jethro drew a silent breath of relief as he saw First Senator Silvermain standing on the insulated walkway of the battlement's parapet. He was gazing down the sloped iron walls, the smell of ozone strong from the deadly charge flowing down the barrier. Little forks of electric energy rippled over the surface, angry green serpents where the steam mists rolling across the ground outside stimulated the killing charge into visibility.

'Our friends,' the First Senator called loudly, seeing Jethro emerging out onto the parapet. 'Our clever Jackelian soul mate and his loyal servant.'

'Your Excellency,' acknowledged Jethro, giving a little bow.

'Just the fellow,' said the First Senator. 'How is your search for the conspirators progressing? Has Jago's evil cabal proved a match for your fierce intellect?'

'It continues by-and-by. Early days, I fear,' said Jethro. He reached into his pocket and drew a bag of boiled sweets out. 'Can I offer you a Bunter and Benger's aniseed drop?'

'My food taster is not here. Do not underestimate those who would rob us of our bright, shining age,' warned the First Senator, waving the proffered bag of sweets away. 'Their minds are cunning and their hearts are riddled with the sickness of sedition.' He leered at the steamman. 'What of you, strange creature of the metal? Have you found the enemy yet?'

'I have a simple attitude to such matters,' replied Boxiron. 'I wait for my enemy to reveal himself, then I strike him down.'

'An admirably straightforward method, yes, but the enemy's daggers will not bounce off our skin as well as they would off your hull plating,' laughed the First Senator. 'You will both benefit from seeing the foe at first hand, we believe.' The First Senator signalled to his senatorial rod carrier and the elaborately liveried servant stepped forward and inserted the ruler's staff of office into a control socket in the battlement's floor. 'Open the doors!' commanded the First Senator, 'and send out the prisoners.'

Slipping open a panel on the side of the gold staff, the

servant revealed a line of keys, and sent the order to the machines that controlled the battlement systems. Jethro heard a rusty-sounding ratcheting as a concealed door in the battlements opened, a ramp extending down to the black rock in front of the wall.

Stumbling out across the ramp and onto the dark, mist-shrouded plain below, a group of seven Jagonese were roughly shoved out into the wilderness. They milled around looking confused for a second while the light from the door disappeared behind them. The ramp was pulling back, the door closing.

'What are you doing?' demanded Jethro. 'There are women and children down there. . .'

'They look the same as other citizens, don't they?' said the First Senator. 'But they're not. That's what you're up against with this cursed conspiracy; the enemy could be anyone – anyone at all.'

'They're Jagonese? In the name of the Circle. . .'

The First Senator shook his head. 'They were, until the Senatorial Court stripped them of their citizenship. These villains put themselves beyond society, now society is putting these criminals beyond it. Turnaround is always regarded as fair play back in Jackals, is it not? The most natural form of justice. The two tall ones down there were forgers, producing false papers of travel to Concorzia. The other dogs you can see below were named as the criminals that paid them for the forged documents.'

'Exile,' said Jethro.

'A death sentence,' said Boxiron, hissing out the words.

'What they do beyond the city walls is up to them,' said the First Senator. He leant over the parapet and yelled down. 'They are no longer our society's concern. Off with you. We don't need your kind here. Corrupt filth!'

'For pity's sake,' begged Jethro.

'Some we are told even make it as far as the closest of the abandoned cities,' said the First Senator. 'If they can run fast enough.'

Down below, the shifting currents of steam had swallowed the two forgers as they ran towards a black forest rising out of the sea of white. In the distance there was a muffled drumming. It sounded to the ex-parson of Hundred Locks as though it was coming from the direction of the trees.

'Ursks,' said a mercenary officer walking down the battlements towards the politician. 'They smash bones against the sides of the trees when they smell city folk coming.'

'But not our bones, Stom urs Stom,' said the First Senator. 'Not while we have our loyal Pericurian soldiers protecting the true citizens of Jago.'

Down below, the group of would-be émigrés began yelling as screams sounded from the direction of the forest. Jethro couldn't hear what the exiles were shouting, but the dark shapes he spotted fleeting though the mist spoke volumes for what their cries might be.

'Your bones!' the First Senator yelled down jubilantly. 'It's your bones today!'

The large Pericurian officer jerked a paw towards her soldiers and they unshouldered their turret rifles.

'You are not to shoot them,' shrieked the First Senator. 'Their sentence is exile, not execution.'

'There are cubs down there,' protested the officer as her fighters lowered their rifles. 'The ursks will drag them away alive for burial in their larder caves.'

'They wanted to leave us all behind,' cried the First Senator. 'Well, they have! They're getting exactly what they wanted.'

With a scream, one of the exiled citizens was pulled back into the white vapour, vanishing while dark shapes cut through the mist where he had been standing. Jethro tried to shut his ears to the group's panicked, pleading cries, though he had no choice but to listen to the screams of grief as the remaining adults picked up their children and tossed them into the sloped city battlements, the explosion of energy carrying up past Jethro's face, so intense it almost stopped him seeing the remaining exiles grasping their hands together and hurling themselves forward to create a second blast. They had committed suicide rather than try to outrun what was waiting hungrily for them in the mists.

'You're cheating the exile law,' shrieked the First Senator, his face pursing petulantly.

Jethro leant forward, his knees buckling and involuntarily emptied the contents of his stomach across the insulated grey tiles along the rampart. By the time Boxiron helped him back onto his feet, all that remained of the exiles was the charred smell in his nostrils. Their burnt corpses had already been dragged out of sight by the horrific things prowling through the steam mists.

'We expected a stronger stomach from you,' said the First Senator. 'We know you have sent men and women to the gallows back in Jackals.'

'They were murderers,' coughed Jethro. 'All of them.'

'And so are the members of the conspiracy and their puppets,' said the First Senator. 'The enemy are murdering our society. Every year, every month, we are a little deader on Jago. A little bit emptier, a little nearer being finished. But we will stop them, we will reverse all of their schemes, we will smash their plots, and so—' he jabbed a finger at Jethro, '—will you, my Jackelian friend. Don't bring us the little people, the draft dodgers and the deserters. They are all the colonel's incompetent militia are able to catch to feed our courts, the pathetic stowaways dragged off the boats heading to Pericur. We want the ones organizing the great plot. Find us the cabal behind this evil so we can toss them out of our city before they corrupt any more of our people.' The First Senator pulled a silk handkerchief out of his jacket pocket and tenderly wiped a trace of vomit away from Jethro's mouth as his voice turned threatening. 'And you must work fast. We would hate to see you fall victim to the conspirators' filthy lies, our Jackelian friend. You must prove where your loyalties lie.'

Jethro swayed on his feet, the cold winds mixed with the warm fog from the Fire Sea playing across his face. He was rock. It was as if he was becoming part of Jago here. Merging with its black basalt plains and the fire-warmed cliffs.

'We should come out to the wall more,' said the First Senator, his voice turning sugary again. 'To see the enemy. To remind ourselves of what they look like. It's better when the weather's not so misty, you can see more of what the ursks do to the criminals. And it's so warm when the mists are rising, so warm.'

Jethro watched the First Senator collapse into a sedan chair waiting on the parapet for him, four Jagonese bearers lifting him away. Another man ran alongside the chair with a large fan, energetically cooling the ruler and trying to avoid his feet becoming entangled with the robes of the richly liveried senatorial rod carrier trotting after his master.

'Yes, but who is the enemy?'

'A free company fighter does not ask such a question,' said Stom urs Stom, thinking Jethro's remark was addressed to her. 'We only need to know who is paying us to take to the field.'

'There should always be honour in war,' said Boxiron.

The large mercenary stared at Boxiron, as if seeing the steamman for the first time – a steamman knight's skull incongruously welded to the rattling body of a Catosian mechanical. A broken fighter.

'Yes,' said Stom. 'Yes, you are right. There should be that.'

The mercenary officer followed after the departing retinue, leaving Jethro and Boxiron alone looking into the shifting mist and listening to the distant victorious howling of the ursks.

Jethro was no soldier, but he was bobbed if he could see any honour out there.

CHAPTER EIGHT

'Wait here,' commanded the house's chamberlain, brushing the white-tipped fur on his ancient chin; easily one of the more supercilious of the ursine representatives that comprised the trading mission to Jago. 'I shall check the baroness is ready to receive you.'

Chalph resisted the urge to click his teeth – the ursine equivalent of a tut. Of course the baroness was ready to receive him. If Chalph hadn't shown up exactly on time this evening to present the week's completed trading ledgers, the Master Clerk of Accounts would have had him whipped for his tardiness. Luckily for the young ursine, he was far cleverer than the elders he served usually gave him credit for – able to do his work, and squeeze enough time out of his far-ranging errands to help Hannah. Chalph, isn't he at the docks this morning? No, then he must be out visiting the merchants for returns. Really, but I thought he was with you this afternoon?

Chalph rebalanced the pile of heavy ledgers under his arm as his eyes flicked across to the large double doors the chamberlain had disappeared through into the baroness's receiving room. Above the doors were the crests of each Pericurian house that had held the Jagonese trading licence – the House of Ush's single legendary white oak occupying the right-most position – that line of heraldry a living testament to the twists and turns of politics in their homeland. In much the same way as the Jagonese had managed to capture a slice of their old lives in the deep vaults of the island, the interior of the building the trading mission had occupied since time immemorial boasted the oak flooring, panelling and engraved woodwork of a typical Pericurian dwelling. If the baroness could have got away with adding onion-shaped minarets to the mission's roof, she would have. Then again, perhaps not. These days there was a value in being discreet. There was enough bad feeling towards the Pericurian traders 'getting rich' as the islanders' own fortunes waned, without the house flaunting expensive imported timbers on the outside of their compound.

'Enter now,' said the chamberlain with a false tone of awe, reappearing through the doors and making it sound as if Chalph had just been given news of a large legacy.

The baroness's chamber was dark, the wooden slats of the blinds turned to admit only a half-light from the vault outside – the kind of perpetual twilight you were meant to be able to feel walking through the great forests of Pericur. And there, lying on a low, cushion-lined couch of monstrous proportions was the great dark mass of Laro urs Laro, the twenty-second Baroness of the House of Ush, most humble servant of the nation of Pericur. Among those of her house, those on Jago, she was known simply as the baroness, as if there were no others sitting on the Baronial Council. And as far as Chalph and his fellow bonded workers were concerned, that might have been the scripture's own truth.

'I have the week's accounts, my baroness,' Chalph announced.

'So you do, Chalph urs Chalph,' warbled the baroness from her couch, the silvery black fur around her large belly

165

undulating as she spoke. Here was a true ursine female in all of her middle-aged glory. So heavy that she had to be borne through Hermetica City on a litter carried by eight footmen. A noble mountain of flesh carved in the traditional manner, and the absolute ruler of her realm.

Chalph bowed and stepped forward, placing the ledgers between bowls of honeyed fruit on a low table. Her command of detail and concentration bordered on the supernatural, and woe betide the clerk who came forward with errors in the books after having supposedly double-checked the results that week. The baroness took the first of the ledgers and languidly turned its pages, interspersing her reading of the profit and loss columns with murmured demands for the contents of the table's bowls, stirring little apoplexies of anxiety among the retainers on all sides as they competed to fulfil her whims.

After the baroness had consumed half his ledgers and the same proportion of the honeyed fruit in front of her, she snorted and laid a massive furred finger on one of the line items. 'This charge, my clerk. Three days ago. Six gallons of paint . . . irregular?'

'For the walls of our wholesaler in the Seething Round, my baroness,' explained Chalph. 'It was attacked at night and the building daubed with anti-Pericurian graffiti.'

A sigh emanated from the large mass sprawled across the couch. 'The Seething Round used to be a good neighbourhood.'

Chalph shrugged and he heard the chamberlain cough in annoyance behind him.

'Speak, my clerk. Do not leave things unsaid,' ordered the baroness.

'There are no good neighbourhoods now in Hermetica City, my baroness. Not for the people of Pericur.'

'Oh ho. So that is the way it is, Chalph urs Chalph? I have

ears enough to hear the gibes and insults that are thrown at my chair when I am carried outside the walls of the house.'

'Things are growing worse in the city as the harvest from the domes dwindles, my baroness,' said Chalph, choosing his words carefully. 'If you travelled without the mission's guards, I fear you might have worse than insults thrown at you.'

'I see the counsel you would offer me in the way that you stand and the tone of your voice, even though you don't suggest it.'

'From a clerk who should mind his manners,' hissed the chamberlain behind Chalph.

The baroness raised a slow-moving paw in Chalph's defence. 'I must know what all my people are thinking, not just those in the house's council. It is the trader's curse, my clerk. The wanderer's curse. All those of your age and younger have been raised in this strange foreign city – and you think as much like the Jagonese as you do a proud member of the House of Ush. If the harvest is poor this season, then we shall just make much of the opportunity by bringing in grain from Pericur.'

Chalph bit his tongue. Every coin in profit the house made just fuelled Jagonese resentment against them. There would be no gratitude from the locals for bellies fed that would otherwise have gone empty, just more enmity against the Pericurian ambitions to drive the Jagonese off the island and grow fat off the islanders while they did so. Why couldn't the baroness see that she was imperilling them all by staying here? They would end up selling the Jagonese the same oil and kindling that would be used to burn the mission out when things turned to the worse here. Would she treat a pogrom against them as just another part of the trader's curse?

'Patience, my clerk,' commanded the baroness. 'You will feel the soil of the homeland between your toes before your soul is called; but the House of Ush will not hand the conservatives back home a famous victory by voluntarily forsaking our trading licence here and sailing back to the new archduchess with our tails between our legs. That is *not* how I will meet her.'

Chalph did not agree, but he kept his place and held his tongue this time. Better to leave with their tails between their legs than have those tails cut off and handed back to them by a baying mob. The cunning of the baroness and her ability to plan five moves ahead of her opponents was legendary: how she had taken a backwater trading house and allied it to the rising star of the liberal cause in the Baronial Council, parlayed her growing wealth from the new southern trade routes into the trading licence for Jago. But her star's rise had halted with the death of the last reformist archduchess, and her cunning had landed them here – the renowned wealth of Jago a fading, illusory footnote of history. The flames of the Fire Sea had consumed this place and left only bitter ashes in the grate for their house to rake over. Age, it seemed, wearied everything, and now the Baroness's guile had atrophied into whatever blind stubbornness was keeping them here.

The weekly oversight of the accounts complete, Chalph withdrew with the pile of ledgers, feeling far more despondent than when he had arrived. There was a tiny nagging voice deep inside him that he ignored and then forgot. Which was a pity, as there was a grain of truth in it that he should have listened to.

Blind stubbornness. *Unless the baroness knew something that he didn't.*

The tea-tray rattled as Boxiron brought it towards the table in their hotel suite. It was all right for Jethro Daunt, the Jagonese food and drink might be foreign, but at least it proved mildly palatable to him. Boxiron had no such comfort.

Trying to find high-grade coke in a city run on dark electric energies was proving as difficult as finding the archbishop's elusive killers. There were a few scuttles available from a stall in a small canal-side market that specialized in old imported Jackelian curios, but at a cost that was, quite frankly, bordering close to those charged by the extortion rackets that Boxiron had himself once acted as an enforcer for.

Jethro looked up from the papers and documents spread across the table and gave a wan smile.

'Are we any closer to locating the archbishop's murderer, Jethro softbody?'

'Small steps, small steps,' said the ex-parson. 'The most interesting thing I have found is not among the police files you stole for me, old steamer, but among the more general data that is available from the public records office here.'

'You brought back many tomes from the city's library,' said Boxiron.

'Yes I did,' said Jethro, 'and something is exceedingly wrong with the ballot of draft for the protected professions. There are patterns of citizens being called into guilds that make no sense to me. The gas workers for instance, why are so many of their number being drafted when their trade is already essential to the city?'

'Knowing your race as well as I do, I would expect corruption when it comes to the call into unpopular and dangerous trades,' said Boxiron. 'The rich always find a way of avoiding such duty. You are looking into the draft of the young church girl into the Guild of Valvemen?'

'That is where I started,' said Jethro. 'But there is much more going on here than Alice's ward being press-ganged as leverage to force the archbishop into an unwanted marriage. Context, good friend, context. If only I can find the context, then all the parts of Alice's murder will start to fall into place.'

'I shall check the files from the police militia when I return from the market,' said Boxiron. 'Perhaps I shall find something you missed. My mind is still my own, even if this pathetic body is not. It deserves little better than the overpriced second-rate garbage Hermetica's excuse of a coal merchant sells.'

'Don't worry about the price,' said Jethro, intently sorting the papers. 'The Inquisition will pay.'

But not, Boxiron suspected, before he and the ex-parson paid a far greater price for being here.

Jethro's body twisted, hot and sweaty in the sheets of the hotel bed, while his mind churned, turning over the contents of the police files that he and Chalph urs Chalph had picked up from the capital's records office. The fruits of the steamman's raid had appeared to reveal depressingly little, apart from the cursory nature of the militia's investigation into Alice's death. All the official conclusions pointed to the mercenary force's incompetence in manning the city's defences. As fixed in stone as the weight of the cathedral that poor Alice's body had been discovered inside.

Alice Gray. Don't think of the militia daguerreotype of her headless corpse in situ on the cathedral floor; or of her laid out on the coroner's slab, her few possessions spread out alongside her – the archbishop's robes, the *Book of Common Reflections*.

She was dead, gone. But there was a wrongness to it more than the death of the only woman he had truly loved. A wrongness to all of this. The possessions spread around her, something was missing. What was it?

The realization came to Jethro, but then suddenly he was back among the pews of his church at Hundred Locks. Say a meditation for Alice's soul, cupped back out into the one sea of consciousness. Say a meditation and ignore the arch of fur slowly snuffling around the back of the pews. Surfacing, then sinking, as though it was the conning tower of a u-boat. Ignore the cloying voice of Badger-headed Joseph taunting him.

'You're the man for the job, fiddle-faddle fellow. You're the man.'

'Alice would have cast you out,' snarled Jethro. 'Just one look from her.'

'From a real priest?' snickered the distant prowling voice. 'But she's dead and *you're* the man. The Inquisition's man now.'

'I won't hear you.'

'Did you never wonder why that was? Why the Inquisition wanted you to come to Jago, you of all people.'

'I won't hear you.'

'You don't need to,' hissed the ancient god. 'You hear *them* and because of that you need to believe in something, and we're it. We're the ones that went before your godless church set up empty altars to the reason of humanity. The best. The original and we're still waiting for you. Patiently. Benevolently.'

'I'm not a Circlist parson any more,' howled Jethro.

'Yet the refugees still keep coming to visit you,' said Badger-headed Joseph. 'I can hear them outside your confessional, queuing. Can't you? And it's your duty to see them. Every last runaway escaped over the border from Quatérshift to the safety of the Kingdom of Jackals.'

'Shut up!' Jethro covered up his ears. 'Shut up about the—'

Organized communities – long lines of naked bodies – emaciated – they beat me for the last of the gruel when the food arrived – and I thought they were my friends and neighbours – cleaning out the blood from the blades in the machines – my friends – before they took my children away and made them – but that's not the worst of it, father – when they—

171

'Shut up!'

—*were pulling sacks of processed flesh from the grinding bins – guards forced them to play on flutes while they took the women inside and – are you listening to me, father? When they—*

'Please shut up.'

'Why should they be silent?' laughed Badger-headed Joseph. 'They're the sound of the boundless humanity your Circlists cling to. There wasn't much humanity in the nation next door when the glorious revolution started, was there? The synthetic morality machine, snick-snick-snick. Toss another bag of organs on the manure pile, compatriot. And if you run out of coal for the killing machines, there are always plenty of knives or sticks or stones. But then, why waste good sticks on the enemy when you can just toss them outside the walls and let the beasts eat them?'

'Leave me alone,' begged Jethro.

'What else were you going to believe in after the refugees came to you?' sneered the half-animal god's voice. 'That horse-shit inside your Circlist book. A little light algebra? A koan or two? Bloody koans, more like a children's tale that kicks you in the head at the end of it.'

Jethro tried to crawl away across the floor of the church. 'Why me, why?'

'We're here for you, fiddle-faddle fellow. But we're going to need to hear you say it. Say that you believe in us.'

'You can wait for the Circle's end. I cast you out!'

'And in return we're going to do exactly what the Inquisition expected us to do. We're going to help you.'

'Liar!' Jethro pulled himself towards the altar.

'That's it,' said Badger-headed Joseph. 'Go towards the altar, crawl towards your empty, barren altar.'

The refugees outside his confessional were fading; their

emaciated, scarred bodies disappearing with each hand's length Jethro pulled himself closer to the front of his church.

'That was your clue, by the way,' growled Badger-headed Joseph, releasing a stream of warm, foul-smelling liquid over the back of Jethro's boots. 'Don't you dare look back at me – eyes forward, eyes on the prize. On the altar. The *empty* altar.'

'I – don't – believe – in – you!'

'But you will. And much more, too.'

Jethro touched the altar. It became the headboard of his bed, his fingers clawing the bamboo wood. And as he woke he saw in his mind's eye what was missing from amongst Alice's possessions. What the police should have found but didn't. What had been stolen from her corpse.

There was a breeze blowing in through his room's open window, cooling the sweat-soaked sheets lying across his legs. It was an artificial breeze, the whisper of the vault's machines.

Hannah couldn't believe she was still arguing when they got to the rooms of this great church investigator that Chalph and Father Baine had sworn would be able to help her. She should have risked bringing Chalph along with her to help argue her case, even if the police militia guarding the hotel did get suspicious about his comings and goings.

Why couldn't the commodore and Nandi see that she had to go back to the guild to serve out her last few days' service before sitting the church's entrance exam? Not because of the dangers of being arrested as a draft dodger, or even for the chance of unmasking the guild's head as Alice's killer – but because Hannah's parents might *still be alive*. The discovery of the skipper of the boat that had disappeared with the supposed loss of all hands frozen to death in an abandoned mining station didn't have to mean, as the commodore suspected, that Captain

Maggs had arranged to murder her mother and father, and then been silenced in turn. Her parents might have bribed Maggs to fake their sinking, then disappeared. Hannah's parents could both still be alive!

'You can't go back to the guild,' Nandi insisted as Hannah knocked on the door to the hotel room. 'They tried to kill you. If we hadn't got off that carriage when we did. . .'

'Alice was killed here in the city,' said Hannah. 'In the supposed sanctuary of her own confessional booth inside the cathedral. Besides, you'll be with me for the last few days – you need my help to mine the guild's transaction-engine archive. And I have to find out what really happened to my parents.'

'You'll be safer on the *Purity Queen*,' lass,' begged the commodore. 'Papers or no, you're a Jackelian. We'll stow you in my cabin and let's see which of the black-hearts on this dark isle think themselves big enough to board my boat and take you off. They'll find not all her fangs were pulled before the fleet sea arm was done with her, that much I can promise you.'

Hannah shook her head vehemently. 'I want to join the church here, not start a war between Jago and Jackals.'

'An admirable aim,' announced the beak-nosed gentleman with gently greying hair who opened the door to them. 'As a rule, the church prefers to work towards the preservation of life rather than its extinguishment.'

So this was the man? He didn't look much like an agent of the Inquisition dispatched to investigate the archbishop's death as Father Baine had intimated. But then, he didn't look much like the sort of man that Alice Gray might have once married, either. Ordinary, plain, but with a slightly vulpine face.

Commodore Black bulled his way after Hannah as she entered the room, Nandi following behind them.

'I knew there was a blessed sight more to you than you told us on the voyage over here,' the commodore accused Jethro Daunt.

'I owe a certain amount of discretion to my clients, good captain,' said Jethro. 'Much the same as you do to those whose cargoes you transport in the *Purity Queen's* hold.'

A clunking metal creature entered the room bearing a tray loaded with porcelain cups, a pot and a couple of sliced bamboo pieces. So, that was what one of the Steamman Free State's metal creatures looked like? Hannah's reading on the subject had suggested they might be more . . . elegant, somehow. Or was this creature one of the Jackelian or Catosian manufactured automatics milled by the hands of man?

'I have made tea, as is the fashion here,' the creature's voice projected scratchily from his voicebox. He indicated the short slices of bamboo on the tray, each hollow tube stuffed with drying tea powder for use in the pot.

'Tea will serve perfectly,' said Jethro. 'Put it down there on the table, Boxiron, and let us listen to your story, young Damson Conquest. I am eager to find out why someone would wish Alice Gray's ward dead enough to risk letting a pack of ursks into the city.'

Hannah expanded on what Chalph and Father Baine had said they'd already told the church's agent, reciting to him everything that had happened to her, everything that she suspected. The archbishop's argument with Vardan Flail, Alice's murder, Hannah's enforced guild service, Chalph's discovery of the sabotaged section of the city's wall, locating her parent's research in the guild's transaction-engine vaults, the bomb on the atmospheric carriage, their discovery of the frozen corpse out in the mining station.

Jethro Daunt seemed very interested in the dead skipper, Tomas Maggs, and had just as many questions for Hannah

175

about the nature of her parent's research on Jago – peeling away at everything they had discovered inside the guild's transaction-engine vaults. Then Jethro cast back even further, prying into the circumstances of Hannah's arrival on Jago, her adoption by the church, what she remembered growing up and her ambition to join the ranks of the Circlist church.

By the time Hannah had finished, she felt as if a burden had been lifted from her shoulders. The man she had told her story to, though, looked as if his had been increased.

'Does any of this make any sense to you?' Hannah begged the ex-parson of Hundred Locks.

'A little more than when you came in,' said Jethro. 'Bob me sideways, but there is more to this than just the matter of a high guild master spurned and a murder of passion, that much is obvious to me. A question for you, good damson, which might at first appear not to make much sense. Why would someone be crawling towards an empty altar in a church?'

Hannah was about to answer that she didn't know, when a memory suddenly rose up unbidden. 'An empty altar! The cathedral here in the capital had an empty altar. We had a break-in. Some of our parishioners desperate to emigrate, no doubt. They cleared out all the silver from the altar.'

'When was this?'

'A few weeks before Alice was murdered.'

Jethro Daunt smiled. It was as if he had expected that would be her answer. He removed a little Circlist symbol from underneath his waistcoat, a metal circle in the form of a snake swallowing its own tail – the church's token for the infinite passage of life – dangling from a chain. 'It was Alice who gave me this.'

Hannah hesitantly pulled out an identical symbol of her own. 'I have one too. It matches the one that Alice wore.'

'I was hoping you might,' said Jethro. 'Except that Alice's pendant is missing. It wasn't listed among her possessions on the police report, and none of the fathers at the cathedral found it when they were cleaning up the confessional booth.'

'Nobody would have stolen it,' said Hannah. 'It's made of simple steel, not silver. You can buy one of these for pennies from any of the stalls opposite the cathedral.'

Jethro lifted up his pendant, pinching the snake's head and there was click, the circle swinging open on a concealed hinge to reveal a hollow tube inside. He knocked it against the side of his chair and removed a tiny piece of paper – a daguerreotype image of Alice Gray's face as she had been in her twenties. There was something sad and disapproving about her face, even then, despite her beauty. 'The students in our seminary used the circlets to pass messages to each other behind the monks' back.'

Hannah apprehensively pressed on her own circle as Jethro had done and was rewarded with a small click from the snake's head. 'Did Alice's locket have a picture of you inside it?'

'Once,' said Jethro. He watched her fingers tease out something from inside the hollow space. 'But not, I suspect, for a long, long time.'

Hannah was half-expecting to find a picture of Alice Gray – or perhaps of her parents – inside her circlet, but when she unrolled the stiff square of paper she saw it was a miniature of an oil painting. She recognized the scene instantly; it was a common church illumination, the first of the three images that made up the rational trinity. The tiny painting showed a man wearing white scholar's robes, kneeling down and humbly demonstrating a screw drill before a group of fierce-looking tribesmen, bringing water to the surface.

'Knowledge shall raise you,' whispered Hannah. The first of the church's core beliefs.

'And so it shall,' said Jethro. He held his hand out towards Hannah. 'If I may, damson?'

She passed him the painting while the commodore and Nandi peered over his shoulders to look at it.

'That picture isn't hand painted, is it?' asked Nandi. 'There's too much detail in it.'

'A good assumption,' noted Jethro, playing with the angle of the miniature in front of his eyes. 'The original would have been a full-size illumination. But this was produced by taking a daguerreotype image of the original, shrinking it and running off a miniaturized copy using a rotary gravure press. Forgers turning out high-quality fake bank notes use some of the same techniques.'

'It's a pretty little thing,' said the commodore, 'but what does the blessed picture have to do with keeping a Jackelian lass out of the hands of a wicked crew of murderers.'

'For that, I believe, keener eyes than mine may be able to throw some light on the matter.' He passed the illustration across to Boxiron.

Hannah watched as the steamman held the painting up in front of his image plate, the light that pulsed behind the crystal surface slowing and becoming steadier. There was a series of clicks from inside the steamman's shiny metal skull – his head's sheen such a contrast with the rest of his rusty, hulking body.

'What can you see, old steamer?' asked Jethro.

'Please give me a second. These flat visual interpretations are never easy for my kind to process. Your people always overcomplicate your strange art. I can see that there is a signature in the right-hand corner,' said Boxiron. 'The hand of its creator, I presume? It reads William of Flamewall.'

Hannah gasped. The name they had uncovered in the guild's transaction-engine vaults. The lover – and murderer – of the fiercely brilliant priest Bel Bessant. 'Why would Alice have given me a picture painted by someone that my parents were researching?'

'I believe the answer to that rather depends on what else this illumination may contain. Can you detect any traces of steganography on the surface of the canvas, Boxiron?'

'Searching,' announced the steamman. 'Yes, the desert soil in the painting shows signs of having been coloured in on a pencilled grid. Every tenth pixel on the grid has had its colour base altered.'

'A concealed code,' said Nandi. 'I've heard about the curators at the college museum finding such things hidden in their paintings.'

'The technical term for the art of hiding a code in a picture is steganography, and they are normally quite benign when they've been decoded,' said Jethro. 'Jokes about the stinginess of the patron commissioning the piece or the ugliness of those sitting for their portrait, deprecating comments about rival illuminators. It may be nothing more than a complaint by William of Flamewall that his billet in the cathedral was cold and uncomfortable, but. . .' he looked at Boxiron, meaningfully.

'The stegotext – the code – concealed in this painting is very advanced,' said Boxiron. 'Decrypting something so complex will be an unpredictable undertaking. It could take hours to break it.'

Hannah looked at the rickety creature in amazement. 'You can do that?'

'Boxiron has a talent for such work,' said Jethro. 'A talent that belies his rather basic appearance. You must get to it, old friend.'

'No, we should let it be,' advised the commodore. 'If there's a dark secret hidden away for so long, we should let the mortal thing slumber for a few centuries more. We don't need to be poking our noses into this foul business. Let's go downstairs to this hotel's magnificent dining room instead and test their chef's fare while we plan how to steal young Hannah aboard my precious boat. We can all be away and back to the green shores of Jackals and leave the Jagonese to stew in their dark hole.'

'I'm afraid that's not an option, good captain,' replied Jethro, 'even if we could break out of the harbour without getting blown up by the cannons along the coral line, we could never navigate the Fire Sea without a pilot. People have already been hurt because of this secret. First Hannah's parents, then poor Alice, and now it seems Hannah also.'

'*Knowledge shall raise you*,' said Hannah.

'Ah no, lass,' said the commodore. 'It'll sink us for sure.'

Hannah looked meaningfully at Nandi. 'And now we have another reason for me to go back to the guild's vaults and help you complete your research for the college. We need to find out more about William of Flamewall in the archives.'

'I will not risk your life like that,' insisted Nandi. 'The professor asked me to try and help you while I was here on Jago, not get you killed gadding about the island.'

'I think you should go, good damson,' said Jethro. 'I believe you'll be safe enough in the guild's vaults this time around.'

Hannah nodded her head in acknowledgement, hiding her surprise that the detective was taking her side in this matter.

'Whereas for me, I believe I will need to visit the less salubrious parts of the capital to put my theories about this shadowy affair to the test.'

CHAPTER NINE

Chalph urs Chalph stared nervously down the street – and with just cause. The Lugus Vault was without doubt the poorest area of Hermetica City, and that naturally went hand in hand with it being the riskiest to cross. Not only did its inhabitants resent the Pericurian traders more than the rest of the island's citizenry – as they did anyone with more money than they (almost everyone else in the capital) – but they were gazing at Jethro Daunt's obviously foreign clothes with appraising eyes.

If only the ex-parson had seen fit to bring along his hulking manservant rather than leaving Boxiron behind to process some code from an ancient painting – as strange an excuse as Chalph could imagine for the two of them having to venture into dangerous lanes such as these unprotected. The eccentrically godless church that the Jackelians shared with the Jagonese might embrace pacifism, but judging by the cunning glances he and the investigator had been attracting since entering this vault, the locals of Lugus district weren't regulars in the cathedral's pews. It might have helped if there were fewer locals – but unlike the rest of the capital, depopulation didn't seem to be as much of a problem around the slums. Lacking the money and contacts to emigrate, there was always time enough – it seemed to the young Pericurian – to knock out another litter down here.

Jethro Daunt actually seemed pleased to see the urchins running around the streets – the lively presence of cubs a conspicuous difference from the Seething Round where his hotel was located, near the quality and all their money. Would he be so happy when one of the rascals dipped his wallet, though? No, that would stretch his Circlist tolerance a little too far, Chalph suspected.

In his own manner, the beak-nosed detective was just as obstinate as the matriarch baroness of Chalph's trading house. He might not insist on being carried everywhere by a train of Pericurian serfs on a sedan chair being served sweet-meats while every whim was satisfied *now*; but even as a mere member of the race of man, everything still seemed to work out being done Jethro's way. At least he wasn't presently humming one of his strange songs under his breath.

'You must have a very low opinion of me,' said Chalph, 'thinking that I would know how to meet the kind of people you are looking for.'

'On the contrary, I have an exceedingly high opinion of you,' said Jethro. 'But where there is a tightly regulated and taxed market with only a single point of contact with the outside world, a black market and smuggling always exists. And there's no one else to supply it on Jago but your house.'

Chalph watched a group of men sitting barefoot in a yard cleaning freshly cropped cavern bamboo with machetes. They would bury the bamboo in the vault's ground for three months and it would be soft enough to make a not particularly nourishing gruel when they boiled it after digging it back out. The workers scowled across the street at Chalph and Jethro.

'You're a clever man, Jackelian. But not clever enough to avoid being sent to Jago by the Inquisition.'

'No, bob my soul, not clever enough for that,' smiled Jethro. 'You really don't like living on Jago, do you?'

'Not much more than they do,' said Chalph, throwing a shrug at the bamboo cleaners. 'Are you aware that there are forty-four castes in Pericurian society? I was born a Rig-Juna, that's a male chattel of a bonded merchant. I've been on Jago for as long as I can remember, but I can only leave when the baroness decides there's no more profit here or if the house loses its trading concession. My house may be of a reformist bent, but they're not nearly reforming enough to allow me my freedom.'

'Things will change for you and your people,' said Jethro. 'Change is the only constant in life. Your country has seen how our colonists in Concorzia live, the example of a true multi-racial society. Courageous ursines like Ortin urs Ortin would see your archduchess's rule tempered by a true parliament.'

'Yes, you shipped here with the new ambassador, didn't you? I saw him arrive when he presented himself to the baroness. A high-caste dreamer, indulged by his position, who likes the sound of his own voice far too much. Pericur will never be the Kingdom of Jackals. There is a place for everyone in Pericur and everyone is in their place. I shouldn't complain, it would be taken as ingratitude. Pericur has many noble titles, but the last word of most of them translates as mother. And mother always knows best.'

Jethro's sly eyes narrowed. 'And when you have helped your friend Hannah get the freedom that is denied you, what will be left for you here?'

Chalph growled. He didn't like this foreigner thinking he could see inside his soul with such ease using his godless church's tricks. 'Me, I'll do what I'm ordered, Jackelian, just like I always do. There's a change coming all right, but it's coming here on Jago, not back home. The Jagonese need a scapegoat for their troubles, and my people are it. Not that the opinion of a low-caste ledger keeper means much, but I just hope that the baroness wakes up to what's happening outside the trade mission's gates while our boats are still allowed to dock on Jago. It's going to be a very warm swim back home for us if she doesn't.'

'You shouldn't blame the Jagonese too much,' said Jethro. 'Good people in desperate times are mutable clay to those that would manipulate them.'

'I'll remember that when there's a mob chasing after me as if I'm a killer ursk that's just climbed over the city wall from the wastes outside.' Chalph pointed to the bottom storey of one of the tenements; there, a bow-windowed shop hunkered under a sign painted with the proprietor's name – *Hugh Sworph*. 'That's it.'

The shop's windows were old-style stained glass, an ostentation that pointed to a time when the store might not have been just a pawnshop. An older age when the vault's poor had been lifted up on a rising tide of prosperity. Now Hugh Sworph's windows were filled with faded furniture, carriage clocks, crockery, cutlery, paintings and a few old books. This was the place the city's criminals came to when they had something particularly difficult to fence.

A bell on a spring rang as the two of them entered the shop, but there was no sign of customers or staff inside. Just a maze of discarded debris from Jagonese life put up for sale amidst the swirls of dust and the rainbow illumination pouring in from the tall bay. Chalph and Jethro split up and searched through the crowded bric-a-brac, looking for the missing owner.

'Mister Sworph,' called the Pericurian. 'It's me, Chalph urs Chalph. I haven't come about the extras from the boat, this time. I've got a friend here who would like to talk to you.'

Silence. Odd. The door hadn't been locked and the sign was still twisted to read 'open'.

'Well, I'll be bobbed. Over here, good ursine!' exclaimed Jethro.

Chalph walked around a long rail hung with worn velvet jackets.

Jethro Daunt was kneeling by the proprietor's body, Hugh Sworph recognizable even lying face down thanks to his hairless skull. A dagger emerged from his spine and a puddle of blood pooled across the faded bamboo floorboards.

Murder had been done here.

How odd it seemed to Hannah, to be back among the crimson-hooded ranks of the guild after having briefly returned to the streets of Hermetica City she knew so well. Exchanging the capital's bright, open vaults for the dark corridors and valve-studded canyons of the order that had claimed Hannah as one of its own. But the urge to return to the guild and find out what had happened to her parents had proved even stronger than Nandi and Commodore Black's urging not to risk her life to another sabotaged atmospheric carriage – or similar 'accident'.

The three of them had returned to their allotted study cell. While there was no sign of any guildsmen investigating the matter of the recently overloaded systems, as Hannah had half expected, the valves outside their cell and down on the canyon floor were clearly new – clear as a freshly washed window, rather than stained brown with the dark energies that flowed through the vacuum tubes.

As before, Nandi sat herself in front of the stone screen

while Hannah manned the cell's punch-card writer, typing a tattoo of retrieval commands to bring up the record set she had found before.

The commodore risked a quick glance outside the cell, standing by the balcony overlooking the massive canyon of valves. Then he stepped well back.

'You don't need to worry,' said Hannah. 'That switching storm last time was a freak occurrence. You could wait by that balcony for a century before you'd see another one out there.'

'So you say, lass,' hummed the commodore. 'But fool me once and it's shame on you. Fool me twice and it's shame on me.'

There was a rattle as the injection system carried Hannah's first punch card away. Nandi leant forward, the stone screen changing colour in front of her to show a green oblong filled with text.

'This can't be right,' muttered the young academic.

Hannah turned on her bench. 'What is it?'

'See for yourself.'

Hannah left the punch-card writer and moved behind Nandi. There was a single line repeated over and over down the stone surface – the only response to Hannah's query.

These records do not exist.

'That can't be right,' said Hannah, trying to fight down the impulse to panic.

'Where is your parents' research?' asked Nandi.

'It's been deleted,' said Hannah in shock. 'But nothing is ever deleted from here.'

That was the cardinal rule of the guild. Nothing was *ever* deleted. Archived, yes. Assigned a middling document weight and forgotten along with a million similar records, certainly. But erased? *Never.* Hannah rushed back to the writer and composed another longer query. Injected it and awaited the results.

The stone screen began to fill up with primary code-level iconography similar to the symbols on the keyboard of Hannah's punch-card writer.

'There's not even an audit trail of an erasure,' gasped Hannah. 'It's as if the records were never there in the first place. Nobody can do this, it's simply not possible.'

'As impossible as that dark storm that shouldn't have brewed up outside here,' noted the commodore.

'That's almost a whole year of your parent's work,' uttered Nandi, her voice cracking. 'Is it just the bookmarks assembling everything into a coherent project that have gone, or have the source documents also been destroyed?'

Hannah ran back to the card writer. 'I'll check.'

Hannah had nearly finished composing the query when Nandi called her over again. The image on the surface of the stone screen was reforming. The code-level iconography Hannah had called up was vanishing, to be replaced by a single line sitting in the middle of the green oblong.

Access denied.

'This is outrageous,' spluttered Nandi. 'The college paid good—'

'It's not your line of access that's been pulled,' said Hannah. She grabbed one of the blank punch cards, turned it over and began to scribble across it with a pencil. 'It's mine!'

'What's happening, lass?' asked the commodore. 'Does the guild believe their wicked bomb on the atmospheric carriage did its black business after all and that you're no longer alive?'

There was the sound of a commotion outside their cell, growing louder.

'I knew we were fools for coming back here,' whined the commodore. 'Fearsome transaction engines tended to by equally monstrous guildsmen. We should have stayed in the capital. At least that prison of a hotel has a mortal drop of wine or two in its cellars that's fit to wet my blistering lips with.'

The study cell's door burst open, a small crowd of burly guildsmen wielding discipline staffs rushing in, followed by the one valveman Hannah had been trying to avoid since she got here. Vardan Flail!

'What is the meaning of this?' roared Nandi. 'You are interrupting my work. Work you've been handsomely paid to facilitate.'

'And we are indeed happy to be facilitating it,' smirked the high guild master, 'Damson Tibar-Wellking, is it not? But we will be facilitating it with a different guild archivist from now on.'

The guildsmen lowered their staffs in warning towards Commodore Black's chest as he barged forward shouting, 'Now you let her be!'

'This is an internal guild matter,' warned Vardan Flail. 'We have traced the recent switching storm that took down this vault back to this young lady's sloppy work. An infinite loop hidden in the search layer to avoid detection upon injection.'

'You're lying' accused Hannah. She hadn't written any such loop in any of her queries, let alone a hidden one. Such an act would be sabotage.

'I had such high hopes for you,' said Vardan Flail. 'But now your transaction-engine privileges have been cancelled and we shall have to find an alternative task for you. Something manual, I think, seeing as you have proven yourself unworthy of more stimulating work.'

Hannah slipped the punch card she had been scribbling into one of Nandi's hands behind the young academic's back, hoping that the guildsmen wouldn't notice. 'Don't let them take me.'

'I need Hannah's help for my work,' protested Nandi.

'Not this one,' laughed Vardan Flail. 'She has other engines to attend to now.'

He didn't mean . . . they couldn't do *that* to her? On the high guild master's instructions, two of the valvemen grabbed Hannah and bundled her out of the room, while the others held the commodore and Nandi back with their staffs.

'You can't do this!' shouted Hannah, as she was dragged down the passages that led towards the lower levels – the turbine halls, halls filled with the deadly electric energies that powered Jago. 'I only have days left until I sit the church exams.'

'Really,' said Vardan Flail, as if this thought had only just occurred to him. 'Then you'll be glad of the chance to rest your brain. Although I understand working in the turbine halls can be quite physically exerting.'

'You dirty little jigger,' yelled Hannah. 'You won't stop me. I'll see you hanged for what you've done.'

The guild master shook his head sadly. 'But fortunately, you seem to have more than enough energy to spare.' He nodded to his brutes. 'Tell the charge-master that she's to work double shifts and have no more than two hours' sleep a night.' He smiled at Hannah. 'I understand that you have been boasting to the other guild initiates that you can pass the church exams in your sleep. Let's see how well you can put that into practice.' A pair of steel doors clanked open in front of Hannah, leading to a lifting-room with a mineshaft-long drop down to the guild's vast, heavily shielded turbine rooms. The burly men yanked her inside.

'Do be careful down there, my dear. It can be quite treacherous work.'

Then the doors shut and the lifting room began to descend towards the lowest levels of the guild's vaults. Right alongside the hell the Jagonese denied existed.

* * *

'We can't just let them take her!' Nandi shouted to the commodore, an overwhelming rush of panic overtaking her as she realized that she might never see Hannah again.

'Leave it be, lass,' advised the commodore, glancing warily at the staff-wielding guildsmen penning them in the study cell. 'How many of these crows could we take down? The guild has the law on their side and a cruel mistress she can be. We won't be able to help Hannah from the inside of their police fortress's dungeons.'

'Forget what you promised the professor back in the Kingdom,' said Nandi. 'It's not my safety you need to look after; it's Hannah's. You just have to lift the robes of any of these dolts to see what the radiation of the turbine halls will do to her.'

'I'm not abandoning any Jackelian lass to swing on the guild's yardarm,' said the commodore. 'But there's a time to cut the enemy's line and there's a time to tack for a better position, and we need to aim for the latter if we're to winkle Hannah out of their wicked clutches.'

'What if I decide to do what's right?' said Nandi. 'Here. Now. Will you still follow me?'

'My blade is sharp for it, lass,' said the commodore, 'but don't be confusing winning a battle with winning the war.'

'They'll work her until she drops, she'll have no chance of passing the church's entrance exam. And then they'll have all the time in the world to kill her slowly. You saw what they did to our atmospheric carriage, nearly blowing us all up to get to her. . .' Nandi tried to yell down the corridor, the guild's sentries holding her back. 'We'll get you out of here, Hannah. I promise. We'll get you out of here!'

'As long as we're still alive to do it,' said the commodore, 'you and me both. Still alive to help her.'

The old u-boat man was right, curse him. Every fibre of

Nandi's being was crying at her to push into the corridor and grab Hannah back from Vardan Flail, but they were in the heart of the guild's power here, and a long way from the capital. They had to leave Hannah – at least for now – and try to work for her release through the cathedral, maybe through the Jackelian embassy. Jethro Daunt would know what to do. He had to.

Back home, Nandi had the professor to look after her – and her protector had dispatched the commodore in her stead to fulfil a similar role on Jago. Hannah had nobody now that the woman who had acted as her mother had been murdered, and that wouldn't do, not for a ward of the college.

Nandi was going to save Hannah from the guild, whatever it took and however perilous the price.

CHAPTER TEN

This is outrageous,' protested Nandi as she and Commodore Black were hustled to the waiting atmospheric carriage. 'You are impeding my research! Work you have been generously paid to assist.'

'You will have a new archivist assigned to you tomorrow,' said the guildsman heading the group of staff-wielding toughs escorting them out of the vaults. 'And by that time we will have fully restored operations in the transaction engines outside your study cell.'

The commodore snarled, 'I know the fixing you're planning to do, and it's more of the same rotten work you've already been at: erasing what we've already uncovered inside your wicked thinking machines.'

'The valves hold all, nothing is ever lost,' recited the guildsman.

'Nothing but a poor helpless lass,' said the commodore. 'But you listen well, lad. We had better be finding Damson Hannah Conquest again, and hale with it, or I'll be coming back down here with my crew and a fistful of hull hammers from my precious u-boat, and I'll show you how it is we brew up a switching storm back home.'

The door on their atmospheric carriage slid open and the leader of their escort swept his hand towards its interior. 'Goodbye, Jackelian. Come back tomorrow.'

Commodore Black let Nandi lead him inside the capsule. 'I've marked you, you crow, red cowl or no, your vaults aren't big enough to hide you from me.'

'Take your own advice and leave it be,' said Nandi. 'You were right. If we start a fight with them they'll have a pretext to ban us from the guild vaults permanently.'

'Don't worry, I know when to draw my sabre, lass. And when I do, someone's going to die – either they or I. Not today, though. Those were just a few mortal threats to remind them that Hannah isn't alone and forgotten in their dark vaults.'

The door shut on Nandi and the commodore. Their carriage juddered as it passed through the rubber vacuum curtain before accelerating to its full travel velocity.

'Why did I listen to that fool Jethro Daunt?' moaned the commodore, restlessly pacing the carriage. 'Hannah will be safe enough in the guild, indeed. Just like a blessed churchman, thinking the best of everyone and everything. And now they've got their claws into the poor lass good and proper.'

'But not before she gave me this.' Nandi produced the punch card that Hannah had been scribbling on before the armed guildsmen arrived in their study cell.

Commodore Black twitched as he recognized the long lines of formulae scrawled across the card. 'Ah, she's a clever one, that Hannah is, with a churchwoman's perfect memory. The second iteration of the Joshua Egg we teased out of the guild's archives before the switching storm struck. We'll crack it, Nandi. We'll do it for the lass. I'll run the blessed egg's code through the *Purity Queen's* navigation drums myself until we squeeze the truth from its fiendish symbols.'

Nandi nodded. And if Hannah had remembered the egg's code accurately, then they could discover what it was the guild had been so desperate to stop the three of them from finding out. Perhaps even use the research left by Hannah's parents to force the guild to release the press-ganged girl from their service.

Chalph urs Chalph watched Jethro gently roll over the pawn-shop's murdered proprietor. It was definitely him – Hugh Sworph – but Chalph had been wrong about the man being dead, despite the dagger stuck in his spine.

The shop owner's eyes flickered open and Chalph thought he saw a glint of recognition in them.

'Who did this to you?' Chalph demanded. 'Old man, who—'

The pawnshop's owner reached up and pressed something into Jethro Daunt's fingers. He tried to speak, but bubbles of blood came out instead. The blade must have punctured his lungs. Chalph saw that there were other wounds on the man's chest – the knife had seen plenty of work before being buried in his spine.

Jethro Daunt knelt in close and Hugh Sworph hissed something that started as a whisper but ended as a hacking cough. Then the shopkeeper groaned and Chalph sensed the last breath of life departing the man's mangled body.

Jethro listened to the man's chest then laid him back on the floor. 'No, the poor fellow's gone now, may serenity welcome his soul along the Circle's turn.'

Chalph glanced around the room, sniffing at the air. Not a single active scent. They were alone in here. The murderer had left a good while before the two of them had entered the pawnshop. Poor Hugh. It was symptomatic of how long Chalph had been around the race of man that he could look at the corpse and not wonder at the strangeness of the furless

194

body, instead noting how pale the man had become. How lifeless. 'How your people can see something like this and not believe in the scriptures, I'll never understand.'

'Life is all around, good ursine,' said Jethro. 'Energy is never lost, only its pattern changed. Hugh Sworph's soul has poured back into the one sea of consciousness and will be recupped into all the lives yet to come. That is the true crime of murder, for whoever killed him has only succeeded in murdering themselves.'

Somehow, Chalph doubted that. 'What did he whisper to you?'

'Twelve ten,' replied Jethro. He opened his hand to reveal what had been pressed into it. A tiny key made of iron, not much longer than a fingernail.

'A tenement apartment number to go along with the key?'

'Not with this type of key, good Pericurian,' said Jethro. 'It is too small. Did you tell anyone you were coming here?'

'I informed some of the people in my house that I was going to see Sworph about a mistake I found in the books for the supplies we ran to him,' said Chalph. 'But it wasn't one of us that did for him. The only scents in here are from the race of man. There's been no ursine bodies inside this shop for at least a week.'

Jethro glanced around the store, rolling the tiny key between his fingers. 'Well, there's no dolls houses for sale here, but. . .'

He walked over to a brick wall lined with grandfather clocks, each as tall as the ex-parson himself. None of the timepieces appeared to be in working order, though. All of their clock faces were reading different times and their pendulum rods hung silent and unmoving behind trunk doors. Jethro tapped the wooden plinth of each pendulum clock until he got to one that made a slightly different sound. Then he went up to its glass dial plate and inserted the dead shop owner's tiny key in a small keyhole there, swinging open the glass door and twisting the hands to ten minutes past twelve. A second after he had readjusted the dial, a door in the grandfather clock's base swung out revealing a crawl space little bigger than a chimney cut through the wall. Chalph could see that there was light at the other end of the short passage.

Chalph went through on all fours after Jethro Daunt, coming out of the claustrophobic passage just behind the man and into a workshop at least half the size of the shop front they had left behind. Shelves and cupboards lined the walls, filled with the fruits of Hugh Sworph's real trade – fencing stolen goods for the capital's thieves and its desperate poor, with a lucrative sideline in black-market commodities. Chalph suspected the only things missing among the jewels, gold watches, rare metals, silver cutlery and imported spirits he could see stored about here were their customs duty, the stained senate's taxes and any genuine receipts.

Jethro went over to one of the work benches littered with the tools of a jeweller and picked up a metal block. 'Something to stamp a false mark of provenance on re-smelted silver.' He checked the drawers of the bench and lifted out a tray of silver ornaments, church candles and a Circlist hoop, a much larger version of the one that Jethro wore himself.

'They're smashed,' said Chalph.

Jethro pointed to the metal kiln in the corner of the hidden storeroom. 'They were being broken apart to fit inside his kiln. Except that this circle didn't need to be sawn into pieces, it was meant to be opened.' He held the ornament up, indicating how it could be split open on concealed hinges, pushing a hand into the hollow empty tubing inside. 'These are the altar ornaments that were stolen from inside the cathedral.'

'What was kept inside the circle?'

'What indeed?' echoed Jethro, putting the circle back down.

'What indeed, to have acted as the catalyst for so many deaths. Yes, everything started with the theft of this from the cathedral.' Jethro walked over to a lithographic printing press behind the bench and tapped the press bed. 'Your Mister Sworph would have used this to print off catalogues of stolen items for sale for his clients. The criminals back in Jackals call them steal-sheets. Let's see if we can't find some of them while we're here, and Mister Sworph's real set of ledgers if he kept such a thing.'

'I think he would have,' said Chalph. 'He struck me as a most careful man, he was meticulous about everything we sold to him.'

Chalph started opening drawers and cupboards, rummaging through coins and medals and assorted bric-a-brac. It was obvious that the Jackelian ex-parson had been expecting to find the cathedral's stolen altar ornaments inside the shop. What was the canny foreigner playing at? He continued searching.

In one of the lower drawers, Chalph came across a pile of catalogues – stiff, bleached, white bamboo sheets hole-punched and held together with string ties – discovering them at the same time as Jethro came across the set of leather-bound ledgers. They laid them both down on the workbench. Jethro examined the catalogues first: daguerreotype images of items that were worth more intact than they were as smelted and recast silver and gold goblets, page after page of fine crystal decanters, priceless books, family heirlooms and antiques. Only the good stuff. As Jethro reached the final page his mouth cracked into a smile. Chalph leant in for a closer look. It was a painting, a Circlist illumination similar in style to any one of a thousand stained glass windows that could be found gracing the buildings inside Jago's capital. The painting showed a mountain, clearly the Horn of Jago, surrounded by a wall of druids. A group of Circlists had broken through the line, making room for one of their number, a pilgrim, to run through and approach the mountain. A Circlist priest was running after the pilgrim and pointing to the top of the Horn of Jago, indicating his way.

'This painting, good ursine, is what was concealed inside the altar ornament,' said Jethro.

'It is just a Circlist image,' said Chalph.

'The illumination is based on the third belief of the rational trinity,' said Jethro. '*You climb the mountain alone.*'

'Why would your strange church without gods want to encourage its followers to climb to the top of a mountain?' asked Chalph.

'It is a metaphor, good Pericurian. Every religion the world has known places itself between the worshipper and the mountain – which in this illustration stands for enlightenment – ranks of priests demanding the right to interpret and impose their truths on you. In Circlism, you must find the truth yourself without help. You must climb the mountain alone, with your bare hands. Truth is never given to you, you can only seek it.'

'Old Sworph did not think this painting was very valuable,' snorted Chalph, reading the text underneath the image. 'It is at the back of his catalogue. A miniature by William of Flamewall. Price on application. That means he would have accepted the best price for it, a low price.'

'No, it had the highest price of all,' said Jethro. 'It cost him his life.' The ex-parson rolled up the catalogue and slipped it inside his jacket. 'But you are correct. Our poor Mister Sworph did not know the painting's true value. But he suspected it had some, given he had found it hidden inside an expensive silver ornament stolen from the cathedral.'

Jethro opened the fence's ledgers and scanned through them

for a couple of minutes before passing one to Chalph. 'You help keep your house's ledgers. What do you make of these?'

Chalph flicked through the book, finding neat hand-lined pages inside, black ink on bamboo paper. 'It's a purchase ledger. Items by date – prices paid, sellers, estimated value. Detailed work. Accurate.'

'You see, you were right, he was a careful man,' said Jethro. 'You can tell that by the fact that he printed off his own catalogues. A lazier fellow would have given the steal-sheets to a printer to run off and risked one of the ink mixers getting drunk at a tavern and boasting about their "special work" to someone who might have tried to profit from having heard it.'

'But there's nothing in here about who Sworph sold the items to.'

Jethro hummed and took back the book. 'No, the sales ledger is, I suspect, no longer under this roof. I believe whoever killed our Mister Sworph made him hand his sales ledger over. Then the poor fellow was murdered anyway to stop him from talking.' Jethro ran his furless fingers down the margins of the pages until he found what he was looking for. 'Here is the purchase record for what was stolen from the cathedral. Circlist silver. Meltable. Paid two marks and twelve pence. The good man certainly didn't believe in overpaying for what he received, did he?'

'But the name of the seller has been crossed out,' observed Chalph. And there was something written in black ink above the crossings out. Hugh Sworph had written the word *"Dead!!!"*

'Yes, he'd heard something,' said Jethro. 'My pennies would be placed on something unpleasantly fatal occurring to the thieves who broke into the cathedral and fenced him the altar ornaments. Our friend suspected he was the next in line to be silenced.'

'What's so special about this damn painting,' asked Chalph, 'that people are willing to kill for it?'

Jethro held up three of his fingers. 'Three paintings, good Pericurian. The rational trinity is composed of three paintings. Whoever killed Alice and tried to murder Hannah now has two of them.'

Chalph's eyes narrowed in his bear-like face. Seeing what the killers had already done to get the first two paintings, Chalph didn't need to be an investigator like Jethro Daunt to know that they would be coming back for the last one.

Coming back whoever or whatever stood in their way.

While his minions called the pot-bellied man who ruled the guild's deep turbine halls the *charge-master*, Hannah quickly realized he might just as well have been the demon king of this buried dominion.

Like everyone else down in the turbine halls he had shaved his head and he strutted around the induction vault with his cowl – unusually for the guild – folded down.

The charge-master eyed the chain of new arrivals suspiciously and laid a hand on one of the great iron suits lined up behind him against the wall. 'Which of you grubs,' he boomed, 'can tell me what this is?'

It seemed all the new recruits were 'grubs' until they graduated through sheer sweat and survival into fully-fledged turbine men, or 'termites'.

'It's one of the machines the trappers use to ride outside the city,' announced someone from within their line – Hannah didn't see who had been brave enough to answer back.

'Trappers, yes and city workers too when they have to clear the culverts and the aqueducts beyond the battlements.'

It looked to Hannah's eyes like a massive version of Boxiron, or a rusty suit of armour made for a twenty-foot giant. She had heard the recruits talking about them before she came in. How you needed a lucky suit, one passed down through the generations that hadn't killed any of its owners. One that wasn't possessed by a suit-ghost.

'To the trappers up top this is a Rigid Armour Motile suit, or RAM suit. But down here, it's just *iron*, and pushing iron is what keeps you healthy.' He rapped the legs of the metal giant. 'There's a thousand ways to die working the turbine halls – steam flash, gas build-up, false current reversals – but one thing you grubs won't get sick from is the electric field. Sick is what you get being tickled by constant background exposure to the transaction engines upstairs. But this is the guild's real work down here. We don't wear lined cowls inside the halls; we don't wear those toy lead chainmail vests the guild passes out to visiting senators. There's a foot of lead inside your iron, and that's thicker than your grub heads. And thick is what you are, or you wouldn't have been given to me.'

The charge-master rested his foot on a platform and struck a rubber button, the platform lifting him out and up and towards the centre of the suit where a vault-like door had swivelled out, revealing a man shaped cockpit. Their master's suit was painted in a distinctive red and black chequerboard pattern.

'The suit is slaved to your movement,' he called down to the line of initiates from inside the cockpit. 'You move, it moves. All the extra controls are down by your right thumb.'

The door in the centre of the suit's chest was closing, sealing the charge-master inside. The suit stomped forward, shaking the cavern floor and making the initiates jump back in fright and scatter before the towering metal creature. There was a thick dome on top of the suit and Hannah could just see the charge-master's beady eyes gazing down at them through the crystal slit. His voice boomed out of a voicebox built into the chest as he swung a massive arm to point to the hangar-style door at the opposite end of the cavern. 'When that door lifts up in two minutes, any of you not inside your suits are going to fry. Any of you grubs who are too stupid to be able to copy what I just did are too dangerous to be allowed to work alongside me.'

There was a mad scramble towards their suits as the initiates realized they only had seconds left to emulate the charge-master or be cooked by the violence of the turbine halls. Hannah was barely into her suit, slipping her arms and legs through a cantilevered iron frame surrounded by soft red leather in the centre of the chest, when lanterns on the vault wall behind them began to flash in warning.

She was not the only one cutting it fine judging by the cries of alarm in the chamber – but luckily for the initiates, simply occupying the suit was enough to trigger the closure mechanism and Hannah found herself sealed inside her cockpit, trying to ignore the stale smell of the previous occupant, her view of the outside world abbreviated to what she could see through the glass slit of the dome that had lowered over her head. The iron suit really was designed for the lowest common denominator of operator, Hannah realised; moving her limbs within the cage inside the suit dragged the massive legs and arms clunking around outside. But it was strenuous work. Everywhere around her, the other initiates were taking faltering steps and the cavern floor echoed with the crash of feet carrying a tonne of metal with each step.

'Move away from the wall,' ordered the charge-master's voice sounding inside her helmet. 'Nobody is to try anything fancy today. Just follow my lead and learn fast. Your suit is dialled down so you're moving heavy and slow. Stay away from each other's feet. Anyone who puts a dent in their suit today will have me to answer to.'

The door lifted up into the ceiling and Hannah's view opened out onto a short metal ramp down to hell. A vast cavern floor littered with turbines and massive machinery barely visible through the sea of hissing steam. It was as bad as on the surface after a storm had blown in off the Fire Sea. Guildsmen in their heavy suits cut through the mist as though they were ships, navigating around the condensers, core-cooling pumps, pressurizers and borated-water storage tanks. And this – she had been told – was just one of dozens of turbine halls buried on this level. The experienced termites' suits had been painted a chequerboard yellow and black, a bright contrast to the green and black that Hannah and the other initiates wore.

It was only because the charge-master was able to speak inside Hannah's dome that she could hear him above the roar of the turbines and generators. 'Follow me to the stables.'

Circle, but it was hard pushing her suit after the charge-master. Hannah hoped that when the suits were dialled up to full strength, the simple act of moving around wouldn't be so similar to lifting weights.

'I see you there, initiate Conquest,' whispered the charge-master inside her suit's earpiece. 'You think you're too good for us. You think you can escape the guild just because you've got well-placed friends inside the church. What do you think that does for the morale of everyone else that has to work with you? You're a walking disaster waiting to happen. I know your sort, girl. Soft. Pampered. The high guild master should have sent you down to us on the first day you stepped into our vaults.'

If the charge-master was so concerned with morale, then maybe he shouldn't have kicked one of the initiates to the floor earlier in the day just because they had sniggered at something he had been barking. Hannah said nothing. She had already noted the temper on this beast.

What the charge-master called the stables was no more than a low tunnel sealed with an iron door. As the group approached it, the door opened and six ab-locks emerged from the near darkness, the stunted simian creatures loping out and blinking up at the machine suits in front of them.

'Once you're trained, each of you will get six ab-locks,' said the charge-master. 'What we call a hand. After your suit they're your next most important possession. Treat the abs well and they'll live up to nine years before the electric field down here kills them. We have to trap them young, break them, and train them in basic turbine lore, and that's an art none of you grubs will ever appreciate. If I hear from the stable-master that you're responsible for unnecessary wastage of abs then I'll have you crawling around the steam lines in a scald suit and see how long you last before you get sick. But—' the charge-master triggered a flail to emerge dangling from his suit's right arm, its lashes crackling with raw electricity, '—that doesn't mean you spare the rod with them. Abs are natural shirkers.'

His own hand of abs seemed to know what they could expect from their master right enough. Hannah watched as they fanned out before him, picking up pieces of equipment racked outside the stable.

The rest of the day's training was a blur of swirling mists and the brutal lessons. How to get ab-locks to crawl under, over and inside the massive turbines, steam lines and block valves. Which pieces of turbine equipment needed lubricants applied by the abs' spray guns to stop them burning up, where the electric energies were dangerously high and how to read the trip recorders that would indicate rogue current reversals. Which jobs were too heavy for the abs – such as turning the vast wheels in the water injection pumps – and which ones automatically required the intervention of the guildsmen.

And through it all the charge-master's contempt for the guildsmen who tended the transaction engines above them was apparent: puny coders. The real power was down *here*. Here were the muscles of Jagonese society and here were to be found the real men and women that worked them. The turbines that kept the vaults of Hermetica City powered with light, that charged their very defences and kept the island's monsters at bay.

Now that Hannah could see what the ab-locks had to put up with, she began to regret having defended their employment in front of Nandi and the commodore. On some of the abs she couldn't even see the numbers branded onto their spines, so bad were the flail burns. These weren't beasts of burden, these were slaves. Jago's position in the shifting ocean of magma might mean the island was the one place in the world where the power electric could be tamed enough to be used for mundane purposes rather than merely as a weapon of war, but its taming had a cost. And down here in the turbine halls was where society paid the price for the miracle of their free energy.

Hannah tried to ignore the agonized yells of the ab-lock that lost a leg to the twisting fan of a turbine, or the one that was blinded by a stray squirt of superheated water from a condenser running over-pressurized. Observing how many times the heavy suit she was wearing saved her and the other initiates from similar accidents during her training in the turbine halls, Hannah could see why the charge-master was so obsessive about the care the grubs took of their suits.

The first sign that anything was amiss towards the end of their first shift was the claxon sounding from a bank of machinery against the wall of the vault; the needles on their dials twisting in a paralytic dance as screeching sirens filled the turbine hall.

Hannah and the other grubs were left twisting their necks inside their suits as the guildsmen quickly stomped to their emergency positions in response to the unholy caterwauling, switching turbines to idle while their ab-locks swarmed around the hall, past the suits' iron legs, weaving in and out of the steam as their master's flails goaded them into a frenzy of activity.

The charge-master's suit had clanked into a huddle of senior turbine workers, debating who knows what between themselves on a private channel. Whatever emergency they were discussing, they reached their decision in moments. Worryingly, the charge-master came cutting through the sea of steam towards the initiates.

'You,' he thundered towards Hannah, 'with me. The rest of you grubs bugger off back to the suit hall.'

'What's happening, charge-master?' Hannah asked, being careful to keep up with the man while she was talking. 'Why are the claxons sounding?'

'Hell's happening, grub,' spat the charge-master, leading her across the vault and towards a line of towering brick chimneys that occupied the far end of the machine-carved cavern. Another guildsman was bearing towards the chimneys, a navvy by the look of his suit, covered with slings loaded with equipment crates and strange-looking devices.

'You're going down with him,' the charge-master's voice barked.

'Down?' Hannah looked around. An iron door in one of the chimneys was opening inwards, revealing darkness inside. 'But the turbine halls are as deep as the guild's vaults go.'

'You think?' The charge-master turned towards the other guildsman. 'The grub's supposedly got a brain; they were using her as a cardsharp upstairs. But if you don't bring her back, don't worry, it's one less for training,' He turned and stomped away, shouting orders for everyone to evacuate to the next turbine hall over and seal the blast doors behind them.

Hannah turned towards the navvy. He might be wearing a termite's colours on his hull, but the sweat-slicked face staring at her through the slit of his suit's dome looked awfully young. There was a name stencilled above the eye slit – *Rudge Haredale*.

'What is this?' demanded Hannah, pointing to the open door in the massive chimney.

'Tap nine,' replied the navvy, not bothering to hide the irritation in his voice.

'Tap? As in *steam* tap?'

'Well, it surely ain't the tap for our bathhouse's hot water, grub.' The servos in his iron legs ground away as he ducked down through the open door, then he was inside the chimney, lanterns across his suit flickering on in reaction to the darkness. 'You waiting for an invite?'

Was he insane? This was an actual steam tap. A shaft tunnelling down for miles to funnel the superheated steam rising out of Jago's depths – the same force that powered the erupting geysers across the volcanic island, harnessed to turn the guild's turbines. The only thing that would be waiting for them inside that chimney was a mile-long drop to a char-broiled death. Even their suits couldn't protect the two of them from the violence inside a steam tap. Hannah's cooling mechanism would be overwhelmed and her pilot cabin transformed into a human baking oven.

The navvy called through the voicebox on his chest and an ab-lock came trotting out of the steam and leapt up to take hold of a specially-designed grip on the back of Rudge's suit. Suddenly Hannah realized the words she had just heard the navvy call had been correct after all. *T-face*. Not the number branded on the ab-lock's back, but a nickname based on the steam burns on its face in the shape of a letter 'T'. This creature must have received them young, for they were almost a mottled tan now, in adulthood.

'This ab knows shaft work,' said the navvy. 'Best we got, aren't you, T-face?'

It murmured a whine in response.

'What about the other abs?' asked Hannah. 'I still have room on the back of my suit.'

'One's enough when it's T-face – the rest of the hand would just spook down there.'

They weren't the only ones. Seeing Hannah's hesitation at entering the chimney, Rudge Haredale leant forward and yanked her suit across the portal into the steam tap. 'The shaft's not carrying super-pressure right now, grub. That's the problem. One of the regulator gates deep down inside the shaft is jammed and we've got to fix it.'

Hannah knew the answer to the question even as she asked it. 'And if we don't?'

'Then the bloody pressure builds up behind the gate until it takes the gate off and about a tenth of the guild's turbine capacity with it in the explosion.'

Hannah didn't need any of her church training in mathematics to do the calculations on that sum. A tenth of the guild's turbine capacity, but a hundred per cent of Damson Hannah Conquest.

CHAPTER ELEVEN

Boxiron sat in the middle of his hotel room in the lotus position, the inferior hydraulics of his legs trembling in protest. The steamman ignored the discomfort and concentrated on the task at hand – or rather, mind – running the stegeotext that he had found concealed in Jethro's ancient painting through his brain, parcelling pieces of the code out to the additional specialized processing unit that the criminal lords of Jackals had outfitted him with.

It was an unfamiliar thing, deciphering something so ancient. The Jackelian transaction-engine locks he had cracked were all much of a muchness, but tackling the code hidden in the painting was like breaking an ancient safe – the maths that protected the cipher expressed with an antique elegance, and something else, something that remained intangible and just out of sight. He had been at it for most of the day, crunching and attacking, chipping away pieces of the puzzle. Half of the battle was trying to get inside the mind of the cipher's creator. Pushing at the code to see what gave way and what held firm, modelling how he would have done it and following those avenues to their logical conclusions.

Boxiron was under no illusions about the difficulty of this job. It was as good as being a captain of the Free State's militant orders once more, marshalling his forces and distributing them, testing the enemy, finding the weak spots to overwhelm. Every inch of Boxiron's being knew it had been a member of the Circlist church who had secreted this code within the painting, and not just because the illustration came with the signature of William of Flamewall scrawled across it. The maths were of the highest order, everything balanced with the symmetry that the softbody faith attempted to incorporate into its formula-based moral rules. Yes, that was the weakness of the cipher's creator. Too much symmetry.

Not enough chaos and randomness.

The randomness of—

—the steam from Boxiron's stack drifted across the hotel room. Thickening. Reforming.

It had been so long since they had come. And he wasn't even calling them today. Not a drop of his oil shed. Not a single cog thrown. For which of the Steamo Loas would come for Catosian cogs, which would visit for Jackelian oil? Which of the spirits of his ancestors would manifest themselves for such a desecrated body as was his now?

Radius Patternkeeper, Lord of the Ravenous Fire.

The words of the Loa came out like a snake's hiss, echoing from the distant plane occupied by the people of the metal's ancestors. 'Do not attempt to do this thing.'

'Who are you to make requests of me?' spat Boxiron at the smoking form swaying in front of him. 'I who am a desecration in your eyes. I who have gone unaided by King Steam in this living hell of a body my mind has been condemned to join with.'

'Yet you *have* called us,' said Radius Patternkeeper. 'Filling a mind that was once of the people with the dark cipher that must not be decrypted. You have summoned me as surely as if you spilled your own oil and tossed your own cogs in the ritual of gear-gi-ju.'

The steamman got to his feet, angrily. 'I am still of the people. I am Boxiron, even if I am a shadow of what I once was. I abide.'

'No. Boxiron died well on the Fulven Fields,' said the Loa. 'His corpse piled with the bodies of our enemies, his knight's lance broken through those that would have destroyed our land.'

'Then you should not have allowed Jackelian grave robbers to staple his skull onto this mockery of a body they fashioned in a Catosian manufactory.'

'The army searched,' hissed the Loa. 'But there were so many bodies, so many corpses. And the mechomancers' grave robbers came like carrion on the wind after the battle.'

'You should have searched better,' retorted Boxiron. 'And then we would surely not be having this discussion now.'

'Erase the steganographic code within your mind,' ordered the Loa. 'Then destroy the painting you took it from.'

'Tell me why I should.' demanded Boxiron.

'It is not upon you to question the will of the Steamo Loa.'

'As it is not upon you to order me to do this. My friend Jethro Daunt requires the cipher to be broken.'

'The softbody is called by his people's gods. Ancient ones that have been long forgotten,' hissed the twisting steam shape manifesting from his stack fumes. 'Forgotten with good reason. The great pattern can only be woven forwards; it can never be woven backwards. Your friend cannot be trusted.'

'Easy words,' Boxiron growled. 'But I choose to judge on actions. Jethro Daunt helped save me from what I had become when my own people would not even look me in the vision plate as I begged for high-grade boiler coke outside our temples. I will trust his judgement over yours, Radius Patternkeeper. You who will not even trust me with the truth when you would order my obedience.'

The shape in the smoke danced from side to side like an angry cobra. 'You are beyond the pale, desecration, that is the truth I see in your defiance!' Spears of smoke hardened in the air between them, darting threateningly towards Boxiron.

'You,' swore the hulking steamman, 'can go back to the flaming furnace of Lord Two-Tar and suck on his pipe.'

'I shall ride!' the Loa's voice exploded from the smoke like a banshee scream and the manifestation hurled itself at Boxiron, the steamman stumbling back and flailing at the powerful ancestral spirit as it entered through the ill-fitting joins of his body, curling into his metal as though he were a magnet and the Loa a cloud of metallic filings. Filling him, possessing him. His inferior body becoming a host for the Steamo Loa to ride.

Boxiron was left caulked, blundering across the room. Burning. Burning. The Loa was reaching for his mind, reaching for his brain's nanomechanical network swirling with the fruit of so many long hours of cipher breaking. Reaching to burn the last traces of his mind from the face of the world.

The steammen gods had finally come to bring Boxiron his second, final death.

Even the young guild navvy Hannah was following down the oblong-shaped shaft seemed impressed at how easily she had taken to the art of shaft walking – pushing the back of her RAM suit against one wall and using the leverage of her armoured legs against the opposite one to ease her way slowly and steadily downwards. Yet this whole situation seemed odd to Hannah; it was almost as if her suit was anticipating her needs and helping her. Though unless the ghost of some guildsman who had died inside the suit's cockpit had possessed it, she didn't know how that could be. Their suits were inanimate; they relied on their occupants to provide direction and intelligence. She shivered as she recalled the tales the other grubs had told each other. They were just stories, surely.

There was still the occasional spear of steam rising up past them from tiny cracks in the shaft, but the regulator gate they were heading for looked to be well and truly immobilized. They had already passed several working gates – iron frames containing motorized vanes that could be opened or shut depending on how much superheated steam was rising up from the island's depths. The power needs of the turbine halls were carefully balanced with the pressure from below and the engineering tolerance of the gates themselves.

'My first day,' Hannah muttered, 'and he's already trying to kill me.'

'Don't flatter yourself,' the young navvy's voice sounded inside her helmet. 'The charge-master thinks a lot more about keeping the turbine halls intact than he does about teaching some fancy-piece a lesson, just because she thinks she should be chopping punch cards upstairs rather than pushing iron with the lads down below.'

'Then why's he sending me down here with a—' Hannah had to stop herself from saying *a boy*. 'A navvy.'

'Because I'm the best he's got for shaft work,' said young Rudge. 'And he must think you're the best he's got for transaction-engine work, or you wouldn't be here, either.' The navvy pointed at the small transaction engine attached to the gate they were passing through – still functional enough to close its vanes and withdraw into the wall when we triggered it.

Hannah looked more closely at the transaction engine on the gate, blinking in surprise. It was the kind of thing she had seen in Jackelian picture books. 'It's got no valves. That's a transaction-engine drum rotating inside it – it's steam-driven!'

'Isn't that just like a cardsharp,' snorted Rudge. 'You love your head games with numbers, but you haven't got a clue about the iron you need to run them on. This shaft is normally full of superheated steam. How long do you think a glass valve would last down here? Primitive works just fine inside a steam tap, especially given there's usually enough steam flowing past here to power every paddle steamer in the world. Our pressure regulator gates operate autonomously. They're not on the guild's network, understand?'

'I'm here because I'm the best,' Hannah repeated the words, hardly believing them. And not because Vardan Flail had instructed the charge-master to ensure that she was dropped down the first conveniently deep shaft.

'The charge-master comes across as a right bastard, but that's only because unless you temper young metal well, it breaks before it becomes steel. If you're not made into the best you can be down here, you'll never survive to get your own suit, and you'll as like take more than a few good people with you when you die. What the charge-master does, he does for a reason.'

The deeper they travelled down the shaft towards the jammed gate, the more erratic her suit appeared to get, the frame that surrounded her body inside the cabin juddering and getting harder to control.

'My suit's stopping working,' called Hannah.

'Mine too,' said the navvy. 'We're going to crack the doors on our armour manually and tie an abseil line to our suits' legs and then rappel the rest of the way down. I'll distribute the gate gear between you, me and T-face.'

'Both our suits can't be malfunctioning at the same time,' Hannah protested.

The navvy's reply came as if he was talking to an idiot. 'It's not a malfunction, grub. We're reaching the electric limit.' He grunted in annoyance at Hannah's silence and continued. 'We're too deep, girl. Whatever spells the Fire Sea casts on the power electric topside don't stretch this far down. A couple more yards further and you might as well be back in the Kingdom of Jackals. The current in our suits is getting irregular, it's spiking and cascading in random amplifications. If we go any deeper wearing our armour, we'll burn out both our suits, and then we'll have one hell of a climb getting back up to the turbine halls.'

Hannah swore at the insanity of what she was being asked to do. 'Maybe you could find a way to run one of these suits on steam for the next time we come down.'

The navvy laughed. 'That's not a bad idea, grub. But then I heard you're the girl that's got Jackelian blood. Using steam should be second nature to you. And we need to tame the steam down here too, if we're going to make it back up to the turbine halls.'

When Hannah cracked the door to her suit, the heat came rushing in like a flood. Even with the concrete shaft clear of steam, it was still as febrile as a kettle outside. Hannah's plain cotton skin-garb was quickly soaked through with humid moisture while her nose was dripping itching beads of sweat onto the burning hot exterior of her RAM suit.

They had halted their suits next to each other like two bridges wedged in the shaft, and as Hannah climbed from her cockpit she looked nervously across to where Rudge was slinging equipment around himself and his ab-lock, tying up his abseiling lines as securely as if their lives depended in it – which they surely did. Out of his cockpit and standing on the chest of his horizontal suit, Rudge was a burly-looking six-foot – with a poorly cropped mop of ginger hair soaked by sweat. The ab-lock was making a low crooning sound beside him, as it too was loaded down with satchels and equipment.

'T-face doesn't sound much like the ab-locks outside the wall,' said Hannah.

'They have their vocal chords removed when they're caught by the trappers,' Rudge called back as he sorted out the gear that Hannah was no doubt to carry the rest of the way down. 'Good job, too, the racket they'd make in the stables otherwise. But T-face is all right; I was with my father when a current reversal blew out a turbine and half the pipes in hall four. It was us that pulled T-face out of there. We saved his life and he knows it right enough.'

'Father? You don't bear children in the turbine halls do you?'

Rudge snorted. 'Of course not. The plating in our suits might be enough to hold off the worst of the deformities, but working in the turbine halls removes the lead from your pencil right enough. No, you have to get a double on the ballot – two from the same family called into the guild. It's less rare than you'd think now there's so few names in the cities to be called.'

Cities. He had been labouring down here long enough not to hear, then. It was just the capital now on Jago. Hermetica. The last city.

Rudge jumped across the gap between the two RAM suits wedged next to each other in the shaft, bringing Hannah's load across.

'A punch card writer for you,' said the navvy, slinging her a heavy sack. 'In case it's a coding problem on the gate.' He tapped the two glass torpedoes slung under his arm, filled with swirling liquid explosives separated by an ignition membrane and a clockwork timer. 'Charges to blow the gate open if it's a physical jam that can't be cleared with my tools.'

He wound a line of powdered tape around Hannah's hands and fitted a climber's sling across her chest, making sure that it was properly connected to the line that she was going to use to abseil down.

'What if the lines aren't long enough?'

The navvy shook his head in annoyance. 'This is your first time, grub, not mine or T-face's. I've been counting the distance all the way down here. You just hold onto your line and keep your gear secure.'

He cast her line off the side of her suit, jumped back to his own machine and then lit a chemical flare belted onto his sling to augment the light of the suits' lanterns.

Down the three of them went, another thirty foot, the powdered bandages on Hannah's hand gripping the abseil line's pulley-like mechanism, the machine droning as she fell. Rudge's calculations were right on the money, though, the three lines playing out a foot above the jammed pressure gate below them.

'Don't touch the surface, grub, and stay on your line. It's burning hot.'

Hannah hardly needed his shouted warning. The gate below was trembling under the pressure of the superheated steam building up on the other side of its heavy vanes, metal plates steaming with moisture from the incredible heat being held back.

Rudge pointed to the stone handholds laddering down the shaft and indicated that Hannah should use them to get to the transaction engine built into the wall. At close quarters the thinking machine was every bit as primitive looking as Hannah had been told by the navvy. A flared trumpet sucked in the passing steam, while a bank of transaction-engine drums rotated to perform the basic calculations needed to help regulate the flow. Under the machine was a tiny stone platform where maintenance work could be done. This must be what working with transaction engines back in the Kingdom of Jackals was like.

'See if the fault's inside there,' ordered Rudge, as he and T-face lowered themselves further down towards the metal gate. 'We're going to check each vane for rusted bearings.' He removed a small hammer and began to tap across the gate's surface, listening to the returning clangs with all the intent of a safe cracker, while T-face held his line steady above him.

Hannah brought out the portable punch card writer that she had been given and rattled out a basic diagnostics query then levered off the cork plug that protected the brutish machine's injection reader from the steam that would usually be powering up this shaft. She quickly became absorbed into her work, forgetting there were others in the tap working alongside her. Checking the transaction engine carefully, Hannah calculated there was enough residual steam in its reservoir for about ten minutes worth of operation time. The inconvenience of having to read the symbolic results directly off the rotating drums was going to be the least of her problems down here.

In the end, it was the garbled nature of the symbols coming up on the transaction-engine drums that gave the fault away and Hannah allowed herself a brief thrill of elation. The gate's transaction engine had recorded a spike of steam well beyond the bounds its guild programmer had originally allowed, so the engine had tried to cope by resetting its ceiling values itself. But it had set them too far beyond the normal parameters, and now the gate that the thinking machine controlled was permanently locked, convinced that the killing pressure building up below was only a slight up-draft that it wasn't even worth the bother of harnessing.

Hannah rattled out another punch card with a more realistic set of pressure peaks and troughs for the control mechanism to follow – factoring in enough time for them to exit the shaft before the gate reopened. She had injected the punch card and re-corked the engine, but the self-congratulatory words of praise she was about to call across to Rudge were lost as one of the rivets exploded from the gate below – blasted away by a pressure front far more intense than the gate's safety margins allowed for. A geyser of steam discharged through the tiny hole that had been opened – knocking the three of them swinging around the shaft on their rappel lines. There was a crashing sound as the spear of steam dislodged one of the RAM suits wedged in the shaft above. The suit came tumbling down like a landslide of metal and crashed into the gate. For a terrible moment Hannah thought the impact was going to smash the gate open, but it proved to be made of tougher stuff. The fallen RAM suit lay over the hole left by the dislodged rivet, temporarily sealing the leak. However, if sealing the leak had spared the three of them from steam burns, it had done no other favours for Rudge. The dislodged suit had brought his line down with it, and now the young navvy was pinned under the knee joins of his own suit, the arch of the leg trapping him with all the weight of a two-tonne foundry-forged tree trunk.

T-face was off his line, whining and pushing hopelessly at the massive suit's leg. Rudge was still conscious enough to see Hannah trying to climb up into his downed suit's pilot cage.

'Suit – won't work,' he coughed up at her. 'Not this – far down the – shaft.'

'It might,' Hannah called down. 'I just need enough power to lift the leg off you.'

'You'll as like – crush me, grub. You're the – only one with a line left tied to – a working suit. Climb back up and – take T-face with you.'

Hannah tried not to gag. She could smell Rudge's skin burning where it was touching the gate. 'I've found the fault, you idiot. The gate's vanes are going to open up underneath you.'

'Good job, girl. Then there's only one – way me and my – suit are going, and that's straight down.'

There was a loud creaking noise from underneath them. The gate wasn't going to hold together long enough for Hannah to get out before the flow of super-pressurized steam resumed. It looked as if Vardan Flail had got his way. He was going to buy Hannah's silence with her death after all.

Burning. Burning, as he rolled across the hotel room's floor. Boxiron's body was burning, but not as fiercely as his mind. The Steamo Loa that his people knew as Radius Patternmaster was reaching into his brain and filling it, preparing to swell and crack his nanomechanical neural channels and burn out each and every memory that Boxiron possessed. Not just the almost-decrypted code hidden inside Jethro's church painting, but everything that made Boxiron a distinct being. His inferior, man-milled body was finally going to get the mind it deserved – that of an idiot savant.

Something deep inside Boxiron struggled and writhed in reaction to the pain – a vomit-like reflex that was trying to emerge and fight the possession of the Loa. What was it? A routine that had been hidden inside him by the flash mob? The cunning mechomancers who knew that there was always a danger that one of the steamman's gods might strike at the abomination they had created for their Jackelian criminal masters. But whatever defences the crime lords had secreted inside his body felt too far away and the weight of the Loa riding him too intense for him to connect with it—

—as he felt Jethro's shadow falling over his body, the gear lever on his back slid squealing up to five. *Top gear*.

Now it was the Steamo Loa's turn to shriek as the cobbled-together firewall the flash mob's hirelings had inserted inside Boxiron connected with his mind. Blocks were raised on every circuit he possessed, the Loa that was trying to ride him cut into a million separate, self-aware splinters, steam leaking out of his joints. The manifestation of Radius Patternmaster tried to seethe out of Boxiron's body, broken and mangled beyond recognition, attempting to reform . . . but merely dissipating in the air of the hotel room.

Boxiron pulled himself groggily to his feet, trying to avoid placing a heavy iron foot on Jethro's toes as he swayed to and fro. Jethro was standing there before him, as was the young ursine Chalph urs Chalph.

'That was one your people's gods, was it not, old steamer?'

'A Loa – I rejected him,' said Boxiron, 'much as you reject your gods.'

'I am not much of a standard to aspire to,' said Jethro.

'You are more than they.'

A coldness flowed through Boxiron, as if every crystal board and node inside his body was hardening after being freed of the corrupting hold of the Loa. But it was not the aftershock of cleansing himself of the possession he felt. *It was the cipher from the painting*.

Assembling. Assembling. The last of the flash mob's crooked processing units came back online passing him the final clue he needed to crack the steganographic code – one third of the mathematical weapon that the priest Bel Bessant had crafted so many centuries earlier. It was like nothing that Boxiron had been expecting.

But then, neither was the explosion of pain as the terrible, cold, alien thing unfolded within his consciousness. . .

CHAPTER TWELVE

'I've never seen the like,' said the commodore to Nandi as they emerged from the conning tower. He waved the punch card containing the Joshua Egg in the air as if he was still trying to clear the smoking ruin the card had left of his transaction engine's navigation drums. 'This blessed egg is jinxed, right enough. Raising a switching storm in the dark valves of those guild dogs, then roasting the transaction engine on my precious boat. It'll take my crew weeks to repair this mess, and Jagonese tugs guiding us out or no, I won't be sailing the Fire Sea blind without my navigation drums. We're as good as beached here until the navigation room is fixed.'

'It's a coincidence,' said Nandi. 'I know that u-boat men are superstitious, but you can't believe a few lines of code are cursed.'

'I believe it, lass. This whole wicked isle is cursed. Jackelians find nothing but bad luck here, and look at the Jagonese. They were as good as us, once, and now see what they've become. Pale-faced lickspittles tending their infernal turbines and hiding in their mortal caves. Milksops raised on bamboo soup where once they would have swigged beer and eaten beef as proudly as any Jackelian.'

223

'Just a coincidence,' said Nandi again, trying to make herself believe it.

The commodore crossed the gantry over to the dock. 'No, lass. This dark isle is a vampire land. It's sucked the vigour out of a whole nation. Why do you think the Fire Sea surrounds it? There's not one good island sitting in this whole damned sea and I've visited a few of them. Old Lord Tridentscale is the master of the oceans and he knew what he was doing when he sealed the black cliffs of Jago off behind the shifting magma. Yes, I'll be right glad to swap the dark vaults of this place for the queer wooden towers and oak minarets of Pericur.'

Nandi started. Of course, the other end of the commodore's voyage. Pericur.

'That's it!' said Nandi. 'I know how to run the Joshua Egg.'

'Don't be asking me to solve the numbers of its formula by hand,' whined the u-boat man. 'Not that my genius isn't up to the task, mind, but I can feel it in my bones – anyone who attempts to solve that dark code will go mad. Don't ask old Blacky to end up in an asylum for this lunatic chase you're on.'

'I'll prove it to you,' said Nandi. 'That what we have here is only a complex code without a single supernatural expression in its formula; and I'll do it with the help of Ambassador Ortin. Your cargo, Jared, transaction-engine parts bound for Pericur – and the ambassador took a good few crates of them for installation in his embassy.'

'Ah, lass,' said the commodore, 'if that fur-skinned fellow has a need for processing power that's not satisfied by the monstrous thinking machines of the guild, it is only because he doesn't trust the Jagonese with what he's handling. Cipher work, Nandi. You'll find his blessed embassy's transaction engines come with an officer of the Pericurian secret police attached to them.'

Nandi shrugged. She didn't give a damn about Pericurian politics, and if the ambassador's transaction engines came configured for cipher work, so much the better. What was in here was going to save Hannah from the guild and Nandi would burn out every transaction engine on Jago if it meant saving the young church girl from her tormentors.

The transaction-engine room inside the Pericurian embassy was a lot more advanced than Nandi had been expecting. In fact, it was a lot more advanced than it had any right to be. How many customs officials on the Jackelian docks had Commodore Black bribed to look the other way while their most advanced transaction-engine models were hustled out of the country for export to the rising power across the sea?

The rattling, steam-driven drums on the Jackelian machinery looked out of place in this chamber, decorated in the Pericurian style with richly carved hardwood panelling across the walls and floors. The windows here were in the circular wooden-framed style known as bulls' eyes back in Jackals. The stained glass obscured the view beyond, but that had probably been intentional. All of the embassies were clustered together in a ring on the hollowed-out level of the Horn of Jago know as Embassy Circle, and had a clear view of the concrete artillery domes around the foot of the mountain. A not-so-subtle reminder of Hermetica City's ability to drop a shell on any unauthorized boat trying to breach the coral line defending the island.

'You're a fine fellow, Ortin,' said the commodore. 'Helping your old shipmates out of a blessed tight spot like this. I'll give you a free berth to Pericur for your troubles, Ambassador, when you want it.'

'What I want is of little consequence, dear boy.' The Pericurian ambassador was still dressed like a Jackelian squire.

Perhaps the Jagonese tailor hadn't come to see him yet. 'The only way I'm getting out of my posting here is if the liberal houses come back into power, and I hardly judge that likely at the moment. Besides, annoying the ineptly disguised intelligence officer the archduchess has watching my every step by allowing you inside our embassy is worth every ill word in the report she's furiously drafting right now.'

With the machine's operator dismissed from the room, Ortin urs Ortin took an almost childish delight in taking charge of the transaction engine himself, his eyes glinting with manic glee as he transcribed the Joshua Egg's second iteration and sprayed water onto the rotating drums when they started running hot. He put Nandi in mind of her mother watering the roses that wound around the trellises at the back of her cottage, all concentration, lost to the world.

As Nandi had predicted, if there was a curse on the Joshua Egg, it was a particularly Jackelian one, because the engine room in the Pericurian embassy seemed markedly unaffected by it. The results came rattling back on a large Rutledge Rotator, an abacus-like board of rotating squares. A more detailed breakdown appeared on a winding reel of paper tape, its wheels poorly oiled and squealing like suckling piglets competing for a mother's teat.

When the results were flowing back from the third iteration of the Joshua Egg, Nandi didn't hesitate. She urged the ambassador to toss the newly reformed code back into the decryption run – she would have enough time later to leaf through the data spooling out. Nandi might not be as convinced of a curse as the commodore, but she didn't want to tempt fate if there was some mathematical quirk in the code that led to transaction engines overloading as they were teasing meaning out of it.

Again the next level of the Joshua Egg was solved, more

data thrown out along with another iteration and she tossed the new code back like a fish that was too small. By the fifth iteration, the Joshua Egg was exhausted. No more iterative pearls to be uncovered, no more compressed data to be drawn out.

Nandi spread the unfurled rolls of printed data across a heavy table meant for use by the engine's cardsharps. Here it was, then. The last legacy of the two Doctors Conquest. Would there be anything in the pages of records they had printed out to help save the daughter they had hardly known? Would there be anything in them to allow Nandi to prove she was at least the equal of every one of the pampered popinjays who had bought their way into Saint Vine's rarefied halls of academia? As Nandi started reading, she was calmly intent on finding out what the guild was so bent on preventing her from discovering. By the time she had finished, though, her hands were shaking and her skin was cold with sweat.

'What is it, lass?' asked the commodore. 'Say this blessed evil code hasn't given you a fever. . .'

'Not the code,' said Nandi. 'What is inside it. We have to get to Hannah, Jared. We have to get her out of the guild's vaults to hear what I've found here. . .'

The superstitious commodore was backing away without even realizing it, nearly treading on the riding boots of the large Pericurian ambassador.

'. . . because she's not going to believe this,' said Nandi.

Jethro Daunt came running back into the hotel room with more thick cream bamboo paper to replace the pile that Boxiron had already used up. The pencil clutched in the steamman's iron fingers moved across the paper so fast it was as if the numbers of the formula he was writing were flowing out of a breached dam. Chalph urs Chalph was gathering up the completed papers, standing back from Boxiron as the steamman moaned about the pain of holding whatever he had found in the painting in his head before it vomited across the papers.

At last the steamman stopped scribbling. He rolled across the floor, whimpering, his stack emitting wheezing bursts of smoke. 'It is gone. It is gone.'

'It has,' reassured Jethro. 'It is all down here, now. On paper.'

'Such a thing is not meant to be held within a mind,' hissed Boxiron.

'Not held incomplete,' said Jethro. 'Not without being balanced by the other two parts.'

'No!' said the steamman, so loudly it was almost a warning. 'It is not what you think it is. I should have listened to the Steamo Loa when it came to me. Read the formula, Jethro softbody, see the symmetry of what has been wrought here.'

Jethro took the papers being neatly piled by Chalph urs Chalph and started to read through them, slowly at first, then more frantically – almost disbelieving – flicking through the sheets and turning them over, tracing the formulae between pages and jumping back and forth until the ex-parson was perspiring. 'This cannot be!'

'What is it?' asked Chalph. 'Is it something to do with the machine spirit that was trying to possess your metal friend?'

'So obscene,' said Jethro. 'So obvious. Such a fearful symmetry.'

'What was hidden in the painting?' demanded Chalph.

'How do you slay a god?' asked Jethro, pushing the formula-strewn papers back, sadly, towards Chalph. 'Why, the easiest way in the world. By becoming a god yourself, a *stronger* god.'

'Become a god?' Chalph sounded shocked. 'Such a thing is not possible.'

Boxiron cleared his voicebox. 'It should not be. Yet I was burning with just a third of this horror held within my mind.'

'Sentience is a function of complexity,' said Jethro, regretfully. 'To an ant, good ursine, you would look like a god. To an animalcule living on a slide under a microscope, the ant would seem like a god. The purpose of this god-formula would appear to be to focus the complexity of the universe inside a mortal mind and keep on folding it in an infinite loop: infinitely wise, infinitely knowing, and the Circle preserve us, I have no doubt, infinitely mad. And what would emerge from such a fearful recursion would be as far beyond that which we are, as we are beyond an unthinking mote of dust.'

'I have never encountered such mathematics before,' admitted Boxiron, his voicebox trembling with awe. 'The clarity of it, using paradoxes to refocus the great pattern and turn the threads of existence inwards on themselves.'

Jethro sighed. 'Oh, Bel Bessant. Such genius. But such arrogance to believe her mind could have held the entirety of such a thing and not ended up as dangerous as the divine monsters she had been asked to protect Jago from. A god-formula, of all the things for a Circlist priest to want to create. A *god-formula*.'

'She had to die,' said the steamman, simply.

'Poor William of Flamewall. Close enough to his lover to see what she wanted to become. Close enough to poison Bel Bessant before she could use the formula on herself. Loving enough to take the blame for a crime of passion rather than circulating the dangerous truth behind her work any wider. To go on the run as a murderer rather than being hailed as the hero he deserved to be.'

'William of Flamewall, he is the one that concealed the code in the painting?' asked Chalph.

Jethro nodded.

'If he was willing to murder his own mate to stop the god-formula being used, why preserve it within a series of paintings, why not destroy it instead?'

'Once created, weapons are never uninvented, they are never forgotten' said Jethro. 'If someone was to use this or something similar to raise themselves to godhood, the understanding of the god-formula would be the sole way to stop them – it is virus and vaccine both.'

Boxiron picked up one of the sheets and waved it angrily 'The Inquisition knew this abomination was here.'

'It is possible, good steamman. The Inquisition might have held onto this terrible secret for millennia. Why else would they ensure the archbishop of Jago was always one of their officers? But I rather think the recent rediscovery of the god-formula, its unearthing, was the work of the two Doctors Conquest. And Alice was involved somehow; dear Circle, I do hope it wasn't her that killed Hannah's parents.'

Chalph shook his head. 'Come on Jackelian, the archbishop was strict, but—'

Jethro interrupted. 'You can only ever know yourself, and then barely. Alice was an officer of the Inquisition. If it meant protecting William of Flamewall's secret, I have little doubt she would have killed everyone in this room to achieve that end.'

'I have never voiced misgivings about the work you have accepted before,' said Boxiron, 'but. . .'

Jethro spread the sheets containing their painting's third of the god-formula out in front of him. 'There is something about this. Something wrong.'

'Beyond the alarming concept of a completely unworthy mortal transfiguring themselves into a god?' asked Boxiron.

'Yes indeed, but bob me sideways, what is it?' Jethro looked as if he had remembered something, and pulled out the catalogue he had found in the murdered fence's hidden storeroom, passing it to his friend. 'You will find a painting on the last page, old steamer. Another of William of Flamewall's works.'

'This is a picture of a picture,' complained the steamman, leafing to the end of the catalogue. 'A third-generation copy.'

'Your best efforts, if you please.'

Boxiron raised the page in front of his vision plate and waited a couple of seconds while he resolved its details. After a moment's stillness he shuddered back to life. 'There is nothing there. No sign of steganographic concealment within the image. It is just a simple painting.'

'You are certain?'

'As certain as the signature of William of Flamewall scrawled in its right-hand corner. The print quality of the catalogue is such that I would not be able to resolve the detail of a code in the painting, but I *can* see there is no trace of one hidden anywhere on this canvas.'

Jethro smiled. 'Of course, why would there be?'

'Old man Sworph was killed for this and there isn't even a code in it?' said Chalph, disbelievingly.

'Not a steganographic code,' continued Jethro, 'which makes a strange kind of sense to me. What did you do with the last part of the god-formula, William? Where did you hide it?'

'I'm glad this affair makes sense to you, Jackelian,' said Chalph. 'Because the only thing that makes sense to me right now is getting off Jago before one of the locals skins me for a rug.'

'This painting is blank,' explained Jethro, 'because if it wasn't, our murderous adversary would have all three parts of the code in his possession and would have already used it to transmigrate, to ascend towards the godhead.'

'Is it possible that the Inquisition destroyed the third part of the god-formula?' asked Boxiron. 'If they were only keeping the god-formula as a potential counter weapon, then could not two thirds of it have served that purpose? Destroying the third component would ensure the god-formula was never used.'

'That is so,' admitted Jethro. 'But I rather fear the Inquisition was only holding onto two parts of the god-formula because that is all they ever had. The third part has been lost to them, to the world, since its creator was killed.'

'Your logic is faultless, yet I have to concur with our Pericurian friend,' said Boxiron. 'What do you owe the Inquisition that would mean we need to stay here on Jago? It is time, as your people say, to let discretion be the better part of valour. We should leave the island.'

'This isn't for them anymore. No, I need just a little longer,' said Jethro, almost pleading. 'Just long enough to slay a god.'

CHAPTER THIRTEEN

Hannah tried to ignore the young navvy's cries as the heat seeped through the pressure gate and scalded his back. She climbed over the fallen suit to reach the transaction engine. Time to find out if she had fixed it as well as she believed she had.

'What are you doing?' cried Rudge, his head barely able to follow her from his position wedged under the suit's leg. 'I told you to get back up the shaft. I ordered—'

'Be quiet,' retorted Hannah. 'The charge-master sent me down here because I've got a brain and I'm going to use it.'

'You're not going to think a couple of tonnes of suit off me, grub. You've done the job we came down here to do, so get out of the shaft now!'

She was at the controls of the primitive steam-driven thinking machine, ignoring the navvy's shouts while she put the small portable punch-card writer to good use. One more card. One last chance. There was another creak from the gate underneath them. It was getting noticeably noisier – the pressure building up below. 'T-face,' Hannah shouted down to the ab-lock pacing behind his fallen master. 'Get ready to pull him out.'

'You're not going to do what I think you. . .?'

Hannah inserted the punch card. 'What do you care? You're going to die anyway if this doesn't work.'

The drums in the transaction engine on the wall began to rotate as her punch card instructions were received and processed. Please, let there still be enough steam left in its reservoir to do the job.

Rudge was tearing the sleeve off his body suit, wrapping the material around his eyes. 'Cover your face, grub.'

Hannah ripped a line of cotton material off her own body suit, bundling the makeshift sweat-soaked bandanna around her eyes.

The tolerances. It was all down to the tolerances now. Her best guess at the weight of the suit and the intense pressure of the steam tap below the gate, and. . .

The blast came like a lightning bolt cast from the gates of the hell they denied.

. . . how wide the opening of a single vane would have to be to shift the suit, and. . .

Hannah was thrown back into the wall, blind behind her bandanna, deafened by the crash of the displaced suit.

. . . how long to leave it open without cooking the three of them. . .

Hannah yelled as she realized she had fallen forward onto the oven-hot pressure gate, the thick iron burning into her hands as she pushed herself up and tore off her blindfold. It was like being inside a surface mist, now, but she could see that T-face was dragging Rudge away – his fallen suit shifted over to the other side of the shaft by the force of the volcano of steam Hannah had briefly allowed through that single open vane.

Some piece of gear on Rudge's suit had smacked him when it had shifted, though. Rudge was bleeding from the head and unconscious. Hannah climbed back up to the transaction-engine platform, closely followed by T-face bearing the weight of his master's body, and she was about to reach for the single dangling rappel line attached to her suit, when she realized that it had vanished. Oh, sweet Circle. It was on the metal gate below her – her line must have become dislodged when she steam-blasted Rudge's suit away from his broken body. Hannah's suit was still lodged far above them, though. Far enough that there was no way she was going to be able to climb up the shaft's smooth walls to reach it. T-face was shifting from foot to foot, moaning as he took in their hopeless predicament. Hannah fought down the sense of mounting panic. How to get out? She couldn't signal the turbine workers with the transaction engine to call for help. That was the whole point of it. An independent steam-driven node with only one purpose, controlling the gate. Could she open the pressure gate again, blast herself, Rudge and the ab-lock up to her suit, using Rudge's suit as a lifting platform? No, that was suicide. Just a second with a single vane being opened had nearly killed them both. She might reach her suit, but it would be without her skin.

'Damn you!' Hannah yelled up the shaft. 'Damn you for sending me down here to die.' Was that for Vardan Flail? For the master of the turbine halls? For everyone on Jago who needed the dark energy that was going to end up killing her? It hardly mattered anymore. Rudge was starting to wake, but not to full sensibility, drifting in and out of a shivering half-awareness. He was muttering something, and Hannah bent down to hear him better.

'*Winch.*'

She looked up at her suit, its flickering lantern signalling teasingly to her. There was a winch hook on the right leg of the suit. It was designed for dragging broken turbines out of the way on the floor of the halls above, but if she could get it to lower itself down, then they could shimmy up the line. The winch's activation lever was up there too. Thirty feet above her head, but it might as well have been in the clouds for all that she could reach it. Unless . . . Leaping down onto the burning hot gate, Hannah retrieved Rudge's tool kit and brought it back to her ledge. She rifled through the contents of until she found it, a lone signal flare.

'One shot,' mumbled Rudge.

One shot. She had better make it a good one. Hannah pointed the red tube up at the winch lever, aiming it as well as she could without a sight, and pressed down on the trigger, the recoil of the escaping firework nearly sending the tube leaping out of her sweating fingers. Arcing up, the flare hit near the winch drum and went spinning off to the side of the shaft, a useless sparking comet.

Hannah growled through gritted teeth. 'Missed!'

But Rudge didn't hear her, he had passed out again. If he was lucky, maybe he would stay unconscious through their deaths too. T-face howled in surprise as the hook of the winch came plummeting down from the suit's leg and bounced off the pressure gate as the metal line whipped dangerously across the passage. Hannah stared up in amazement. She had missed the winch lever, missed it by a country mile, she could have sworn she had, and yet it had . . . the stories of the suit-ghosts came back to her.

She looked at the ab-lock, who seemed as spooked by the winch activating as she was. 'Can you carry him up to my suit? You'll need to hold onto him as I climb up the shaft – the cabin only fits one.' Did he understand her? To emphasize the words, she pointed at Rudge and then mimicked climbing up the rope with the young man tossed over a shoulder.

Hannah realized how desperate she sounded and how

dangerous the situation was. What did she know of ab-locks and their taming? If T-face turned feral now, she didn't even have a suit whip to lash him into line.

T-face responded by slinging the passed-out navvy across his back, his leathery scarred face wobbling from side to side as he emitted a stream of growls. It almost sounded as if the creature was trying to say something back to her, the noises from its mangled throat rising and falling in a mockery of speech. The ab-lock seemed to grasp what was needed for them all to survive, though, seizing the winch line and shinning back up with his master.

Below Hannah's ledge the gate gave a hungry anticipatory shudder.

Hannah leapt off the transaction-engine platform and caught the winch cable, clambering up the line after T-face and Rudge, abandoning the mobile punch-card writer, Rudge's tools and his fallen suit down below. How far did the steam tap travel towards the centre of the earth? Hannah didn't intend to be around to find out when the gate retracted.

Hannah pushed her suit out of the steam tap, into the turbine hall, the clangs of a dozen retracted pressure gates still ringing in her ears. Her hands were so sweaty now that the control cage inside her suit's cabin had begun slipping off her skin. The chimney door was shutting behind her when the lights on the vault's wall began to flash, the steam tap returning to operation. Blast doors pulled into the ceiling at the other end of the vault and a mob of suited workers returned from the safety of the adjoining turbine hall. She had done it. All around Hannah, the turbines were spinning back into life, the eerily silent hall filling with the racket of rotating blades. Fingers of vapour were already leaking from the pipes. Soon, the hall would once again be the steam-filled hell she had stepped out into earlier in the day.

T-face leapt down from the perch moulded onto the suit's back, landing on the floor with the still-unconscious navvy.

At the head of the gang of returning guildsmen was the red chequerboard-patterned hull of the charge-master. 'You're down a suit.' His bluff voice echoed from Hannah's earphones.

'A steam spill sent Rudge's suit crashing down the shaft, well below the electric limit of its circuits, charge-master.'

The head of the turbine hall grunted and turned to one of his retinue. 'Do you slackers think you're still on a break? Take our lad down to the infirmary before the field begins to build back up.' The charge-master swivelled his head dome down to stare at T-face and made a jabbing motion back to the other end of the chamber. 'Return to stables. Chop-chop. Assigned to another hand while boss man in infirmary.' He ejected his whip in case the ab-lock hadn't got the message,

T-face bent his head sadly and trotted off.

Hannah thought she saw the charge-master's eyes staring at her through the dome on top of his suit. 'Adequate for your first day. For a *coder*.'

He walked off, leaving Hannah unsure whether she was meant to go back to the suiting hall or continue her training with the rest of the workers out here.

Something about the charge-master's words stayed with her. *Our lad.*

Young Rudge never had got round to telling her who his father was in the turbine halls.

Our lad.

Nandi stepped out of the transport capsule and down onto the platform of the guild's atmospheric station, the young priest from the cathedral, Father Baine, close on her heels.

Vardan Flail was waiting for them in front of the lockers holding the guild's visitors' suits, a retinue of red-cowled guildsmen standing behind the high guild master's twisted form.

One of the guildsmen stepped forward as she approached. 'Damson Tibar-Wellking, I will be your assistant for the rest of your research session within the great archive. I am archivist Trope.'

'That's very kind of you,' smiled Nandi, looking meaningfully at the high guild master. 'But I believe my research will be taking me a little further afield than the guild's transaction-engine vaults. And that's not why I'm here today, as I suspect you well know.' She indicated the young priest following behind her.

Baine caught up with Nandi and stopped in front of Vardan Flail. 'By the authority of the unified arch-diocese of Jago and the rational order of the Circlist church I present an examination notice for Damson Hannah Conquest.'

Vardan Flail looked irritated. 'If it's an observance of the formalities you want, perhaps the cathedral should have sent Father Blackwater to me rather than a mere pup.'

'The examination notice duly ratified and sealed by order of the stained senate,' added the young priest, not rising to the insult.

'Oh, very well,' snapped Vardan Flail. 'Your examination notice is accepted and I do hereby authorize release of Initiate Conquest of the Guild of Valvemen into your custody.' He clicked his fingers for one of his minions to fetch the girl. 'The *temporary* release, pending the results of the church examination.'

'The church examination which will be marked manually for this test,' Nandi added. 'Rather than by your transaction engines.'

'Manually! Isn't that quaint. I still expect to see the results

239

myself,' snapped Vardan Flail. 'To ensure that there is no favouritism in the grading of one of my initiates.'

'Perish the thought,' said Father Baine.

'You probably still remember the test yourself,' said Vardan Flail. 'You hardly look old enough to shave.'

'I remember the test as being very easy. Anyone can pass, really.'

A group of staff-wielding guildsmen entered the station hall and parted to reveal Hannah Conquest, still wearing the grey cotton body suit of a turbine hall worker. She was soaked with sweat and swaying slightly on her feet.

'What have you done to her?' cried Father Baine. 'She looks like she hasn't slept in a week.'

'The city demands much of the guild,' retorted Vardan Flail. 'It is only dedicated toil that keeps the turbine halls running. Perhaps the church authorities might remember that in future, rather than twisting the law to try to circumvent the draft ballot for their favourites.'

Nandi grabbed one of Hannah's arms while Father Baine supported her other side, leading the girl stumbling towards the transport capsule.

'Don't worry,' Vardan Flail sneered after them. 'The church examinations are easy, anyone can pass them.'

Nandi shook her head in disgust and shut off her view of the high guild master's hooded face with the closing of the carriage's door.

Her arm still held by Father Baine, Hannah straightened up, wiping the sweat off her face as though she was a drunk who had suddenly transitioned into stone-cold sobriety.

Hannah winked towards the shocked young priest and Nandi. 'Well, my suit was logging double shifts down in the turbine halls, but it doesn't mean that it always had to be me inside it.' With a shudder, the carriage entered the airless atmospheric tunnel, leaving the guild's vaults. 'It's good to have friends, isn't it?'

'Quick,' Jethro said to Hannah, 'your favourite hymn from the cathedral. . .?'

'*My knowledge, my soul*,' said Hannah, looking at the books spread across the table in the inquisition agent's hotel room. 'Will that be part of the church's entrance exam?'

'No,' said Jethro. 'I just wanted to see which hymn you liked best. That question can reveal a lot about a candidate.'

And he could see; he could see Alice's mark all over the young girl, little reflections of the things he remembered and loved about his ex-fiancée. The way Hannah thought, the way she acted. Truly, Alice had been the mother than Hannah had lost, and for Alice, perhaps, the daughter that Jethro's defrocking and the breaking of their engagement had denied her. Denied *them*.

'Then it won't help me pass,' said Hannah. 'I hear you sing to yourself all the time, Mister Daunt. But only tavern songs, never Circlist hymns.'

'No, I don't sing those any more,' admitted the ex-parson. 'I don't feel I have the right to them. And you should call me Jethro.' He picked up the books they had been cramming from, borrowed from the acting archbishop's office. 'You have an exceedingly good mind – first rate, in fact. The way you can pick apart the components of synthetic morality and put them back together again puts me in mind of Alice.'

'Alice was the cleverest person I'd ever met.'

'Myself also,' said Jethro. *Until now, that is*, his mind silently retorted. 'But she had her weaknesses and I think you share them too. Circlism is not just about knowledge and enlightenment. It is about embracing our humanity. Each of us is cupped out from the one sea of consciousness and poured into these mortal vessels. You – I – everyone we know is the same. It is only the nature of reality that makes us feel alone, which tricks us into seeing difference where none exists. But it is a false illusion, for when you pour a cup of water back into the river, where do the cup's contents end and the river's begin? All is motion, all is the river.'

'Even for Alice's killers?' asked Hannah.

'A Circlist would say the killer only killed themselves. Lack of knowledge tends to do that.'

'I don't think I can ever see them as part of me enough to forgive them.'

'We are all but human,' said Jethro.

'What they did to Alice,' said Hannah quietly, looking down at the tome in front of her as if it was all of her world. 'It wasn't just to make it look like an ursk attack, was it? She was tortured to try and find out something.'

'I won't let the killer touch you,' promised Jethro. 'I arrived here too late to save Alice, but I'm just in time for you.' The girl that Alice had raised as her own, the child that should have been theirs. 'Isn't that right, old steamer?'

The steamman was standing in the doorway bearing a tray of steaming tea cups procured from the hotel's staff.

'Indeed it is, Hannah softbody,' said Boxiron. 'We have faced evil and criminals many times together, yet by combining my intellect and Jethro Daunt's famous brawn, we have always triumphed.'

'You are exceedingly obliging,' said Jethro, taking the tray. 'With both your refreshments and your humour.'

Boxiron tapped the armour on his chest, the transaction-engine drum buried there slowly rotating. 'My 'intellect' is, I fear, a little scratched by the Jackelian underworld's pistols I'm sure you will forgive me.'

'Let's get back to your studying,' said Jethro, tapping the

tomes in front of Hannah. For if Hannah failed to gain entrance to the church, the next place she would be going was straight back to the Guild of Valvemen and into the clutches of Vardan Flail.

And that was no longer something Jethro could allow – not for Alice's sake or his own.

Jethro Daunt found it hard to suppress a smile when he saw the number of people gathered in the cathedral's testing room – rarely, he suspected, would it have been busier than this. Not just with those sitting the examination, their heads swelled to gargantuan size by the Entick machinery, but with the observers trying not to trip over the trailing cables or get in the way of the priests behind the testing tables. There were twelve examinees sitting the tests this day, but only one of them was responsible for drawing in all these extra people. Commodore Black, Nandi, Boxiron, Chalph urs Chalph, Ortin urs Ortin, half the cathedral's off-duty staff – all to see if Damson Hannah Conquest could throw off the guild's shackles – with a few of the crimson-robed crows sitting silently in the corner. Briefed, Jethro was sure, to try and detect the slightest deviation from the usual form of the church's examination. Anything that would allow the guild to nullify the results of the test.

And the results were hardly in doubt, for Hannah Conquest had both nature and nurture on her side. The offspring of two of the brightest scholars Jackelian academia had ever produced, tutored by Alice in every mathematical nuance of synthetic morality. Even so, Jethro could sense the amazement the priests testing Hannah felt at the speed she was going through the large leather-bound tomes of questions piled on top of each table. Knocking down their questions as fast as they could fire them at her. And the scariest thing of all was that it was obvious to him that she wasn't even trying. This was just what Hannah Conquest needed, to earn what she believed would be a life of quiet contemplation. To get everyone off her back for good.

Jethro glanced across at Nandi and the commodore. Of course, the young academic had been right. None of them could tell Hannah what they had discovered in the Pericurian embassy, not before she'd sat the exam. There was no telling how Hannah would react, and she needed her head clear and focused right now. Able to conjure up, as she was at the moment, a formula to prove how allocation of food to female children during a time of famine would prove the optimum stabilising force within a democracy – with a sidebar question on how the allocation would need to change for a classic autocracy.

Jethro winced. He remembered that question from his own examination. So, the priests administering the Entick test had reached the nineteenth book of synthetic morality, *Saint Solomon and the Questions of Functional Savagery*. There were no easy answers in that book, and the trick was often to reply with the heart as much as the head. Sometimes the wrong answer was the right answer, and sometimes it was better not to ask the question at all.

'And every so often, it's time for you to stand up and take responsibility for your own actions.'

Jethro's eyes darted around the testing room. That voice. The stench of sulphur and wet animal hide in the room. Was that a glimpse of fur he saw slipping behind Boxiron? The people around him to seemed to slow down, as if moving through treacle, as the exotic presence forced its way into their world.

'I take responsibility for my own actions!'

'But do you?' hissed the voice of Badger-headed Joseph

from somewhere on the other side of the room. 'All that death and misery in your little kingdom, and now the Jackelians can't even be bothered to pray to us to make it better. What have you done of late to make the world a better place?'

'Life is lived by the one and one.'

'Oh, that's pat,' laughed the voice. 'And all of your trite Circlist excuses appear to be made the same way. You know what your people created here on Jago now, you must know what you could do with the god-formula. The good that you could achieve.'

'What Bel Bessant was creating was wrong,' insisted Jethro. 'No mortal mind is meant to have that level of understanding of the universe. Not without going insane.'

'Oh, but that's the twist: the world's already insane. If you understood it a little better, maybe you could do something about it. Put your world towards the mend, instead of hiding yourself away from life with the all distractions of your investigations and the smugness of your false humanist cleverness. Maybe you could stop and pull your cowardly head out of the sand just the once.'

'Leave me alone.'

'Time is just a tree to be pruned, all the infinite possibilities branching out. The whisper of a butterfly's wings on the other side of the world and a good king takes the throne rather than his evil uncle. Plenty rather than famine. Health rather than plague. A little push here, a little nudge there. It's so very easy to do. You could do it, you could use the god-formula to remake your world as a paradise.'

'No one has that right.'

'One branch of potential, another branch next door, you're going to have to travel down one of them in the end anyway. The tree's always growing, even we can't stop that. All the branches look much the same from a higher perspective.

Why not pick the road that leads to a nice warm bed rather than a swamp? A comfortable parsonage back in the Kingdom, the cosy fire stoked by Alice Gray. Isn't that the world you always wanted?'

'Those are words of temptation. I refuse you.'

'Refuse us? I expect you to join us, fiddle-faddle man. Time to step up. Time to be like your funny half-steamman friend – time for you to go all the way up to top gear!'

Time lurched forward again and Jethro felt Boxiron's metal fingers on his shoulder. 'Didn't you hear me, Jethro softbody? Hannah Conquest has finished her tests. It is time.'

'Yes,' coughed Jethro, 'that it most certainly is, old steamer.'

Jethro stepped over to the table where the priest was storing away the pile of tomes filled with questions that Hannah had finished answering. The examinees were slipping off their Entick helmets and wiping away the grease marks the brass goggles had left on their faces, looking groggy from the intensity of the questioning and sudden influx of light.

'Father?' Jethro coughed.

'There is little doubt,' said the priest behind the examination table. 'Our result tabulation is just a formality now. Hannah Conquest had passed the entrance threshold by the third book. Even the Guild of Valvemen will not be able to gainsay these results.'

Jethro shook the priest's hand in thanks and went over to where Hannah was using a tissue lent to her by Nandi to remove the grease from her cheeks.

It was time for young Damson Hannah Conquest to hear the truth. . .

Hannah took the chair that Jethro Daunt offered her with trepidation, sitting just behind Boxiron. After what Father Baine had told her about how the cathedral fathers believed

246

she had done in the tests, this should have been a time of celebration, but instead there was an almost funereal air of expectation on the faces of the commodore, Nandi and Chalph. And what was the large ursine she had been introduced to as the new Pericurian ambassador doing in the ex-parson's hotel room? Her escape from the guild's draft was surely not the business of Jago's distant neighbours on the opposite shores of the Fire Sea. . .

'The guild hasn't found a way to forbid me to enter the church?' asked Hannah.

'No,' said Jethro. 'You are free of the guild's call on you. But we have discovered some important things while you have been in their servitude.'

'The evidence that it was Vardan Flail who murdered Alice?'

'Why she was murdered, at least,' said Jethro. He reached into his pocket and drew out a paper bag of boiled sweets, popping one in his mouth before offering the bag to Hannah.

Hannah demurred. 'The senate banned the import of those from the Kingdom years ago.'

'Lucky I never offered one to the colonel, then,' said Jethro, patting Hannah's hand. 'The weapon that Bel Bessant was developing to defend Jago from the Chimecan Empire's gods was not designed to push them beyond the walls of our world as we thought, but to transform Bel Bessant into a god, to allow her to meet the dark deities on the gods' own terms. That is what the cipher on the painting inside your locket was . . . it was one third of such a weapon, a god-formula. I believe the second piece of the god-formula was inside Alice's missing locket. The third was concealed in the silver infinity circle that was stolen from the cathedral's altar. These three paintings were uncovered by your parents during their research in the guild's vaults.'

Hannah was left reeling from the ex-parson's words.

To become a god! There were people of power in the world who thought they already were. And murder would be the least of what they would stoop to, to make their delusions a reality beyond the confines of their own twisted minds. Dogs like Vardan Flail.

Chalph stopped prowling the hotel room. 'But the painting that was stolen from the cathedral did not contain a cipher?'

'Precisely,' said Jethro. 'Yet it was that theft that led to Alice being murdered. And who would be in a position to know what that picture meant? Only someone who already had possession of one or more of the paintings with Bel Bessant's god-formula concealed inside them. Someone who had pursued your parents for the copies of the images they found in the guild's archives.'

'I am not sure I understand,' said Chalph.

Hannah shook her head. She didn't either.

'That is because you don't yet see all of the picture,' explained Jethro. 'But Damson Tibar-Wellking, I believe, holds some of the missing pieces of the puzzle.'

Nandi produced the punch card with Hannah's writing on the reverse side. 'You did a very good job remembering your mother's Joshua Egg from the guild's archive. We ran its remaining iterations on Ambassador Ortin's transaction engines and recovered the final pieces of your parents' research.'

'I knew it,' said Hannah. Hope rose within her. 'I knew there would be more.'

'Much of what was compressed inside the Joshua Egg your mother left us concerns the priest, William of Flamewall,' explained Jethro. 'Although the most important items your parents left behind for us are the first two parts of the god-formula. It seems your parents found images of all three paintings of the rational trinity within the guild's transaction engines and your mother broke the steganography concealed within the images. Like us, they found that the first two paintings contained parts of the god-formula, and that the third was a ruse, blank of steganographic code.'

Hannah gasped. 'So it was Vardan Flail who destroyed my parents' records on the guild's engines. The jigger realized that my mother had left hidden copies of the god-formula. Destroying my mother's secret backup was just removing the evidence of his crimes.'

'The evidence may have gone, but we now have two of the three parts of the god-formula,' said Jethro.

'Which of the three paintings of the rational trinity did you recover from the Joshua Egg?' asked Hannah.

'The second,' said Jethro. '*Discard your beliefs*.'

Hannah murmured in appreciation. That image was captured in stained glass back in the cathedral. A man sitting cross-legged in a hall surrounded by the broken idols of a thousand religions, prophets and messiahs. 'So we have two pieces of the god-formula. But why would Bel Bessant leave two pieces of the code for us to find but not the third?'

'You will get there shortly. Once you understand what Bel Bessant was creating,' Jethro continued, 'you will understand why even a Circlist priest could be driven to commit murder – why William felt he had no choice but to kill his lover when he found out. I have little doubt that just developing the god-formula would have left Bel Bessant dangerously deranged. She may even have started manifesting supernatural powers as a side effect of her work. By the time William realized what Bel was doing, physical violence was probably the only way he could have stopped her before she ascended towards godhood. I fear that towards her end she was no longer right or rational. Your parents uncovered more facts about William in their research, history they decided to bury extremely proficiently. For example, William of Flamewall never actually went on the run from the police when his crime was discovered; he had already set off into the wilderness, acting as the priest on an expedition into Jago's interior. He was following in the footsteps of Bel Bessant, who had filled much the same position herself with a party of trappers before she began developing the god-formula.'

'Going outside the city walls with the trappers? That's dangerous work,' said Hannah. 'Was William trying to get himself killed out of some sense of guilt for what he did to Bel?'

'A little more than that. One of the documents your parents left us was transcribed in something distantly related to ancient Pericurian. It was discovered among Bel Bessant's possessions during the militia's investigation into her murder.' Jethro pointed to Ortin. 'The good ambassador here was kind enough to have it translated for us.'

'Yes,' said Ortin, excitedly. 'It appears to be the text of a previously unknown tablet from the scripture of the Divine Quad.'

'*We* know what it is,' added Nandi, 'and your father with his skills would probably have been able to translate it, but the text would have been a complete mystery to William of Flamewall and Bel Bessant. The Jagonese of their era weren't to lay eyes on an actual Pericurian until many centuries later. Ortin and Chalph's ancestors believed that Jago was a lost paradise sealed away by their gods somewhere inside the Fire Sea.' Nandi dug into her satchel and pulled out a reel of paper that looked as if it had been spooled off a transaction engine. Dusting it off, she handed it hesitantly to Hannah. 'Please read this. It was also among the contents of the Joshua Egg and will clear up a great deal for you, I think. It's the last document your mother wrote for us, taken from her journal.'

Hannah unfurled the tape and began reading.

*   *   *

This is my last entry before I must leave Hermetica City. It seems as if our fears about who to trust were well-founded and not mere paranoia. George's boat has been reported lost in the Fire Sea. I can only thank the Circle that our decision to keep Hannah safe here on the island with me was the right one.

The local newspapers say it was an unpredicted peristaltic flow that cut off the boat and then overwhelmed the craft. If that were true, then it would have been a very easy thing for the guild here to arrange. A small alteration in their model of the lava flows, and my darling husband would have been murdered as smoothly as sliding a stiletto blade into his back.

But I am not so sure that this is how the murder was done. I could swear that I saw the face of Tomas Maggs today, the skipper of the boat we had paid to take George back home. It was the look of astonishment on his face at seeing me alive, no doubt mirroring my own, that confirmed it was indeed the same treacherous little jigger. If Maggs was paid to abandon his vessel to the lava flows, then those who gave him the coin to do it must now know that I am not a sea-sick corpse locked in my cabin as George was pretending, but that I am very much alive and still on Jago, albeit as a widow.

Maggs will no doubt have stolen all three paintings and the first two parts of the god-formula from George before abandoning his boat to the Fire Sea, and Maggs' paymasters will seek my death to put an end to the affair. If they realize quickly enough that William of Flamewall's last painting was a hoax, then they will surely try to take me alive to torture the true location of Bel Bessant's terrible creation from me. The first two parts of the god-formula are worthless without the third, so it seems I must follow William of Flamewall's trail into the dark heart of Jago, towards the Cade Mountains and beyond. I wonder if he ever found the corpses of Bel Bessant's original expedition at Amajanur? I wonder if I will find William of Flamewall's own body frozen out there? But most of all, I wonder if I will find the third part of Bel Bessant's horrific legacy – and what I shall do with it when I do?

They say it is cold beyond the capital's walls, far beyond the shoreline of the Fire Sea and the steam storms, but it is as nothing compared to the coldness inside my heart for those that have murdered George. If I can find the god-formula, they will have reason to fear my fury and regret having threatened my family. They *all* will.

Hannah found her hand was trembling as she got to the end of the entry; tears dripping against the rough transaction-engine tape it had been printed out on.

'She's alive!' And the converse was also true. Hannah's father was truly dead. But her mother hadn't been on the u-boat when it was crushed by the shifting walls of magma – scuttled by Maggs, who was no doubt paid to do the terrible deed by Vardan Flail.

'Your mother *was* alive,' cautioned Jethro. 'A decade ago. That is the only hope you can trust.'

'What was the expedition at Amajanur she mentioned?' asked Hannah.

'Amajanur was spoken of in the Pericurian scripture found in Bel Bessant's possession, dear girl,' said Ambassador Ortin, enthusiastically. 'It sounds exceedingly similar to one of the chapters in my people's scriptures: *The Gateway of Amaja*, the tunnel that Reckin urs Reckin and his wife used to escape his treacherous brother and sister-in-law's city after the war of the heavens.'

'It's a gateway to trouble, lad,' said the commodore. 'That much I know – and you so happy, ambassador, you'd think you'd found a long-lost uncle's will and discovered yourself rich from it.'

'It is indeed a legacy,' said the ambassador. 'But one for all of my people. Proof that our scriptures have a historical basis as well as a religious one will allow the reformers to gain the upper hand in the court once more.'

'The Jagonese have been living on this island for thousands of years,' said Nandi. 'If we can find evidence of a Pericurian settlement on Jago that predates settlement by the race of man, then our history books will have to be completely rewritten.'

'History, dear girl, I will leave to the sweep of time and the pens of archaeologists such as yourself,' said the ambassador. 'But if I can change the present of my nation for the better, then I must seize the chance.'

The commodore shook his head ruefully. 'You want to seize the chance, but I can see that it's poor old Blacky that's going to be asked to do the bleeding for Pericur's bright new future.'

'You're going after my mother!' exclaimed Hannah.

'Ah, lass, it's a pretty pickle,' complained the commodore. 'William of Flamewall goes off exploring after the trail of his murdered lover, your mother follows him, and now we're to be emulating the whole pack of them – when not a blessed soul ever came back to boast of it.'

'I'm coming too,' Hannah blurted. 'My mother's still hiding out there somewhere, I can feel it.'

'Yes, you are,' said Jethro.

Hannah was about to start arguing when she actually processed the words and gawped in amazement at the ex-parson.

'Going will be no less dangerous for you than staying here,' said Jethro. 'Alice wasn't holding onto the two active pieces of the god-formula because she wanted to use them. She was keeping them in case the Inquisition needed to develop a counter-weapon against anyone who actually tried to use the code to attain godhood. She was murdered to stop her doing that, and her killer came after you on the mere chance that you had seen what was inside your locket. There is a ruthlessness and coldness to these acts that is rare to see, even by such as Boxiron and myself with the cases that we have worked on. That peril still holds true. In fact, it now holds true for *all* of us. Each of us is in terrible danger every day that we stay here.'

There was something in Jethro Daunt's voice that unsettled Hannah. 'You're not coming with us, are you?'

Jethro shook his head. 'There's something about sitting the church's exams – you're already thinking in the manner of a Circlist priest, Hannah. You are correct. I must stay here in the capital with Boxiron. I was sent to Jago to uncover Alice's murderer, and that is what I intend to do. We have a great advantage over her killer, or killers, now. We know that William of Flamewall and your mother both travelled into the island's interior. They don't. Alice's murderer is still here in the capital and this is where I must stay to uncover them.'

Hannah was surprised to find the ex-parson was right – insights did seem to be forming more quickly ever since she'd sat the cathedral's exams. It was as if the grease in the Entick helmet had lubricated the cogs of her mind; her brain running so much faster, with a diamond-sharp clarity. Hannah stopped Jethro Daunt wasn't saying everything. He — *he didn't trust himself with the god-formula*.

Jethro fixed her with his sad eyes. 'If you find the third piece of the god-formula, you must destroy it. We are all weak, Hannah. A dead child or a sick wife, which of us wouldn't be tempted to change such a misfortune? You'd just bring them back and then instantly relinquish your power, that's what you'd tell yourself. Do that one small thing and then you could go back to the way things were before. Except—'

Hannah thought she understood. 'Until the first time you saw a hungry urchin in the Lugus Vaults, until you saw an act of cruelty you knew you could stop, a war you could halt, a leader elected to the senate you didn't agree with.'

'There would be no end to it,' agreed Jethro. 'Everything fixed to your will, more and more to be rectified, growing angrier and angrier with those that defied you. Until you started acting as a real god, and then you wouldn't be able to stop, not without abandoning your absolute grip on your perfect, burning world. The first two parts of the god-formula will have to be enough for us to preserve in case the Inquisition ever needs to develop a counter-weapon. The third part must be destroyed forever.'

Hannah nodded. It had taken both her parents from her, Alice too. The god-formula deserved to be destroyed. Unless, whispered a nagging voice from somewhere deep within her, she could use it. Use it to bring Alice back, to right all that was wrong with Jago.

'Alice's killer,' said Hannah, 'they want to be become more than just human. They would use the god-formula to gain ultimate knowledge and ultimate power.'

'*Just* human,' sighed Jethro. 'And they would be wrong. Infinitely folded in on themselves and out into the universe, the ultimate paradox given living expression. But lacking the wisdom of an infinite lifetime. *Just* human with ultimate knowledge. What an angel of fire that would be, and what a hell they would make of Earth if they chose to stay here.'

'But a truly good person might be able to control it?' asked Hannah, hopefully. 'Couldn't they change things for the better?'

Jethro smiled grimly. 'It's a temptation, isn't it? Thousands of years ago, Bel Bessant thought she was pure enough to survive it and still be human enough to end the dark reign of terror the Chimecan Empire and their bloodthirsty gods were threatening Jago with. Thank the Circle she had a man who loved her enough to kill her. I doubt that the person who killed Alice has such a love in their life. No, the third part of the weapon must be destroyed, never used. The Inquisition was always sure to appoint its officers to the archbishop's seat on Jago, Hannah, but I suspect that they never knew the full details of the secret. Only that a terrible weapon existed here and that their incomplete portion of it had to be kept hidden by their brightest and their best. Alice was such a woman. The secret would have been passed from archbishop to archbishop, limiting the temptation of taking the godhead to a bare minimum. We know Alice's killer is seeking the god-formula and so now it must be extinguished forever. Do this for the church you're about to be sworn into, Hannah, and do it for me.'

And she would do it for her father. Her *dead* father.

It was going to be strange to be in one of the giant iron walking machines with the open sky above her head, rather than the roof of the turbine halls, Hannah mused. The trapper Tobias Raffold and his men moved with the same easy confidence in their RAM suits that the charge-master's staff had shown in theirs. The expedition was lucky to have secured Raffold's services, thanks to the significant financial backing of Ambassador Ortin and some truly magnificent humble-pie eating on the part of Commodore Black – the old u-boat captain muttering under his breath about the fact that his precious boat would be hauling animals across the seas for Raffold for the next decade to satisfy the trapper's bargain.

Including herself, Nandi, the commodore and Ortin urs Ortin, there would be twenty members of the expedition to find the final resting places of her mother and William of

Flamewall. Most of those men were lounging around behind the safety of Hermetica City's main gates, rolling dice on the rocky ground while their RAM suits received their final checks from the city's lodge of mechomancers. Bales of supplies and crates of victuals were being winched up and belted around the hulls of their machines by a crowd of merchants.

The iron plating of the RAM suits had been painted with a geometric patchwork of purple, white and grey mottling to blend in with the territory outside. And if their camouflage failed its purpose, the right arm of each suit would be brought to bear – mounted with a magnetic catapult and circular ammunition drums of sharpened disks. There were other subtle differences between these suits and the ones used down in the turbine halls. The domes that covered the pilot's heads contained more glass for better visibility in the mist-shrouded wilds, but the suits had less armour plating since they were not being exposed to the electric fields that dominated life in the turbine halls. And these suits were bigger and taller, the better to cover rough terrain quickly.

Chalph urs Chalph emerged from the gatehouse and Hannah waved to attract his attention as he glanced up at the Pericurian mercenaries patrolling the battlements above.

'I'm glad to see you managed to get here in the end,' Hannah called.

'One last chance to try to convince you not to go,' said Chalph. 'You've got everything you wanted – entry into the church, a chance to be free. Why do you need to go on this fool expedition?'

'You know why,' said Hannah. 'My mother's out there.'

Chalph shook his large furred head in irritation. 'She didn't come back. Just like your ancient phantom, William of Flamewall. Neither of them ever returned.'

'I will,' Hannah promised. 'You'll see.'

'I might not be around to see.'

'What do you mean?' Hannah demanded.

Chalph's lips cracked into a ferocious smile, flashing his ursine fangs. 'The house's boat from Pericur has just docked and I got the news straight from its first officer. They've couriered the baroness an order from the archduchess herself. Our house's trading licence for Jago has been cancelled. We're going home, Hannah Conquest! A few weeks to settle our commercial affairs and the next boat that comes here will be to take us all off.'

So much change, so quickly. The happiness that Hannah felt for her friend was tempered by the knowledge that things would never be the same for him – or her – again.

'Then you've got what you wanted, too.'

'Don't look so glum,' said Chalph. 'Even the archduchess and her new conservative-packed council can't deny the House of Ush a new trading licence *somewhere*. Most of our people here speak your furless tongue better than we do our own. We'll end up with the trading caravans down south doing business overland with the settlers in Concorzia. You could find yourself a parsonage down that way after your training. . .'

Leave Jago? Well, it wouldn't be the same without Chalph or Alice, with herself in the seminary of the rational orders. And when all the visitors like Jethro, Nandi and the commodore had gone home, what would be left? Dour old Father Blackwater and the resentment of every member of the Guild of Valvemen she happened across? Perhaps a new start had its attractions after all. And there wasn't much of a seminary programme on Jago any more. She might well find herself assigned to a cathedral in the Kingdom of Jackals, or to one of the fledgling orders in Concorzia, whether she wanted to stay on Jago or not.

'I still have to go out there,' said Hannah. 'I have to know!'

Chalph didn't look as if he understood, but then ursines had large litters and only female cubs were truly prized by the mother – the father was uninvolved beyond his initial contribution. It was the house that mattered in Pericurian society, not the parents.

'I don't want to leave this damn island without knowing whether you're even dead or alive,' said Chalph.

'But you'll leave anyway,' said Hannah. 'You won't have any choice and soon enough you won't have much to complain about. Not the smell of the canals or the taste of dome-grown food or being called a dirty wet-snout by the Jagonese.'

'That'll be a thing to see,' agreed Chalph. 'Real forests, with a real sky above filled with stars you can actually glimpse at night. Cities raised from Pericurian oak and streets teeming with hundreds of thousands of ursine. And you could see them too. . .'

'I will, one day.'

Just then, the man engaged to make sure she lived long enough to keep that promise stepped out of the gatehouse behind Chalph. Tobias Raffold's bulldog face was set in its habitual frown as he strode up to Ortin urs Ortin and the commodore.

'We can't wait for the last of the supplies,' said the trapper. 'We have to bleeding leave now.'

'I'm sure the expedition's letters of credit are good for the required provisions, dear boy,' said Ortin urs Ortin, tipping out his monocle to clean it.

'You just worry about *my* bleeding payment,' warned the trapper. 'First Senator Silvermain is trying to get my hunting concession revoked, but he needs a sitting of the senate to do it. He's putting one together as we speak.'

'We're not just paying you for your skills, lad,' said the

commodore. 'It's your connections we need. I thought you and the lord of this dark place were meant to be firm shipmates.'

'He's heard about your expedition and the paranoid old bugger thinks that it's a foreign plot to scout out where his new cities are going to be built, a conspiracy between Jackals and Pericur to nip his plans in the bud, the rest of the world being jealous of the island's greatness'n all. I don't think he wants me to lead you outside the city.'

'I say,' coughed the ambassador, 'you're not convinced by that lunacy, I trust?'

'It don't matter to me, matey. It's lunacy to go as deep into the island's interior as you're set on, and frankly, I don't give a tinker's cuss if you're going out there to toss bombs down into his empty city caverns or you're looking to find the lost tomb of some bleeding heathen Pericurian deity. You're paying me enough to be able to get off Jago and never worry about coming back again. I was in Quatérshift before the revolution, working in the forests for their king, and that country had the same bad stink in the air as this, right before the nobles started getting tossed into the mincer.'

'Old Blacky can see that you're nobody's fool, Tobias Raffold. You can smell the way the wind's turning out here. Once this little jaunt's done, I'll only too happy to cast off from Jago with you and never set foot on these black shores again.'

A flurry of activity followed the trapper's warning, the mechomancers making final checks to the suits being shooed away lest the expedition fold before it had even departed. Chalph helped Hannah raise her supplies up to the loading platform behind her RAM suit, pulleys squealing as sacks flew upwards. Hannah slipped the harness belts over her suit as though she had been born a trapper.

Hannah thought they had beaten the senate leader's mad whim to cancel their journey when the captain of the Pericurian mercenaries, Stom urs Stom, came jogging out of the gatehouse towards them, a line of her soldiers following, each ursine weighed down by a turret gun, with its massive ammunition drum and brass tank of compressed air.

'There's no bleeding way there's been a full and legal sitting of the senate yet!' the trapper growled at Stom urs Stom.

'There has not,' said the captain, 'but you would be well advised to consider who your master is on Jago.'

'The difference between you and me, matey, is that I get to hunt for more than one person.'

'First Senator Silvermain considers the contract between you and he to be of an exclusive nature.'

'He can consider what he likes,' spat the trapper, placing himself squarely between the officer and her massive troops. 'I've brought in abs for him and for the guild and for anyone else with the coin to pay me. Now, unless you're carrying a legal revocation of my fully paid-up hunting concession, you can sod off back to guarding the ramparts.'

'He's got balls,' hissed Chalph to Hannah. 'I've never seen a Pericurian talk to her like that, let alone one of your people.'

Hannah shushed him – she wanted to hear this. They crept closer, near enough to see the shine on the massive Pericurian's black leather armour. The outcome of this standoff might decide whether Hannah would find her mother or not.

Ambassador Ortin came over to attempt to mediate. 'Now see here, Stom urs Stom, you know there's as much chance that I'm going venturing into the wild to drop grenades down some empty cavern the First Senator thinks will be his new city, as there is of the archduchess selecting me to be one of her new husbands.'

'What I believe is not of relevance here, ambassador,' said

Stom. She produced a wax-sealed envelope addressed to Ortin urs Ortin. 'You will acknowledge receipt of your express instructions from the First Senator. If you venture anywhere near the plains you and your staff will be immediately expelled from Jago, and the stained senate will request a new diplomatic mission be dispatched to the capital from Pericur.'

'Please assure your master I am ever his servant,' said Ortin. 'I have no intention of leaving the island in disgrace. We won't be heading anywhere close to the plains or the coast – quite the opposite, in fact. We are heading deep into the interior on a purely archaeological mission.'

Stom glanced doubtfully at the archaeologist, Nandi standing alongside her RAM suit. 'If that is the case, ambassador, then I would say that your mission has a very slim chance of returning.'

Her warning delivered, the captain and her troops turned and left, the slow stamping of their march echoing around the gate yard. Hannah realized she had been holding her breath. She was going after her mother after all, as long as they could depart in the next few minutes while Tobias Raffold still had his papers to operate on Jago.

'There was something strange about that,' said Chalph.

Hannah glanced across and mistook her friend's narrowed eyes for worry over her own chances of coming back. 'She was just trying to intimidate us into not leaving.'

'No, it was the letter, I think—' Chalph shook his head 'I'm tired. I've been up since dawn checking the boat's manifest. But it's the last trading boat I'm ever going to have to wake up for on Jago.'

Hannah hugged her friend, his fur soft and silken against the skin of her arms. 'I hope that Pericur is everything you thought it would be.'

'You just stay alive,' chided Chalph. 'Stay away from Vardan

Flail and his people. What is it that your godless priests say to each other in your cathedral?'

'May serenity find you,' mouthed Hannah, her eyes moistening.

Yes. And it would only find her when she knew what had really happened to her mother, somewhere out there. In the cold dark heart of Jago.

CHAPTER FOURTEEN

Perhaps naively, Hannah had assumed that climbing the capital's air vents with Chalph to watch the u-boats from Jago's black cliffs had made her into something of an expert on conditions above ground. Her first few days in the company of the trapper Tobias Raffold soon expunged any superiority she'd felt over the vast majority of Jagonese who were only too glad never to leave the regulated comfort of their vaults.

As the expedition pushed towards the interior, they left behind the heat of the Fire Sea, and Hannah came to realize that it was no accident that almost all of Jago's cities had been cast like a necklace around the coastline, attracted to the warmth of the magma. Or how much of the tinted light on the surface came from the vast undulating currents of molten rock, painting the Horn of Jago crimson even when the steam storms had obliterated the milky sun behind the clouds.

Ironically, the worst of the danger seemed to have been awaiting the expedition immediately beyond the battlements – where hordes of animals appeared drawn to the wall's electric field like moths to a lantern's flame. The trappers had exited the city with their magnetic catapult arms pointed upwards, and a few chattering bursts of razor-edged disks into the air had quickly marked their rights to the territory, sending the creatures lurking in the mists scampering back towards the dark, stunted pine forests. The beasts were intelligent enough to know the difference between Jagonese in RAM suits and the exiles that were thrown out on foot.

The expedition followed the iron girders of the great eastern aqueduct through the forests and up into the low foothills. Bright yellow lights embedded behind protective metal mesh lined the aqueduct's high ridges, making it easy to follow despite the murkiness of the daylight.

One of the controls inside Hannah's suit was a set of temperature adjusters and she became engaged in a continual battle to keep the heater at its optimum level. Too cold and she would feel the tips of her toes growing numb from frostbite; too warm, and the transparent dome on top of the suit would mist up with condensation. The trappers leading them had either cracked the balance through long experience out here, or they were men of iron, impervious to the chill. Hannah could tell from the clear crystal on top which of the RAM suits held a trapper and which – misted up like her own – held Nandi, the commodore and the Pericurian ambassador.

Halfway along the aqueduct they had come across the rusting shell of an abandoned RAM suit – a more primitive model, larger and less streamlined than theirs – possibly hundreds of years old. Tobias Raffold had pointed to the top of the aqueduct and explained how ursks would climb the structure, block the water's flow, and then wait for a group of maintenance workers to come out from the city before trying to smash their viewing domes with rocks. In this case they had obviously succeeded, cracking the suit like an egg.

The aqueduct maintenance workers still passed down the tales – an object lesson in never underestimating the animal cunning of the creatures of the interior. The trapper didn't say what had happened to the unlucky city worker and Hannah was content not to know the person's grisly fate – remembering the hot, foetid breath of the ursk that had broken into Tom Putt Park, she could imagine well enough.

Shortly after the expedition had reached the wolds, the aqueduct ended in a large sealed concrete pumping station and Hannah felt a twinge of unease that they were leaving behind the last visible sign of the race of man's presence on the island. It was only an ugly iron construction, but she had become used to the aqueduct's yellow lights leading the way through the mists. Now it really did feel as if they were entering the unknown. Had her mother followed the same route all those years ago? Had she felt the same twinge of fear when she looked back and saw that last yellow dot of civilization dwindling to nothing?

Hannah's mother would have been travelling out this way when Alice Gray had been trying to explain to a young child how her parents had moved along the Circle and wouldn't be coming back to collect her. How the church would be her family now. It can't have been an easy thing for the archbishop to have done, Hannah realized, and she still remembered her guileless response. One that only a child could make. That it was all right. If Hannah were taken to see her parent's bodies she would kiss them on the forehead and they would come alive again, just like in the stories that her mother had read her. A *kiss to bring them back to life*. But the Fire Sea didn't leave bodies in the water, only ashes. And nor did Vardan Flail's schemes. Well, Hannah had cheated him of a life of servitude within the guild, and if she could follow her mother's trail in the footsteps of William of Flamewall, she would cheat

Vardan Flail out of getting his filthy hands on the last piece of the god-formula, too.

After they made camp in the foothills, Hannah saw why Tobias Raffold had been so particular about the location of their site – and discovered the purpose of the large steel components that two of the trappers had been lugging distributed across their suits, a heavy load even with a RAM suit's amplified strength. The parts were assembled into a circular frame holding a turbine vane, pieced together over a steam blowhole that had been previously marked by the trappers with a fluttering pennant. After heavy rubber cables had been attached to the device, the ends of the leads were plugged into their RAM suits' chemical batteries. With the portable turbine whining as the steam hole drove it into action, a stench of bad eggs began to circulate within the confines of Hannah's suit. Circling the disk-capped blowhole, connected by the cables, the twenty suits would have seemed to observers like some strange variety of iron flower, a night orchid emitting a bizarre stench as they recharged their batteries.

The increased size of the trappers' RAM suits wasn't just to accommodate the larger batteries needed to cover great distances – it had other uses, too, such as allowing the pilot frame to rotate back into a sleeping position, the lightly cushioned spine making a serviceable, if not particularly comfortable, bed. Hannah was selfishly glad that the number of trappers the expedition had engaged was large enough that she wouldn't be required to stand a turn on sentry duty – not that the hard, taciturn trappers were likely to have trusted her even if she had offered. They stood duty two at a time, the sensing mechanisms in their suits set to violently judder the pilot cage if they detected a lack of movement consistent with sleep.

After a hard day pushing the suit forward over endless

miles of terrain – harder even than duty in the turbine halls – sleep was really not a problem. It swallowed Hannah up, rising out of the suit like a spinning vortex and cutting off the smell of sweat, oil and recharging battery packs.

In the days that followed, most of the places where they made camp were the same: low rocky wolds with enough of a view of the surrounding landscape for them to ensure that stalking ursks weren't trying to crawl up on the resting RAM suits – although when the mist filled the low valleys, it was as if they were sitting on an island surrounded by smoking white rivers. And who knew what nightmares were swimming through their depths?

There was one site that got Nandi excited, a hill where the blowhole they were using to tap the steam lay in a dip and the crest of the hill was a rock formation that resembled a cup melted along one side. The archaeologist swore that there were tell-tale signs the rock had once been the foundations of a building and pointed down into the valley to indicate contours which she said were further indications that there had once been constructions on the surface.

'I'm not so sure, lass,' said the commodore, his RAM suit turned to face the ridges on the hill opposite. 'There's no bricks or mortar on this slab of rock – it looks as blasted and natural as the black cliffs on the coast to me – and those ridges could be where the storms have carved the soil away from the top of the hill.'

'That's because you don't know what to look for,' insisted the archaeologist.

'Well, I've spent more of my life sandwiched between the hull of a boat than I have between the shelves of the library at St Vines College and I'm no doubt the worse for it,' said the commodore, 'but old Blacky's seen the sunken streets of the city of Lost Angels on the seabed, and scoured by the tides though the ruins were, they still had the look of streets to his tired old eyes.' He called across to Ortin urs Ortin's RAM suit– their domes retracted as they took in the fresh cold air. 'What say you, ambassador?'

'I say it may be,' said Ortin urs Ortin. 'The deeper we push into the island the more I see echoes from the scripture of the Divine Quad. The blasted plains of paradise and the crumbled cities that our people once inhabited.'

'As I understand Pericurian scripture,' said Hannah, 'the race of man shouldn't be here at all.'

The ambassador smiled. 'I see that the Circlist church has indoctrinated you well in its efforts to deny our gods, dear girl.' He quoted from the relevant passage. '"And the paradise that had fallen shall be forever more sealed in a sea of punishing fire, denied to all that would seek it. In sin was the land destroyed and only the wicked shall suffer its cursed acres." As we push deeper into Jago, a joke that is told in the court of the archduchess comes to mind. That inside every liberal's fur there are little conservative fleas waiting to climb out. The deeper we drive into this land, the closer this trip seems to blasphemy to me.'

'Blasphemy is a good start,' said Hannah, quoting one of Alice's favourite sayings.

'Perhaps to your peculiar church without gods, dear girl,' said the ambassador. 'But I would not tempt the wrath of Reckin urs Reckin so readily.'

'Ah, we're all tempting fate by being here,' moaned the commodore. 'You would think the world had had enough of throwing poor old Blacky into peril, but no, it understands that by tricking me into promising I'll keep young Nandi Tibar-Wellking safe it can have me off chasing through Jago's dark wastes after some long-lost invention of the church, when all that I deserve is the chance to spend my last few miserable years gently revisiting the ports of my youth in my precious boat, hauling an honest cargo or two to help put a little beer in my flagon and a cut of roast beef on my table. This dark chase, this is my punishment.'

'Punishment for what?' asked Hannah.

'For supporting the ambassador's liberal friends on the other side of the Fire Sea,' whined Commodore Black. 'Running cargoes of Porterbrook steam engines and enough transaction engines to allow their great houses to count every tree in their forests twice over.'

'Helping Pericur drag itself into the modern age hardly counts as a sin deserving punishment, dear boy,' said the ambassador.

'So you say now. But let's see if you can look me in the eye and say as much in a generation or so – when you'll have petty rules and large taxes set by small minds with nothing but malice for what once made you great and unique. When your forests are felled and you're choking on the likes of a Middlesteel smog, when you've created a legion of jealous little shopkeepers who'll drag your archduchess to a scaffold rogues who'll cut off the grand old lady's arms in case she shakes a fist at them and styles their stealing and scheming for what it really is.'

'That is not Pericur,' protested the ambassador.

'It wasn't the Kingdom of Jackals either, once,' said the commodore. 'But my great grandfather saw it happen there just as I watched the revolution in Quatérshift let fly across the Jackelian border. That's the way of a revolution; it's like the blessed circle of existence our church keeps banging on about, always turning round and round. It'll turn for your people too, and crush a mortal few of your nation under its rim I have no doubt.'

The four friends fell to silence until Tobias Raffold called from behind that the portable steam tap was ready to begin charging, ordering them to seal their suits and drop their shield hoods.

The trouble started shortly after they left the ridged valley the next morning. Tobias Raffold's men opened a cage built into the back of one of the RAM suits and started unloading crates of unfamiliar-looking equipment.

'Mister Raffold,' called Ortin urs Ortin. 'That's not what I think it is?'

Raffold's RAM suit turned to face the Pericurian ambassador. 'If you're thinking it's an ab-lock snare, then you're bang on.'

'I say, old fruit, this is hardly what my fee for this expedition was intended to cover.'

The trapper jerked his head towards the commodore. 'Your fee and the sea-dog's u-boat are my ticket home, but I still owe the guild's stable-master one last catch of abs. They're bleeding sticky about contracts here, and I don't want the First Senator using the breech of one as an excuse to stick me and my crew in his dungeons when we get back. He's going to be narked enough at me and my lads when we get back for taking you outside the wall.'

'We still have a long way to go to reach the Cade Mountains,' complained Ortin urs Ortin.

'That's unknown territory,' said the trapper. 'These wolds I know, and they're prime ab-taking land.'

Hannah sighed to herself. It seemed the expedition wasn't going to be making as much headway this day as she'd hoped. Ortin urs Ortin appeared content to use the unlooked-for spare time to read the scriptures of the Divine Quad he had stored in his suit's pilot cabin, finding echoes of his people's ancient writings in the landscape all around them; while Nandi seemed happy to do much the same with the research Hannah's parents had gleaned from the guild archives.

With nothing else to do, Hannah watched the trappers move out to set their snares. They used mats of rubber with surfaces that had been shaped and painted to mimic the coarse green alpine grass that grew in the soil between the ugly basalt rocks of the wolds. Onto this the trappers placed bricks of bone-white sugar, before connecting the rubber mats to a battery pack that they would then bury. More than enough power to shock an ab-lock cub into unconsciousness when the damp wind carried the smell of the sugar to them and sent them scurrying to locate its source. Sugar was something it appeared the creatures loved to gnaw away at. And whereas adult ab-locks were canny enough to recognize the rubber traps and remove the sugar with branches torn from nearby pine trees, their cubs had no such experience and would happily blunder onto the shock mats, triggering both the stunning charge and a whistle to announce a capture – of which there were quite a few. Tobias Raffold chuckled as his trappers piled the insensible ab-lock cubs in front of a man using a branding iron to stamp a guild mark and number on their backs, before moving the young abs into the cage.

Hannah tried to imagine the confused cubs waking up in the charge-master's turbine halls, to be mercilessly drilled in the care and maintenance of the massive power plant's machinery until one day – if they lived long enough – they might end up like T-face: broken, obedient and grateful for any day that didn't end in a flogging. Hannah's brooding on the ab-locks' fate was broken by one of the distant snare's whistles combined with something she hadn't heard before – a shrieking like a wounded cat.

'That's not an ab-lock!' Hannah called.

'Too bleeding right it's not,' Tobias Raffold shouted back from the crest of the hill. He snapped shut his suit's skull dome and pulled down an amplification plate, peering in the direction of the caterwauling. 'It's a bloody ursk cub – the little runt's got one of its paws stuck through the mat and the charge is driving it wild. None of our snares are set for a catch of its bulk.'

'You said we would be avoiding ursk territory,' said Hannah accusingly.

'What is and isn't their territory is settled between the ursks and the abs by tooth and claw, girl,' spat the trapper. 'It's been a dry season, the ursks must be pushing up from the southern plains towards the lakes.' The trapper raised his RAM suit's right arm and the cantilevered steel of his magnetic catapult extended out to full rifle length. There was a clang on his arm's drum as a razored disk was fed into the breech, followed by the evil twang of a projectile cutting through the air. Tobias Raffold's aim was true, for the terrified screeching in the distance halted instantly. But it was too late; echoing from around the hills came an eerie throaty song that Hannah recognized only too well from the hordes of creatures drawn to the killing field of Hermetica's battlements. Ursk song.

Tobias Raffold was screaming for his crew to come back from the snares and form a circle around the steam tap. One of his trappers came stamping past Hannah and clanged his left arm's manipulator hand against her suit, manually activating her magnetic catapult. Fixed on the end of a rod, an iron circle with a crosshair in its centre snapped down in front of Hannah's face, floating above the exterior of her skull dome in synchronization with her catapult arm's movement. A mechanical sight for the catapult! Something resembling a copper clock face extended out of the suit's control panel, a single hand pointing upwards on a dial of sharpened disk icons. A full drum of killing disks, for the moment.

'Ah, this is wicked bad,' came the commodore's words inside Hannah's pilot frame. 'All this way for my brave bones to end up being gnawed by a pack of oversized bears. This is where staying true to an oath's course has landed poor old Blacky.'

'Ursks know the weak spots of our RAM suits.' Tobias Raffold's warning cut in. 'They'll run in low and try to go for the rubberized seals around our legs. If they claw your seals open they can bite through the hydraulics and bring your suit down to the ground. They'll skirt the mists, circling to start with to try and make us waste our ammunition. Ambassador, you and your people save your fire until they're coming over the rise here and are bearing straight for you.'

'Their wicked teeth can't bite through this crystal noggin of mine, can they?' asked the commodore.

'They're right good at waiting around a downed suit,' warned the trapper. 'They'll wait until your water runs out and you're desperate enough to pop your lid and make a bolt for the nearest spring.'

'The ursks outside the battlements ran away when you shot in the air,' said Hannah.

'The ursks around the battlements know what those artillery emplacements around the Horn of Jago are good for. This far out, we're all just canned food as far as an ursk pack is concerned.'

But it wasn't a pack. Hannah saw the long wave of howling black crest the line of hills in front of them, throwing themselves down into the mists flowing along the valley. Not a pack. A migration!

Hannah's fingers were trembling as they closed around the trigger of the catapult inside her suit's weapon arm. Her skill was mathematics, not gunnery, and she realized immediately that the expedition didn't have nearly enough razored disks to deal with such vast numbers. Hannah's ammunition drum would be empty long before the exodus heading directly for her suit abated.

CHAPTER FIFTEEN

Father Baine looked up as he heard footsteps coming down the corridor to the chancery office. The cathedral's architects had built the passage to specification, he suspected. Nobody could ever sneak up on the archbishop's office while it was occupied. Not that the owner of the approaching footsteps would find much if subterfuge was their intent. Only the unappreciated clerk working into the early evening to clear the backlog of paperwork that came from trying to run a cathedral without a sitting archbishop to oversee the dioceses' official bureaucracy.

There was a knock and the door opened to admit one of the novices who was meant to be standing duty on the cathedral's main bridge.

'Father,' said the novice, 'the ursine Chalph urs Chalph is outside asking for you.'

Father Baine looked up at the carriage clock at the edge of his desk, just visible behind a pile of profiles of those who had recently passed the church's entrance exams, each mind as unique as the whorls of skin on their fingertips.

'He said it was urgent,' noted the novice, 'and relating to a private matter between the two of you.'

Father Baine cleared his throat and made to stand. 'Ha. So.'

'He is a believer,' said the novice, as if this revelation wouldn't have occurred to Father Baine at some point.

'We all believe in something,' sighed the father. 'Even if it's something slightly more sensible than the Divine Quad. Such as what is right and rational.'

Chalph was waiting at the edge of the Grand Canal. Father Baine left the novice at the midpoint of the main bridge and crossed to where the ursine was loitering – in some agitation, if he interpreted the creature's body language correctly.

'Father Baine,' called Chalph, 'is Jethro Daunt with you?'

'He was – but he left. He spent a good few hours poring over the records of the draft ballots in my office, although why he should bother escapes me. Even if Hannah's induction into the Guild of Valvemen was crooked, she is marked for the rational orders now.'

'I have to see him immediately,' demanded Chalph. 'Where did he go?'

'I think he went to see if his steamman friend was still working in the public records office, though much good will it do them. Everything filed with the office as paper documents is first released by and filtered through the guild's transaction engines. Vardan Flail is too canny to allow details of his feud with the archbishop to be openly catalogued. Is this urgency related to Alice Gray's death?'

'No,' growled Chalph. 'It's far worse than that. I have to see him. Tell him I've been doing my own investigating and what I've found – it's unbelievable!'

He was turning to jog away.

'Can I help?' Father Baine called after him.

'Only if you've started to work for your people's Inquisition,' Chalph shouted back. 'I don't even know if Jethro Daunt and his metal friend can do anything about this.'

'Is there no more that I can tell him?'

'Tell him it's about a letter that was given to the expedition.'

Father Baine watched the young ursine run off, wondering if the foreign trader was entirely in possession of his senses.

Jethro was walking alongside Boxiron across one of the waterways close to the Grand Canal, ignoring the hopeful cries of the street vendors, when the pair ran into a force they couldn't so readily ignore. Stom urs Stom, the commander of the mercenaries, flanked by four of her fighters.

'They look as if they mean business,' whispered Boxiron.

'None that is good for us, I fear, old steamer,' said Jethro.

Stom urs Stom raised a large paw to stop them, close enough to Jethro's face that he could smell the well-worn leather of her Pericurian war jacket. It would have been a mildly pleasant smell under other circumstances.

'No need to go any further, Jackelian.'

'Good captain,' said Jethro. 'I presume your employer is interested in another update on our progress?'

'Not this time,' said the hulking ursine. Two of her mercenary fighters stepped forward, seizing Jethro while the other two levelled their massive weapons at Boxiron, the copper segments of the gas pipes on their turret guns jangling as loudly as the steamman's limbs jerking in surprise. Boxiron scanned the soldiers intently, looking for any break in their concentration.

'Do not attempt to interfere,' the mercenary officer warned Boxiron. 'You may possess the strength of the life metal, but the steel pitons in our rifles will drive through your body as easily as they would man-flesh.'

'What is the meaning of this?' demanded Jethro.

'Your letter of credit was found lodged with a merchant in support of the outfitting of a recent expedition which left the capital. One led by the Jackelian trapper Tobias Raffold and crewed by various Jackelians who arrived with you here.'

'Yes,' said Jethro resignedly, adding, 'what of it?'

'Your letter of credit has the backing of your church, and more specifically, the militant order known as the Circlist League of the Rational Court.'

Jethro groaned to himself. He was a fool. Of course someone with the First Senator's resources could trace the origin of Jethro's funds within the capital's banking system.

'The recent expedition is on a mission of sabotage, one which the First Senator has discovered is acting as a tool of foreign interests.'

'This is ludicrous,' spluttered Jethro. 'You have my word that my friends have embarked on an archaeological expedition, no more. You cannot believe these accusations. . .'

'What I believe is not at issue,' said the mercenary commander. 'The First Senator has requested that I sever both your arms as a statement of his disappointment and displeasure at your betrayal of his trust.'

Jethro struggled in the grip of the two soldiers while the other two jabbed Boxiron back with their turret rifles' barrels.

'Where is the process of law in this?' demanded Boxiron.

'The First Senator is invoking the ancient law of extra-territorial reciprocity,' said the mercenary commander. 'In this case, the Jackelian law where the ruling monarch has their arms incapacitated to stop them being raised against the people.'

Jethro groaned in agony. The massive paws were pinning his arms in place, as tight as iron bands. Extra-territorial reciprocity was intended to automatically trigger corresponding trade duties when a foreign power slapped extra tariffs on a category of goods, but the mad ruler of Jago had obviously found a loophole to stretch a particularly nasty Jackelian tradition to him.

A curious crowd had gathered on the canal-side street. There would be no shortage of witnesses to the First Senator's savage revenge – even if it wasn't going to be quite up to the standards of the baying mob that assembled in Parliament Square to see the surgeon royal remove the new Jackelian monarch's arms.

'I demand to see an official from my embassy.'

'My apologies, Jackelian,' said Stom. 'This is not personal. You may crawl up to the embassy circle after we have fulfilled our liege-lord's orders.'

The two mercenaries on either side of Jethro shoved him down onto the cobbles and Stom drew out her short sword from the scabbard strapped to her leg. She raised it high. It looked every bit as sharp as the First Senator's wrath.

Drifting clouds of steam distorted the terrifying howls of the ursks circling around the expedition, as though a siren tied to a cable was being spun around their camp on the hilltop. Tobias Raffold's trappers held their nerves and their fire, not expending ammunition into the white sea that surrounded them, waiting until the ursks exploded roaring from the mist, launching themselves at the camp from multiple directions.

Then the noise was unbelievable – the shouts of the trappers intermingled with Raffold's barked orders through the speakers in Hannah's suit as magnetic catapults exploded into action all around her. Hannah held her fire as she had been ordered, but tried to direct her target sight onto the ursks breaking out of the mist. There were fractional seconds when the crosshairs coincided with the position of one of the massive black shapes leaping towards their camp – but they were more accidental than intentional, despite her best efforts. Short of holding down the trigger and keeping it depressed until the ammunition drum on her arm was depleted, Hannah wasn't going to hit a thing with her magnetic catapult.

The wolds opposite their camp ran dark with loping ursks diving down into the mist of the surrounding valley. Again and again they came at the camp, heedless of the whining arcs of flying steel cutting them down and sending them flying back into the mists. The expedition's defiance just seemed to enrage the ursks more, as if they expected the trappers simply to lie down and let the horde overwhelm them.

Hannah heard the warning yell over her speakers just as a dark shape covered her skull dome. The ursks must have found a weak spot in the circled RAM suits! Hannah could feel the extra weight of the suit's left leg as she swivelled, trying to throw off the beasts clawing at her – and she remembered the head trapper's warning. One of the creatures was trying to gnaw through the rubber seal of her knee joins, trying to bring her suit crashing down onto the rocks.

Someone else's suit came lumbering past Hannah, a leg lashing out and briefly clanging off hers. The ursk on her leg was sent flying and then the dark mass clambering over her head unit was picked off and tossed flailing into the mist of the valley. Hannah saw the pilot in the RAM suit that had rescued her. It was Ortin urs Ortin. She mumbled shocked thanks into the voicebox on her pilot frame, but the sound was lost in the roar of stone chips flying up and ricocheting off both their suits' armour. More ursks had broken through and the trappers were firing their magnetic catapults down towards them. Hannah joined in the shooting in a mixture of panic and revulsion; as though madly brushing off insects crawling up her legs. Was she hitting anything? It was impossible to tell, but there was shrieking as her razored disks found targets among the river of maddened fur flowing around her legs.

Tobias Raffold shouted a command to cease fire and a relative silence fell, leaving only the muted growls and whines of dying ursks and the crackle of recharging catapult arms. Ursks were still circling them down in the mist-covered valley, but their attempt to overrun the camp had failed. Hannah looked over at the distant wolds and saw more and more ursks flooding towards them. The next attack couldn't be far away.

'Retreat back to the steam tap, lass,' urged the commodore's voice. 'You too, Nandi.'

'Ammunition count,' ordered Tobias Raffold.

Shouts rang out with the number of disks each suit had left in their ammunition drums. Hannah glanced at her dial – its hand had rotated around to red. She was empty! And she wasn't the only one.

'The ammunition crates are next to the steam tap,' announced Tobias Raffold.

Hannah glanced back to the pile of supply bales and crates that had been slung around the trappers' suits during their march.

'Lowest charge goes down.'

The truth of the situation dawned on Hannah. They were going to have to send someone down there, out of their suit to crack open the crates and load up the drums. The manipulator claws that acted as the RAM suits' hands were fine for lifting heavy loads, but the claws didn't have the flexibility needed to break open the crates and slide the rolls of steel disks into their ammunition drums. There was a cruel logic to the choice of the poor unfortunate who was going to have to slide their canopy open – the RAM suit with the lowest battery charge was least likely to survive being pursued by the ursks.

Their luckless candidate selected – one of the trappers – the other RAM suits formed a tight circle around the crates giving the trapper as little ground to cover as possible.

Then Tobias Raffold shouted a command that Hannah didn't catch, but the cage on the back of one of the RAM suits sprang open and a handful of terrified ab-lock cubs leap for the ground and scattered in all directions. As the mad diversion was released, the selected trapper slid his canopy open and began scrambling down the handholds on his suit's chest, leaping the last few feet towards the supplies below. The tenor of the ursk song rising up through the mist changed, indicating their confusion as the sudden outbreak of ab-locks pelted past them in the valley. There was a truly hideous screeching sound as some of the young ab-locks fell to the claws of their much larger adversaries.

'Hold fire,' Tobias Raffold ordered. 'Let's keep the ursks focused on the bloody abs, not us.'

Once the first of the ammunition crates was cracked open, the RAM suits lowered their catapult arms towards the ground, the trapper on foot striking the top of each drum to spring them open, then frantically pushing rolls of razored disks into the rotation feeders that lay exposed inside. The trapper had reloaded perhaps half of his colleague's catapults when the feint came, three ursks running in from the west side of the hill. The suits' catapult rails roared in answer, spitting spinning steel at the charging beasts. Seconds later, and almost too quickly to follow, another black shape flashed between their legs and the loader vanished without even a cry. Hannah moaned. The ursks' second assault began in earnest.

Hannah raised her empty catapult arm towards the creatures' attack, as if the whine of the magnetic accelerator alone would be enough to stop them.

CHAPTER SIXTEEN

Jethro looked up, near hypnotized by the shining steel short sword about to be brought down on his shoulder by Stom urs Stom. From nowhere a spinning bottle knocked the mercenary's blade aside and yells of anger erupted from the watching Jagonese crowd, breaking Jethro's focus.

'Filthy wet-snouts!'

'We don't need your justice here, we're a civilized people!'

'Go home, you jiggers!'

One of the mercenaries holding Jethro released her grip on him and raised her turret rifle towards the swelling mob, threatening a response to the growing hail of garbage and the insults of the locals. The mercenaries menacing Boxiron with their weapons glanced nervously between the steamman and the rabble surrounding them.

Just as it seemed as if the situation was going to boil completely out of control, Colonel Knipe and a group of police militia stepped out of the crowd, pistols drawn from the belts under their velvet-lined cloaks.

'Do not hinder us,' Stom urs Stom warned the police militia. 'This is the will of the First Senator.'

'I have no doubt it is,' barked the colonel. 'But those that hold to the police oath follow the laws of two millennia of Jagonese civilization, and you can remind Silvermain that the staff of office his senatorial rod carrier bears for him is not yet a dictator's sceptre.'

'Your orders?' the mercenary pinning Jethro down asked Stom. The ex-parson had a painful view of the barrels facing each other to either side of him. Hand-sized police pistols versus the mercenaries' massive turret rifles. He knew who would come off worse if matters escalated on the street. Jethro and Boxiron's rescuers would be cut to ribbons.

'Your writ only extends to guarding the battlements and the coral line,' snarled the colonel. 'Hermetica's streets are still under police jurisdiction, unless the senate wishes to vote for martial law to be imposed.'

There were loud ugly bays of agreement from the mob standing behind the militia officers and Jethro sensed a riot about to break out if the Pericurian officer didn't back down.

'Withdraw,' said Stom, sheathing her short sword. Her mercenary fighters kept their weapons trained on the crowd and the militiamen as they backed away. 'You can be ordered to follow the will of the First Senator as well as I, colonel.'

'I'll be sure to follow any legitimate written order of the senate, as long as it bears the high judiciary seal of three judges. We're not Pericurian savages here, ursine. Vendetta and assassination are classed as murder on Jago, not politics. Now sod off back to your master like a good little wet-snout.'

The mercenaries warily withdrew back down the street, the colonel's officers forming a line of connected staffs to prevent the mob of townspeople from following after the soldiers. Jethro felt the tension leave the Jagonese crowd as if it were air escaping from a balloon.

Boxiron lurched over to where Jethro was picking himself up from the cobbles. 'I am going to need to have my body seriously upgraded with heavy plate if we're to be dodging turret-rifle fire, Jethro softbody.'

'Be sure to buy a couple of pounds of reinforced steel to cover my arms,' said Jethro.

Colonel Knipe approached the pair. 'What have you been doing to have the First Senator set his pets on you, Jackelian?'

'I'm afraid, good colonel, I have entirely failed to discover the identity of the cabal of plotters intent on destroying the First Senator's new cities.'

'There's a coincidence,' sighed the commander of the militia, nervously tapping his mechanical leg with his pistol barrel, 'you won't find those plotters inside our cells, either. It'll take the First Senator about a week to fix the judiciary list to have three of his lickspittles sitting on the court bench at the same time. That's how long you've got to leave Jago unless you would see your soul following that of the archbishop along the Circle.'

'Sound advice, good colonel.'

'Take it, Jackelian,' urged Knipe. 'Otherwise the wet-snouts will be feeding you to the creatures beyond the wall and all I'll be able to do about it is try to find that drunken sop of an ambassador your people have posted here and urge him to lodge a diplomatic protest about your treatment.'

With the colonel's stern rebuke ringing in his ears, Jethro was following Boxiron as he used his bulk to push open a path through the Jagonese crowd – still jeering after the departing mercenaries – when he spotted Father Baine moving through the crush towards them.

'Jethro Daunt!' The priest raised a hand through the jostling mob. 'Over here.'

Moving to the side of the street, Jethro listened to the young father's description of a panicked message from Chalph urs Chalph and how the ursine was desperate to find him.

'I sent Chalph looking for you at the records office,' the churchman concluded breathlessly. 'Do you have any idea what he might have meant by the things he said, Mister Daunt? What letter he was talking about? He is always quick to anger, that one, but I've never seen Chalph looking so out of sorts before.'

Jethro glanced at Boxiron, then at the young priest. 'It is nothing that augurs well, I fear. We'll search for him back at the records office, then at our hotel. You look for him at the trade mission, good father, and anywhere else you think he might be.'

'Is this to do with the archbishop's murder?' asked Boxiron as they ran back towards the records office.

'More than our young ursine friend realizes, I believe,' said Jethro. 'We need to find him as badly as he thinks he needs to find us.'

'Running low—'

'I'm out—'

'There's one on your leg—'

Hannah flailed an iron foot at the pair of charging ursks, her leg inside the pilot frame having to push twice just to get the RAM suit's limb to move – she was leaking hydraulic fluid from a torn knee seal, flecks of black oil splattering her skull dome as the suit's foot finally responded and piled into the snarling monsters launching themselves against her.

'Get behind me, lass.' The commodore's voice echoed inside the cabin, his suit looming up by her side. 'Old Blacky's still got a couple of these wicked sharp disks left.' As if to prove his point, a rotating silver shard cut down one of the ursks trying to clamber up her leg. 'And I don't need the sights on these metal coffins we've been fitted for to see my aim true.'

'We've got to get out of here!' cried Hannah. 'The trappers are almost out of ammunition.'

'Not down there, Hannah,' said the commodore. 'Don't ask that of me. If the mist did not hide their terrible sight from us, you would see the valley's running black with ursks. Ah, I've faced many dangers before, but this is as dark as any of them. My brave body stuffed into this strange foreign walking machine like a juicy filling in a steak pie for thousands of wicked sharp-clawed monsters to pick at.'

Hannah was about to shout back that the expedition's camp was only seconds away from being completely overrun, but an eerie wail sounded over the brow of their hill, cutting her words off, followed by another wail answering in the distance. Then another and another, each further away.

The commodore's voice echoed in her cabin. 'What in the name of the seventeen seas is that fearful racket?'

Tobias Raffold laughed. 'That's what the hollowed-out skull of an ursk sounds like when you blow a tune through it, you old sea dog.'

Was it Hannah's imagination, or were the waves of ursks coming at them abating? Yes, the attack was tapering off, the shapes skirting the edge of the mist slinking away. Then, a sudden wave of bamboo spears came leaping out of the mist like flying fish. An ursk rolled into sight at the edge of their hill, growling ferociously at two adult ab-locks, the pair of abs howling back and thrusting at the ursk with their bamboo spikes. Hannah realized that the trappers' release of the ab-lock cubs from the cage earlier had been more than a temporary diversion – they'd been sending terrified adolescents reeking of ursk scent back to the ab-lock caverns nearby.

'Stow your supplies,' ordered Tobias Raffold. 'Pack up the steam tap. The abs and ursks are running on instinct now, and we need to take off while their lust to taste each other's blood is still running stronger than the urge to crack open a handful of RAM suits.'

The grips on the large iron feet of Hannah's suit started slipping on the gore of the slain ursks littering the cold basalt around the camp. Hannah was never gladder to pack up her share of supplies and follow the line of trappers into the whirling white cover hugging the wolds' slopes. Leaving behind the muffled echo of a full-scale battle between the ab-locks and the ursks rising from the hidden depths of the valley.

Everything east of the wolds where the ab-locks made their home was virgin territory to the trappers, becoming colder and colder the further away the expedition travelled from the shores of the Fire Sea. Their progress slowed as the trappers had to scout out suitable blowholes for their portable steam tap to recharge the RAM suits. Occasionally Tobias Raffold would stop and point towards some track or rock and make noises indicating that another party might have passed this way a long time ago.

To Hannah, these signs looked just like the rest of the landscape. They were relying as much on her mother's notes of where she thought William of Flamewall had headed, and, perhaps more worryingly, the fragments of lost Pericurian scripture that had been recovered from his lover's original voyage into the interior's darks. Hannah hoped it was just her Circlist distaste for following prophecy and scripture making her hackles rise every time Ortin urs Ortin pointed at some feature of the landscape and announced a match corresponding to the holy fragments in his possession. How had Hannah's mother felt coming this way all those years before? Unless she had run into the ursks or the ab-locks and not – no, better not to dwell on that possibility. There were so many dangers out here. A storm the day before had nearly separated them, and Nandi had needed to use the flare launcher on her suit's ankle to shoot a bright burning star into the mist to warn the others she was in danger of becoming lost.

After two more days of travel, the dark outlines of the Cade Mountains loomed large on the horizon and Tobias Raffold announced that the expedition had now travelled as deep into the interior as anyone had ever journeyed and returned to tell of.

'Here be monsters,' the commodore announced, miserably. That drew a laugh from the trappers – the hard, coarse men knew that you didn't have to venture beyond the capital's battlements to come across those.

The Cade Mountains formed a circular range that had been reached by explorers from all four points of the compass when the Jagonese civilization had been at its height during the long age of ice. It was a sobering thought that even at the height of their nation's glory, the Jagonese hadn't explored beyond this point. Snow and ice covered the bleak, rocky plains leading up to the foothills, long billowing lances of heated steam marking the presence of geysers and blowholes from deep below the surface. Some small comfort when traversing the bleak landscape – it was as if arrows were pointing to each recharge point for their suit's foul-smelling chemical batteries.

Approaching the mountain range, the expedition's members took the most direct route across the ground in front to increase the chances that they were following a trail others might have chosen before them. They hardly needed the Pericurian ambassador's interpretation of his people's scriptures to identify the next landmark on their travels.

'The Eye of Adarn!' said Ortin urs Ortin, excitedly. 'I say it must be.'

Hannah raised the magnification array in front of her eyes to get a better view of the incredible sight. And there it was.

Hannah wasn't hallucinating. There really was an eye staring down on them from one of the slopes of the Cade Mountains, a single lidless orb as milky white as a maggot, a dark pupil lazily floating inside. The horrific detached eyeball had to be size of a house, a nest of throbbing white fleshy creepers dangling below it, anchoring the thing to the rocks and flowing down the jagged slope of the mountain.

'And Adarn urs Adarn, seeing the horror of what his children had wrought, plucked out his eye and set it down on the slopes to forever watch over the dark lands his progeny had made of their green forests. Then he cast himself into the fires of the sea, bearing the guilt of his kindred no more.'

'The eye,' whined Commodore Black, 'the evil eye.'

'I have never seen anything like it,' said Tobias Raffold. 'That thing looks like an animal, not a plant. But what in the name of the Circle is it living on up there?'

There were superstitious mutters from his trappers, the crude men giving voice to their fears; forebodings pretty much in line with the commodore's feelings. Tobias Raffold cursed his workers for girls and shouted at them to hold their peace. Perhaps, Hannah pondered, he was considering the price he might extract from the Jackelian Zoological Society if he could manage to transport such a uniquely hideous thing back to the capital.

'It's looking at us right now,' said Nandi. 'I swear it is.'

'We have our way,' announced Ortin urs Ortin. 'The Gateway of Amaja is watched over by the Eye of Adarn. Our passage lies below that eye.'

Hannah felt a frisson of fear shiver down her spine at the thought of trekking towards the foot of the Cade Mountains with that terror gazing at them every step of the way.

As if confirming the ambassador's directions, a flight of cawing birds arrowed overhead, heading towards the slope and the sickly white orb staring at the expedition. Hannah cursed her suit's sticky, malfunctioning leg and she forced it forward to follow the trappers.

Jethro Daunt's first thought when he and Boxiron returned to his hotel to find the door already open, was that Stom urs Stom and her free company soldiers had used the hours he had been searching for Chalph to circle back and attempt another arrest. But although their door had been forced, there was no sign of Stom's mercenaries inside.

A bone-like crack echoed around the room as Boxiron slipped up a gear in response to the obvious ransacking of their quarters. Tables lay overturned, drawers pulled out, their contents and those of Jethro's travel chest discarded in random piles across the floor. The steamman's skull turned quickly as he scanned the room, working his way through his combat senses, before he pointed an iron finger towards the large ursk skin that had been sent to them by the colonel of police. 'A residual heat signature, Jethro softbody. Someone is hiding there. . .'

Despite having been discovered, nobody moved from underneath the fur. Boxiron drew closer and grabbed the edge of the hide, still spotted with dried blood from where the ursk had been shot down by the city's defenders, giving it a fierce yank. The fur pulled back to reveal the limp body of Chalph urs Chalph lying on his side. A pair of ornamental duelling rapiers that had been displayed on Jethro's wall had been ripped off and used to skewer the poor young ursine, one through the stomach, one through the spine.

Jethro knelt down and felt for a pulse on Chalph's thick-furred wrist. Much to Jethro's surprise, his touch was answered by a faint throb, a flutter slowing to an end that was close.

'Chalph,' said Jethro. 'Can you hear me? Who did this to you?'

The ursine said nothing, but his eyes slowly focussed on Jethro Daunt, as if seeing him from the other side of the world. Chalph's mouth opened, a stream of blood released, running down his chin. 'I – am—'

'I am here with you, Chalph,' said Jethro, trying to recall what he knew of the Pericurian people's faith. 'I am standing witness for you outside the hall of Reckin urs Reckin.'

'Sorry,' hissed Chalph, the single word escaping through clenched fangs as though it was the whisper of his departing soul.

Jethro shook his head. 'Not your fault.'

The ex-parson waited for almost a minute, holding the unstirring body, saying nothing. At last Jethro gently shut his friend's eyelids. 'May your next vessel pass along a happier path.' The ex-parson glanced up at Boxiron, the steamman standing as motionless as a statue, and slowly made the sign of the Circle over his heart. 'He's moved along the Circle's turn, there's nothing we can do for him.'

'There is,' said Boxiron, his voicebox quivering with contained rage. 'When we find the ones responsible for this. But you know who caused his death, do you not? I see it by the way you are not moving to search our chambers for traces of his killer's identity.'

'Working revenge in Chalph's name will not benefit him,' said Jethro, sadly, standing up over the corpse. 'I'm sorry, good ursine. I believed you would live to see this affair through, live to walk through your home's glades.'

'Was it the free company brutes?' demanded the steamman. 'Did they come here looking for us, only to find this poor young softbody instead? Or was it the guild's thugs paying him back for helping his church friend escape their service?'

The ex-parson of Hundred Locks said nothing and the steamman pulled the blades out of the body and started to roll the corpse up inside the large ursk skin. Jethro's troubled eyes turned to vexation. 'Old steamer, please tell me you're not planning to dump his body?'

'The dark canals of this warren of a city are at least good for that,' said Boxiron.

Jethro walked to the window and pulled aside the curtain, glancing down into Hermetica's streets. 'We shall certainly not just dump Chalph's body. The scriptures of the Divine Quad contain exceedingly specific burial rites.'

'You deny his gods. . .' said Boxiron.

'His gods, but not his right to believe in them. The Pericurian trade mission should receive his remains.'

'If we are found with a corpse in our rooms we will be handing the First Senator another excuse to toss us over his battlements.'

'His paranoia needs no excuses now,' said Jethro, 'and we have a duty to the living as well as the dead. We have to find Father Baine exceedingly quickly.'

'Is our foe eliminating everyone who has helped us?' growled Boxiron.

Jethro Daunt sighed, popping a Bunter and Benger's aniseed drop in his mouth. 'If I am correct in my fears, good steamman, then the killings in this city have barely even begun.'

A mile from the jagged rise of the Cade Mountains, the expedition members were labouring through the tail of a steam storm blown far inland by the howling winds, the heat of it melting the snow on the rocky plain, leaving knives of treacherous ice in its wake. One small mercy emerged from the storm: the waves of billowing steam blocked the ever-watching gaze of the terrible massive eye halfway up the mountain slope.

It was during the storm that Hannah stumbled unexpectedly across something frozen in the ice – an oval of rusting girders jutting out like whale bones on top of broken caterpillar tracks, the decayed treads so eroded some of them were little more than shadows of rubble in the snow.

'I've seen one of these before,' said Tobias Raffold, his dome, like Hannah's, retracted for a better look, despite the bitingly cold wind. 'Outside one of the empty cities down south. It's a land hauler – like one of our horseless carriages back in the Kingdom. The Jagonese used them to cross the wilds once.'

'Around the time of William of Flamewall,' said Nandi, excitedly. 'Look how little is left of its hull – that level of corrosion puts it squarely in the period we're interested in.'

'Ah, the poor wretches,' sighed the commodore. 'And we're to end up sharing the same fate.'

'Chin up,' observed Ortin urs Ortin. 'We have the advantages of modern RAM suits and rapid-fire weaponry on our side.'

'You've a blessed unhealthy faith in the trappings of modernity,' said the commodore. 'In my experience a foot of sharp steel is your best friend in a tight spot, no capacitor to decharge on you when your back's against the wall, no clockwork lock to jam on your rifle.'

'An easy comment to make, dear boy, when your nation is the sole keeper of a navy of airships ready to pummel all your foes to pieces from the sky.'

'Not in my mortal name,' the commodore muttered.

Hannah looked ahead. The storm was changing direction, the rise of the towering Cade Mountains revealed through the shifting curtain. The baleful eye was still watching the expedition from on high and there was something else revealed at the foot of the slope. An oval of darkness bordered by something that appeared too regular to be a natural rock formation.

'There!' called Hannah.

It was what they were looking for, it had to be.

Hannah pushed her RAM suit as fast as she dared across the treacherous ground until she was standing in the shadow of the mountain, the Gateway of Amaja revealed as a lightless tunnel sixty feet across its entrance. The portal was bordered with raised mouldings around its rim, mouldings of winged cherubs holding hands – children of the race of man alternating with ursine cubs – all of them with curled hair and fur clearly marked against a panel of what appeared to be grape vines.

Hannah watched Nandi retract her skull dome, reaching out of her suit to touch the mouldings with her own fingers. 'It's hardly weathered at all. I've never felt anything like it before – a ceramic of some sort, but mixed with metal? And it's cold to the touch – the mountain stone is warm in comparison.'

Hannah spotted something. 'There's something scratched on it over here. I think it's written in old Jagonese.'

Nandi brought her suit alongside Hannah's. 'It is old Jagonese.' The academic looked closer, mouthing the translation out loud as she read. 'To. Enter. Is. To. Die.'

'A warning from William of Flamewall,' said the commodore, dejectedly. 'Ah, but who among us is wise enough to heed his omen?'

'I don't think it was William that scratched out this message,' said Nandi. 'Old Jagonese used different verbs depending on whether the writer was male or female. "Die", here, is in the female form. I think this was scratched by Bel Bessant – it dates back to her original expedition.'

The ambassador stared up at the line of cherubs. 'And the Angels of Airdia came as a host to bear away all of the dying children that had been burnt by the fires of the last war, for they wore their innocence as their mantle.'

Hannah looked into the inky darkness of the tunnel. All things considered, if their path took them inside the mountain, Hannah was happier to be wearing the armour of the RAM suit as *her* mantle.

To enter is to die.

There had nearly been a mutiny among Tobias Raffold's crew of trappers when he had ordered them into the tunnel through the Cade Mountains. Only the Pericurian ambassador's promise of a large bonus upon their return to Hermetica City overcame the trappers' unease enough to activate their RAM suits' lanterns and file inside.

With the two lights mounted on the shoulders of Hannah's RAM suit throwing twin yellow beams forward, she could twist her machine's chest above its hip gimble to focus in on sections of the tunnel. She had grown up in vaults bored and enlarged by the Jagonese Lodge of Engineer Diggers and the smoothness of this tunnel surpassed anything she had seen down in Hermetica. It was as if the walls had been carved out true by the rays of a sun and then layered with the same strange substance that formed the mouldings bordering the entrance.

Dozens of gutters, alcoves, ledges and air vents emerged under Hannah's beams, signalling that this was no natural excavation. Whether there had once been a source of light along its length she could not say. There didn't appear to be any lantern grates she could see, or anything resembling the LED panels lining Hermetica's roof vaults.

When twin lights blinked into life in front of them, Hannah's first thought was that the trapper scouting the way had turned to signal back to them. But then she realized that the points of light ahead were glowing demon red. Suddenly the tunnel was filled with the lead trapper's screams as his machine came stumbling backwards before collapsing in front of them, a molten hole burning in its chest armour.

'The Angel of Airdia,' the dying trapper croaked.

One of Alice Gray's sayings echoed in Hannah's mind. *Given enough time, all angels prove to be diabolic.*

CHAPTER SEVENTEEN

Jethro's heart sank when he saw the police militia standing on the cathedral's bridge.

Boxiron jumped to the same conclusion. 'Father Baine has been murdered and—'

They both stopped as a company of green-uniformed militia led the young priest out of the cathedral's main entrance, his hands in chains. He was still alive!

Jethro shouted and waved at the young priest to attract his attention, but when he saw the ex-parson of Hundred Locks standing there with Boxiron his face turned towards the ground with an embarrassed expression. Jethro pursed his lips. Guilt, or something exceedingly close to it? What had Father Baine done? Before Jethro could call out to ask, the lead militiamen hustling the prisoner out of the cathedral had spotted the pair on the edge of the bridge. Leaving the priest in the custody of their compatriots, they came sprinting towards Jethro and Boxiron, pushing their velvet capes back to draw pistols on the two of them. They were soon surrounded, their way impeded by police staffs.

'Why do you have Father Baine in shackles?' Jethro

demanded. 'You are violating the rational ground of the church by your actions.'

'If that were the least of the violations here I would be a happy man,' said Colonel Knipe, emerging from behind his circle of militiamen. 'When I heard that fool Silvermain's charges against you I hardly gave them credence. But then upon further investigation and with a little encouragement, Father Baine here confessed everything to us. And against the weight of all past experience, it seems that idiot in senatorial robes has actually struck a vein of truth! It would have been far better if you had told me what you were really here for when you arrived, Jethro Daunt. We have enough problems on Jago already – we do not need foreign powers thinking they can send their agents to our shores to operate with impunity.'

Jethro looked at the priest being led away, his face bruised from the local police's 'encouragement' to volunteer what he knew. 'The League of the Rational Court is an arm of the Circlist church, good colonel, it holds no civil power or temporal authority in Jackelian affairs.'

'Oh, please.' The police commander waved Jethro's objections away. 'Save your semantics for someone trained enough in church logic to care to debate with you. You two have been up to your necks in it here in the capital with your Inquisition mischief.'

Boxiron's voicebox shook with barely contained fury. 'Do you call it mischief to try to find out who murdered Alice Gray?'

'You've got the ursk fur of the archbishop's killer hanging in your rooms, steamman, and your justification for being here makes a sorry excuse for interference with evidence, disruption of lawful ballot service, suspected involvement in the death of the merchant Hugh Sworph, failure to declare true intent to our customs officers and multiple counts of espionage against the Jagonese state.'

'I assure you that we are on the side of what is right and rational,' Jethro insisted.

'That is as may be,' said the colonel. 'But you're also on the wrong side of the Fire Sea to be practising your true trade.'

Colonel Knipe signalled to his men and they locked metal shackles across Jethro and Boxiron's wrists. Boxiron suffered the manacles restraining him, but Jethro knew the police militia had to be sorely aware they would need chains a lot thicker to stop his hulking body from snapping his fetters in a second if he chose to break free.

'I shall do you and your metal brute a favour, Jackelian. Call it a professional courtesy. I'm going to hold both of you for deportation. The next boat that comes in will find itself with two extra passengers – and if either of you two rascals ever try to set foot on Jago again, I'll let the First Senator's wet-snouts throw you outside the wall and our diplomatic relations with the Kingdom be hanged.'

'I must protest this treatment,' said Jethro as the militia dragged him away.

'Of course you must,' said the colonel. 'Everyone always does, and you haven't even enjoyed the hospitality of our cells under the police fortress yet.'

Jethro exchanged glances with Boxiron, the light on the steamman's vision plate pulsing uncertainly. It seemed as if their investigation on Jago had come to an abrupt end.

Hannah ducked as the buzzing sound passed over her RAM suit's skull dome, chips of the tunnel lining raining across her. The trappers fired their weapon arms wildly up into the darkness, the whirling circles of light cast by their lanterns trying to pick out the creature assaulting them. Only the blinking red orbs – its eyes? – betrayed the fleeting presence of the attacker, rapidly skimming over their heads as though an enraged mosquito was harrying them. Except that this mosquito carried a sting capable of piercing the armour of a RAM suit.

One of the trappers in front of Hannah turned, and she caught sight of the creature in her beams – it was clinging to the back of the trapper's suit with two tiny bony legs and plunging its other two limbs – long piston-like lances – into the suit's battery pack as spouts of green acid gushed out. Attached to two circular wings, the creature's body could almost have passed for human were it not for its transparent skin revealing pumping, pulsing organs within.

Hannah's lantern beams were only on the monster fleetingly – it leapt off the disabled trapper, leaving the man's paralysed suit sparking electric energy from a damaged spine plate. The thing's eyes were twin telescopic tubes mounted on its skull, irising open and shut to blink out an evil red semaphore at her. Hannah ducked her suit as the humming of the monster's wings bounced off the tunnel walls. The creature could be circling around and heading straight for the blind spot on her suit's back right now.

Hannah's brain desperately churned; there was something about the way the creature had shied away from the lantern beams, its telescope eyes casting diffuse red light. The sort that enabled it to hunt inside the dark tunnels?

Hannah tugged the handle down by her knee inside the pilot frame, the handle that would activate her – 'Leg flares!' she yelled. 'Light up the tunnel!'

Fizzing out of the tube of her suit, a flare ricocheted off the roof well before its parachute could deploy and went spinning across the tunnel like an angry firework, painting the shadows with its sodium glare. Then, all around Hannah came the sound of flares firing, and every shadow in the darkness was instantly banished, the sudden brightness making her eyes water with its ferocity; her eyes that were born to see daylight. For the murderous Angel of Airdia it must have been a different sort of pain altogether, the creature lashing around between the vaults above their heads, blindly trying to find a way out. But not before the maddened trappers raised their magnetic catapults and scored a dozen direct strikes on the thing, the creature's massive, disk-like wings torn to shreds, sending it dropping, mewling, in front of them. Lurching forward, the nearest RAM suit connected its metal foot with the creature's head – the crack from the amplified strength of the trapper's strike carrying all the way through the armoured crystal of Hannah's skull dome.

The creature was finished now for sure, laying sprawled on the tunnel floor, energy from its long, lance-like arms sparking across the space while one of their flares spun madly around inches from it, illuminating the organs visible deep inside its transparent chest.

'Nothing like this has ever been recorded attacking the battlements,' said Tobias Raffold, gingerly pushing at one of the monster's limp lance arms. 'Not that I've bleeding heard of, at any rate.'

'It was waiting in ambush,' said Nandi, looking with fascination at the mangled beast, 'as if it knew we were coming.'

'That wicked eye on the slopes behind us, lass,' said the commodore. 'It was that eye that ratted us out for sure. They're an evil pair, watchman and sentry, waiting for innocent travellers to enter their lair before slaughtering them and divvying up the meat.'

Hannah watched Nandi looking more closely at the thing.

There were cables hanging out of one of the broken tubes the creature had been using for its eyes.

'It's a metal-flesher, an animal-machine hybrid,' observed Nandi.

'Made for war,' whispered the commodore. 'Aye, and sure I've seen many of the same dark arts practised down Cassarabia-way by their womb mages. But this is an ancient thing, Hannah Conquest, as foul and old as that beastly eyeball up on the mountain slopes. You wanted to know what happened to William of Flamewall and his lover's terrible god-creating design, I say it ended here, in the clear belly of that tube-eyed horror.'

'No,' insisted Hannah, firmly. 'Bel Bessant travelled past this point centuries ago and she, at least, lived to return to Hermetica to create the god-formula. William of Flamewall followed her trail here, and not just to ensure the last part of the god-formula was placed beyond the hands of the race of man. He could have simply jumped into the Fire Sea to achieve that. William came here for another reason, and whatever that reason may be, this tunnel leads towards it.'

Yes. Bel Bessant had survived this creature. Might Hannah's mother also have lived, her brave, resourceful mother? Her mother had to have survived, she simply had to.

'Ah, lass,' Commodore Black said to Hannah, 'you're sounding more and more like that rascal Jethro Daunt every day. So forward it is, though against all sense it be. Your blessed scripture talks of a paradise fallen to war, ambassador; if this flying devil was one of its soldiers, then it must have been a mortal hellish affair indeed.'

'You see the evidence of the ruins around you, captain. Darkness enveloped our paradise, and darkness is all that we are left with. I must agree with the young damson,' Ortin urs Ortin said. 'The fragments of scripture that Bel Bessant retrieved were found beyond here, beyond the angel's hunting ground.'

They moved down the tunnel even more carefully now, in case there were more survivors from the Pericurians' ancient war lurking in the arches and alcoves. Three destroyed RAM suits and dead trappers lay behind them, sporting smoking holes where the angel had administered its fatal blessing.

Shortly before Hannah reached the end of the tunnel, the alcoves that intermittently lined the walls turned into full side-chambers connected by corridors that were too narrow and low to follow inside a RAM suit. Rather than explore the passages immediately, the expedition members conferred and decided to follow the distant suggestion of natural light to the end. And there she saw *it*.

The expedition had passed right underneath the towering mass of the Cade Mountains, emerging clear on the other side, and if Hannah had lived to be a thousand years old, she would never have expected to find the shocking sight that was waiting for her outside.

Hester stood in front of the tug's pilothouse, cursing her luck as the febrile waters of the boils on either side of the craft spouted angry geysers, their burning vapours keeping her rubber scald suit uncomfortably hot. The channel the Jagonese tug was bouncing along felt dangerously narrow, seventy feet of boiling water shadowed by slowly shifting walls of magma to either side. But the channel's increasing narrowness was precisely why the tug had been dispatched from Hermetica. The great model of molten flows contained in the guild's transaction engines had predicted weeks ago that this channel was going to close, the boils of water squeezed into non-existence, and the Jagonese tug service still had a way station at the other end that needed towing to a safer mooring.

Well, as bad as the task of keeping forward watch on this maintenance run was, Hester considered, at least she hadn't yet been assigned the lonely duty of buoy keeper. Waiting on one of the stone platforms for non-existent trading vessels that hadn't needed to be guided through the hellish sea since the southwest passage had opened up. How many solo hands of cards could you play in the confined quarters of one of the granite buoy platforms before you went mad? The service ran rich with the stories of insanity that its old hands were only too glad to inflict on a newly drafted unfortunate whose natural inclinations leaned towards fine embroidery. But the milliner's shop that belonged to Hester's mother wasn't a protected profession so here she was. Keeping watch for any of the myriad tell-tale signs of unpredicted magma shifts that had so recently been carefully drilled into her while the boils spat searing needles of water at her.

A pod of Fire Sea dolphins was following in the tug's wake, drawn by the fish that the turbulence of the craft's passage stirred up, their granite-thick skins slapping down as they arced through the boils to enjoy their supper.

Oddly, the tug was drawing to a halt, the paddles on her side slowing their rotation as the door to the pilothouse clanged open. The tug master himself stepped out in his bright orange scald suit slashed with the black bars of a captain – not that his manner ever left any doubt about who was master and commander of this vessel.

'Nothing to report, sir,' Hester ventured.

'I'm not here to inspect the watch, tugman. This is where our way station should be anchored.'

Hester gazed out across the searing channel, thinking of all the stories she had heard of buoy keepers who had gone mad and cut their moorings to allow their stations to be sucked into the flow of magma, welcoming the fury of the Fire Sea as if it was a warm blanket in winter.

'Check to starboard for wreckage,' ordered her skipper, scanning the bubbling boils on his side of the tug.

'Nothing, sir. No wreckage in the water.'

But they expected that, the currents of the shifting molten rock sucked in everything not under power, which was why failing to make the mandatory engine checks before a voyage was a court martial offence.

'Diving stations,' barked the captain. 'We need to check the seabed.'

Hester felt a twinge of fear. That was something else she'd had drummed into her – that these floating engines they piloted were safely submersible only in the vicinity of the docks – their craft weren't full u-boats. If their tug's seals failed this far from Jago, the way station wasn't going to be the only thing missing from the service's lists.

On the surface of the boils, the dolphins watched the craft that had been flushing fish towards them sink away, the pod's disappointment turning to fear as a massive geyser of water erupted from the surface where the tug had been sinking out of sight moments before.

One of the dolphins curiously nosed Hester's yellow rubber-skinned body when it came floating up to bob face-down on the steaming surface. The dolphin watched the body and the scattered burning metal that had been the tug rotating around, swirling into the wall of magma, before it noticed the angry clicks from the rest of the pod. There was a painful wall of sound flowing under the water, making their highly attuned sense of hearing pinch with irritation.

None of the dolphins had ever heard anything like the terrible resonance before and the entire pod fled back down the magma-walled channel.

There was a good reason the dolphins had never encountered anything quite like what they were hearing. The Fire Sea hadn't heard the likes of *this* before, not once in two millennia.

CHAPTER EIGHTEEN

Behind Hannah lay the rise of the Cade Mountains and the tunnel's exit. In front of her lay a hundred yards of basalt rubble and rock, then perhaps a mile of smooth dark glassy material, as though a giant glass blower had discarded one of his works halfway through the process, leaving a slick of black frozen surf across the floor. But it was what lay beyond the band of glassy territory that caught Hannah's attention as she stepped out of the dark tunnel.

The ground there was heavily fissured and in between the vast cracks stood a dense thorny maze of emerald green, almost a jungle, thriving in the heat and clinging to what looked like the ruins of a city. But if a city it had been, the place had fallen prey to some unknown malady – towers a hundred storeys high stood twisted and melted, the squares of windows distorted into disfigured orifices. Half-dissolved foundation pillars broke the canopy of the thick jungle, thousands of stone fingers branching out in a beseeching spread. The place had taken on the look of a sweep of colossal, malformed anthills, covered by bush, thorns and creepers while hissing waves of steam rose up from the land and channelled through its ruins.

Nandi's voice sounded over the speakers. 'There's more behind us.'

Hannah turned and saw that the young academic was right. The slopes of the Cade Mountains were studded with buildings – not overgrown with vegetation like those on the steaming plain ahead of them, but still wrecked and mangled almost beyond recognition. The ruins looked to be made of the same queer ceramic that formed the interior of the tunnel, but twisted and distorted as if by intense heat. Rivers of the bone-white material had flowed down to the foot of the mountain as liquid, and then cooled back to rock, before being worn away to become the rim of rubble from which they were currently surveying the scene. Higher up the mountain the structures looked to be better preserved, closer perhaps to their original state.

'What could melt stone like that?' asked Tobias Raffold in amazement.

The ambassador swivelled his suit to face the trapper's 'The wrath of Reckin urs Reckin. The same tears that formed the Fire Sea.'

Hannah sighed. The ambassador might make a good show of affecting the manners of a modern Jackelian gentleman but his heart still belonged to the savage deep forests of his homeland, it seemed.

'A prickly fellow to have done all of this, then,' muttered the commodore.

'The terrain across there looks volcanic,' said Nandi. 'I've never read of ruins in such a strange condition in any of the texts back in Saint Vine's. The damage doesn't match what I've read of pyroclastic flows.'

There were signs that someone had visited the foot of the mountains before their expedition, wooden planks laid like a pier across the band of glassy ground, stopping halfway out at an oval circle of ground, almost an island, formed of a lighter-coloured rock than the black surf. There were piles of discarded garbage to Hannah's right, opened food cans rusting by the remains of a fire.

'A decade old, I reckon' said Tobias Raffold, examining the circle of rocks that had contained the fire. 'Give or take.'

Hannah's heart leapt. Around the same time her mother would have arrived here!

Nandi pointed back to the tunnel. 'There might be more inside those side corridors we passed. I'm going to dismount and have a poke around on foot.'

Commodore Black reluctantly opened his suit and climbed down after her, a long-barrelled rifle slung over his shoulder, sabre and holstered pistol hanging from his wide girth. Hannah pushed open her canopy and joined them while Tobias Raffold ordered two suited trappers to stand guard at the mouth of the tunnel so nothing could slink after his clients, and a couple more to wait a hundred feet inside to ensure that their weapon arms' firepower was available should they need it.

Hannah held a lantern she had unclipped from her suit, flickering light dancing from the tight featureless corridors and antechambers. She shivered. Was it fear, or excitement at what she might find?

A couple of chambers back from the tunnel the three of them discovered a pile of supplies that Nandi dated to the era of William of Flamewall. A barrel of dried food – little more than desiccated leather now – and spindly rifles with intricate engravings on their imported beech-wood butts that spoke of an age of wealth and opulence.

In the chamber behind they made another discovery, one that made Hannah recoil as her lantern revealed the shape of a camp table with a shining white skeleton sitting at a chair behind it, a silent sentinel watching the open arch they had just walked through. The remains of tattered clothes clung to its bones and there was a splint attached to the left leg. On the table in front of it were a dust-covered satchel and a pistol with crystal charges scattered about.

Commodore Black picked up the pistol and rubbed its clockwork hammer mechanism clean. 'A Buford and Armstrong lady's pattern. This is a Jackelian gun.'

Nandi collected the satchel, and Hannah saw the young academic wince as she noticed something on the satchel's flap. Nandi lifted out a number of books, placing them carefully on the tabletop.

Hannah was staring so intently at the satchel's flap – the same arms of Saint Vine's College that decorated Nandi's own bag – that it took a couple of seconds for her to notice the young academic holding out one of the books to her in an almost apologetic fashion.

'No!'

The initials on the diary's leather cover.

Hannah's eyes ran with tears, blurring the figure in the chair. In no way was this the reunion that she had been planning with her mother.

'It's all right.' Hannah leant forward to kiss the skull's forehead, but nothing happened: her mother's skeleton was still a skeleton. A *kiss to bring them back to life.* But all the magic had fled.

Hannah's hands were still gently trembling as she read the pages of her mother's diary. She felt a mixture of shock and denial that the bones behind the camp table belonged to the woman who had given birth to her – denial even when Nandi had examined the pelvis and declared it was a woman's, even when Hannah had come to the page in the diary that described the ursk attack on the other side of the Cade Mountains and the wound on her mother's leg exactly where the skeleton's splint had been set. The writing grew shakier page by page as the infection spread and the medicines Hannah's mother was carrying failed to heal it.

Hannah's mother, the redoubtable Doctor Jennifer Conquest, must have been feverish even as she arrived where the expedition was now camped. She described how she'd made friends with a gentle translucent flying creature in the tunnel under the mountain, and there were long rambling pages written to her husband whom she must have known was dead. More details on how she had found William of Flamewall's remains on something she called Bloodglass Island, and then burnt the priest's papers and notes so no one else could get them; her description of how the third part of the god-formula had not been among William's possessions – the one thing she could have used to rise above her mortally fatal affliction. After that, the diary was filled with pages and pages of mathematics. Mad mathematics, symbols that Hannah didn't recognize blended with formulae that seemed to run contrary to any of the accepted rules she had been taught. At first Hannah thought her mother must have been trying to recreate the third section of the god-formula herself, but as bizarre as the formulae in her mother's diary were, their structure didn't seem to match either of the first two parts of the god-formula she had seen. Had the fever sent her mother insane? Later, the lines of mathematics were interspersed with descriptions of songs of siren beauty, her mother's hand getting scratchier and scratchier. They seemed to make a sense – but only in the way that you could gaze at abstract patterns on wallpapers and start to see meaningful pictures as you let your mind wonder.

Nandi came around the corner, the glow of her lantern announcing her presence long before she appeared. 'It is done. Do you want to see where we buried her?'

'That wasn't my mother,' said Hannah. 'They were just the clothes she wore, is all.' Hannah realized that the young academic had probably interpreted what she just said as a Circlist homily. 'No, I mean *this* is her.' Hannah raised the diary. 'What she believed in. What she thought. Not the dust that's left behind.'

Nandi lifted the satchel she had found. 'I've been looking through your mother's other notebooks. There are more complete descriptions of what she and your father discovered in the guild's transaction-engine rooms – material she chose not to compress into the Joshua's Egg she hid for us. Your mother believed that William of Flamewall came here to destroy something.'

'Not the missing section of the god-formula,' said Hannah. 'William was a priest of the rational orders; the ritual of coming all the way out here to where his lover had preceded him to burn the last piece of Bel's work wouldn't have appealed to him.'

'Well, Bel Bessant retrieved her fragments of Pericurian scripture from here, but the Circle knows where or how. I've just returned from climbing up to the buildings on the slopes above us – this place is an archaeologist's worst nightmare. Just empty rooms, thousands of them, twisted out of shape. Whatever was hot enough to melt stone turned everything to ashes here. No furniture, no bones, no pottery, no doors or windows. Certainly no manuscripts.'

'The city beyond the glass plain might be in better condition.'

'No,' said Nandi. 'I've studied it through my telescope; if anything, it's in a far worse state. It was closer to whatever killed this civilization and there's a whole new ecos clinging to the steam fissures across there. Nothing destroys a good dig site like weeds and creepers.'

There was a distant ringing from camp, a dinner call being sounded.

'Do you want to eat?'

Hannah shook her head in answer.

'Finding your mother's bones makes it real, doesn't it? The fact that she's dead.'

'I don't want to talk about her.'

'When my mother told me my father was dead, I never believed it. It never felt real to me – I would always catch myself expecting him to come through the door to our home.'

'How did your father die?' asked Hannah.

'Much as your mother did,' said Nandi. 'About the business of St. Vines' college. He was on an unauthorized dig in Cassarabia, and when the caliph's soldiers found him there, they shot him as a grave robber.'

'Did you ever stop thinking about him?'

'Never,' said Nandi. 'But when I was older, the head of the school of archaeology took me down into the southern desert to show me where she had buried his body. I still think about him, but now I know he won't be coming through the door.'

'If we find the last piece of the god-formula here we could use it to bring him back. . .'

'What would such a thing be but a poorly formed simulacra of how I remembered my father?' Nandi tapped her head. 'And he is already inside my mind like that now, in how I remember and honour him.'

'I think it would be more than that,' said Hannah. 'If you had the powers of a god.'

'My father had a near-perfect memory, crammed full of stories which I used to love to hear,' said Nandi. 'One of his favourites he would tell me many times. It's from one of the Circlist books of koans: *The Koan of the Wondrous Thing*. Have you heard it?'

Hannah shook her head.

'Then I shall tell it to you,' said Nandi. 'There was a young boy who was said to have been born enlightened, although many did not believe it and continually tested him. They would try to goad him by filling his shoes with crumpled pages torn out of the *Book of Common Reflections*.'

'There's a few like that in the cathedral school here,' said Hannah.

'Back at St. Vines, also,' said Nandi. 'Anyway, the day came when the boy had to attend the funeral of his grandmother and the Circlist vicar leading the service noticed that of all the mourners there, the boy was the only one not crying. So the vicar approaches the boy after the service and says to him, "Lad, why do you not cry? Did you not love your grandmother?"'

'And what did the boy say?' asked Hannah.

'He said, "Of course I loved her, but this is a wondrous thing." The vicar was naturally very curious about this and asked the boy to explain. The boy gave this explanation: if his grandmother had not died, she would have seen her sons and daughters die before her. If she had not died she would also have had to see her grandchildren die before her and borne the pain of that. She moved along the Circle in harmony with the natural order of the universe and that is a wondrous thing.'

Hannah nodded in understanding. At its core, Circlism was just a humanist way to underscore the mathematical truth that reality's strings were so closely woven together that there was no difference between one person's life and another's. She and Nandi really were the same, both here to find the same thing, their fates intertwined and their future bound up in the same outcome. *People are all you have*, that was another of Alice's favourite sayings. Her mother had come here alone.

but Hannah hadn't. She was with a young woman so alike they might have been sisters; there were the trappers and the commodore and Ambassador Ortin to watch over them. Her mother's essence might have been cupped back into the one sea of consciousness, but she lived on in Hannah, and her daughter wasn't done yet. Not by a long chalk.

'I like your father's story. But there is one thing – Koans normally make three points,' said Hannah. 'That one only had two. It feels as if there is something missing.'

'Yes,' said Nandi. 'But that's the thing about the death of someone you loved. It always leaves something missing.'

Hannah's lips twisted into a small smile. And that too, perhaps, was a wondrous thing.

Hannah and Nandi left the tunnel chambers and emerged into the open. The expedition had fanned their RAM suits facing outwards towards the island's newly discovered interior. It was the first time since they had left the battlements behind that their trapper guides had felt secure enough to pitch tents and sleep outside of the closed but safe confines of their suit armour. And little wonder. Hannah watched as a red cord was pegged in a wide circle around the camp. Then the trappers uncrated and assembled a portable transaction engine along with a series of brass boxes studded with flared trumpets that looked like steammen hearing manifolds, carefully placing the boxes down just inside the perimeter of the red line. Finally, they connected the RAM suits, transaction engine and trumpet boxes together with long black cables.

'You don't move beyond the red cord,' Tobias Raffold instructed Hannah, the commodore, Nandi and the ambassador, 'and here's for why. . .'

He tossed a rock beyond the line and the trumpet-studded boxes made a series of whistling noise like kettles, the nearest RAM suit swivelling automatically, its magnetic catapult hissing once while the rock the trapper had tossed erupted into a shower of dust mid-air.

'Anything bigger than a gnat comes towards us night or day, and the suits will put a disk right through its bleeding heart.'

Commodore Black stared uncomfortably at the blinking valves on the Jagonese transaction engine controlling their suits' weapon arms. 'You'll be trusting our safety to that blinking box of lights?'

'What am I, new to this?' retorted the trapper. 'We still post manual sentries, two at a time. But when you're sleeping outside your suit, you'll be glad you have old Bessie there as an extra pair of eyes.'

Grumbling, the commodore accepted the presence of the machine picket. Hannah followed the ambassador's gaze out across the glass plain to the jungle-swallowed city. 'Is that the city of your scriptures?'

Ortin urs Ortin polished his monocle, his eyes glinting sadly. 'I don't think any of us have found what we were expecting here, dear girl.'

'No.'

Hannah ignored the newly turned ground marked with a circle of boulders where her mother's bones lay and went inside her tent to try to puzzle some sense out of the pages of mathematics in the diary.

Her mother's diary and the mind she had left Hannah were all the legacy she needed.

When sleep came for Hannah, it was a hot claustrophobic thing. She was tumbling through waves of alien numbers until Tobias Raffold came into view and started catching the numbers and throwing them beyond the red cord, where rotating shards of deadly steel burst them into black dust.

'What are you doing?' she demanded.

'This is the only thing we're going to trap this trip, girl,' said Raffold. 'And they're no good to me. You can't put an equation in a zoo, or skin it for profit.'

She tried to get him to stop, but he only laughed all the harder, throwing more numbers into the RAM suits' arc of fire. Then the tenor of the dream changed, a bright light expanding from the hail of falling formulae, clearing away the darkness – burning and burning – and out of the fiery nimbus Hannah saw the shape of a figure resolving, a familiar silhouette.

Hannah held up a hand to protect her eyes from the glare. 'Chalph, is that you?'

'It is,' answered the familiar voice. 'I am in the great forest of Azrar-bur, waiting for Reckin urs Reckin to lead me to his glades.'

'But,' Hannah stumbled over the implication, 'that means you're dead?'

'I found out too much, Hannah, and the knowing of it was not good for me.'

'What was it, Chalph, what did you discover?'

'That history repeats itself, much like the circle of existence your people's strange church puts so much faith in. Going round and round. It spun too fast for me and I fell off.'

Hannah rushed forward as the light began to dwindle.

'Don't leave me, Chalph. My mother's gone now – there's just you and me left.'

'Your mother saw too little,' whispered the voice from the fading light. 'You need to see more, but not too much more. Not unless you want to join me. There's so much green here. Just like Pericur. Just like I imagined a real forest.'

'Don't—' she begged.

Follow
the
song

Hannah,
but
not
too
far.'

'—go!'

Hannah woke with a start. Light outside the tent canvas indicated morning had arrived.

Oh Chalph! Chalph was dead, he had to be. Or why else was the alien melody of a song drifting outside Hannah's tent?

Hannah stared in amazement. A series of small white structures had risen out of the ground on the island in the middle of the glassy plain. It was from these buildings that the song Hannah had heard in her tent seemed to issue – albeit with no voiceboxes visible to carry the eerie tune. The harmony sounded like a blend of voices from the races of man and ursine, though in no language that Hannah recognized.

Ortin urs Ortin appeared, seemingly as entranced as Hannah by the strange melody drifting across the plain of glass. 'I say, it's a hymn, it has to be.'

Nandi appeared from her tent. 'Where did those buildings come from?'

'Like a Catosian city-state reconfiguring its streets for war, lass,' said the commodore. 'I saw them. They just rose out of the ground at dawn.'

'Some of the words in the song sound familiar,' said Nandi. 'I think there might be phonetic germs to some modern words in their roots. Those buildings are too small to contain much, though, unless they're shrines.'

'Let's have a look,' said Hannah, but Tobias Raffold grabbed her arm and pointed down to the glassy plain she was about to step onto.

'You don't have to stop me. You've switched your gun control off, Mister Raffold, I can see that the transaction engine's valves are powered down.'

'Not our guns, girl,' said the trapper. 'There's something under the glass. I've seen shadows moving beneath it and whatever they are, I'm betting it's the reason there's planks laid out to that land. Go out along the walkway.'

A couple of the trappers mounted up and trained their suits' magnetic catapult arms on the glass while Commodore Black led the way across the shaky planking using his rifle for balance. Nandi, Hannah and the ambassador followed, with Tobias Raffold at the rear, his long-barrelled Jackelian hunting gun sweeping over the crystallized ground. There *were* things moving under the glass. Long sinuous shapes like grubs, and they appeared to be circling higher towards the expedition members' shadows on the surface. What had her mother called this place in her diary? *Bloodglass Island*. Hannah carefully kept her footing lest she discover why her mother had labelled it with such an ominous name.

Reaching the island, Hannah saw that it was filled with seven single-storey structures, windowless and constructed of a light-blue material patterned with thin grey lattices. The ground of the island seemed to be made of a solidified puddle of the same material and walking on the surface sent a gentle tingle through the soles of Hannah's boots. The notes of the song were definitely coming from the structures, louder as the expedition approached them. When they were a couple of feet from the nearest structure a hole suddenly appeared in its side, expanding to a size capable of admitting a single member of the expedition within.

'Ah, we're blessed mice now,' said Commodore Black. 'And here stands the trap that's been set for us.'

Hannah wasn't so certain. Her mother had come here before

their expedition and she had died alone in one of the chambers off the mountain tunnel, not out here.

Follow the song.

'It's led me here, Chalph,' Hannah whispered to herself.

As Hannah approached the threshold, she could hear panicked shouts behind her. Ignoring them, she stepped through and found herself standing in a windowless corridor that might have been one of tunnel's anterooms underneath the Cade Mountains; except that the structure she had stepped into was far too small to contain this space she had entered – but somehow the building had taken her here all the same. Hannah was deep below the ground; she knew that, could sense the weight of the world pressing down above her. The walls around Hannah were as black as night, but when she laid a hand on one of them, they turned translucent and alien calligraphy began to crawl down their surface. No, not writing. Numbers. The same alien characters that were interspersed across her mother's diary. Hannah walked along the corridor until she came to its end, the whole structure no more than a hundred feet in length.

Commodore Black came running up behind her. 'You're taking your life in your hands, Hannah Conquest. Jumping into this dark black tomb as if there's a warm meal and a soft bed waiting for you in here.'

'This isn't a tomb,' said Hannah, running her fingers across the surface while formulae floated around them like ripples in a lake. 'I think these structures are tools.'

'Tools? Tools to work what mortal terrible labours?'

'I think that's what my mother was trying to find out, but her bad leg finished her before she managed to complete the work. Someone came here and uncovered their secret, though, and that person was Bel Bessant. This is where she got the inspiration to create the god-formula, I know it was! I can feel the strangeness of these alien characters in the weave of her work. These corridors were the muse for her creation.'

Commodore Black looked around the tight walls, horrified, as if Hannah had just told him they had jumped into a plague pit. 'Let's be out of here then, lass, before the same queer sickness leaps into my noggin and I start trying to raise the spirit of Lord Tridentscale and take it upon myself to declare old Blacky the Monarch of the Seas.'

Reassured by Hannah and the commodore's safe return from inside the structure, the other members of the expedition set about exploring the remaining buildings. The interiors of two of them had not survived the wear of ages; they were filled with rubble, their dark walls dead. Inside the fourth structure the reason for the destruction of the previous two become clear. The cave-in here had only affected two-thirds of the corridor's length and under its rubble lay a half-buried human skeleton, not a trace of clothes left.

Commodore Black kicked the shards of broken glass on the floor. 'The bones are male. Whoever this poor soul was, he was no expert with blasting tubes. He mixed the liquid explosives too early and brought the mortal place crashing down around him.'

Hannah knelt down by the bones, spotting something hidden under the dust. It was a church infinity circle on a chain. 'William of Flamewall, I presume. So, this is what he came here to do – demolish the source of Bel Bessant's inspiration, the genesis that he blamed for his lover's transfiguration.'

'He's done that alright,' said the commodore looking at the debris. 'Whatever secrets were scrawled on the walls of this tunnel and those other two buildings have been scuppered good and proper, just as the third part of the god-formula died with William of Flamewall. That rascal Jethro Daunt is the only one who is going to be happy with the results of this wicked trek into danger. The secrets his Inquisition woman strove to keep untold have been erased. These melted anthills of a city are of no use to Nandi Tibar-Wellking, and if there were ever holy Pericurian tablets in these tunnels, William of Flamewall blew them to bits centuries ago.'

Hannah stared sadly at the priest's skeleton. So it seemed on the face of it, but then her mother had discovered the same scene of destruction over a decade ago, and she had still been trying to achieve something here, to – that was *it*! Hannah urgently flicked open her mother's diary, the meaning of the pages of badly scribbled mathematics becoming clear.

It was a key. Her mother had been using the expressions on the tunnel walls that had echoes in modern Jackelian mathematics to guide her to the meaning of the unknown symbols. She had been translating the ancient mathematical language. Her mother had so nearly completed her work, too. But the fever had got to her, or perhaps she'd lacked the final insights that the codified structures of Circlist synthetic morality would have given her. This was bread and butter to Hannah.

She could complete her mother's work after all!

Alien numbers stirred around Hannah's fingers as she pushed the characters around the wall. She glanced down at her mother's notebook for reassurance; she had never attempted anything so difficult. It wasn't just that the characters were foreign – it was the fact that half of the mathematical concepts used in these underground passages seemed to have no comparative reference points in the Circlist doctrine that she'd had drummed into her during her cathedral studies. The base understanding appeared to be the same as synthetic morality – that everything that existed could be defined and modelled in numbers and that as you changed the inputs you changed the results – but, even given the difficulties of translation, what Hannah was attempting to grapple with was so much more advanced than anything else she had ever tackled. There were formulae for waves and strings that seemed to demand to be integrated into everything Hannah worked on, before being parsed into algorithms that rendered them into something else entirely. Layer upon layer of complexity – perversely growing simpler and simpler the higher up the layers these results of calculations were passed.

Hannah knew what this wall was now – no different from the dials and mechanical switches on the pilot frame of her clunking RAM suit. But what a control panel it was – designed to be operated by minds so advanced it pained her to consider them. Already, Hannah had pushed far beyond her mother's work – come to grips with the concepts that had eluded her mother's fever-racked mind. But what Hannah couldn't grasp was what these structures were for – a tool, certainly, but a tool to what end? Each building had a slightly different purpose, that much Hannah had gleaned. And she suspected that they were linked, like a series of baths in one of Hermetica's public pools – starting cold with each steam chamber growing slightly warmer – each building more difficult to comprehend. William of Flamewall had started at the unfathomable end of the chain in the building he had selected to demolish first, working his way down the scale of complexity until he had died within his premature explosion inside one of the structures. His starting point had been no accident. William of Flamewall had chosen to wreck the most advanced art of this lost civilization first, working his way down to the constructions containing the most simple concepts. The material that had inspired his lover Bel Bessant to create her terrible work was lost to the world forever now. That much Hannah had already discovered for Jethro Daunt and the Circlist church – with the help of a long-dead priest of the rational orders.

Hannah was toying with one of the symbols – something like a lightning flash that seemed to have different functions depending on the position of its insertion point within a formula. She whisked it around with her forefinger, allowing it to follow her like a curious goldfish in a pool tracking a hand. Then the idea struck her. What she was grappling with here wasn't flat: the underlying base of the characters was multi-relational – the symbols she had been puzzling over were links between the disparate formulae and functions. That was why their insertion points mattered so much – they were like the gates that controlled Hermetica's canals – shutting off or opening a single tributary would create knock-on effects all the way down the channels it opened out into!

With almost frenzied haste Hannah began rearranging the concepts she had been lining up on the wall, setting up a structure of theoretical pipes and struts between the formulae to allow the results that had always seemed twisted beyond recognition to follow a logical sequence. A sequence that might prove she was intelligent enough to be allowed to operate this mysterious tool? Hannah thrust the little lightning-bolt symbol into the middle of the line of alien symbols as if it was a real bolt of power. The characters began to rearrange themselves around her finger as though they were insects performing a mating dance, then the symbols started swirling in a vortex and Hannah felt her knees buckle as the room dissolved. Her hands lurched out to grab at something solid, anything, but all of her physical reference points had vanished.

Hannah was flying as if in a dream, skimming over mountains that clearly belonged to the Cade Range; but the land around her, below her, it was all so different – Jago's sky a brilliant diamond blue, the only clouds above her thin white fingers scratched high under a warm, inviting sun. Below Hannah lay well-tended woodland and a chequerboard of farms, dark arrow-straight roads leading to a city that was barely recognizable as the petrified jungle-covered anthills that Hannah had glimpsed after emerging from the tunnel. So many towers shining in the light, ethereal shapes so beautiful they were as much art as architecture – delicate arches and parapets with insubstantial transparent walkways bridging them – separated by sculpted parkland in rich emerald green. Hannah's course altered and she found herself swooping down across the city at ground level, a ghost observing a lost past.

Moving walkways underneath Hannah were filled with ursine and the race of man, both peoples happily intermingling and wearing the same style of flimsy clothes – silks and muslins in a rainbow assortment of pastel hues, arms and shoulders left bare. Many of the crowd had illustrations printed on their clothes and amazingly the pictures were moving and changing in an animated dance. Hannah was so taken aback by the sight that she nearly didn't notice that there were other races mixed in on the walkways – less numerous that the ursine and men, but walking proudly through the masses nevertheless. Tall feline-faced creatures with legs so long and bony they could have been walking on stilts, and a crimson-coloured race that had an insectoid appearance with compound eyes, were just two of the species she spotted. This was a true multiracial society, as diverse and as vibrant as that of the Kingdom of Jackals today. The invisible currents pulling Hannah tugged her towards the centre of the vast city, over a temple with priests leading a ritual in front of a sea of worshippers – the crowd and the priests made up of the same scattering of races she had already noted. But this was no worship of gods or ancestors Hannah was seeing. The ancient mass these priests were leading was more in the way of a public science experiment.

Understanding filtered through Hannah, rising to her unbidden from the ancient machines of Bloodglass Island. Science, power, the control of nature – but mastery of the outer untempered by any understanding of the inner. Dear Circle, she could have told these ancients they were walking a dangerous path, she could have called out to them over the ages. *Understand your own nature before you understand the world.* But there was no time for any warning, nor voice to be found within Hannah's throat.

The scene changed, moving forward in time – the fashions subtly altered. The manicured parks between the towers had fallen into disrepair, while the energies of the city's inhabitants were now diverted into the skirmishing of street battles as gangs of ursine clashed with thugs from the race of man, youths on both sides raised to hatred while the priests of science hectored and cursed their rivals as heretics. More time passed. The violence grew increasingly organized, bands of cloth tied around heads transforming into uniforms, fists and sticks replaced by dart-firing pistols and rifles – sedatives inside the crystal ammunition giving way to fatal toxins.

Then there was war. Full war, total war, long years of it, growing darker and more desperate. But *what* a war. Artificially created death spores and sicknesses and blights. Thousands of soldiers in armour rising from trenches and running at each other in clouds of killing particles that attempted to melt and destroy their protective suits, hideous monsters brought to life by dark science leaping out from craters like spiders to impale troops. Other creatures gliding down from the dark poison clouds to disgorge sacks of acids across the helmets of their foe, ursine and man writhing in agony, shooting and hacking at each other with blades as hot as furnaces, weapons easily capable of chopping each other's armour into pieces.

It was only ursine versus man now, the other less fecund races exterminated after being caught on one side of the conflict or the other. The war on the island continent lasted centuries until, in a final orgy of destruction, one of the sides unleashed truly terrible weapons – hell-fire impacting the earth, storms that melted stone and incinerated both races, forces that cracked the ground and warped the fabric of the world; great tracts of land turned to liquid flame, the sea itself burning as magma seeped out of the world's wounds.

Hannah was left floating above a land blanketed by eternal winter, and then she noticed the Cade Mountains. There were eyes there, identical to the hideous sentinel that had observed her enter the tunnel, but these eyes were on the other side of the slope, still watching: watching the melted, steaming city as drain covers and survival centre doors lifted up and those who by accident or design had been fortunate enough to be underground when the sun storms scoured the land above them emerged.

Time flickered forward again and Hannah watched as each generation that succeeded the survivors of the conflict fell further from the condition of civilization their forefathers had reached. Scrabbling simply to eke out an existence in the freezing lands about them. But then, something completely unexpected. Hannah was whisked deep under the mountains to a machine-lined chamber filled with ice-covered coffins, their lids retracting to reveal a group of healthy, full-sized ursine. As the cloud of frost dissipated, these last scientist-priests rose as though they were gods returning from an earlier age. A breakaway ursine faction planted like drought seeds to reawaken and rebuild civilization.

However, the land the scientist-priests found waiting for them was far beyond repair, beyond even their worst pre-dictions of the ravages the war would wreak. They tried to resettle the island but it proved too difficult. The tunnel was the sole remaining legacy of that time, leading from nowhere and going nowhere. A fresh start in a new land was the only way their society could live again. Many of the creatures of war given life by their twisted science had become predators, preying on the primitive descendents clinging onto the land, a land too barren to support meaningful agriculture. And there was a worse revelation still to come. Dark energies released in the war had poisoned the very soil that once supported its people. Those that subsisted on the land were poisoned in turn, their flesh twisting and mutating, and in response the scientist-priests did the only thing they could. They created a centre of healing using the last of their hoarded science. *Bloodglass Island*. With a small handful of ursine descendents healed, the priests summoned the flying scouts that had once served them. Their last loyal servants. The Angels of Airdia arrived and bore the healed ursine away to a domain far beyond their ruined home, across the sea to a nation that would become Pericur.

Still the hideous eyes on the mountain watched, recording the march of ages, filling the machines hidden far underground with their recordings of the slow sweep of history. Century upon century – millennia upon millennia. The twisted, broken race of man hammered into primitive, voiceless savages, poison seeping across the generations until the dark energies dissipated and only the ab-locks were left. Tears fell from Hannah's eyes. And while the race of man shrank and became wizened ab-locks, the unhealed ursine left behind had swollen and grown bestial, larger and larger, claws and fangs replacing reasoning and morality. They had become the monstrous race of ursks. Both of those races that had once completely mastered nature fallen victim to the random whittling of an untrammelled creation run wild and merciless. The sole legacy left by their civilization was a deep revulsion between the two races, an ancient war without end turned to nothing more than savage territorial instinct. That and a land locked in fire and circled by a sea of burning magma, its ground echoing to the clashing howls of their devolved descendents.

A geological age later, other offshoots of the race of man had returned to Jago, eventually reencountering the people of Pericur across the sea – the hairless devils of ursine mythology, scorched of all fur by their sins. Another of Alice Gray's sayings came back to Hannah. *Those who failed to learn history are doomed to repeat it.* The Pericurians scheming to evict the Jagonese from their sacred soil, the Jagonese hostility towards their nearest neighbours across the sea, all just a mirror to the thoughtless skirmishes of the ab-locks and ursks. A circle turning and repeating, a memory distorted through Pericurian scripture. That was all that was left of their legacy now. That and – Hannah took a step backwards. *The ancient healing centre on Bloodglass Island.* Capable of restoring degenerate flesh – but Hannah was neither an ab-lock nor an ursk. Her mind was no simple poisoned husk that needed evolving back to full sentience. She tried to will away the ancient vision of knowledge that had possessed her, to return to the walls of the chamber crawling with ancient formulae, but she was firmly held in the tool's grasp now and it had not finished with her. It had barely even started.

Hannah screamed as her brain began to heat up, her every thought a burning dagger as molten as the fires of Jago. Changing her, remaking her. Healing her and killing her. . .

CHAPTER NINETEEN

With eight bearers on either side, strapping ursine adults all, the litter belonging to Baroness Laro urs Laro of the House of Ush, head of the Pericurean trade mission, was borne with careful dignity and some difficulty through the tight entrance to the cavernous senatorial banqueting hall and towards the senate's best imitation of a Pericurian feast.

Despite their best efforts at courtliness, the bearers deposited the Baroness in front of the piled food as if she were another haunch of meat being added to the feast. First Senator Silvermain's free company mercenaries took position along the wall, guns and armour jangling, two food tasters emerging from a doorway to flank the politician and his noble guest – both the food tasters kin of the kitchen staff, as was the Jagonese tradition. The possibility of poison aside, the two food tasters looked as happy to be sampling the foreign food as the First Senator's favoured courtiers and cronies. They were trying not to make it too obvious as they covered their noses with silk handkerchiefs in distaste at the fare in front of them. There were a few disgusted mutters of *wet-snout food* whispered by the courtiers forced to sit down with this foreign savage.

Banging the First Senator's staff of office on the stone floor, the senatorial rod carrier declared the state occasion open with all the flowery language expected of him and extended the senate's official leave-taking to the baroness of Pericur, expressing the senate's deep regret at her recall to her noble homeland. As the man's last words echoed away, waiting staff emerged in force to remove heavy glass domes from platters of food, revealing roast meats spread across beds of sugared rice, all smothered with a pungent honeyed sauce made from rotting fish entrails. Steam rose up towards the stained glass windows in the arches above.

'Remind us, how long has the House of Ush held the trading licence for Jago, baroness?' First Senator Silvermain solicitously enquired as he waved sweet wine towards his guest of honour, who had already started pulling honey-soaked baked hams off the table and towards her razor sharp teeth.

'Seventeen years, noble excellency,' said the baroness from the horizontal comfort of her litter, wiping her face with the fur on the back of her huge wrists.

'Yes, we remember now,' said the First Senator. 'It seems like only yesterday we assumed the mantle of our position – a couple of years before the House of Ush replaced the incumbent trading house. And now the wheel has turned. Your house's boat is due today, is it not? By tomorrow you shall be sailing for your homeland.'

'The boat will be here by this afternoon,' agreed the baroness, holding out one of her people's traditional leather cups for the senatorial staff to fill with sweet wine.

'You seem to be bearing your house's loss of its trading licence with admirable equanimity,' said Silvermain.

'Life is change.'

'Change, indeed,' said the First Senator. 'A good Circlist sentiment. Your previous archduchess was a great reformer;

ruling with ambition and vision, cut much from our own cloth. The loss of your patron is not just mourned by the House of Ush; it is Jago's loss also.'

The baroness shrugged, sending great ripples of fur rolling down her body. 'Forests have been felled and mills built, with many minor merchant houses raised on the tide of their industry. Not even the conservatives can so easily turn the clock back on our advances. There is a time for everything and our house's star will be resurgent again.'

'Capital. If only you had been born within the race of man, baroness,' trilled the First Senator. 'Such vim! No whining or complaining. If we had a hundred such as you sitting by our side in the hall of the stained senate, then our future could not be denied!'

The baroness raised her overflowing wine cup in a toast. 'To futures that cannot be denied.'

The First Senator was delighted to join in the toast, before calling out for Stom urs Stom. The mercenary officer appeared and was dispatched with a company of her hulking soldiers to bring back the architect's model of the planned new capital. The mercenaries returned, struggling under the immense weight of a section of the scale model, and lowered it to the floor in front of the table.

'These are the docks for New Titus,' said the First Senator, his hand sweeping proudly over the diorama. 'U-boat pens with space enough to accept freighters from all over the world, for who will not want to visit us to see the wonders we will construct anew on Jago? And here—' he indicated a vast stretch of marble buildings lining the underwater harbour '—will sit the new Pericurian trading mission. After you return home, you must spread word among your liberal allies in the baronial council that as Pericur is now becoming a great power in the world, we shall be building them a trade mission worthy of your people's ambitions. We shall prosper together, Jago and Pericur, as an apprentice and an old tradesman prosper in their shared labours, participating in the glory of the great venture we are planning here.'

There was an enthusiastic round of applause from Silvermain's favoured senators and courtiers as Baroness Laro urs Laro bowed her head in recognition of the First Senator's flattery.

'And will your trading boat from Pericur be bringing word of which house the archduchess has decided to favour with the new grant of the Jagonese commercial concession?'

'I do not think so,' said the Baroness, picking a string of bacon fat out of her teeth.

'But surely the archduchess will want to award it to one of her political allies? That is the way of patronage, is it not?'

'It is a matter of economics, not patronage,' said the baroness, with the same tone that a mother might use in telling a truculent child that there would be no supper for the night. 'Have you never been shown your trade minister's accounts? Since the opening of the southwest passage diverted all the shipping away from Jago, your coffers have been running down to empty over the last few years. There is simply no margin for us now here on Jago.'

'But,' the shocked First Senator had abandoned all pretence of nibbling at the pungent foreign dishes, 'we have been given assurances from the archduchess through your embassy. The trading license will be passed onto a new house just as it always has.'

'I would be surprised if she hadn't made such assurances to you,' said the baroness. 'Maybe she even believes her own words. But there is something else to consider. . .'

'What?' the First Senator pressed.

'It is a confidence,' said the baroness. 'I would like to share it with you, but first, I must admit, I am most curious. I have heard that you have the gift of reading the lines of your people's feet in the manner of a wise woman, that you can ascertain much about the person, even their future.'

'We do possess that gift,' said the First Senator, the anxiety in his voice mixed with a sliver of satisfaction that word of his second sight had passed as far as the foreign traders.

'I heard as much soon after I first arrived on Jago,' said the baroness, 'and ever since I discovered it, I have often wondered if your gift might extend to an ursine's feet as well as those of the race of man.' She clicked her fat furred fingers and one of her retainers jumped forward to slip off her enormous dark leather boots. 'Will you do me this honour, noble excellency? In return I shall pass on some small intelligence I have come into possession of, a morsel that will prove of great advantage to you'

'It is said that fair exchange is no robbery,' said the First Senator, kneeling down to run his hands along the two fur-covered slabs of flesh that had been revealed. The ranks of Jagonese courtiers suppressed their scandalized coughs and whispers at the lack of decorum in the situation, lest their dangerously erratic master overhear them. Silvermain examined the limbs of the baroness and poked and prodded at her soles for a minute before he appeared to give up. 'We fear these are too unlike the feet of our people for our talent to be brought to bear. We can see no future here.'

The baroness nodded thoughtfully and bent forward. 'Well, you tried, so I shall tell you the few facts I know. The assurances of the present archduchess are worthless. I fear her reign will be short. You see, she is close to being replaced.'

A shocked hush fell over the table at this sudden revelation.

'What faction could take power so quickly?' asked the First Senator. 'Who is to be installed as the new archduchess?'

Baroness Laro urs Laro looked distrustfully at the staring faces of the First Senator's lackeys around the table. 'I will whisper the name to you.'

The First Senator came forward, climbing up between the sprawling noble's legs as the baroness bent forward on her litter, pushing aside the politician's hair around his ears and drawing his head in close to her voluminous belly.

'Me,' she whispered, pushing the First Senator's face down flat onto the great folds of furred flesh. Silvermain's yell of surprise was smothered by the vast tract of flesh blocking his nose and mouth, his spine pressed down by the full strength of the massive ursine female.

There was a moment when the courtiers lining the table opposite looked at the jerking, struggling body of the First Senator being suffocated as though this might be some surreal prank being played on them by their insane ruler. But there was little disguising the reality of Silvermain's violent spasms. A clang sounded through the hall as the door to the banqueting chamber was locked from inside.

The First Senator's rod bearer ran up to the advancing free company soldiers. 'She's lost her bloody mind, beat her off, bring her down. Kill her if you have to.'

'I am loath to do so,' said Stom urs Stom.

'But I'm ordering you,' spluttered the official. 'That's your sworn liege-lord!' He stumbled back, looking dumbfounded at the short sword thrust into his chest.

'That would depend,' said Stom, unhooking her turret rifle from the brass tank on her back, 'on who commanded the oath to start with.'

Rifles burst into action, courtiers and senators sent sprawling as heavy piton heads struck them. None of the Jagonese was permitted arms in the presence of their First Senator, and they scrambled away in terror from the table, ploughing into serving staff trying to escape down the passage to the kitchens, only to find its doors bolted by those that were meant to be guarding them. The serving staff died with more dignity than their politician masters, turning and throwing themselves at the guns of the mercenaries rather than clawing in useless desperation at the thick oak doors blocking their exit. In the narrow confines of the corridor concentrated weapons fire tore the fleeing throng to shreds without discrimination.

Great pawed hands reached under the stone table to pull out a few remaining, cowering senators, tossing more targets into the open. The politicians had hardly got to their feet when they were cut down again in a hail of heavy pitons. They lay twitching on the stone floor as the last few embers of life departed.

Laro urs Laro, Baroness of the House of Ush, pulled herself to her feet, casually discarding the blue-faced corpse of the First Senator as she surveyed with satisfaction the dozens of bodies strewn across the banqueting hall.

She addressed Stom urs Stom. 'I believe I won our wager.'

'Baroness?'

'It seems the First Senator had the gift after all.' Her foot stepped down on the scale model of Titus City abandoned on the floor, splintering a whole district with her weight.

We can see no future here.

The feverish air on top of the coral rise surrounding Jago resounded to the crack of the work crew's sledgehammers chipping away at the growth. The Jagonese had long ago realized that the best way to control the width of their protective coral line was to prune the height of the great rise – topping it forced its growth out horizontally instead, thickening the defences.

Theirs was hard, hot, dirty work, judged vital by the lessons of history – the coral line had turned back the long wooden ships of the polar barbarians, the wheel-powered dreadnaughts of the Chimecan Empire – every foe who had been attracted by the wealth and power of the island nation in centuries past.

It was always a welcome part of the work gang's routine to take pause for a water break when the trading boat from Pericur arrived in front of the massive gates cut into the rise, the sight of the machines drawing open the doors below, an awe-inspiring sight, as well as an excuse to halt their back-breaking labours. But the crew knew enough about the comings and goings of the trading vessel to recognize that a thrashing in the water didn't normally precede its arrival as the thick-skinned dolphins that inhabited the boils tried to flee before the iron hull. And if the merchant u-boat below had an escort of dolphins, it was missing the accompanying tug that would have normally guaranteed it safe passage through the Fire Sea's shifting flows of magma.

The coral line's portcullis master and his workers must have shared the work crew's sense that something was out of place, as the gates that had started to open were now slowly shutting in the face of the trading boat. The work crew's feelings turned from apprehension to panic as they saw gate staff being tossed out of balconies along the gate's control cabins below, tiny bodies bouncing and tumbling off the coral line's slopes before being absorbed by the searing waters of the channel they were meant to be protecting.

Behind the Pericurian trading boat, the bowsprit of a u-boat broke the steaming water's surface, then another and another, ugly black lines of men-o'war masked by the steaming wash flowing off a forest of conning towers; hundreds of submersibles rising up from the depths of the channel leading to Jago's entrance. And to the work crew's horror, the gate's closure had now halted, the rumble of the machines accelerating as they powered up again to open the gates wide, admitting the dark-hulled armada into their realm. None of the snub-nosed mortars and cannons on the bastions of the coral line's gun emplacements were moving into position, let alone shaking the air with the ear-splitting fury of their weekly gunnery practice. The free company soldiers that the work crew could see on the emplacements below seemed unconcerned by the massive fleet's arrival.

Impotently clutching their sledgehammers, the workers on the summit could only look on in stunned disbelief as the first successful breach of Jago's sea defences sailed through the coral line completely unopposed.

CHAPTER TWENTY

Hannah groaned, gasping for breath as Tobias Raffold withdrew a foully reeking bottle of smelling salts from under her nose.

'Ah, lass,' wheezed the commodore, coming into blurred view and offering her a canteen of water. 'I thought you'd had it there for sure. But old Blacky was near enough to hear your screams and pull you out of your tunnel, covered though you were in wicked lights dancing around you like a swarm of angry hornets.'

She was lying down on the ground outside one of the singing buildings, her head aching – not with pain, but with perfect clarity. 'Nandi and the ambassador, get them out of the buildings.'

'They're not inside,' said the trapper's leader. 'It was only you in there.'

'Nandi and Ortin are off. They've made another discovery, lass,' explained the commodore. 'A set of stairs under the floor of one of the tunnel chambers in the mountain, corkscrewing deep underground. There's a lead-lined tabernacle down there filled with scraps of Ortin urs Ortin's blessed scripture and a

circle of coffins that looks like a pack of bloodsuckers could
have made their nest inside the hall.'

'Not vampires,' coughed Hannah. 'Only forgotten dreams
and dust down there now. She went into the buildings, she
went inside them all.'

'Who, lass?'

'Bel Bessant. She passed through every last one of these
buildings. The machines thought they were healing her, but
they were changing her, making her intelligent enough to be
able to create something as obscene as the god-formula.'

'You're not making any blessed sense.'

Hannah grabbed the commodore's jacket. 'That's because I
can see more clearly now. Don't you see! They destroyed paradise over this, over whether it was right to alter your mind and
your body – raise yourself so far and fast ahead of everyone
else you wouldn't even be able to recognize yourself by the
time you'd finished. Changing the template of your creation.
Their minds, new minds, building weapons, so terrible.'

'Your forehead, now,' said the commodore extending a worried
palm. 'Your temperature is running wild.'

'Connections, more connections,' spluttered Hannah.' But
they're settling down, the density, cooling.'

'Let's take her back to her tent,' Tobias Raffold said to the
commodore, looking around nervously. 'Hang me, but I'm
getting as superstitious about this damn place as you are.'

'No!' shouted Hannah. 'We've got to blow the remaining
buildings, finish the work that William of Flamewall began.
None of them can be allowed to stand, none of them!'

Hannah watched the smoke rise out of the buildings on
Bloodglass Island from the other side of the glassy plain. Their
song had changed now, discordant and ugly after the last
explosion had rocked the final building – the same structure

342

that had recounted the tale of Jago's lost paradise to her. She still didn't know if it was the race of man or the ursine who had been in favour of advancing their minds into something so ingenious and alien that those that remained behind must have seemed as insignificant as insects.

It hardly mattered. That dream was an abomination and she, like William of Flamewall, had decided that the buildings had to be destroyed. Would Hannah have made the same decision if she had been able to pass through each building in turn, each one pushing her further and further away from the template she had been born to? Bel Bessant clearly hadn't. She had made a different choice. The rest of humanity must have appeared like drooling household pets to her as she worked on her god-formula – still not satisfied with being so far ahead of the rest of her kind. She had wanted to accelerate the process with another step-change of complexity and raise herself to the status of godhood without a backward glance to those she would have abandoned to their mortality. Following her course even having seen the wreckage of what had been lost. Would Hannah's mother have resisted the same temptation if her leg hadn't killed her before she could unlock the buildings' secrets? Hannah suspected not. Her mother couldn't have gone quite as far as Bel Bessant, not with William of Flamewall's vandalism of the last few chambers. But driven by revenge she might have gone far enough. Hannah looked sadly at her mother's grave. Perhaps the fever of that mangled leg had done her mother a favour after all?

The expedition's RAM suits needed to be charged on the other side of the mountain tunnel and they were finished here. Hannah had lived up to the trust that Jethro Daunt had placed in her, and the Pericurian ambassador was ecstatic that he had his fragments from a tabernacle to prove there were literal as well as spiritual dimensions to his people's liturgy. Hannah did not disabuse him. She did not tell him that the earliest writings of his people's faith were the distorted ramblings of sixth generation survivors of an ancient war, living like beasts in caves, poisoned and degenerate and not yet healed by their sleeping scientist-priests. Well, the Pericurian faith was as good as any other religion, she supposed. Power without wisdom. Science fallen to superstition. The ancients who had lived here had come so close. If only they had tempered their mastery of the world with an equal understanding of their own nature, what a world they might have built around them!

And Ortin urs Ortin wasn't the only happy one. Nandi now carried with her the ground-shaking revelation of a prior civilization that predated the migrant Jagonese by so many millennia that it was impossible even to calculate the time scale of their existence. The commodore was simply happy that Nandi's research had run its course and his precious u-boat would soon be able to sail away leaving the black cliffs of Jago behind him.

What Hannah still hadn't told any of her friends was that her dangerously quick new brain had worked out the final resting place of the missing third section of the god-formula, and it certainly wasn't ashes left over from an incineration centuries earlier, blowing as dust around the bones of William of Flamewall. *It was back in Hermetica City.*

Tobias Raffold's RAM suit stopped under the wan light of the aqueduct's lamps, the other members of the expedition slowing to a halt behind the trapper.

Commodore Black was standing next to Hannah. The u-boat man's voice echoed around her pilot cabin. 'Not more beasts? Can they not leave us alone now that we're nearly out of the wilderness?'

'There's free company soldiers ahead, some in suits and some on foot,' announced the trapper, examining the scene through a magnification plate.

'Protecting the city's maintenance workers?' asked Hannah.

'I can just see the soldiers,' said the trapper, lowering the plate from his face. 'No workers.'

'Are they waiting for us, then?' wondered the commodore. 'With a warrant of arrest from the prickly madman that rules this place? Ah, that's too bad. No doubt one of his blessed new vaults has caved in while we've been off journeying and he wants to lock us all up as saboteurs.'

'I say we don't find out,' said Tobias Raffold, 'we bypass them through the forest and—'

His plan was interrupted by the hiss of a flare from the leg of one of the suits, a shimmering red umbrella of light extending over the expedition as the burning tube drifted in the mist-fingered wind above their heads. There were shouts from lower down the aqueduct's course, the free company soldiers turning towards the expedition's position.

'Which bloody idiot. . .?' the trapper shouted.

'My apologies, dear boy,' called the ambassador. 'The flare handle caught on my sleeve as I was trying to bring my magnification plate up. These machines really aren't built for someone of my bulk.'

'You've paid for us to be out here,' said the trapper, angrily, 'and if Silvermain's pets are waiting for us, you might just have put paid to us too with your clumsiness.'

'Those were idle threats made against us before we left,' said the ambassador. 'I carry diplomatic immunity. I'm sure there is nothing here that cannot be reasonably negotiated.' He passed the trapper and walked down towards the advancing free company soldiers.

'Fine for him,' the commodore muttered to Hannah and

Nandi. 'It's just the mortal rest of us that'll end up rotting in the senate's dungeons.'

A couple of minutes later the ambassador returned, followed by a free company officer in a RAM suit. 'There we are. Nobody has been posted to arrest us. An ursk pack has been carrying stones to the top of the aqueduct to block the water supply in the hope of luring out a meal from the city to fix it. This unit has arrived to clear the blockage. Not only shall we be back at Hermetica City shortly, we now have an armed escort to protect us on the remainder of our journey.'

'How far are we from the city? Hannah asked the free company officer.

'She only understands Pericurian, dear girl,' the ambassador answered for the soldier.

'Oh,' said Hannah. That was odd. Most of the free company soldiers had picked up at least a smattering of Jagonese during their time on the island.

'We're close enough to home,' said the trapper.

Close enough. Yes. How good it would be to leave the sweat-stained confines of her RAM suit's cabin behind at last. Stretch her legs on the streets of Hermetica. Sit down at a tea table and watch the traffic of the Grand Canal without worrying about ursks and ab-locks hiding in ambush around the corner. And to think she used to believe that her mattress back at the cathedral was hard.

As they moved past the unit of soldiers, Nandi's RAM suit slowed in front of Hannah, stopping in front of the aqueduct. The young archaeologist leaned in for a closer look before popping her skull dome to inspect a series of cords dangling from the construction.

'This is wrong!' Nandi called.

The others in the expedition halted, the free company soldiers at the front of the aqueduct backing away from them.

Nandi indicated the hanging cords to the soldiers. 'You can't use this many blasting tubes to clear a blockage up there. You'll bring the whole thing down on top of you.'

The soldiers were shouting up at the archaeologist's open canopy. Hannah's grasp of Pericurian was shaky, but she was sure they were telling the archaeologist to step back.

'I've used blasting tubes to open up tombs,' Nandi insisted, waving at them. Their shouts were getting louder and angrier, as was the young archaeologist's tone. 'You fools, you're going to be showering pieces of aqueduct down for miles if you detonate this.'

Striding towards Nandi, the free company officer in the RAM suit raised her arm and the air hissed as a razored disk slashed into Nandi's open pilot cabin, a splash of blood spitting across the visor of Hannah's canopy. Hannah stood still, transfixed as Nandi's blood rolled down her glass, hardly hearing the shouts of the free company soldiers surrounding the expedition, or the yells of the trappers they aimed their guns at. Inside the pilot cage of Nandi's machine, the young academic's body had fallen back and the suit translated its occupant's motion, tumbling back and collapsing onto the hard, snow-covered ground.

'I am sorry,' called Ortin urs Ortin, his RAM suit returning from the head of the column. 'They did not understand what she was trying to do. It was an accident!'

Hannah was out of her suit and down beside the fallen machine before she was aware of what she was doing, clambering up towards Nandi's cockpit. She found that Commodore Black was already on the ground and there before her.

'Don't be looking inside, lass.' He pushed Hannah back, shaking himself – whether in anger or shock she couldn't say.

'Nandi!'

'Her head's been taken off. Ah my oath, my word to the

347

professor and this brave girl here with her head taken off. All this way, all this way for *this*. Nandi Tibar-Wellking, you poor blessed thing.'

'You jiggers!' Hannah screamed at the free company troops advancing on them. 'She was just trying to help you!'

Commodore Black had his empty palms in the air, showing the soldiers he was holding no weapons. 'Quiet now, Hannah. The blood of these brutes is running hot on a hair trigger and you can't help Nandi by joining her along the Circle's turn.'

Ortin urs Ortin was barking at the soldiers in Pericurian, but whatever the ambassador was shouting didn't seem to be calming them down.

'I want this wet-snout on charges,' Tobias Raffold yelled, thrusting his suit's fist towards the free company officer. 'I want this—'

His demands ended as a volley of turret-rifle fire jounced off his suit's armour, the canopy shattering in a storm of crystal as the free company fighters opened up on the trapper from all directions. Hannah was left scrambling over the cold ground, the whine of metal pitons mixed with the sound of splintering iron from the aqueduct behind her. The commodore knocked Hannah down to the icy soil as she was desperately weighing up her options – running for the cover of the ursk-haunted forest or the relative safety of her own RAM suit – a piton flying across where she'd just been standing.

Jared Black was trying to help Hannah to her feet when the hulking free company soldiers overtook them and they both went down in a flurry of blows from the iron grips of turret rifle butts. Hannah was still reeling from the pain when a blunt weapon connected with her head and she lost consciousness.

Hannah had a variety of agonies to choose from when she began to regain consciousness, and it was a few seconds before she was able to separate the throbbing in her head from the thud of explosions she could hear around her. She was next to Commodore Black in a cage on the back of one of the trapper's RAM suits, the machine lurching heavily over the landscape.

Then Hannah remembered Nandi and the swollen bruised skin around her eyes stung with tears. Nandi, poor Nandi. She was gone. Her corpse abandoned behind them somewhere in the wilderness. Hannah had never had that many friends on Jago, and now she was left with one less – except that the pain of the memory stung worse, like losing a sister she had never had. Nandi had risked her life to save Hannah from service in the guild, and how badly fate had rewarded the young academic. One second alive and vibrant, the next shot dead. Was this their deadly punishment for disobeying the senatorial will and mounting an expedition to Jago's interior in spite of the insane First Senator's opposition to it? It should have been Hannah who had died, but then, the secret of the final part of the god-formula would have died with her. The secret she could use to fix all this, to bring Nandi back to life. The memory of Nandi's voice echoed in her mind over the sounds of battle outside. '*What would such a thing be but a poorly formed simulacra?*'

'Those noises,' Hannah coughed.

'Mortars, rifles and cannons. We're in a shooting war, lass. And I think I know whose. . .'

Whose soon became clear. The plain outside Hermetica City's battlements was full of Pericurian soldiery, the capital's wall standing silent without the killing hum of electricity that usually flowed along its surface. Rows of tents and makeshift palisades were being raised in its lee. Massive iron cranes had been driven into the top of the black cliffs of Jago, lifting up more Pericurian formations and supplies onto the dark basalt plain from a fleet that lay out of sight below. Every gate in the sloped iron battlements that Hannah could see was wide open, ursine troops marching through.

Commodore Black pointed to a line of new pennants raised from one of the wall's sentry stations. Dozens of triangles of fabric fluttered in the chill arctic wind, each a different colour, each bearing a different tree — oaks, sycamores, blackthorns, camwoods.

'There's the blessed answer, flapping in the breeze. Pericur!

But the capital was yet to fall entirely. Whatever the state of affairs above ground, there were puffs of rifle smoke rising from the structures built into the slopes of the Horn of Jago answered by the roar of cannon fire from the Pericurian siege below.

Reaching the lee of the capital's silent battlements, Hannah and the commodore's cage was lowered towards the ground and when the door was sprung, they found themselves facing Ortin urs Ortin, with a ring of Pericurian soldiers pointing turret rifles at them.

'Put your guns down now,' wheezed the commodore. 'There's just me and the girl and I've no weapons nor figh left in me besides.'

'Where's everyone else?' asked Hannah. 'Where are the trappers?'

'They opened fire when Tobias Raffold went down,' whis pered the commodore. 'The wet-snouts killed them all. We were only spared because we were out of our suits and already beaten into the snow for our troubles. The ursine weren' there to clear the aqueduct, Hannah. They were there to cu off the city's drinking water supply. The brutes blew it to pieces after they shoved you and me into the cage.'

Hannah looked angrily at the ambassador. 'This is badly done.'

'It is necessary,' said Ortin urs Ortin, motioning at the troops to lower their massive weapons.

Commodore Black indicated the pennants raised above the capital's battlements. 'Those are the flags of the great liberal houses, ambassador. Not the wicked firebrands that follow the archduchess, but your people!'

'It is the only way to secure our fortunes, dear boy,' said the ambassador. 'We will present the baronial council with something no one in history had been able to do before – the removal of all interlopers from the sacred soil of Jago.'

'How can you do this?' Hannah pleaded. 'To Nandi, to the Jagonese?'

'How could we not, young lady?' The ambassador pointed at the lead tabernacle that had been recovered from the chamber deep under the Cade Mountains. 'How can you even ask that after everything that we saw on the other side of the mountains? This land is cursed, nothing can prosper here. Its poisons have infected the Jagonese and your society has been on its deathbed for centuries. Pericur is not here to conquer; we are here as *liberators*. When we've defeated the nobles who are your jailors, do you think we will need to drag the common people out of their vaults, crying, kicking and fighting at the tips of our sabres? No, we will point to the empty holds of our freighters and offer your people free passage to the colonies across the sea and they will flood away. No more ballot, no more protected professions, no more exile into the wastes for those caught trying to stow away for just the chance of a better life.'

'Spare us your cant, lad,' said the commodore. 'You're doing this for politics, not for the people here.'

'Nobody's hands are clean, dear boy,' said the ambassador. 'Especially not yours. What do you think our houses needed all those transaction engines for? Why do you think our last archduchess was willing to give a ship of the *Purity Queen*'s reputation a trading licence?'

Hannah's heart sank. So much processing power. Enough, perhaps, to approach the power of the transaction-engine vaults of the guild, if not the sophistication of the guild's valve-based engines. 'You were modelling the flows of the Fire Sea.'

'Safe passage through the magma,' smiled Ortin urs Ortin. 'For the greatest war fleet our nation has ever raised.'

Commodore Black's eyes blazed in anger, but Hannah could only shake her head in disgust. How long had Jago's neighbour on the other side of the Fire Sea been planning this holy war of theirs? As she pondered, a figure she recognized came striding out of a gate opened in the battlements. The First Senator's pet, Stom urs Stom.

The head of the free company fighters marched up to the survivors of the expedition and her eyes widened when she saw the lead tabernacle retrieved by the ambassador. 'The Divine Quad has smiled upon you, my ambassador.'

There was a light in those eyes, Hannah realized, a light that had been well hidden before. The glare of a fanatic.

'Just so, my captain,' said the ambassador. 'I have seen such things out in the wilderness. The ruin of paradise. The words of the scripture are true, all of them. How long have our forces been camped here?'

'A day only.'

'I did not anticipate quite so much activity on the surface,' said the ambassador, looking across their camped legions.

'The tug service jammed the lifting rooms on the seabed. We weren't able to enter the harbour with the fleet. It is only a small set-back.' Stom urs Stom indicated her forces massing in front of the wall. 'We have taken the coral line; we have taken the city wall and secured all the gun emplacements

352

protecting the capital. The Jagonese have no reply to our cannons except a few police militia pistols and rifles on the slopes of the mountain. With all the airshafts under our control on the surface we can drop down into the city vaults at any point, as we will.'

Ortin looked up at the Horn of Jago. 'You have troops enough to assault the slopes?'

'Only a few scared policemen shelter behind the stained glass windows,' said the officer triumphantly. 'Without even the counsel of their leaders now that the head of the snake has been decapitated.'

'Traitor!' shouted Hannah. 'Traitor to the oath of the free company.'

'Keep her quiet,' snapped Stom. 'Or I will cut out her tongue.'

'These are no mere free company fighters,' said Ortin urs Ortin. 'During my years in the Kingdom of Jackals I played my own small part in that ruse. Paying corrupt pensmen working on the Kingdom's newssheets to plant false stories concerning the exploits of the continent's most successful band of ursine mercenaries. The free company's activities were legendary, making them the natural choice for the First Senator to hire when he decided to engage his own private army to cling onto power.'

'You're a clever fellow,' said the commodore, 'taking by subterfuge what you could not take by force.'

'Not bad for a savage, you mean, old fruit? Not bad for a simple wet-snout? You really shouldn't have underestimated our people so, and the Guild of Valvemen shouldn't have recorded in their archives everything that they read in quite so unquestioning a manner.'

'We are the chosen,' said Stom, proudly pointing to the army's pennants. She growled another word Hannah didn't

353

recognize. 'The bodyguards of the great houses. Shock troops. Our loyalty cannot be questioned. It was just, unfortunately for the Jagonese, never your First Senator's to command.'

'Please don't do this, Ortin,' said Hannah. 'Don't let your people do this. I know that you're not bad, but this terrible thing is not right or rational.'

'It is entirely right, dear girl,' said the ambassador. 'We have the righteousness of the scriptures as well as the weight of the large guns on our side. Your people's time here desecrating our forbidden soil is at an end, and not even your own commoners will mourn your age's end.'

Religion, always religion. Hannah shook her head. This disease was too deep for any other course to run here.

'We don't despise you,' said Stom, watching her soldiers step forward and manacle Hannah and the commodore's hands. 'We pity you. Your forefathers were burnt of their fur for their sins. It is only natural you should be attracted back but staying here is an offence against the Divine Quad. Your presence on this bitter ground is twisting your people to ruin, soiling your symmetry, until one day you will become demonic enough to call down another Armageddon upon the world.'

'Well, that's mortal big of you to feel sorry on our account,' spat the commodore. 'After you and your traitorous diploma friend have taken the life of a girl who was under my protection. Someone who had not an ounce of wickedness in her bones, nor any cause against your people.'

'Someone who has sailed the world should not be so naïve,' said the ambassador. 'There are always innocent casualties in these affairs, dear boy.'

'I'm always ready to be disappointed, and sure enough the world's always obliged me there,' said the commodore. 'But I'll trade you your pity for your corpse. Toss me a sabre and I'll pit what I've learnt on my voyages against you and your chosen brutes here. Line them up and let's see how well your filthy scripture protects a gang of cowards.'

Stom urs Stom angrily drew her short sword and looked ready to grant the commodore his match, but the ambassador pushed the blade back into her scabbard for her. 'The great houses would much prefer to choose their wars, my dear captain, rather than have them forced upon them. Let's try not to kill any more Jackelians today. Lock these two up in the fleet's brig. After we've captured the Jackelian embassy staff, they will all be given safe passage across to their colonies.'

Hannah coughed as a wave of pungent cannon smoke drifted over them. The Pericurian formations were moving into position to attack the city; perhaps as many soldiers as there were citizens of Hermetica City. Their black leather uniforms were weighed down with ammunition belts, blades and the brass tanks to power their turret rifles. Hannah choked down her despair. And against what? Shoemakers and gondola men, storekeepers and merchants. Many of whom, it was true, would be only too glad to accept their conqueror's offer of passage away from Jago if they survived this war.

Their time here was at an end.

CHAPTER TWENTY-ONE

Part of Jethro Daunt knew where he was, shivering inside the cell of the militia fortress, his sleep disturbed by the muffled cries of agony that could be heard at night in any house of correction. And other sounds, too. Otherworldly sounds. Jethro could hear Badger-headed Joseph snuffling around outside the cell door, just as real as the wan light thrown from the single electric lantern in the ceiling.

'Such a disappointment,' snuffled the ancient god. 'Not even brave enough to put your principles to the test. Pushing a little girl out into the darkness just so you wouldn't have to suffer temptation.'

'The frustration in your voice is enough to tell me that I made the rational choice,' Jethro called to the voice behind the cell door.

'What makes you think that yours wasn't exactly the decision we wanted?' growled the ancient god. 'Your young friend hasn't had a good time out there in the wilderness, fiddle-faddle man. Do you think we had to line up behind Bel Bessant and push and prod her into creating the god-formula? No, she saw what the veneration of science over nature leads to, logic over spirit, learning without play, laws without passion.' There was a noise like a shudder of relief. 'And now your young friend's returned cleverer than you. Just like Bel Bessant. Clever enough to see things without the pipe-smoke of your pious humanist humbug. Soon, she won't be looking into the core of humanity for answers; she'll be looking to us. Joining us!'

So, young Hannah Conquest was safely returned. Perhaps the gods had been looking after her.

'All she needs now is to see her people as they really are, and there's nothing like a good war to put a shine on your kind's true nature.'

There was a moment's silence as Badger-headed Joseph waited for a reaction from the ex-parson. But the ancient spirit was to be disappointed. 'Have you not even the breath to deny us?'

'Not today, good emissary,' said Jethro. 'This day, I'm going to do the one thing your kind truly can't suffer. I'm going to forget you, and by the time I'm finished on this island, you're going to be just another echo lost in history, your idols three-penny curiosities in an antique shop – good for a bookend or a doorstop.' Jethro started laughing and the voice hissed in anger at his mockery, the hiss transforming into the steam escaping from Boxiron's stack.

The steamman was shaking Jethro awake. 'I'm glad you can find some amusement in our confinement. Clear your eyes of sleep. Something is happening outside. Cell doors are being opened up along the corridor and I have heard gunfire in the distance.'

Jethro rubbed his tired eyes. 'It's a war.'

'Jago is unassailable, Jethro softbody,' said Boxiron. 'If I wore my old war frame and had every steamman knight that ever served King Steam given to my command, I would still not wish to assault this place.'

'Perhaps,' said Jethro, touching his heart. 'But that's not where the war that matters is going to be fought.'

From outside their cell came a clanking, then the door was pushed inward and the space filled by a fat militiaman. 'It's your lucky day, my bucks. Follow the others up the stairs to the courtyard level. Draw a rifle. You're going to get to fight for your freedom.'

'I'm not a soldier,' said Jethro.

'Everyone's a soldier today, friend.'

'Who is the foe?' asked Boxiron.

'It's the wet-snouts, metal shanks. Seems they got tired of bleeding us dry slowly with their trading boats. Now they're here to finish the job fast with their armies.'

'We are Jackelian citizens,' protested Jethro.

'The wet-snouts are climbing down the shafts and killing everyone they come across,' said the militiaman, impatiently jingling his keys and kicking straw on the floor at them. 'When they find you they won't see a kingdom man, they'll see meat to decorate the end of their bayonet. Now get out – any prisoner who's not joining up today, we're hanging.'

Jethro noted the evidence of that in front of the police fortress, a gallows erected between two statues of mastiffs, the granite hunting hounds carved with leather hoods covering their eyes. The statues might have been symbolically blinded to the status of those the police pursued, but Jethro needed to turn his face away from the figures hanging in warning from their ropes – militiamen tugging at the boots of one of the recent thrashing additions, a recalcitrant who clearly hadn't been cleanly finished by the drop from the trapdoor. Was Jethro's reaction hypocritical, he wondered? He had worked with Ham Yard back in Jackals to send many a killer to such a fate. But he had never joined the crowds outside Bonegate Prison on a hanging day to see the final result of his labours.

Filing to a table set up in the shadow of the gallows with the other prisoners, Jethro found a long rifle pushed into his hands, an ugly length of steel with an intricate clockwork firing mechanism mounted on an engraved brass lock-plate.

'This still has oil on it,' Jethro said to the bald militiaman lifting the long guns out of wooden crates piled behind the table.

'It's new. Wipe the barrel clean on your sleeve and then sod off.'

Jethro was shoved forward by one of the militiamen guarding them, the slippery gun almost falling out of his hands. Yes. New rifles for a *surprise* attack by Pericur.

Behind him, Boxiron was thrusting his rifle back at the militiaman behind the table. 'The trigger will not accommodate my fingers. Your weapons mill has made them too small.'

'Beg your pardon, my lord,' spat the militiaman. 'We'll get our gunsmith to commission you your own personal piece in gold. In the meantime, you'll bloody fight like everyone else.'

Boxiron reached behind the table and picked up one of the sledgehammers the militiamen had been using to crack open the wooden rifle crates.

'That's just a hammer,' said the militiaman.

'In your hands, perhaps,' corrected Boxiron, his body hulking above the militiaman's frame. 'In mine it is a *warhammer*.'

'You are too eager, old steamer,' Jethro said to Boxiron as they cleared the line. 'This is not our fight and you know your hands shake too much for a gun to be of use to you.'

'I will not let us die here, Jethro softbody. I know you won't raise your rifle to protect yourself, there is too much of the parson left in you.'

'As I fear there is too much of a steamman knight left in you.'

'I still have a head for war,' agreed Boxiron.

That was what Jethro feared, that and a hulking body that had been used for murder before Boxiron had allowed himself to be saved from the flash mob's clutches by a young ex-parson recently defrocked from the rational orders.

'I have exceedingly few friends left who do not shun me,' said Jethro. 'I would not see that number dwindle still further, good steamman.'

'Avert your eyes, Jethro softbody. You will find this distasteful.' The steamman fell to his knees, his voicebox echoing in machine song with the names of his ancestors, the Loas of his people – Steelbhalah Waldo, Legba of the Valves, Magnet-e-rouge. But he never prayed to his Loas anymore, not to those that had forsaken him. . .

'They did not come,' said Jethro as his friend fell silent and stood up.

'I did not ask them to,' said Boxiron. 'For all your studies of religions to deny, I think you still do not understand what it is to believe.'

All around them, the lines of released prisoners were being formed into companies and dispatched to various vaults, given the names of streets where barricades had been set up and airshafts where the police militia expected the Pericurians to strike next. The two of them were assigned to a group of perhaps twenty convicts who – with the exception of the hammer-wielding steamman – were each given a pouch of rifle charges. Then they marched through the streets to their position. Along all of the canal sides, the capital's inhabitants were being led away in the opposite direction – women carrying wailing infants, old men with sacks filled with hastily collected family silver, money and whatever other valuables they could snatch before the militiamen banging on their doors lost patience.

'They are heading back towards the stairs leading up into the Horn of Jago,' said Jethro.

'A sound strategy,' said Boxiron, 'considering the foe have control of the surface. Once the surface is gained, the vaults of this city are not defensible. The Pericurians can strike at will through the airshafts and if the invaders blocked the vents, the city's inhabitants would slowly suffocate. Inside the mountain the defenders have air, windows to snipe from and a high slope that must be stormed. They will not be easily taken there.'

'You needn't sound so pleased about it,' said one of the convicts shuffling alongside them. 'We're the poor buggers they're asking to hold the vaults. What did you two foreign lads get taken for? Killing a sailor, smuggling, taking on board stowaways?'

'Nothing,' said Jethro. 'We are innocent.'

'Me too,' guffawed the convict. 'It's just that one of the police fell on a knife when I was filling my pockets. Clumsy bastard. The very best I had waiting for me if a judge took pity on me was the senator's picnic outside the walls. But now? I reckon they'll give me a medal if I stick a few wet-snouts the same as I did Knipe's man.' He flicked the bayonet fitted on the end of his rifle and made a crude slurping noise as he imagined his blade piercing an ursine body.

Jethro wrinkled his nose in distaste. This was the sort of man that prospered in the chaos of war. One week a murderer, the next a war hero. It was only society's judgement that separated the two.

'I recognize this canal,' said Jethro. 'This is the way we came down from the harbour.'

Boxiron nodded. 'The *Purity Queen*. She must still be docked in Jago's u-boat pens or we would have been extra-dited on her.'

361

The convict by their side sneered. 'Did they have you two lads in solitary? Haven't you heard? You aren't sailing out of here. Knipe jammed the sea locks to stop the wet-snouts sailing into the city. And even if the locks weren't jiggered, there's the whole wet-snout fleet sitting out under the cliffs. You're bottled up here same as us. Best you keep your eyes on the main chance. Slit a few wet-snout throats and put your hand up for a pardon when it's done.'

'And what makes you think Jago is going to win, good sir?' asked Jethro.

'Wet-snouts, they're just savages,' said the convict, shaking his head at Jethro's ignorance. 'They only got this far because the free company swapped sides. Bastard traitors let the fleet sail through the coral line yesterday, is what I heard. Stuck the First Senator's head on a pole on the battlements. No loss there, eh? But now they're fighting the people, not a bunch of gold-pursed idiots sitting around in senator's robes. Wet snouts think the sky's going to fall on their heads if we stay on this island. Ignorant heathens. Been here two thousand years, ain't we, and we'll make the world end all right. For any dimwit wet-snout jigger left on Jago!'

Shouts of indignant anger were raised all along the line of convicts in support of this foul-mouthed oratory.

'I don't know what these people will do to the Pericurians,' Jethro said to Boxiron, 'but by the Circle, I know that they scare me.'

Commodore Black brushed his fingers along the warm iron wall of the brig, wiping off the tears of water crying out of the rivets. 'This is second-rate work, lass. They've got water as hot as the Fire Sea right off the coast of Pericur, and the Pericurians can't even fit their boats out with a cooling system worth a spit.'

Hannah found it hard to find words to answer with. Her mother's loss, Alice's murder, Nandi's body lying dead and abandoned in the wastes. All gone now. Even her country was going to be taken away from her.

The commodore banged the hull and listened to the echo of the metal. 'But still, when I was a lad the wet-snouts couldn't have done this. You could still see wooden submersibles in their ports in those days, like blessed oak bathtubs they were. Someone has been helping the ursine and you don't have to look far to see who. This tub is a bad copy of a Cassarabian *Ad-Dukhan* class boat. Aye, the caliph's boys have been up to mischief across the sea in Pericur. A strong Pericur on the borders of the Jackelian colonies causing trouble for us will suit the caliph just fine.'

'It hardly matters,' said Hannah. 'Does it?'

'Take heart now, Hannah Conquest,' said the commodore, trying to put a brave face on their plight. 'We've got your mortal clever church-trained mind to rely on, and these ursine might have faced a few foes in their time, but they've never had Jared Black against them before.'

From outside their cell door there was the sound of the viewing panel being drawn back. Ortin urs Ortin's face appeared at the gap.

'The author of our wicked misfortunes,' said the commodore. 'Have you come to gloat over us, ambassador?'

'I see little misfortune in your situation, old fruit. You are under our protection and safe with the fleet. Given the alternative for you is being caught up in the reconquest of the island, you have little to complain about.' He waved Hannah forward. 'I am afraid I am the bearer of bad news for you. In the expedition's absence, the body of Chalph urs Chalph of the House of Ush was handed over to us. He had been murdered, knifed to death. The capital's grain dole ran empty when we were away and there were a number of attacks on members of the trade mission and its warehouses. I suspect Chalph urs Chalph's death can be counted among the disturbance's fatalities.'

'I knew it,' sobbed Hannah, falling to her knees while the swollen skin of her cheeks burned. 'Chalph came to me in a dream. He told me that he was dead.'

The ambassador's eyes widened in appreciation through the viewing slit. 'Reckin urs Reckin allows favoured souls a final moment of their choosing. You have been blessed.'

'Let us count our bloody blessings alone,' growled the commodore.

'You have my condolences, dear girl,' said the ambassador. 'I will ask the vessel's master to take you off prisoner's rations. You shall be the fleet's guests until you are repatriated.' His footsteps echoed away down the corridor.

'Guests,' spat the commodore. 'With three inches of steel to keep us safe and a bucket to relieve our bowels.'

Hannah stood up, the last tears she would shed falling onto the deck. Her very last tears. 'I have to do it!'

'What, lass?'

'Nandi, Alice, Chalph, my mother. I can save them all. Bring them all back. End this insane holy war.'

'Sit down, Hannah. Those wet-snouts must have rattled your head mortal bad when they gave us our pistol whipping.'

'Everything is my fault. Nandi was killed because I got her involved in my life, but I can make everything right again. I can save Nandi. I can save Chalph, I can resurrect all of them. I know where it is!' said Hannah. 'The last piece of Bel Bessant's god-formula. If I can get to it, I can use it. I'll make everything right.'

Hannah had to. Nandi had risked everything to save her

from the guild and Vardan Flail; and if Hannah could just bring the young academic back, then she could make everything right again.

'You don't, lass,' said the commodore. 'Say you don't know where it is. Say that wicked scrap of dark mathematical art rotted to dust under the bones of William of Flamewall.'

'It didn't,' said Hannah. 'It was always concealed here. It never left Hermetica City – the secret was hidden in the third painting all the time.'

Commodore Black was shaking. 'It was blank! The third painting was blank of any cipher.'

'No,' said Hannah. 'We just didn't look deep enough.'

'Don't do this thing,' begged the commodore. 'That terrible weapon isn't meant for us. You knew that back on Bloodglass Island when you had us blow those queer singing buildings to pieces.'

'We didn't look hard enough,' said Hannah. 'Just like you've been keeping your eyes off this cell's transaction-engine lock since they threw us in here. All your boasts, your stories about how there isn't a lock that can stand up to the genius of the great Jared Black.'

'We're safe here, lass. The ambassador's a double-dealing jigger, but he had that much right. We could die outside in their terrible war.'

'Nandi already died for us,' pleaded Hannah. 'You were sworn to protect her, to help her, and I can bring her back when I complete the god-formula,'

Commodore Black sobbed and he seemed to crumple before her, placing himself over the transaction engine lock. 'An oath taken. It always comes down to duty. Poor old Blacky, he's been crushed by it. Everything lost to it.'

Hannah watched curiously as the old u-boat man pulled off one of his jacket's buttons, using the edge of the metal circle to lever out the nails holding down his boot's heel. But the nails were longer than they should have been, with ridges and serrations and wardings along their length. He used one of them, a long flat piece of metal, to lever open the escutcheon protecting the lock's cylinders, then got to work inside the mechanism of the frame plate that had been exposed. Hannah stared suspiciously when she saw how smoothly he removed the plate to expose the transaction engine's punch-card injector, and her suspicions turned to incredulity when he pulled a strip of leather off his boot heel and began punching holes through it with one of the tools that had been concealed as a nail.

'This is too easy!'

'Don't doubt my genius, lass.'

'Genius be hanged,' said Hannah. 'A punch card concealed within a heel? This is one of the transaction engines you supplied the Pericurians with from Jackals and it's been tampered with, hasn't it? What's going on here?'

'A fine church mind,' whispered the commodore, not taking his eyes off his task. 'As tight as a trap and wasted on all that Circlist cant. The state back home has something heavy on me, lass, and they've been using it to blackmail an old fool out of his much deserved rest. The great liberal houses in Pericur might have their hands on the Kingdom's transaction engines, but they're still the *Kingdom's* engines.'

'You're a spy!' said Hannah.

'Not a willing one,' said the commodore, grunting as he slipped his makeshift punch card into the lock's engine. 'A poor fool caught up in the great game. A dupe. Pericur would have got their hands on transaction engines anyway; if not from us, from the Cassarabians. And if the information that whispers across the drums of Pericur's engines can be picked up by card-sharps in the employ of the state's intelligencers, well, supplying the infernal contraptions still turned a little profit for me. A sorry recompense for what the wet-snouts would have done to me if they discovered I was playing them false.'

He finished his work with a flourish, the pick from his shoe briefly a conductor's baton, before he placed his ear to the bulkhead. 'I can hear the throb of the boat's engines. We're not on the blessed surface.' He picked up one of the drops of water crying from the rivets and let it roll down his thumb. 'And we're running not too shallow with it.'

Hannah looked horrified. 'We're not leaving Jago already?'

They couldn't! Everything depended on her being able to get to the final piece of the god-formula.

Commodore Black shook his head. 'No. You stay close to the surface of the boils to keep an eye on the magma shifting, never out of periscope depth. My guess is the Pericurians have sappers in dive gear working to clear the entrance to the harbour on the seabed. If they can sail this wicked fleet of theirs right into Hermetica City's submarine pens, then they can open up a second front, come at the poor blessed Jagonese from below and above at the same time.'

'If the fleet can get into the city that way,' said Hannah, 'then so can we.'

'I would not pick the waters of the Fire Sea to give you your first diving lesson, lass. We'll need insulated suits, heavy gear, and there will be Pericurian navy divers in the water, while the crabs on Jago's coast scuttle about as large as carts and as mean as a Jackelian mountain lion.'

He saw the look she gave him and moaned as if he was mired in the scalding waters already. 'Then it is to be duty. So be it and I've come to expect nothing better, curse my unlucky stars. I'll do it for you and the chance to bring poor Nandi back.'

Hannah listened carefully to the instructions the old u-boat man imparted to her. The commodore assured her that in the case of the Cassarabian-designed submarine they were imprisoned on, their uncomfortable brig would be located between the boat's orlop deck and the bilges, and that the diving chamber should lie just down the corridor from them. The two of them waited for the next meal of thin gruel to be slotted through the feeding vent in the bottom of the door. Not because, as Hannah first suspected, the commodore wanted to escape on a full belly – but as an indicator that the boat's mess would also be fully occupied, with as many of the Pericurian sailors off the decks as they could hope for.

Minutes after the footsteps of the sailor charged with feeding them had died away, the commodore sprang the lock and the door retracted into the ceiling. There were no marines inside the small brig office outside, nor a master of arms – all the fighters were otherwise occupied on Jago. The commodore managed to break open the locker where their belongings had been stowed, retrieving his sabre while cursing the thieving paws of the ursine that had stolen the expensive pistol he kept concealed inside his great coat.

As the commodore had promised, it was only a short way down the corridor to the diving chamber, both Hannah and the u-boat man's strength needed to spin the iron wheel on the door in the deck to reveal a simmering pool of water in the middle of the floor. There were diving costumes racked on the wall – triple-insulated canvas. The massive brass helmets shaped like shark heads had hard crystal lenses where the sharks' eyes would have been. Commodore Black lifted the complex arrangement of lead weighted belts, buoyancy compensators and auto-inflation hoses over Hannah after she had donned her ridiculously large suit – cut for an ursine, not for someone of her slight build. Then he bid Hannah sit on the edge of the frothing water as he lifted the tank and regulator onto her back; her spine almost crumpling from the weight of it.

Donning an arrangement similar in almost every way apart from the better fit on his almost ursine-sized frame, the commodore lifted a spear gun out of the rack and pilfered a couple of underwater flares, then, with a final check on the air hose's connection to the back of Hannah's helmet, they both dropped through the tight enclosure of the airlock pool. Circle's teeth, it was hot inside, even with the protective layers of the suit going rigid around Hannah's legs, arms and chest. Then they were dropping down into the burning waters of Jago proper, the dark hull of the Pericurian u-boat squatting ominously above them, the green fronds of an underwater forest rippling below. Forward of their position lay the basalt rocks of the island's submerged harbour, the alien-looking buildings fronting the tunnels that led away from the underwater harbour lit by the flares of enemy divers and u-boat lanterns. Dozens of vessels were suspended in the sea in front of the underwater cliffs, their lights making the beads of sweat rolling down Hannah's eyepieces glint like stars.

Hannah's breathing inside the helmet sounded unnaturally loud, echoed by the rasping of the regulator, as though she was sharing the suit with someone else. Distracted by the noise, she almost lost sight of the commodore, unused to the sensation of moving and locating someone in the three dimensions of this hot, viscous world. How unlike the experience of swimming in the city's public baths, or jumping off bridges into canals on festival days this was – it must be how a bird felt when flying. Hannah spotted the commodore below her. He was waving at her to move down, to follow the fronds of the strange underwater forest towards the harbour tunnels. As they got closer to the island's submerged base, the commodore slowly angled around and pointed to the dozens of Pericurian divers in front of them, tiny shapes marked by the flash of their underwater cutting gear, cables running back to the u-boats at their rear. Hannah followed the old u-boat man into the undulating seaweed that would cover their approach, colourful fish as large as shields dodging effortlessly out of their way. They emerged from the underwater forest at the foot of one of the metal carvings to the side of the ornamental entrance to the harbour created by the ancient Jagonese. It was a bronze devilfish, ninety feet tall, sitting on a row of scallops, each shell bearing the arms of an ancient senatorial seat. The devilfish's metal tentacles were rolled up around it and Hannah saw that the suckers of its arms were actually pipe-ends capped by grilles. The discoloration in the water told her exactly what this was – a sewage outlet for the city, Hermetica's machines still dumbly following the pattern of their creation even during the surprise assault on the holy war forced upon Jago.

Commodore Black tested one of the grilles with his diving suit's gloves, but despite using all his strength he wasn't able to dislodge the thing. Hannah nervously checked for Pericurian divers off to their right. She and the commodore hadn't been spotted yet. No, the Pericurians weren't interested in sewage outlets barely large enough to admit a single diver – they needed to open the way for their entire war fleet to enter the capital en masse.

Hannah attempted to help the commodore, who was using his spear gun as a lever to try to force open one of the grilles but the barnacle-encrusted bars had been as good as welded shut by the rust and wear of age. Her suit's interior was beginning to burn her now, the layers of insulation starting to be overwhelmed by the searing heat of the boils. Hannah felt a twinge of panic. How long before they were spotted and hauled back to the fleet's brig? Her toes inside her fins felt as if they had been jabbed into a fire grate. If they swam to the surface, could the pair of them scale the towering black cliffs of Jago – in full view of the enemy fleet, with the surface crowded by Pericurian soldiers waiting to engage the enemy? This escape was looking more and more like madness, the commodore's warnings deadly prophetic. Hannah was still struggling with the drain cover when a stream of brown dust and coral debris rained down on her helmet. She looked up. The siphon on the side of the devilfish's head had opened up above them, figures in the bright orange rubbers of modified scald suits arrowing out of the opening. It was a maintenance tunnel hatch and it was disgorging Jago's defenders – tug service divers, the merchant marine and harbour repair crews, come to ensure the underwater gateway stayed sealed to the invader's fleet!

The commodore pulled her back just as the lance of a spear gun bubbled past, entering the sewage grille they had been trying to force open. That shot had come from above. Of course! She and the commodore were wearing Pericurian suits. A choice of outfit that looked as though it was going to get them both killed. A couple of divers from the ragtag army raised in Jago's defence were zeroing in on Hannah and the commodore, breaking off from the main force swimming towards the sappers attempting to clear the harbour entrance. Wicked barbed lances were exchanged between the Pericurian invaders and Jagonese, seemingly slow in the water, but powering fast enough to skewer a handful of the defenders – explosions of red mist under the sea where the spears found their mark.

Another barbed bolt cut through the water, this time only an inch from Hannah's chest. Then the two divers from the city were upon them, the commodore releasing his spear gun's

single round into the two attackers. The diver the commodore
shot was carried back by the spear's impact, clutching the
metal barb that had impaled his gut. Hannah desperately
tapped her helmet, trying to indicate that her eyes were those
of the race of man, not ursine. But the surviving attacker was
beyond noticing, closing in on the commodore with a dagger
drawn from his leg sheath. Jared Black had his own Pericurian
diver's blade drawn and the two figures twisted and turned
in the water as they grappled and fought for purchase.

Hannah kicked over to the two figures thrashing in slow
motion. She pulled on the handle of her knife, freeing it from
her leg sheath in time to slash at the back of the Jagonese diver's
seashell-shaped helmet, cutting a wedge out of the air hose
connecting his helmet to its tank. As the lion's share of the
defender's air supply began to ladder upwards, the commodore
pushed their attacker away and allowed the figure to swim
desperately up towards the surface. Hannah was watching the
weight belt their attacker had just detached sink towards her
when she felt something as powerful as a whale slam into her
shoulder, sending her corkscrewing back through the water.

Hannah just caught a glimpse of the rotating propeller on
the back of a Pericurian torpedo ploughing forward to slam into
the cliff, before the first shockwaves of the explosion reached
her and blew her into a bottomless chasm of darkness.

CHAPTER TWENTY-TWO

'He ain't firing,' shouted the convict, his voice lost behind the barricade, lost against the hymn-like howling of the Pericurian soldiers, their fierce war songs given counterpoint by the crash of turret rifles against the brass tanks of compressed gas that powered their weapons.

'I cannot!' said Jethro, squatting sadly against his unfired rifle as though it was a crutch. 'I cannot take a life in this way. Every death is my own.'

'It will be your bloody own, alright,' said the convict, sighting down his rifle. 'The wet-snouts are coming forward a second time.'

'Bayonets!' yelled someone behind them. 'Get your cutlery fixed.'

'It is not his way,' said Boxiron, watching the tide of fur, fang and claw storming down the street at them. The attackers were firing wildly, pitons smashing through the barricade and hurling the kneeling ranks of those freed from the prison off their feet with each impact.

'He ain't firing,' repeated the convict, as if this was the only thing that mattered, his bravado fleeing now the defenders

373

had made contact with the terrifying ranks of their massive enemy. The convict might have been a steamman himself, stuck in a loop with fear.

'You seem more in control,' Jethro said to his steamman friend, sounding surprised. 'Before we voyaged here you would have slipped into a fury by now.'

Boxiron stood up, his right arm turning the massive hammer slowly in preparation. 'This is my way. This is what I am for, but I will require your help.'

'He ain't firing,' protested the convict by their side, fumbling for another charge to slip into his smoking breech.

'Don't worry,' said Boxiron, laying his left hand upon the convict's shoulder. 'I am to claim his share.' He looked down at Jethro. 'It is time.'

'He ain't firing,' the convict coughed at the huge ursine who had smashed through the barricade and pushed a bayonet through his ribs. Howling with victory, the giant invader shot the man once, the impact of the piton throwing the corpse off her blooded blade and clearing her turret rifle.

Jethro heard the clack of the Pericurian's turret rifle drum as its barrel swept around towards the steamman and the ursine fed a fresh piton into her breech. 'Forgive me,' Jethro whispered as he seized the lever on the back of Boxiron's spine and shoved it up to five. *Top gear.* Boxiron jolted straight as if he had been struck by lightning, rotating the hammer in an uppercut that lifted the ursine off her feet and sent her sailing into the bow window of a deserted shop. Too panicked to reload their rifles now that they were thrusting and cutting at the enemy through the crumbling barricade, a handful of the Jagonese convicts turned and ran, yelling in fear, the first to flee collapsing as one of the police militiamen shot him in the back with a pistol.

'Coward!' yelled Boxiron, striking forward to sink the flat

374

of his hammer into the policeman's gut. 'This is how you lead!' He stepped over the groaning officer's body and vaulted the collapsing barrier, his massive weight clanking into the middle of the Pericurian assault, clearing a circle of broken bones with his warhammer. Shocked ursine stumbled back as this huge iron brute landed in their midst and lashed out at them. 'Take only those that I leave!'

Jethro looked at his hand in horror as the Jagonese defenders vaulted the blockade and threw themselves down at the stalled, hesitating assault. The hand that had just turned the clock back on everything he had accomplished since rescuing his friend from the influence of the criminal flash mobs in the slums of the Jackelian capital. Jethro pushed through the barricade, just behind the melee, the only evidence of his steamman friend the brief flash of a hammerhead among the screams and shouts. The convicts pressed forward taking Boxiron at his word and impaling the wounded soldiers trying to crawl away along the ground.

'Please,' Jethro begged them. 'Take them prisoner. Enough, they are wounded.'

'*Savages. Filthy, treacherous wet-snouts. Savage. Savage. Savage.*'

The convicts pushed the ex-parson away as he tried to restrain them. Jethro Daunt stumbled to his knees. 'This is wrong. Wrong.'

A fist as strong as steel gripped the back of Jethro's neck, pulling him off his knees. It was one of the Pericurians. A fierce scarred grey-furred face stared into his own. The beast was lying on the ground with a sabre driven through her back – mortally wounded, no doubt, but still with enough strength left to crush him. Blood was streaming out of the corner of her mouth. 'This – is – *war!*'

She dragged Jethro astride her, her arms pulling him down

towards the bloody blade jutting out of her own dark leather armour.

'For me – and – you!'

Jethro grunted in agony as he tried to resist his stomach's inevitable inching descent onto the sabre's tip. He was being pulled down to join her in death.

Hannah woke up to a darkness filled with spots of light. Was she blind, lying on the seabed with a dwindling reservoir of air, perhaps? No, she could hear the water, but it sounded like the gentle splash of a paddle on the surface. As she stirred, a hand reached out and covered her mouth. A hand covered with rough, bare skin, not ursine fur.

'Keep your voice down,' whispered the silhouette in the darkness. 'There are Pericurian soldiers on these streets.'

Hannah realized she was staring up at the LED panels of a vault roof, malfunctioning by the look of them, dark except for a few flares of light dancing along what was left of the imitation sky. 'Where am I?'

'The Augustine Vault,' said the shadow bending over her. Was that a police militiaman's cloak she could see behind the figure? 'The wet-snouts have taken most of the city now. We're following the Augustine canal east to get to the Seething Round and the Horn of Jago.'

Hannah tried to move, but her shoulder felt as though someone had been using it for a pincushion and left the pins inside. Gradually, her eyes grew accustomed to the dark. She was horizontal on the deck of a gondola, warm canal water soaking her clothes. Her diving suit had gone. The crew were using oars rather than poles to move the gondola forward, keeping their profile low down on the water.

'Commodore,' she whispered. 'Are you here?'

'Just you,' said the silhouette, his cloak shifting behind him as he continued to paddle. 'One of the tugmen found you and brought you inside Hermetica. We were expecting a wet-snout to interrogate. Got quite a surprise when we found a missing church girl.'

'My friend,' mumbled Hannah. 'He was in the water with me. We had escaped from the Pericurian fleet.'

'We just found you,' repeated the shadowed figure. 'There's a lot of bodies off the coast now, our *and* theirs. Our divers got a few mines into their fleet and sent a couple of wet-snout boats down onto the coral. Hah.'

Was the commodore dead? She remembered seeing the torpedo go past, and Commodore Black would have been closer to the underwater blast than her. Another stupid, useless death served up to the altar of religious-motivated conflict? She had to get to the final piece of the god-formula! If she could just do that, she could put everything right. Hannah was distracted by screams in the distance carrying to the canal, followed by a burst of turret-rifle fire.

'Poor fools,' hissed the militiaman. 'People hiding in their houses even after we told them to withdraw back to the Horn.'

'Why is it so dark in here?' Hannah asked quietly.

'Wet-snouts have blown the power lines. Half the city is in darkness now, or running on battery light.'

But it was a darkness that protected the boat from the sentries set by the Pericurian army. Slowly but silently their gondola followed the course of the canal through the blacked-out vault, lit only by the malfunctioning ceiling and the occasional fire from a burning street in the distance. Under empty bridges and past deserted boulevards and squares. Hannah had never seen the city so empty. Even in the near-deserted quarters of Hermetica you could always hear the barking of a dog or smell the distant oven of some solitary resident still living in the home their family had occupied for generations. A lone holdout. There was always the chance of meeting a policeman on patrol, or the city workers out crop-ping bamboo to ensure it didn't overrun a near-empty vault. But *this*. This wasn't emptiness, this was desolation. A grim reminder of how Pericur would abandon the capital to the ursks and the ab-locks and the other monsters of the wilds once they had evicted the race of man. Hannah remembered the dusty, empty atmospheric station of the mining town at Worleyn where she, Nandi and the commodore had nearly died; icy winds blowing through cracked roof domes. Was this to be their fate now? She might have been better off staying a prisoner on the Pericurian fleet after all. At least she would have been left with her memories of Hermetica City, as it had been when she and Chalph played across its streets. When Alice Gray had been there to admonish her for missing lessons in the cathedral's school.

Sliding through the darkness, not even daring to cough, Hannah squatted low as the gondola took her across what had once been the city she had known as home. Eventually they entered a tunnel carrying a bad reek, one of the sanita-tion passages that kept the canal waters moving and clear of refuse that fell in. When the channel became too narrow, the gondola men lifted their vessel out of the water and hauled it up onto one of the walkways, following the dark tunnel on foot to an opening in the next chamber across, before laying the craft down in the next canal and recommencing their voyage.

If seeing the empty war-ravaged vaults had come as a shock, Hannah found the sight of the familiar streets of the Seething Round even more painful, filled with barricades and terrified volunteers pointing rifles towards the increasingly loud explo-sions and weapons' fire from the neighbouring vaults. Here at least there was light, and all pretence at stealth was abandoned. The chemical battery on the back of the gondola was given noisy life and the prow of their vessel tilted up as they sailed past wrecked canal boats and skips scuppered by their hundred to deny them to the invaders. There at last was the cathedral, but its magnificent stained-glass windows were dark and the bridge over the Grand Canal part-fortified and manned by what appeared to be anyone willing to carry a gun, pike or sabre.

Tying up the boat outside her home, the militiamen led Hannah up the steps into the Horn of Jago and here too was something she had never thought to see on Jago. Crowds. Corridors and passageways crammed with miserable-looking citizens, squatting and sitting, filling up every available space in the once-exclusive district that had belonged to the capital's wealthy, its merchants and administrators and politicians. Now it was home to refugees and everyone who had heeded the call to abandon the vaults below. Almost the entire city was squeezed into its chambers and corridors. She stepped over squabbling children, their mothers shouting at them, and the shell-shocked huddles of the elderly that made up so much of their population. Here was the real face of war, in the grim hopelessness of lined old faces wondering if their few grandchildren would live to see tomorrow.

Hannah was home, but it had never looked so different.

CHAPTER TWENTY-THREE

Down and down, every second closer to the sabre's tip. Jethro was so close to the ursine soldier now that he could smell her breath. She was choking to death on her own blood as she drew him near to her, the matted fur on her face contorted with anger.

'I forgive you,' whispered Jethro, kissing the Pericurian's brow as the sword's tip began to press through his waistcoat.

Her eyes widened in shock at his words, as though the touch of his lips had loosed her dying soul to move along the Circle, freeing it into the one sea of consciousness to mingle with all life, waiting to be cupped out again into those yet to be born. She went limp; the stutter of her furnace breath growing silent, and her head fell back. Jethro pulled himself up and rolled off the ursine's corpse. Strangely, he felt no happiness at being alive; he barely knew he was. Standing in the smoke from the rifle fire, the sounds of the melee washing over him, he felt outside of himself, protected by the gun smoke, an observer hovering above the buildings burning all down the street, covering him with soot. Now he was the Jagonese convict thrusting a bayonet forward. He was the Pericurian meeting the thrust with tooth and claw, with steel that had been sharpened in distant glades. He was the ursine lying dead at his feet. And he was himself again.

The sounds of battle slowly began to creep into his consciousness. The hiss of a steamman's stacks burning too hot to handle, the crack of a warhammer answered by howling ursine.

Jethro came alive and entered the fog of war to find Boxiron.

Hannah followed the soldiers through the besieged city folk packed into the halls inside the Horn of Jago, coming to a lifting room, its once-opulent interior stained with the gore of wounded Jagonese borne down from the slopes being bombarded by the Pericurian artillery. While medical orderlies lifted out the wounded, Hannah was taken inside and the lifting room ascended up into the senatorial levels. The blood-spattered doors drew back to reveal a long corridor lined with statues of senators, massive busts familiar from the tedium of her history lessons and the annals the priests used to throw at her when she was daydreaming. This was the entrance to the senate, but it had found a new use now, transformed into the military headquarters for the defence of Jago. The famous windows had been smashed, the brightly coloured glass lying on the marble floor, and militiamen stood on makeshift fire steps, pointing rifles or telescopes down the peak, shouting orders to runners waiting behind them as they detailed where the Pericurians were massing, where the bombardment was falling, and which chambers of the mountainside below were likely to be assaulted next.

There was a canteen-style table laid out with maps and plans and Hannah recognized two of the people behind it.

One was Colonel Knipe, the police commander looking haggard and tired, and the other was Father Blackwater, the acting archbishop wearing the same baffled expression she recalled from his synthetic morality lessons – as if the ability of any pupil to draw a meaningful equation might be a miracle beyond expectation.

Colonel Knipe glanced up at Hannah and wiped the weariness out of his eyes. 'Your name is on the First Senator's arrest list.'

Hannah looked askance.

'Don't worry,' said the colonel. 'That fool Silvermain's head is on a pole down on the battlements now. Sometimes I take one of the spotter's telescopes and look at his surprised eyes just to help keep me going.'

A shell shook the slopes below the senatorial palace and the colonel pushed his maps aside. 'But not, I suspect, for much longer. Your arrival is well timed, young Damson Conquest. Father Blackwater here was just explaining to me how he knew nothing about the Inquisition helping to finance an expedition by the Pericurian diplomatic service into the interior.'

'The League of the Rational Court,' protested the father 'does not answer to that vulgar—'

'Enough!' Colonel Knipe silenced the old priest. 'I trust damson, you too will not insult my intelligence by pretending that your presence with the Pericurian expedition was a coincidence.'

'It was not,' said Hannah, jumping slightly as a roar of voices rumbled down the corridor from the direction of two massive doors.

'Excellent,' said the colonel. 'Don't mind the noise. The senate is currently debating what to do about the crisis.' He grimaced. 'With any luck, we'll have some legislation freezing all Pericurian trading assets on Jago within the hour. It's something of a rump senate, however, given that many of their noble elected heads are on poles next to Silvermain's, but we can but hope they overcome such trifles in time for victory.'

'The Pericurian ambassador was looking for evidence of the truth of their scriptures out there,' said Hannah. 'It was an archaeological mission.'

'To justify the war?' said the colonel. 'Most wet-snouts can find that drivel in their priests' imaginations readily enough without resorting to archaeology. And the Inquisition's involvement, damson?'

'There is a weapon, a mathematical weapon, devised by the church over a thousand years ago,' said Hannah. 'Its pieces are scattered. With it we can turn back the Pericurians.'

'Oh, please,' said the colonel. 'It'll take more than a church formula to disprove the force of the legions the wet-snouts have landed on Jago.'

'It's true!' insisted Hannah. 'We've already found two pieces of the weapon. We call it the god-formula, and when it's completed, the invasion could be turned back in the second it takes to think of it. The Inquisition's agent – Jethro Daunt – financed the expedition so we could track down the last missing piece.'

'And did you find it?' asked Colonel Knipe.

'No,' said Hannah 'It wasn't there, but—'

Colonel Knipe waved her away. 'This fancy is madness! We need soldiers, cannons, charges, not ancient church legends.' He motioned a militiaman patiently waiting behind Hannah to step forward. The soldier carried a large leather backpack and a dangling speaker-tube. 'I have contact with the guild, colonel.'

'Good man; so, let us see what that fool Vardan Flail has to say.'

Vardan Flail! Hannah's eyes narrowed. That was all she needed.

'Do you have good news for me, guildsman?' barked the colonel into the speaking trumpet.

'I will not transfer the First Senator's command functions to your staff of office,' said an obsequious voice issuing from speakers on the side of the backpack. 'Not without the due ratification of the senate.'

'Don't you play politics here, you little worm,' spat the colonel. 'I need those functions to prosecute the war. With them I can seal fire-doors on vaults the wet-snouts have overrun, I can—'

'You get the senate to vote for it,' replied the warbling voice, 'and the functions will be yours.'

'Do you think you are safe in your deep hole?' shouted the colonel. 'When the wet-snouts have finished with us here, they'll be straight over to the guild's vaults and turbine halls – down after you like weasels in a rabbit warren.'

'We are not in our vaults,' came the voice. 'We are marching on Hermetica City in our RAM suits and we will be with you within the hour!'

Colonel Knipe cut the voice off and slammed the speaking trumpet into the table. 'Worm. Filthy worm. Vardan Flail thinks that if he comes here with his guildsmen the senate we be so relieved they'll hail him as the new First Senator.'

'The turbine workers are a tough crew, colonel,' said the communications officer.

'RAM suits are fine for turning aside ursk claws and the poison of an electric field,' said the colonel, 'but not a shell from a wet-snout howitzer.'

'Please,' Hannah begged the head of the capital's militia. 'I can fix this, all of this. The war, everyone who has died. I have two pieces of the god-formula and I know where the third part is hidden. It's here in the city, Bel Bessant hid it here in the capital! The ambassador and his people don't know about the existence of the third piece.'

Father Blackwater's eyes widened in shock. 'Bel Bessant! You mean the horror she wanted to develop to use against the Chimecan gods? It doesn't exist, it is just a legend.'

'But it does,' said Hannah. 'The Inquisition knew. Alice Gray was an agent of the League of the Rational Court! She knew about the god-formula before any of us did. The Inquisition has been protecting the secret for centuries.'

'You know better than this,' said the priest. 'If that horror exists you must swear silence on the matter. You must allow yourself to be tortured rather than pass it over to hands touched by mortal weakness.'

'But I can fix it, stop the war and the deaths,' begged Hannah. 'I can see so clearly now. Everything the Circlist church has taught me, all of synthetic morality. I'm strong enough to endure being given the godhead. I won't stay a god long, just long enough to stop the war and bring back the dead that didn't have to—'

'Enough, child!' Father Blackwater slapped her. 'This is vanity. Your grief has unbalanced you.'

'The archbishop was a member of the Inquisition?' Colonel Knipe mouthed the words, hardly believing them. 'I can see there has been a merry dance being played here on Jago behind our backs. Girl, if you really know of something that will stop the wet-snouts, you must use it. To do otherwise would be madness.'

Father Blackwater tried to grab Hannah's arm, but the colonel barked and his militiamen grabbed the Circlist priest, dragging him away as he begged them not to do this terrible thing.

There was a whisper in the corridor, lost in the rattle of a falling shell across the slopes outside. If Hannah had listened harder she might have heard the triumphant hiss of Badger-headed Joseph.

'Soon. Soon.'

Jethro Daunt stumbled along the street after Boxiron, the steamman's stacks releasing spears of smoke into the water cascading down around them. When a serious fire gripped the streets at the centre of their vault, a line of brass nozzles had pushed up and out of the canals, raining water down across the buildings, while canals refilled with boiling seawater pumped in from the harbour to enhance the flows of the seeping water table.

The ex-parson of Hundred Locks knew little of war, little beyond the antiquarian history texts he had inherited from an uncle long passed away. Their coloured plates full of manoeuvring oblongs and squares, arrows indicating the sweep of companies and cavalry units, bore little resemblance to the confusion of war on the ground. No illustration could convey the taste of gun smoke or the acrid churning pit of fear in each fighter's gut. In this environment, of falling water and billowing steam, Jethro was little more than bait, the scent of the race of man necessary to bring the Pericurians running into the blunt end of Boxiron's warhammer. They were lost in a surreal nightmare. Separated from the other convict fighters in the confusion, they ran from forces large enough to rout the two of them, attacking smaller groups, once glimpsing a marching column of militiamen through the smoke, a ghost company whose existence Jethro was beginning to doubt.

Almost as strange a sight as the familiar-looking figure revealed when the smoke parted in the breeze, a man sitting by the canal side, legs dangling down as though he was waiting for someone to bring him an angler's rod and tackle.

'Commodore Black!' said Jethro. 'Dear Circle, good captain, what are you doing here?'

The commodore turned towards them and Jethro noted that the old u-boat man's left arm was in a makeshift sling, the remains of a torn diving costume shredded around his shoulder. Boxiron followed after Jethro, the steamman's gear assembly slipping back into second naturally, without the ex-parson having to intervene as he so often had in the past.

'Trying to get my breathing tank off, Mister Daunt,' said the commodore. 'A wicked hard task with the use of only one arm, and me hoping I can do it before a Pericurian spots me and puts a sharp bolt through my ill-starred skull.'

'You are wounded,' said Boxiron.

'My diving suit was torn out in the boils beyond the harbour, leaving my arm here as rare as I have my roast beef served back home.'

'The harbour?' Jethro helped Boxiron to unstrap the large air tank from the commodore's back. 'But the expedition, Hannah and Nandi – what were you doing at sea?'

'Trying to get out of it, lad. That jigger Ortin urs Ortin handed us over to the great fleet of Pericur. Poor Nandi and the others didn't have the luck to survive our greeting by the wet-snouts. Hannah Conquest is alive, though. I saw her dragged away by Jagonese divers – taken back into the city. Poor old Blacky would have had it away with them too, were it not for being half-buried under the Black Cliffs of Jago thanks to a wet-snout torpedo. But there's a game or two left for fate to play against me, or she wouldn't have blown the grille off a sewer pipe and laughed at me as I dug myself out from under the rubble and then swam through most of the shit of this city.'

'Did you find William of Flamewall's body?' said Jethro, desperately. 'The third part of the god-formula?'

'Ah, we found your murdering runaway priest for you,' said the commodore. 'And a lot more besides. But not your church's wicked weapon.'

Jethro listened as the commodore explained all that had happened to the expedition in the wilds, and made the stunning revelation that the secret of the third piece of the god-formula had been concealed in the final painting of the rational trinity all the time.

'It cannot be,' interrupted Boxiron. 'I scanned the image of the third painting – it was blank of any concealed steganography. It was merely a hoax by William of Flamewall.'

'I only know what Hannah said, old steamer,' wheezed the commodore, rotating his wounded arm now that it was out from under his air tank's weight. 'We just didn't look deep enough. Who's to say it's not a fancy of young Hannah's mind after all that we've been through, eh? Surviving the terrors of the wilds beyond the wall, the poor girl finding her mother's bones and Nandi being added to the butcher's bill. And for what? Just so the wet-snouts can call time on the last Jagonese clinging onto their terrible isle. Maybe the existence of this mortal fancy is only what she needs to make the world make sense? Poor mad Hannah, crying that she's going to save us all from our troubles.'

'*We just didn't look deep enough,*' said Jethro. He slapped his forehead in annoyance. 'Of course! She saw it and I should have too. The painting doesn't contain the third section of the god-formula, it's a clue to the location of the missing piece. Here in the capital, all this time, hang my foolishness.'

'Then I'm a fool along with you,' said the commodore, 'for I still don't see it.'

'Jethro softbody,' said Boxiron. 'If she is close to the third section of the god-formula and she intends to try to use it. . .'

'She is in danger, greater even than she knows,' said Jethro.

'The third section of the god-formula will be encrypted in a steganographic cipher similar to that of the first two. We have as long as it takes her to find and decrypt the missing piece to stop this thing!'

Jethro touched Boxiron's shoulder and pointed to the tank of air they had removed from the commodore's back. 'Lift that cylinder up if you please. I fear we will have use for it soon.'

'I'm done diving, Mister Daunt,' said the commodore.

'We have the Circle's work to do,' said Jethro, 'but it's not at sea.'

Boxiron and the commodore followed the ex-parson of Hundred Locks as he sprinted off into the billowing smoke.

Coming along the corridor leading up to the stained senate, the militiaman saluted Colonel Knipe and held out a pouch of papers – the first two parts of the god-formula that had been locked up by Jethro Daunt in the safe of the Hotel Westerkerk. 'It was where the damson said it would be, colonel.'

Colonel Knipe's eyes narrowed. 'So, it's true after all. Damn the Inquisition's eyes. All this time they knew, playing us for fools.'

'The church was guarding the first two parts,' said Hannah, feeling that she had to explain on behalf of her dead guardian. 'And those only kept for a counter-weapon to be developed.'

'Damn Circlist fools,' said the colonel. 'They are as bad as the city guilds with their plotting and scheming and secrets.' He saw the hurt look in Hannah's eyes and placed a hand on her shoulder. 'I know the church was to be your calling and what I am asking you to do is not an easy thing. You may not have been born in our vaults, but your heart is Jagonese, and by your actions here you have declared yourself as much a patriot as any of us here fighting for our liberty.'

'I just want to save us,' said Hannah. 'To bring back those that didn't need to be hurt by this stupid war.'

'We must trust that you can,' said the colonel. 'I lost my wife and children during the collapse of one of our cities. You, I, our people, we have all paid too much to stay on Jago to allow ourselves to become slaves of those bloody savages on the surface.'

As if underlining his words, the booming thunder of the invaders' bombardment grew heavier. Pieces of cracked glass crashed down from the lintels that had been turned into fire steps for the riflemen. At the other end of the corridor the lifting room doors opened and three runners emerged, their militia uniforms torn and covered in dust and blood. They ran up to the colonel and delivered their reports. Hannah listened intently to the grim news. Almost all of the vaults were cut off from each other and overrun, the bulk of the Pericurian legions down inside Hermetica City now, the Seething Round itself being assaulted, the officer below advising that they needed to make a staged retreat to the mountain fastness of the Horn of Jago and seal the mountain levels off while they still could.

Soon the police militia would be fighting the Pericurians off the steps leading into the mountain as well as shooting down the assaults being led up the Horn's slopes. The only good news was that the Guild of Valvemen's forces had been sighted moving towards the city from the north.

'Too little too late,' sighed Colonel Knipe. 'Damson,' he said, looking into Hannah's eyes. 'The third part of your church weapon, which vault is it hidden in?'

'It's not in the city below,' said Hannah. 'It's here in the Horn of Jago. I know more or less where it is, but—'

'Begin searching now,' said the colonel. He clicked his fingers and two of his officers stepped forward. 'Guard this girl's life as if all of our fortunes depended on it. I will join you after our final defences are put in place.'

Colonel Knipe watched the young churchwoman leave with his two guards, and then he motioned his commanders to the table. 'It is time, gentlemen. Withdraw the militia units back to the mountain, then seal the doors below.'

'There are still people fighting in the vaults, colonel.'

'Convicts, the scrapings of our gutter,' said Colonel Knipe. 'Their deaths will give society the service their miserable lives did not.' He motioned for his staff of office to be brought to him and he pushed it into a socket, exposing the control keys running along its length. Colonel Knipe looked at his men and the edge of his mouth turned up into a grim smile. 'Those heathen savages put such faith in their scriptures; let us do the Pericurians one final kindness. Let us reunite the wet-snouts with their barbaric gods in the sky!'

His fingers began to play across the keys. And everything changed.

CHAPTER TWENTY-FOUR

Boxiron shoulder-charged the two Pericurian soldiers who had stumbled out of the smoke, smashing in the skull of one with his warhammer while landing a large iron fist in the other's stomach, the black leather armour crumpling under the impact as the Pericurian soldier fell unconscious – or perhaps lifeless – under the brute strength of the massive steamman.

'That way!' shouted Jethro, pointing over one of the bridges. The water level appeared to be rising now, the machines that regulated the water table of the subterranean city disabled in the fighting. Not even draining the water to fight the fires could halt the coming flood down here.

'We must be close to the Horn of Jago,' wheezed the commodore as he wearily waved his sabre down the burning street. 'Let us rest a little, Jethro Daunt. I have a few years on your legs and lack the stout boiler heart of the old steamer here.'

'I fear we cannot,' said Jethro. 'A minute may cost us our lives.'

'So you say, so you say. Poor old Blacky, driven out of his

rest by the corrupt officials of the Jackelian state, dragged through the evil wilds of Jago, burnt by the Fire Sea and crushed by rocks, crawling through turds for the sake of his precious duty, and now forced to run through a burning city while Pericurian brutes take pot-shots at him. Just a minute's respite, that's not much to ask for. A small rest while I hope for the fires of this flaming city to pass me by.'

As if listening to his complaints, there was a sound almost like a sigh from the burning buildings along the street the three of them were heading down, the fires seeming to bank down, some of the flames in the upper windows winking out altogether.

Commodore Black shook his head in amazement. 'Has Lord Tridentscale listened to an old seadrinker's prayers?'

'If he has, then he has answered them with your death,' warned Jethro. 'Run! Run, good captain, run for your life!'

All around them the fires were dying out, flickering away as the vault's air was replaced with something else, something that reeked of rot and their final demise.

Ortin urs Ortin winced within the protection of the ring of fortifications surrounding the Horn of Jago. Deep, thick walls of concrete might be enough to protect its occupants from the police militia bullets flying down the slopes, but it wasn't enough to preserve those inside from the fury of Stom urs Stom berating her officers for failing to take the mountain.

'Are you cubs?' she shouted at her lieutenants, 'When you have three divisions of artillery at your rear? No, you are the chosen, and a few furless devils with police rifles are stalling your advance. You dare give me such news!'

'We have taken almost all of the city below,' protested one of her fighters. 'Their soft belly is nearly exposed to our claws.'

Stom urs Stom shook her head in anger. 'Can you smell

that scent? It is the fear of those inside the mountain. Have the guards of each house raise their standards and prepare to charge the slopes. I shall lead the final push myself.'

'Without too many casualties, dear captain,' added Ortin urs Ortin. 'We will not serve our purpose in the eyes of the other nations if Jago's fall becomes a massacre. We need live Jagonese to land on the colonies.'

'We shall slay any of the cursed furless spawn of Amaja urs Amaja raising a weapon against us. For this I have the authority of the House of Ush.'

'You must minimize the loss of life,' insisted Ortin.

'You show weakness, Ambassador. Do you think this is a consular negotiation we are executing? We wage only one sort of war, and it comes with victory attached to it. Speak with the baroness if you would have it otherwise. She is waiting at the foot of the slopes with the general staff. Within the hour I shall hand her the reconquest of our sacred soil as if it was the coronation sceptre of the archduchess itself.'

'That is precisely what it shall be,' said Ortin. 'But only if we do this thing well.'

As Ortin started to follow the advance party out of the bunker he could hear the clanging of multiple blast doors closing throughout the fortifications. Pericurian soldiers locked on the other side of the steel doors Ortin had just exited began to bang and shout in confusion as the mechanical loading arms of the great mortars and cannon emplacements they had thought themselves masters of, instead proved to be subservient to the will of the automated machinery of the capital. Out on the surface, steel barrels jutting twenty feet high swivelled on hundreds of concrete domes and lowered into place.

Ortin did not yet know it, but the automatic action of the bristling fortifications ringing the Horn of Jago was being mirrored by the massive gun emplacements out on the coral line, vast cannons that had scared away so many invaders in the past now lowering to face the hundreds of Pericurian u-boats anchored in the shadow of the black headland of Jago. Ortin was almost out of the fort's entrance when the shuddering of the ground knocked him off his feet, his eardrums near perforated as the titanic gunnery of Jago spoke in anger for the first time in close to a thousand years. The ambassador was left just about sensible enough to drag his shaking body upright in time to watch dark dots swelling larger in the sky above him.

Being a subterranean civilization, the burghers of Jago hadn't needed to worry about the potential casualties that would be caused by shells as large as carts spitting out of their cannons and landing on their own soil. The blast from the bombardment's first wave threw Ortin back into the fort's entrance, as the air filled with shrapnel and pulverized basalt rock fragments. Boom after boom, fire and fury, intense enough to suck the air out of his lungs, the single minute of that salvo seemed like an entire day to the ambassador. Then silence. Everything still except for the sad pattering rain of smoking debris falling.

Outside, one of the pennants that hadn't been shredded by the explosions fluttered through the air on fire, carried by the cold wind into the boils off the coast. There it landed, ignored by the hundreds of screaming sailors treading the boiling water, unnoticed by those jumping out of exploding, sinking, splitting u-boats. Some of the sailors were trying to swim towards the boats that hadn't been wrecked in the rain of hell, but the surviving vessels were submerging, a few trying to turn back towards the coral ring holding back the worst of the Fire Sea's lapping magma. Those that reached its shadow found the great gates of the harbour had been closed on them, trapping the u-boats inside the killing zone. Those that didn't soon discovered that the automated magazines of the coral line hadn't just been loaded with shells.

They contained depth charges too.

'I suppose,' said Colonel Knipe to his men, closing the panel on his staff of office, 'that to a savage, one set of buttons must look quite like another.'

He walked to the fire step, mounted it, and then extended his telescope, scanning the smoking carnage below. Out on the walls, he noted that the severed heads of the First Senator and his lackeys hadn't been dislodged from the pikes where they had been mounted by the wet-snouts. But then the city's fire control systems were programmed never to directly hit the battlements, even if the basalt plains behind and in front of the wall had been reduced to smoking, cratered ruins littered with the invaders' carcasses.

'A bigger fool than anyone suspected,' Knipe muttered to himself.

Especially if Silvermain had thought that any commander of the police militia would voluntarily surrender the real master control functions of the capital's defences to a bunch of dirty wet-snouts for hire.

Even Boxiron was starting to falter, stumbling under the weight of the commodore's Pericurian dive tank. Jethro and the old u-boat man were sharing the regulator at the end of the air hose as they coughed and blundered their way through the Seething Round. It wasn't smoke they were pushing through now. It was thick, choking clouds of gas, forcing the air out of the vaults and entering Jethro's lungs as a rasping fire between each sweet suck on the diving tank's reserves. They had been luckier than the bodies they were nearly tripping over, though, Pericurian soldiers and Jagonese alike. Luckier than them.

Boxiron was stalling, Jethro could tell that. It wasn't just the weight of the tank. The steamman might lack lungs, but his powerful boiler heart needed to inject supercharged air into his valves, not this poisonous soup suffocating the city.

Jethro was sucking on the regulator when the commodore grunted, still holding his breath and pointed to their right. Beyond the great inverted spires of Jago's cathedral hanging from the vault's ceiling, lost in the swirling clouds of poison, was the large stone staircase that led up into the wealthy centre of Hermetica City, up into the hollowed mountain. They were almost too late. At the staircase's top, vast fire doors were rolling shut, a dwindling strip of light left by the doors' rumbling closure.

As the three companions redoubled their speed in a last desperate sprint towards the top of the stairs, each tread an agony, Jethro heard the shouts of police militiamen from inside the mountain heart of the capital.

Boxiron had abandoned the heavy air tank and was dragging Jethro now, the commodore ahead of both of them, developing a turn of speed that was quite unexpected from a man of his bulk. Jethro and Boxiron crashed through the closing gap, Jethro feeling the door barge painfully into his shoulder as they cleared the closing wall of steel with barely an inch to spare. There was a resounding clang from behind them as the doors sealed shut. The three of them collapsed onto their knees, Jethro and Commodore Black hacking and coughing their guts out while the lid of Boxiron's stacks spat out great swathes of dirty smoke as he opened up all his bodily systems again.

One of the militiamen pushed his pistol back into his holster and helped Jethro to his feet. 'I won't be playing cards against any of you three. You're the luckiest bastards on Jago.'

'Lucky is it?' hacked the commodore, pulling himself up. He stopped for a second to catch another clean breath. 'Is that what you call it, to be smoked out of the city like a wicked swarm of wasps?'

'Gas,' said the militiaman, 'not smoke. The colonel worked out a way to tank the gas bleeds and pump the whole lot of it back into the vaults.'

'How fortunate,' said Jethro, 'for such a work to be completed quickly enough – and with the majority of the Pericurian army bottled up inside the city.'

Boxiron's voicebox shook as the steamman found his feet too. 'As fortunate as you insisting I carry the burden of a diver's tank through the heart of a battle.'

'Quite so,' Jethro attempted a smile, wiping the spittle away from the corner of his mouth with a trembling hand. 'You never know when one will come in useful.'

Boxiron looked up at the shaking ceiling of the magnificent entrance chamber they found themselves in. 'What is going on here, Jethro softbody? Those are the reports of the fortress-mounted guns above us.'

Before the ex-parson of Hundred Locks could answer, a pair of militiamen rapidly descended one of staircases leading up into the mountain, pushing past the refugees huddling on the steps. 'All able to fight!' the soldiers shouted. 'All able to fight, up to the fourth-level galleries.'

'We've locked the invaders out,' called back the militiaman by Jethro's side. 'They're trapped in the vaults.'

'Tell that to the wet-snouts that have reached the slopes,' his compatriot called down the staircase. 'What's left of their army is beyond the arc of our cannons and out of range of the coral line's guns. They're charging up the slopes and they don't look happy. All able to fight, with us now. Defend the Horn. For your city, for your freedom, for your lives!'

'I'll have you lucky lads with me,' said the militiaman, as all around them the police and armed citizens peeled away from the entrance's barricades. 'And may some of it rub off on me.' He joined the others clearing a way up the stairs.

'I'm too old for this,' wheezed the commodore.

'Bob my soul, but we have to find Hannah like the deuce,' Jethro told Boxiron and the commodore. 'Or *this* is all going to change, and not for the better!'

'Ah, lad,' said the commodore, 'tell me that Hannah can survive using the god-formula on herself if it comes to it. Tell me that she'll bring Nandi and Chalph back to life, scare this wicked war to a stop and then go back to being just a mortal lass again.'

'Nothing will survive of anyone who uses the god-formula,' said Jethro, 'not as we know them. But there is more at stake than a single life. No man or woman was meant to take on the powers of a god.'

'There's gods a-plenty out in the world,' said the commodore. 'You can't sail for a yard without tripping over them – the Steamo Loas of our metal friend here, the gods of the wind the lashlites bend their knee to, the grand smiting fellow that the Cassarabian sects worship. What's one more or one less?'

'Those are merely manifestations of our belief in them,' warned Jethro. 'What power they have is received through our belief, it is limited by our humanity – but this thing, a creature raised in our pattern, given absolute power so as to corrupt absolutely . . . no, the person who takes such a thing will not survive within that burning fire, and I fear that neither will the rest of us.'

His ears still ringing, Ortin urs Ortin left the cover of the large basalt boulder he was sheltering behind and ran across the gap to the next rock, angry hornets buzzing past his ears as the rifles of the slope's defenders tried to bring him down.

The ambassador might have been beyond the arc of fire of the emplacements below, the guns and barrels of the vast cannons ringing the mountain set in the wrong direction, but there was a long stretch of near coverless ground above him before he reached the first buildings and windows carved out of the Horn of Jago. The Pericurian advance had stalled, their own artillery rendered silent, cannons and gun trains left scattered across the blasted, cratered surface. Not even the damned weather favoured them – no cover from the steam storms off the sea. As though the weather and the world was holding its breath to see who won this day.

Ortin braved the open ground, still slippery with his people's blood, sprinting beyond his boulder to reach the standard bearer's party kneeling under the next ridge, the wounded figure of Stom urs Stom lying spread-eagled below the rocks.

'Do you see,' Stom urs Stom hissed at the ambassador, 'where your weakness has led us? A trap. We thought it was ours, but it was theirs! Theirs!'

'Be still,' commanded the medical orderly trying to stem the blood gushing out of the officer's torn leather armour.

Ortin looked at her and the orderly shook her head. 'The surgeon's tents were in front of the walls with the camp. Gone with everything else.'

'Gone with the baroness,' coughed Stom. 'All gone. This is your pity's harvest; this is your compassion's prize. Their dark hearts, the cursed spawn of Amaja urs Amaja. They brought us here to slaughter us, to pave the road to Armageddon with the bones of all those pure enough to try to stop them!'

It was true, Ortin could not deny it. Their people's corpses littered the ground both inside and outside the capital's walls, raked by shells from the coral line, the hail of bullets from the defenders – the storm of fire – now passing over their prone, uncaring forms where they had fallen in the smoking rubble. Outside in the harbour the torn corpses bobbing in the steaming red waters were so thick the ambassador could have used their shrapnel-studded bodies as a carpet to walk between the burning wreckage of the fleet. This had been a trap and the ursine had walked blithely into it, naively counting themselves the new masters of Jago. All they had wanted to do was to free the people of the island from the shackles of their oppressors, allow them their freedom away from this god-cursed place. This was their reward for trying to follow the word of the Divine Quad. Sent to hell by those who believed in none. What fools they had been. The darkness here had changed the people of Jago, twisted them into something inhuman. The heathen beasts' mortars were still peppering the harbour waters, the screams of exhausted survivors trying to struggle out of the bloodstained water echoing out of the scene of hell. Their fur burnt off their bodies by their sin. No, not their sins. The sins of the humans, of the race of *man*.

'I was wrong,' cried Ortin urs Ortin trying not to look at the staggering field of carnage behind him.

Stom urs Stom raised a massive blooded paw. 'This is the world's end and this is – your war – now.'

Ortin grasped the soldier's fingers tight, but she was no longer there to feel his grip.

Moaning in dirge, one of Stom's soldiers covered her body with the standard she had been carrying, but the ambassador growled and lifted the banner off her corpse. 'You do not lower your flag to honour a Pericurian! Lift it up, lift them all!'

The ambassador slid Stom's sabre out of her belt and stood up, letting the shots of the Jagonese ring off the rocks around him like a bell calling the people to prayer. 'Infidel!' he yelled. 'Infidel!' He turned up towards the slope and lowered the sabre. 'Put tooth and claw in every last one of them. Not one of the cursed of Amaja urs Amaja to be left alive. Salt their ruins and clean your wounds in their blood!'

Close to sixty thousand Pericurians had arrived at the island's shores. The sole thousand that had survived rose up as one and followed their ambassador in his charge up the Horn of Jago.

CHAPTER TWENTY-FIVE

The narrow windowless passage Hannah was taking opened up into a raised gantry crossing the side of the senate's octagonal chamber, high above the heads of those debating Jago's future below. Colonel Knipe had joined the guards protecting her, leading the way while his two militiamen took the rear. The sounds of the heated sitting of the senate carried up towards them, the oratory continuing apace despite the rattle of gunfire and explosions from outside the mountain.

'*Change with responsibility, responsible change.*'

'*We will stand with every vault, with every district.*'

'*Ideals given form with our sacrifice.*'

'*Set up a committee, hold a hearing!*'

Hannah stopped a second on the gantry, almost mesmerized by the hypnotic cadence of the sound. You could be tricked to sleep listening to such a surreal song.

'They are not Jago,' said Colonel Knipe, seeing that she had stopped. 'Once, but no more. Now it is you, damson. You are the light that will lead us through the steam storms.'

'Am I?' said Hannah. If she was, she didn't feel like it.

Uncertainties about her course of action were replacing the confidence she had felt as a prisoner of the Pericurian fleet.

She followed the clacking stamp of Colonel Knipe's artificial leg across the gantry, into another maze of narrow service corridors, before they entered a long hall. It was old, floored with expensive imported wood dating from the capital's halcyon days. But the hall hadn't been dusted in a long time, spider webs hung between hundreds of marble statues and busts of senators and notables, removed from the city and stored away, assigned to obscurity with the shifts of political fashion. Walking down the aisle between their blank, unpainted eyes, it was as though all the island's ghosts had lined up to pass judgement on Hannah's decision to grasp the legacy of Bel Bessant. There were no windows in this hall, only an ancient LED panel that hadn't been replaced for so long that its light had turned blue, washing the hall with its cold glow.

They were halfway along the hall when two guildsmen stepped out of the shadows. To the side of Hannah, the pair of militia guards pushed their cloaks back to pull out their pistols, but they had barely cleared their holsters before double arcs of forked lightning leapt out of the dark between the statues, striking the police officers and sending them hurtling back into the masonry, jerking and twitching as electric energy chased over their bodies. As more initiates of the Guild of Valvemen stepped out, Hannah saw they were holding onto steel lances with oversized rubber gloves, the lances connected to large capacitor packs strapped over their robes. They were followed out of the shadows by a bent, hobbling figure. Vardan Flail!

Colonel Knipe pushed Hannah behind him, shielding her from the guildsmen's deadly weapons. 'Flail!' spat the colonel. 'I might have known a rodent like you would have secret maintenance tunnels to carry you into the Horn of Jago.'

'Tunnels to repair the machines,' hissed Vardan Flail. 'Machines to track you. The Guild are the blood of this city, our transaction engines its brain, our turbine halls its heart.'

'So much power and yet still you want more.'

Vardan Flail stuck a deformed finger out of his robes, pointing it at Hannah. 'You know what I want.'

'Yes,' said the colonel.

Hannah only just heard the click from underneath the militia commander's cloak, his left hand hidden behind his back.

One second.

'And I know what you deserve.'

Two seconds.

Hannah saw the whirring clockwork detonator on the round glass grenade as the colonel hurled it towards the guildsmen before throwing his weight at her, carrying the two of them behind the marble shield of some centuries-dead senator.

Three seconds.

There was a lash of energy burning the stone as Knipe's grenade detonated, the charge of the guildsmen's electric weapons lashing out in a single burst as their backpacks ripped apart, the rain of shrapnel jouncing off the statue shielding Hannah and the colonel. Then there was silence.

Colonel Knipe stepped out from behind the smoking statues, his pistol drawn, and prodded the torn robed bodies lying there. It was hard to distinguish what had been ruined by the corpses' labours in the guild's vaults and what the grenade had wrecked. The pungent scent of mint from their robes mixed with sulphur from the explosion.

Hannah saw that Vardan Flail was still moving across the floor, partially shielded by his men's bodies – but he wouldn't last long, not in the state he was in.

'Sacrifice,' hissed Vardan Flail, 'the god-formula.'

The colonel pointed his pistol at the dying man as if to fire, then he tapped his artificial leg with the gun and holstered it. 'I've sacrificed more than everyone, you rodent. May you live long enough to see the guild's power dwindle to an ember on Jago.'

Colonel Knipe helped Hannah to her feet. 'He can't hurt you now, but there might be more of his guildsmen following him. Are we close?'

Hannah looked at the robed body crawling like a slug across the dusty oak floor, his groans growing more intermittent. Was Alice Gray's ghost resting easier now that the man who had murdered her was passing along the Circle's turn? Not if Hannah's own feelings were any compass. She felt no satisfaction, only pity. That was a surprise. Wasn't this something she had dreamt of when she was a slave of the Guild of Valvemen? Nothing felt quite like it should.

'Yes,' said Hannah. 'It's close.'

Jethro, Boxiron and the commodore were moving through the crowded floor of an assembly room where hundreds of children were sitting cross-legged and frightened on the floor when Jethro heard panicked shouts from the corridor at the other end of the chamber. Out of the passage a townsman emerged using his rifle as a crutch and moving so fast that he was treading on the hands of the children cowering on the floor.

'Careful, man,' cried the commodore, grabbing the townsman by the jacket.

'Let me go! They're coming! The wet-snouts have breached the slopes. They're inside the mountain vaults now, inside!'

The townsman pulled away and resumed his sprint through the huddling crowd of refugee children. Jethro saw the commodore looking at his hands. The u-boat man's palms were covered in the blood that had been soaking the man's dark frock coat.

'Stay and fight, you mortal fool,' the commodore shouted after him. 'There's nowhere left to run to.'

Jethro looked around. There was just himself, the commodore and Boxiron trying to get through the assembly room. No defenders to protect the hundreds of children hiding here. The other fighters had already gone to man the firing lines, leaving the three of them to work their way up ever higher into the honeycombed passages of the Horn of Jago in pursuit of Hannah Conquest.

'Where are you going, good captain?' Jethro called to the commodore as he moved towards the passage. 'We have to keep moving higher.'

'I'm too tired to chase about the tunnels of this blessed mountain, Jethro Daunt. I'm going to sit myself down in this chamber and rest awhile.'

'These children are not our concern,' said Boxiron. 'We have a greater mission.'

'One man and a sabre will make no difference here,' agreed Jethro. 'All the armies of the world will make no difference unless we can get to Hannah before she finds the final section of the god-formula.'

'Does the Circlist church have a formula for that, Mister Daunt? Some equations wrapped up in a homily about the power of the common good?'

They did, but Jethro could sense that the old u-boat man had made up his mind. Not everyone could pick where they died. There were hundreds of children here, hiding terrified in the heart of the Horn of Jago, as safe from the bombardment and fighting outside as they could be.

'Off with you, lad. You and the old steamer have your god-formula to protect and I have my own code I must uphold.'

'May serenity find you, good captain,' said Jethro, passing the commodore his rifle and satchel of charges.

'Maybe she will at that.'

Commodore Black watched Jethro and Boxiron climb up one of the side passages before laying aside his sabre. Sitting wearily down in the assembly room, he raised the barrel of the ex-parson's rifle to his nose and sniffed it. 'As new as a freshly minted coin,' he muttered.

The commodore pulled out a cloth he used for his mumble-weed pipe and began cleaning the grease off the barrel. Two of the children came up to him, a brother and sister perhaps, the girl holding a tiny horse carved out of a single piece of volcanic stone.

'Why did the man run off?' asked the boy.

'He had forgotten to give his wife a kiss before he left home,' said the commodore. 'She'll be blessed angry at him if he doesn't get back to her quickly.'

'We've left home too,' said the sister.

'I thought you had, now. You had that look about you.'

There was a sound down the passage, an echo of rattling brass, and coming out of the flickering artificial light was as bizarre a sight as the commodore had ever expected to see here on Jago. A line of children, but children in militia uniforms, miniature cloaks and full-sized rifles on their shoulders. Most of them barely looked to be in their teens, although the girl marching at their head might have had a year or two on that, along with a good few gangling inches over the troops in her company.

'Cadets, halt!' ordered the girl. She looked suspiciously at the commodore's tattered foreign naval uniform. 'We are here to protect you.'

'That's grand,' said the commodore.

'We wanted to stay on the slopes and fight but the major ordered us back here. She said that the evacuated classes needed to be defended.'

Commodore Black sighed. In the Jackelian New Pattern Army these greenhorns might have passed as drummers. In the Royal Aerostatical Navy, they might have passed as midshipmen or catwalk monkeys for the sailors. Here in the mountain vaults, though, they were just frightened children in stiff uniforms trying to ignore the gestures and calls from the youngsters they had been studying next to the week before.

'Captain Jared Black,' said the commodore, wearily raising his full bulk to his feet. 'You might forget to salute, cadet,' he blustered, leaning over to lock the bayonet under her rifle barrel in place, 'but when you forget to turn-and-twist your cutlery, the first wet-snout you stick with that bayonet is going to end up keeping it in their gut.'

'Sir!' she barked.

Commodore Black stared back down the assembly rooms, calculating the meagre options for their defence. There was the corridor at the rear where he had entered with Jethro and the steamman. That led to the lower levels of the Horn of Jago and those grand doors onto the subterranean city – that should be safe enough. There was the stairway on the side up to the next level – too narrow for a good assault, but maybe good for flanking with a skirmisher or two, he'd have to keep an eye on that. Then there was the entrance in front of them, leading onto the main corridor the cadets had retreated down. Yes, the main corridor, that's where he would assault from, and that's where the mortal Pericurian troops would show their snouts in force.

'Turn over those tables in front of this passage and form two lines behind them. First line kneels and loads, second line fires on command, then you change position. Don't sight your rifles; the passage's width will do your blessed aiming for you. Clear your broken charges cleanly and watch you don't burn yourself on the wadding and residue.'

She saluted. 'We will do our duty, captain.'

Aye, and they would break on it too.

CHAPTER TWENTY-SIX

Hannah opened the door and she and Colonel Knipe stepped out onto the floor of a hoop-shaped passage circling around the metal barrel of the flare-house gun. The two of them had travelled as high as they could climb up the Horn of Jago, to the very tip of the summit itself. It was cold in the narrow passage. It would have been warmer had the flares still been launching like magnesium stars overhead, but the flare bins deep below must have run empty with the loading crews cowering in hiding like everyone else in the mountain vaults.

A ladder had been riveted to the stone wall, rising a man's height to a second gantry, which ran alongside the flare-house's stained glass windows. Each twenty-foot high pane bore a multicoloured illustration based on the rational orders' illuminations, filled with the calligraphy of mathematical philosophy and Circlist imagery from the *Book of Common Reflections*.

'Up here?' said the colonel. 'This is where the third part of the god-formula is hidden?'

'There were three paintings created by William of Flamewall,' said Hannah. 'Two of them held parts of the god-formula hidden in steganographic code. The last painting was blank of any code – it was the third painting of the rational trinity.'

'*You climb the mountain alone,*' said Colonel Knipe.

'William of Flamewall wasn't just an illuminator of manuscripts for the church,' said Hannah, pointing up towards the stained glass. 'He was a glass master. He even used the oxides from his glass dye to murder the priest who had created the god-formula, Bel Bessant.'

Colonel Knipe swivelled on his feet, looking in amazement at the wall of glass surrounding the massive flare cannon.

'The third painting wasn't blank,' said Hannah. 'The Circlist priest in the painting was pointing to the top of the Horn of Jago. We never found an image of William of Flamewall, but I'd wager that his face is that of the priest in the third painting.' She craned her neck up at the images circling them, indicating a panel that represented the third part of the rational trinity. 'And there is the same face on the glass.'

Colonel Knipe climbed the ladder to the second gantry, his cloak brushing Hannah's hair as she followed. 'And this picture will hold the missing piece of the god-formula!'

Hannah looked at the stained glass work, running her hands along the borders of the towering illumination set in crystal, a chequerboard of colourful squares – purples, reds, greens, yellows – all set in a seemingly random pattern that echoed the colours used in the main illustration, priests of a dozen religions being parted by Circlists to make way for a single man to climb the mountain. Alone.

'It's here,' she declared. 'Assign each colour along the border a value, work out the key. This is more steganography.'

'You know what you must do now,' said Colonel Knipe.

'Decipher the code. The archbishop tutored you, you are your mother's child, you must!'

'I didn't crack the first two codes,' said Hannah. 'It was Jethro Daunt and his friend Boxiron – the steamman has special skills in this area.'

'As you love Jago,' pleaded the colonel, 'you must! Our people's time is short.'

Yes, as high as they were, she could still hear the sounds of war drifting up from the slopes below. Hannah's mind raced. She was visualizing things so fast now, she could do this. She had to. For all of them. Hannah reached for the satchel containing the first two sections of the god-formula. She would use the blank sides of the paper to decipher the steganography and tease out the last part of the god-formula. She knelt down to note the sequence of colours on the first of her sheets, suddenly twisting her head to look down onto the lower gantry. 'Did you hear that?'

Colonel Knipe already had his pistol out as he looked down towards the barrel of the flare-house cannon and the instrument room beyond it from where the flares were launched. 'I heard nothing.'

Hannah scowled and went back to work. She could have sworn she had heard an animal grunting below as though it was laughing.

'Look to your locks!' the commodore yelled to the faltering riflemen – though men they were not yet – as their young hands fumbled with their charges. The mortal terrible ranks of ursine charged down the corridor through the press of fire and bolts of steel, smashing into the barricade, splinters tearing into the cadets who cried out with raw, animal fear.

'First line kneel, second line *fire!*'

Another ripple of explosions, glass charges cracking, the sulphur hiss of liquid explosives smoking out of their barrels.

'Clear them! Second line kneel, first line *fire*!'

There were screams and curses from the ursine in the corridor as they clambered over the bodies of the fallen, the dark press of the beasts getting closer to the hundreds of bawling, huddling children crowded behind them in the assembly rooms.

'Look to your locks. Clear them!'

Clear them before the maddened Pericurians broke through the barricade. Soldiers of the great houses that practised vendetta through tooth and claw. Their enemies wiped out down to the third generation.

Tooth and wicked claw.

Hannah's hand brushed against the cold crystal of the stained glass window, her head spinning with the steganographic encryption she was attempting to break.

Her eyes drifted to a transparent pane that had been left undyed, and she gasped as she saw the pall of smoke rising up from the headland in front of the black cliffs of Jago. 'The Pericurian fleet. The fleet is burning at sea!' She swivelled on Colonel Knipe. 'What is this? The Pericurians took the coral line, the battlements, the city vaults. . .?'

'The wet-snouts have taken what they deserved,' said the colonel.

'But the people,' said Hannah, stunned. 'They were in peril. I was doing this for *them*.'

'And they will be saved,' said the colonel, 'when you have decoded the final piece of the god-formula.'

'That is the last thing they will be!' shouted a voice from below.

Hannah looked down onto the lower gantry. It was Jethro

Daunt, standing alongside the hulking mass of a hammer-wielding Boxiron. Hannah felt a cold object resting against her temple and turned. Colonel Knipe was pointing his pistol at her head. 'Stay where you are, Jackelian, you and your metal brute both.'

'What in the name of the Circle are you doing?' asked Hannah.

'Keeping my country safe,' said the colonel.

'That seems to come at a cost,' said Jethro. 'Such as when you paid Tomas Maggs to scuttle the boat carrying Hannah's father back home.'

'No!' whispered Hannah. 'That was down to Vardan Flail.'

'I'm afraid not, damson,' said Colonel Knipe, pushing the barrel of his pistol harder against her skull. 'That fool Vardan Flail is as much a Circlist fanatic as your learned Jackelian friend here. Flail was seeking the god-formula, but he didn't want to use it. He would have destroyed it!'

'And Hannah's parents would have taken it back to Jackals to study,' said Jethro. 'You couldn't allow that to happen either. The Conquests came to you for help, didn't they? They had found images of William's three paintings in the great archives, and they feared that the guild was trying to stop them leaving the island. But you decided to murder the two of them first, steal their find and keep the god-formula to yourself. Just as you killed Alice Gray when you discovered she was also a guardian of copies of William of Flamewall's paintings.'

'I had to torture her after Hugh Sworph came to me, knowing the bounty I was offering for William of Flamewall's works,' said the colonel. 'There was always the chance the archbishop was hiding the third piece of the god-formula somewhere in her cathedral.'

'Your bad luck, then,' said Jethro. 'Alice was only the guardian of what you had already killed Hannah's parents for: two of William's paintings, each containing a piece of the god-formula, and a third seemingly blank. How many people died in the ursk attack you allowed into the city?'

'Alice,' groaned Hannah. 'My father. Murdered by *you*!'

'You should not complain,' said the colonel. 'Your good fortune allowed you to escape twice when you should have died. The first time from the ursk pack, and then from the bomb one of my men planted in your atmospheric carriage – although, to be fair, the second time I was really aiming to kill your meddling Jackelian archaeologist friend before she could uncover your parents' work here. The god-formula is to be mine, and mine alone. That is the way fate intends it to be. Your parents were the first to die, but there have been many others over the years. Explorers, chancers, thieves, local and foreign. Vanished into the stomachs of the beasts outside the wall or found floating drowned in our canals. It was destiny that you survived, young damson, for where would I be without you now? Who would have thought that a mere slip of a girl could succeed where I, with all my resources, failed? You are my fate, girl, and I am yours.'

'But that's not the worst of it.' Jethro pointed beyond the flare-house's walls. 'The Pericurian attack – you knew they were going to invade, and you let it happen. Everyone who died in this senseless war, all on you. You've bobbed us all, used this whole city as your personal plaything.'

'You cannot judge me,' said the colonel. 'I have done what the senate failed to do for centuries. I have united our people with the fear of a common enemy. I did not provoke the wet-snout invasion, I did not arrange it, I merely allowed their attack to happen on my own terms.'

'You lured them into a bloodbath, man!'

'You're a slippery fish, Jackelian. What was it that gave me away?'

'When I was looking over the ballot records for evidence that the guild had falsified Hannah's draft,' said Jethro, 'I noticed the number of people from the lodge of gas workers who had been conscripted into the police militia. And what use could the militia have for those bleeding gas seepage away from the capital? The Pericurians weren't invading Hermetica, they were invading an underground gas chamber!'

'They deserved a quick end, Jackelian, for uniting us and ridding the people of the insane, inbred First Senator and his lickspittles.' He pushed the gun even harder against Hannah's head as Boxiron's warhammer twitched in anger. 'Stay back, or she will die!'

'You wouldn't think twice, would you, good colonel?' Jethro reached into his pocket and drew out a boiled sweet, his cheek swelling as he popped it into his mouth and sucked it thoughtfully. 'You murdered the fence that brought you the church's copies of William of Flamewall's paintings. Just as you killed Chalph urs Chalph when he came to you to tell you his suspicions about the Pericurians' intentions. Chalph had spotted that the envelope Stom urs Stom passed the Pericurian ambassador supposedly warning the expedition not to depart wasn't written in the First Senator's hand, but that of the Baroness of Ush, no doubt apprising the ambassador that their invasion would take place when he was out of the city. Chalph told you this, and you couldn't risk the poor unfortunate ursine informing someone who actually would have tried to stop the invasion.'

'And I would have hanged you for his death,' sneered Knipe, 'eventually.'

'How did you know about the invasion?' asked Jethro. 'That's the one thing I haven't been able to fathom.'

'Look no further than your own countrymen,' said the colonel. 'One of the members of the Jackelian consul here, your Mister Walsingham, came to see me with a packet containing stolen details of a model of the flows and drifts of the Fire Sea. A model sitting on the wet-snouts' transaction engines. I doubt if he is really a diplomat, but then I doubt if your parliament cares one way or another. As long as the Pericurian threat to your colonies' northern borders has its fangs trimmed.'

'And you never passed this intelligence on to the senate?' said Hannah.

The colonel brushed her hair teasingly with the cold barrel of the gun. 'And what would Silvermain have done with the news we were going to be invaded? Passed a bill? Installed one of his hunting hounds as the Senator of War? He was good at dreaming of things that could never be. I, on the other hand, have sacrificed too much to let our land fade. My will shall be done.'

Hannah dropped the pouch of papers she was holding, the half-deciphered code taken from the stained glass vista falling to the stone gantry. 'Alice, my parents, Chalph, they all died for *this*.'

'Continue your work!' Colonel Knipe shouted.

'Go jigger yourself.'

Colonel Knipe's pistol whipped out, striking Hannah on the skull and she fell to the ground, blood gushing from the wound and soaking her hands. She glared up with pure loathing at Knipe. 'I'll never do this for you – pull the trigger!'

'Perhaps you won't after all,' said Colonel Knipe. He turned and shot Jethro in the stomach. The ex-parson was hurled back against the cannon housing, a crimson stain spreading out across his waistcoat. 'Drop the hammer, steamman!' Colonel Knipe shouted, reloading his pistol. 'I'll heal the Jackelian as good as new after I have attained godhead. Come up here and complete the decryption of the code in the stained glass before I put a second bullet through your friend's skull and leave him for the worms.'

Jethro was lying on the lower gantry, clutching his stomach while his blood pooled across the flagstones. 'No. Not . . . for . . . me.'

'I cannot let you die, Jethro.'

'Must!'

Hannah watched the black steel barrel of the colonel's pistol swinging around towards her again. Knipe was going to have to kill them all, for there was no way *she* was going to decrypt the final part of the code for the killer who had stolen everyone she had ever loved from her life, and Boxiron could not be allowed to either.

Even over the clash and fury of rifle fire, Commodore Black heard the screams from the quailing children behind him, terrified by the appearance of two Pericurians crashing down the side-stairs from a higher level within the mountain.

Jared Black had turned and put a bullet through the skull of the soldier carrying a turret rifle before he had even realized that the wet-snout wielding a sabre next to the falling ursine corpse was that of Ortin urs Ortin.

'Spawn of Amaja urs Amaja!' the ambassador yelled. The children crowding the floor scrambled away in panic from this huge monster that had suddenly invaded the assembly room, a fur-covered demon bearing a sword slicked in the blood of their parents.

Commodore Black lowered his sabre at Ortin urs Ortin. 'That and worse, ambassador.'

Ortin charged, pure animal savagery bearing down upon the old u-boat man. Commodore Black stepped forward and met him with a clash of steel.

'You trapped us, tricked us!' Ortin bayed. 'You butchered half the great houses!'

'No, lad, not me.' The commodore fell back, grunting. Ortin's strength was far beyond that of any fighter from the race of man. 'But I'm going to settle for you all the same. For Nandi.'

Ortin struck the commodore's sabre with his steel, again and again, making the commodore's arm ring with the wicked pain of it. There was little room for sophistication in this battle, his parries blunted by the raw swinging power of the Pericurian's massive frame. The commodore's rare bones turned into an anvil from the battering.

As their fight stumbled back and forth across the assembly room, Commodore Black caught a brief glimpse of the barricade where the front line of cadets was thrusting bayonets against the crush of the Pericurian advance, the second line unable to shoot now without hitting their own side. Children, blessed children asked to fight and die like this. To fight for their lives. Their stronghold at the centre of the mountain was seconds away from falling. . .

Commodore Black yelled in surprise as he slipped on the blood of a dead Pericurian soldier and sprawled backwards, his sabre sliding away across the floor. He was weaponless. Ortin urs Ortin moved in and the commodore met the ambassador's insane, glazed eyes as the huge beast raised his blade upwards for the killing stroke.

'Leave . . . me . . . to die.' Jethro coughed.

The steamman shook his visored head at Jethro's wounded form and dropped the warhammer with a clang, mounting the rungs up to the circle of stained glass windows. 'No, I cannot. You must trust me.'

Hannah watched the huge steamman stop in front of the stained glass, drinking in the final hidden section of Bel Bessant's terrible creation. 'Don't do this, Boxiron. I would only have used the god-formula to fix what wasn't meant to be broken. What sort of god will you create by giving such a thing to Knipe? For the love of the Circle, he killed my father, Nandi, Chalph, Alice, he—'

'Be quiet, damson,' threatened the colonel. 'The Inquisition was good enough to send us a machine to break codes, it's only fitting that we use it as they intended.'

'What sort of thing will you be?' Hannah cried.

'A better thing than your precious Circlism,' spat the colonel. 'All this time the church knew what it had here – the means to save our land! And your people buried it away; you forgot it along with our greatness! And the church claims to care for the needs of the people. . .'

'I have completed the steganographic key,' said Boxiron. 'I am ready to begin deciphering the main code.'

Colonel Knipe picked up the first two sections of the god-formula that Hannah had dropped and threw them towards the steamman. 'Pick up the girl's pencil and begin writing on that paper. Quickly! Your Inquisition friend only has a few minutes of life left in him.'

Hannah looked down. Jethro Daunt had fallen silent and was lying with his back against the flare-house cannon, as still as a corpse bar for the trembling of one single leg. The floor below was awash with his blood.

'Jethro Daunt is not a member of the Inquisition,' said Boxiron as he worked. 'He is not even a churchman anymore.'

'So you say. For hire, then. A mercenary, no better than the dirty wet-snouts the senate believed they were buying.'

Boxiron continued to write out the equations of the final piece of the god-formula, his iron fingers moving several times more rapidly than any human hand could. 'Not for hire, for love.'

'He really was going to marry the archbishop?' said Colonel Knipe, sounding surprised. 'Well, I never did get around to checking if that part of his story was true. More fool him. Everything that you love you end up losing. That is the way of life.'

'What will you do with this, colonel?' asked Boxiron. His voicebox sounded as if it was vibrating with pain, as if the mere effort of translating the final section of the god-formula burned at the core of his being.

'I will save your Jackelian friend. I have never broken my word.'

'*Afterwards.*'

'I shall restore Jago to its natural position at the head of the world's nations, just as I shall burn the last wet-snout left on the island into ashes. Fire, then ice!'

Hannah pulled herself up, clutching her bleeding scalp. If that meant what she thought! 'You can't.'

'My will shall be done,' shouted the colonel. 'The world's winter shall be Jago's summer. Our civilization will rise once more. Everyone will want to dwell here again and those who do not will consider themselves cursed. *And they shall be!*'

No. A new age of ice. A winter without end, never the spring again as the world turned.

'Please!' Hannah begged Boxiron to stop what he was doing, but instead the steamman slid the final completed section of the god-formula back towards Colonel Knipe.

'We gave the world everything, little girl,' snarled the colonel. 'And they turned their backs on us, believed us fi only for use as a rock to break the rising wet-snout tide. A mere pawn in the game of our betters. We passed the world the light once, after the age of ice ended, now the torch of their civilizations shall be ours to snuff out again.'

Seizing the completed god-formula, the colonel vaulted over the railing, landing on the lower walkway, then sprinted into the flare-house instrument room and sealed its door behind him.

Hannah was on her feet, groggily climbing down the ladder to the lower level. She picked up Boxiron's hammer and smashed at the door to the instrument room, but its head bounced uselessly off. She screamed for Boxiron to help, but he was standing on the upper gantry as immobile as an iron statue. Had the enormity of what he had done finally begun to sink in? The terrible cost of his friendship with the man who had saved him? She tried to batter the crystal panel in the door, but it had been hardened to withstand a flare misfiring inside the launch barrel. Hannah's strength was draining away. On the other side of the glass, a haze of twisting, turning diamond-sharp panes of light surrounded Colonel Knipe as he read the god-formula, enveloped by energies that were too exotic to be contained by the mortal world. His body was growing translucent, his organs pulsing with light. He was shedding his mortal shell.

Hannah felt fingers circling her ankle.

'Don't . . . let . . . him.'

'It's no good,' said Hannah, kneeling beside the ex-parson. 'The colonel's in there changing. He's taken the godhead.'

'Boxiron! Boxiron!'

'He's frozen,' cried Hannah. 'Please, Jethro, Boxiron's not even moving anymore.'

There was an awful ripping sound behind the instrument

room door, something alien and terrible, the fabric of matter itself tearing.

It was the laughter of a new demigod striding the earth.

Commodore Black heard the cadet commander's yell as she scooped up his sabre and tossed it across to him. He rolled through the blood on the flagstones and speared Ortin urs Ortin squarely through the stomach, the tip of his sabre emerging through the back of the Pericurian ambassador's jacket.

Commodore Black was on his knees, the ambassador looming over him, still trying to move forward despite the wound. At first the commodore could barely hold the ambassador back, but gradually the realization of his imminent death seemed to sink into Ortin urs Ortin, his eyes losing their glare of insanity.

'Well – played – dear – boy.'

The commodore nodded, trying to rise, still keeping both hands on the sabre's grip and preserving the gap between them.

'I – am – *not* – a – savage.'

Commodore Black pulled out his sabre and the ambassador swayed. The old u-boat man raised the steel to his nose in salute as the ambassador crashed onto the flagstones, his monocle rolling away across the floor.

'Just two blessed nobles,' said the commodore, 'living through a savage age as best we can.'

But the ambassador was beyond hearing him.

Commodore Black turned as the barricade cracked open to admit a wave of ab-locks, tools jangling from leather belts, bayonet-fitted rifles at the ready, followed by a pair of men in guildsmen's robes. They looked for all of the world like a couple of hunters taking their hounds out for a walk through the vaults of the mountain.

'Our RAM suits wouldn't fit through the Horn's corridors,' said the nearest of the guildsmen.

'There's a pity,' answered the commodore. He watched the ab-locks fan out across the assembly rooms towards the stairs to the higher levels, followed by the guildsmen. Hunting down creatures that looked and smelt like ursk cubs was something that no doubt came quite naturally to the pack.

'On, T-face,' cried the younger of the two valve-men. 'Smell them out for us, up the stairs, up.'

Commodore Black drew out his mumbleweed pipe and searched for a packet of leaves to light, standing next to the white-faced cadet commander who was starting to tremble in shock now that the combat had ended. He took her rifle from her clenched fingers and set it down on the ground.

'Is this war?' she murmured in horror.

'Not for us, lass,' said the commodore. His eyes moved across the heaps of dead cadets and ursine, bodies locked together in death, mourned by the cries of the shivering children behind them.

'For us, this was campaign experience. For us it's the chance of a medal. It's only war for them.'

Hannah had hold of Jethro's hand, the tremor of his fingers growing weaker as the alien gale of laughter behind the iron door became a storm. The energies being unleashed inside that chamber were leaking through the seals as little flickers of ball lightning.

'Boxiron. He. . .' Jethro gasped. 'Top. Gear.'

Hannah glanced up. The steamman was standing statue-still, transfixed by the scene below. What was the point, what was the point of anything now?

'Bel. Bessant.' Jethro's fingers tightened around Hannah's hand. 'How. Do. You. Fight. Gods?'

425

Hannah stopped. She could see something moving down the corridor, a shadow, the blur of a rooting animal. Or a badger.

She heard the words hiss from the shadows. 'Oh, he's a good one. A real doozy you're brewing up inside there. Your people will all be so glad to come back to us when they see him. You'll beg us. You'll *pray* to us!'

Hannah was desperately pulling herself up the rungs in the wall towards Boxiron, when a diamond-blue figure composed of burning angled planes forming the silhouette of a man walked through the instrument house door as if its steel was as insubstantial as the steam off the sea. Each of its steps turned the stone of the passage into a puddle of hissing liquid magma. The heat on Hannah's back became intense, the nape of her neck burning as she pulled herself up onto the second gantry. Vivid panes of gem-coloured stained glass shook in their frames with the alien pressure of the creature below – a demigod fit for the dark, blasted heart of Jago. Lord of the ruins.

The thing that had been Colonel Knipe looked down at Jethro as if noticing a slug crawling across the dirt. The pond of blood surrounding the ex-parson boiled and frothed on the stone as the demigod knelt down and ran a hand along the man's side. Jethro screamed and jerked in a wild fit as his body re-wove itself under that supernatural touch.

The ripping storm around the silhouette modulated into speech. 'MY WORD.' It raised an arm and Jethro was spun up off the ground and slammed against the steel of the flare-house cannon. 'I NEED PRIESTS TO CARRY MY WORD.'

'No,' groaned Jethro, jowls buffeted by the force emanating from the being that had been Colonel Knipe. 'I deny you.'

426

There was an increase in the gale's intensity, the rippling skin of the universe moving in terrible amusement. 'DID I ASK IF IT PLEASE YOU?'

Jethro's lips started moving in prayer, the words – provided by the colonel – torn unwilling from his lips. But his eyes were his own. Fixed on Hannah, who clutched the railings on the gantry opposite him, with pained urgency. 'My – lord – save – me – who gives – me – life – and – resurrection.'

Hannah lurched towards Boxiron, noting the red dot flaring on the steamman's vision plate, one second a ruby pinprick, the next expanding to fill the whole vision plate with crimson. The steamman's weak, human-milled shell was looping in paralysis. Too weak to contain . . . Bel Bessant knew. She had got that much right. The only way to fight a god. Hannah's hand gripped the lever on the back of the steamman's spine-box and threw it up, all the way. Top gear. Hannah's eyes momentarily fell on the gear panel as the force of the unholy squall below carried her beyond the newly trembling steamman. She saw for the first time the words that had been scratched against the highest of the steamman's gear positions. *Circle save you jiggers.*

Hannah was blown over the railings, landing on the lower gantry with a painful wallop. As the whirling energies carried her further down the gantry she could see Jethro Daunt slide across the cannon's barrelling in front of her, still pinned by the terrible demigod, but his lips and voice his own again. 'A god, so powerful. Truly, a god?'

'YES.'

'Then,' Jethro said, as the skull of the burning silhouette bent forwards towards him, 'it's time for you to go to hell!'

Jago's new dark demigod was pulled back, dragged by the

white tentacles of steam emerging from Boxiron's stacks, the steamman's body vibrating at such a speed that it blurred in and out of sight. The blue figure of fire raised its arms and waves of energy lashed out, only to be absorbed by the steam enveloping it, diluting and ultimately mingling with the demigod, becoming one with it. The flare-house was filled with a scream so primeval that it tore at Hannah's chest, an unholy ripping sound. Hannah was backing away but Jethro was actually crawling towards the agonized demigod. Tighter and tighter the thing that had been Colonel Knipe was compressed, its force becoming brighter and more radiant, shaking with the power of a sun fashioned into a spear of primordial energy.

Jethro extended a finger to point at the teetering shaft of energy. 'Let there be us!'

As if at his bidding, the streak became lightning and leapt upwards, blasting off the roof of the flare-house and raining debris down onto Hannah, Jethro and Boxiron. From the tip of the Horn of Jago a pillar of light stretched up towards the clouds and the stars beyond. Then there were just the three of them. And something else, the steam pouring out from Boxiron's stack forming into a ghostly shape. Alice Gray.

'You look as beautiful as I remember,' said Jethro.

Alice's voice echoed around them, disembodied. 'And you, Jethro, do not look as surprised as you should.'

'I guessed when Hannah's atmospheric carriage was diverted by the machines. Saved from a bomb and taken to find Tomas Maggs' frozen corpse for good measure,' said Jethro. 'Only a valve-mind could arrange that. Vardan Flail didn't murder you, but he did cut your head off your dying body and then put you through the guild's death rites. He loved you well enough for that, to give you his people's

428

machine immortality. And when Boxiron stopped slipping gears and was no longer trying to rip the arms off police militia and free company soldiers, I had my suspicions that he might have brought a hitchhiker back from the guild's transaction-engine vaults. Not all of you, of course. You left enough of your intelligence behind to make Vardan Flail think he still had you in his valves, enough to possess the control circuits of Hannah's suit in the turbine halls, trying to protect her from harm.'

'Alice,' Hannah groaned. The archbishop hadn't just translated the final section of the god-formula as she was hiding inside Boxiron. She had added it to the first two parts. *She had used it on herself.*

The archbishop's laughter came through fainter, the steam starting to disperse. 'If you can keep your head while people all around you are losing theirs. . .'

'Alice!' Hannah pulled herself to her feet. 'What have you done?'

'I incorporated the church's counter-weapon into the final section of the god-formula, child, I took it into myself, just as the colonel did. The archbishops of Jago have had over a thousand years to polish our counter-weapon into perfection. A sabotaged godhead. Expansion without end. Ascending into eternity. Nothing to cling onto. No fixity, no way to reverse the transfiguration.'

'Alice, don't—'

'It's all gone, child. I removed all traces of William and Bel from the guild's transaction-engine vaults, their work and their lives. Just a forgotten dream now. It's time for me to leave, too. Everything else, I leave for you.'

'—go.'

But the smoke was dissipating. Expansion without end. Alice had gone. Forever.

Hannah brushed the tears from her eyes, and not just of mourning. Alice had known where to find Tomas Maggs' corpse, the dead skipper who had scuttled the boat taking Hannah's father home. And the archbishop could only have done that if she had been the one who killed the skipper. Trying to protect the Inquisition's secret, perhaps? Or had Alice known that the boat her father was taking was going to sink, and who else might be involved in the plot? Was Maggs' murder an act of revenge or merely tying up loose ends? How guilty had Alice Gray felt to ensure the cathedral raised a girl pressed into its care by two desperate, fleeing parents? Love and ruthlessness, remorse and compassion. How could you ever choose?

'There are always things we shall never know,' said Jethro, realizing what Hannah was thinking. Perhaps remembering the woman he had loved? 'Notes rise and fall. But the song endures forever, as long as there are people who care to sing it.' He gently patted Hannah's tear-stained hand and looked up at Boxiron. 'Pray tell me that Alice took all three parts of the god-formula with her when she left your body, old steamer?'

Boxiron nodded, his steamman knight's skull trembling with pent-up aggression. 'Jethro softbody, please, I am still running in top gear.'

'Splendid.' He looked over at Hannah. 'Damson Conquest, if you would be so kind. . .'

Hannah went to retrieve the steamman's warhammer. She dragged the hammer over towards the rungs on the wall. There was a shadow moving just out of the corner of her eye and she imagined a frantic howling from a distant, far-off place. Jethro helped her lift up the large hammer to Boxiron's outstretched iron fingers.

'Something best forgotten?' asked Hannah.

'Indeed.'

Outside, the sound of the guns had stilled and the tinkling of shattering stained glass drifted down from the summit of the mountain.

EPILOGUE

Commodore Black was pacing the docks of Hermetica harbour, watching the stevedores haul the cage of ab-locks over to a crane that was making ready to lift it towards the *Purity Queen*'s open cargo holds. Resisting the tempta-tion to bark orders at the dockworkers, Jared Black noted the figure walking towards his u-boat from the buildings behind them. A nondescript fellow in a dark frock coat, wearing a tall stovepipe hat. Where had he seen him before? Ah, the grey little fellow from the Jackelian embassy who had warned him to stay out of trouble when the *Purity Queen* first docked. And hadn't he made a grand job out of that, this voyage?

'A rather raucous cargo, captain,' said Mister Walsingham, stopping to listen to the howl of the ab-locks.

'Bound for the Royal Jackelian Zoological Society, sir,' said the commodore.

'By way of Pericur, I understand.'

'You are very well informed, Mister Walsingham.'

'Our people aren't going to be very popular in Pericur right now, captain. Are you sure you know your friends from your enemies? I foresee trouble.'

'Their war was with the blessed Jagonese, not the Kingdom of Jackals. And I bear trading papers with the seal of the archduchess herself – that's still good for something.'

'So it was,' said the man. 'And so you do.'

Commodore Black watched his sailors taking on board the coffin containing Chalph urs Chalph's body.

'That being the case, captain. . .' The man produced a wax-sealed pouch. 'Some papers for our embassy in the Pericurian capital. They'll pay you very well upon delivery.'

'I dare say so,' said the commodore. 'The crown is always good for it.'

The official sniffed in agreement. 'Did you have a good war, captain?'

'There's no such thing, sir,' said the commodore, 'and anyone who tells you different is trying to get you to vote for them.'

'Oh, I don't know. With everything considered, I would say matters have worked themselves out rather neatly.'

'Is that all, Mister Walsingham?' asked the commodore, irritated.

'For now,' said the man, sitting down on a crate. He glanced back up as he noticed the piqued look playing across the old u-boat man's face. 'Oh, I do apologize, pay me no heed. I'm rather hoping for a boat to come in.'

'You're hoping against experience then, lad,' said the commodore. 'You had better ship out with us. There will be nothing coming in from the continent or the colonies, and any craft from Pericur will be met by a shell whistling down around their ears for the next decade.'

'Well, as long as you are able to sit and wait a while patiently, you never can tell what's going to come along,' smiled the grey little official. 'Something bound for Cassarabia, perhaps?'

Commodore Black snorted. 'And you think *Pericur* will be full of trouble? The caliph's wicked welcome would make the greeting of the archduchess look like a spot of mortal tea with your grandmother.

Jared Black stopped. The cart with Ortin urs Ortin's coffin had arrived – along with Hannah, the ex-parson of Hundred Locks and his brutish old steamer. Thank Lord Tridentscale's beard, that was it then. They would soon be underway and he would be well shot of the wicked land of Jago forever. A quick trip over to Pericur, another journey down the coast to the colonies to drop off Hannah for her seminary training, and then home across the sea to the Kingdom, the blessed Kingdom of Jackals. Green fields and brown ales and a warm log fire burning in the hearth of his rooms at Tock House. Yes, that would be something to look forward to.

The embassy official pointed to the ornate crest of a solitary tree on the side of the coffin. 'Repatriating the bodies of the enemy, captain?'

'No, lad,' said the commodore. 'Just a friend.'

Jared Black walked over to help with the ambassador's coffin and within ten minutes he had totally forgotten about the nondescript man.

Everyone forgot about the man. He had that kind of face, those kinds of clothes.

The *Purity Queen* was away with the tide and cutting through the steaming boils veining the Fire Sea by the time a Jackelian merchantman surfaced outside the coral line, heading for the island and its sole paying passenger.

The passenger waiting ever so patiently.

SIX MONTHS LATER

'Next time,' called Boxiron, pushing open the doors to the massive ballroom, 'might we not restrict the scope of our detections to Jackelian soil?'

Jethro checked behind him to make sure the loyal family retainer was running to safety with the escaped young nobleman through the god-emperor of Kikkosico's palace gardens.

'Splendid advice, old steamer. Do remind me again if we live to accept another case.'

They pushed through the crowd of brilliantly clothed courtiers – all the men resplendent in officers' uniforms, the women in long, flowing gowns – and Jethro jabbed a finger towards the peacock-uniformed boy being led up the red carpet before the god-emperor's throne. 'That is not the Don de Souza!' Jethro yelled. 'Good people, that is an impostor, and he carries an assassin's toxin-gun concealed in his cane!'

The face of the Don's uncle contorted in a snarl, his mob of bodyguards drawing their sabres. Boxiron's gears crashed up to five and Jethro's hand snapped out to drag the lever down to three, stopping the steamman charging towards the pistols presently being drawn by the emperor's loyal guardsmen.

Boxiron had returned to being as hasty as ever after he had shrugged off the god in the machine.

Something of a pity, for surely Jethro never missed *his* gods.

The Archbishop of New Alban moved out of the way of the grizzled master of the wagon train, nearly as wide as he was tall, the dust from the man's riding boots kicking up and joining the mantle of fine powdered dirt swirling around near seventy wagons and their idling line of horses. Many of the people about to depart the city were convicts, unwillingly transported to the colonies, ready to begin a backbreaking life of hard labour out on the farms for as long as their sentence of indentured service lasted. Their sad grimy faces reflected the knowledge of their fate and the archbishop's heart weighed heavy with sympathy for their predicament. Pick a pocket across the ocean, end up over here. Hardly an equitable exchange. Only one of the wagons' occupants directly concerned him, though.

'Are you sure about this?'

'I believe I am,' said the woman he was addressing without looking around, throwing her travel bags into the back of the wagon.

The Archbishop of New Alban made a despondent face at the young woman as she mounted the wagon's rear-plate and turned to face him. 'I'm not sure if I'm entirely comfortable about this, Hannah. Your first vicarage is always test enough as it is, acclimatizing to the responsibilities of the position, the demands of the parishioners, getting to know the people; but the western counties! Dear Circle, that's usually considered a hardship posting. You will have to travel the entire length of the great forest, often without lancer escort, avoid bandits and highwaymen, the creatures of the woods, the aboriginals . . . and there's more trees out where you'll be staying than there are settlers.'

'I'm used enough to empty streets,' Hannah said. 'It's the colony's crowds in the lanes outside the seminary I have more of a problem coping with.'

'There's only a couple of garrisons all the way out there,' said the archbishop. 'If Pericurian mercenaries push south over the border looking for trouble, as like as not you're only going to have a handful of wild woodsmen and miners to stop your church being set on fire.'

'I have learnt enough Pericurian to reason with them.'

Maybe she could reason with the believers at that, but the archbishop had other concerns, ones that ran a little closer to home. 'New Alban isn't that much different from life in a Jackelian city, or the island society you grew up in for that matter, but the forests breed superstition like fallen leaves in autumn. I've seen experienced priests travel out there who have thrown up their hands in despair at what their people claim to see out in the trees, in the dark, deep woods.'

'All the more reason to go where the need is greatest.'

The archbishop sighed. 'Well, I can't stop you. Not with that peculiar letter of commendation from the League of the Rational Court lodged with the cathedral secretary. But seeing as you might have your choice of vacant parishes, I thought something across the ocean in the Kingdom would appeal. Even as a New Alban man, I can say that everyone should see Middlesteel at least once in their life. If only for perspective. Now there's a city. For all our achievements here in recent years, it makes New Alban look like a provincial backwater.'

'Just a larger crowd and more noise.' Hannah smiled and reached down to take the archbishop's hand. 'I'll be safe, your grace. Sometimes, well, sometimes you just have to have a little faith.'

The Archbishop of New Alban's hand fell away from Hannah's as the wagon train began to trundle forward, before rising in a final wave, and he stayed where he was until the last wagon had cleared the city gate.

'I sometimes wonder what we ever have to teach you, anyway?' the archbishop muttered to himself as he grimaced in worry.

Then he turned to walk back home.

Among the other members of the ab-lock clan on Jago, the male was known as *Cutter*, for his skills at sharpening and shaping flints and cutting grooves in the bamboo shafts to hold their spearheads. His eyes were sharp too, and as he left the entrance to the cave system he was the first among the ab-locks to notice the glassy black surface of the ground cracking as heads of wheat pushed through.

He didn't know that the seeds of the wheat he was noticing had blown in from one of the distant city's ruptured farm domes, now emptied of the last of humanity, and he certainly didn't realize that there was a new network of lichen filaments growing under Jago's dark soil, sapping the poisons, cleansing the burnt, barren ground.

Days later, however, when Cutter saw many more of the heads pushing through, he fell to his gnarled knees and muttered guttural sounds of thanks to the goddess of fertility – and in that he was part-right, for it had been a goddess who had created the lichen network – a push here, a nudge there, modifying, with a little hint of irony, the death spores left over from an ancient war to a far better purpose.

But the goddess wasn't around to hear Cutter's prayers any more, nor would she have approved of them if she had been. She might have approved of his next thoughts, though. *If the clan grew these, they wouldn't need to root around in the dark fruitless forests – they wouldn't need to hunt so much.*

And then what might they do?

TOR

Award-winning authors
Compelling stories

Please join us at the website
below for more information
about this author and other great
Tor selections, and to sign up for
our monthly newsletter!